Paul Wankowicz

The Ulysses Flight,

A WWII Aviation Adventure Novel of Aerial Dogfights and Love, with a Glossary

Paul Wankowicz

The Ulysses Flight,

A WWII Aviation Adventure
Novel of Aerial Dogfights and Love,
with a Glossary

Terra Sancta Press
Melbourne, FL 32935
2010

TITLE: **The Ulysses Flight, A WWII Aviation Adventure Novel of Aerial Dogfights and Love, with a Glossary**
AUTHOR: Paul Wankowicz (a.k.a. Paul Wańkowicz) (March 22, 1926 -)
PUBLICATION DATE: June 1, 2010
STREET DATE: May 21, 2010
1st printing, 1st edition, 10 9 8 7 6 5 4 3 2 1
ISBN 97809653467-9-5
EAN BOOKLAND: 52495 $24.95 USD
LCCN PCN: 2010925678
BIP CATEGORIES: BOOK—FICTION— WAR & MILITARY
BOOK—FICTION—ACTION ADVENTURE
BISAC CATEGORY BOOK: HIS027100 HISTORY/ MILITARY/WWII—FICTION
BISAC CATEGORY OF GLOSSARY: TEC002000 Technology & Engineering/
Aeronautics & Astronautics—Aviation
Terminology
PUBLISHER's SAN 854-1388
PUBLISHER: Terra Sancta Press, 304 Royal Palm Drive,
Melbourne FL 32935-6955
PUBLISHER's eMAIL: books4you@cfl.rr.com
PUBLISHER'S WEBSITE: www.terrsanctapress.com

Printed in the U.S.A.
DOLR: 20100513-1700

Publisher's Acknowledgments

Terra Sancta Press expresses its gratitude to the following individuals
whose wonderful teamwork, talents, and energy assisted with the
preparation and publication of this novel.

- Bookcover design: Shirley Grose
- Bookcover execution: Suzanne Witenhafer, Arrow Design
  Solutions, Inc., Rockledge, Florida.
- Webmaster: Chuck James
- Research assistants: Mirinda Hartselle, Dale Muschamp
- Historical memory: U.S. Army Specialist 4 Gerald Nelms
- Historical memory: Lt. Col. Charles E. Pearce for his oral history
  of aviation in the Pacific, and his personal knowledge of how the
  U.S. broke the Japanese Code.
- History of Burma: Emily Rowel Pearce
- Historian: Mark Gager
- Proofreading, research, and/or critiques: Joyce Henderson, Keyon
  J. Jordan, Linda Jump, Richard Leonhart, Dr. Frances Rinaldi,
  Marie E. Roman, David Savarese, Ed von Koenigseck, Katrina
  Thomas, and R. Bradley Witenhafer.
- Critical readers: Joyce Henderson, Linda Jump, Richard Leonhart,
  Janina Kerr-Bryant, Pennie Mager, and Ed von Koenigseck
- Book design, research, and copyediting: Pat McDonough
- Computer technical support: David Garland, Shirley Grose, Robert
  Witenhafer, Sr.
- Components: Symbology, Inc., Maple Grove, Minnesota
- Print specialists: Steve Sirlin, Arla Harrington, and Kyle

Author's Acknowledgments

The author expresses his special thanks to:

- My wife Sue Birnie for being patient with all the years of writing
- Captain Jim Franklin for military technical support
- Janina Kerr Bryant, Sally Chetwynd, and Linda Ornalles for many corrections and general support
- Special thank you to Richard C. Byron for painting the original art which appears on the front cover of *The Ulysses Flight* depicting the three Curtiss P-40 *Warhawk* (a.k.a. *Tomahawk*) fighter planes. As well as being a painter of note, Dick also flew the P-40 against the Germans in WWII (Desert AF)
- For creating the Journey Map of the Ulysses Flight, thanks to Sally Chetwynd (See Appendix III C.)
- Keith W. Miller for his patience and interest in my writing activities.

The Ulysses Flight/ Paul Wankowicz

Content

The Ulysses Flight/ Paul Wankowicz

The Ulysses Flight/ Paul Wankowicz

Publisher's Preface

The Ulysses Flight story takes place from the start of World War II in the China-Burma-India (CBI) and Pacific Theatres of Operation.

In 1960, an unnamed British narrator reminisces, trying to put things into perspective, figure out how his part of the mission fit into the big picture, and bring closure. He is asking what *really* happened and when.

The opportunities to ask these questions and the answers received do not piece together neatly. The answers are supplied as each character develops, often going back to events that shaped them. The narrator has an urgency to find out what happened to the tramp steamer *Nike Victory*, to the three pilots and their friends, and the three U.S. Curtiss P-40 *Tomahawk* planes which were to be delivered to U.S. Clark Airfield in the Philippines.

❖

A **Glossary** lists histories of aircraft and flyers, aeronautical terminology and technical specifications of certain aircraft, and some WWII slang. There is also personal commentary by the author.

❖

A list of the **Characters** appears in Appendix II.

❖

Maps authentic to the period are provided in the Appendix III.

❖

The Ulysses Flight/ Paul Wankowicz

Political geography is more fluid than physical geography. The first draft was originally written in 1961, and presents a story set in the early 1940s. Since that time, the boundaries of many countries have changed, the rulers and forms of governments have changed, and even names of rivers have changed in spelling, if not pronunciation.

For example, Burma was under British control at the time our story opens. Eventually, after several turnovers, Burma obtained independence from British domination, and the name of the country was changed to Myanmar. The name of the Irrawaddy river changed to Ayeyarwady, probably to throw off the Anglicization of the word. Moulmein is now Mawlamyine.

In *The Ulysses Flight*, we used the spelling of place names as they were then, based on authentic WWII maps published in 1942 and 1943.

❖

We have endeavored to make the novel ring true historically, but even recently new information was declassified about the U.S. Navy Department's breaking of the Japanese Code some 48 hours before the Japanese bombed Pearl Harbor. Additional information may yet be declassified, so realize *The Ulysses Flight* is a work of fiction that could have happened this way.

Introduction

On June 22, 1940, France surrendered to Nazi Germany. In the process, Adolph Hitler forced France to cede possession of French Indo-China to its Axis partner Japan. French Indo-China then consisted of what is now Vietnam, Laos, and Cambodia.

August 9th to 12th, 1940, Churchill and Roosevelt held the Atlantic Charter Conference and made what was called the Grand Alliance.

In September 1940, Germany, Italy, and Japan signed the Tri-Partite Pact, officially forming the Axis powers.

The Japanese attack on Malaya on December 8, 1941 Pacific Standard Time, coincided with the December 7, 1941 attacks on Burma and Pearl Harbor, Hawaii. On December 8th, on the other side of the International Date Line, when the Japanese landed in northern Malaya, the battleships H.M.S. *Prince of Wales* and the H.M.S. *Repulse* and four destroyers were sent to attack the Japanese invasion force.

To achieve the conquest of Malaya was identified as part of Japan's *Outline Plan for the Execution of the Emperor's National Policy.* Singapore Island, Malaya, rich in tin and rubber, was considered the Gibraltar of the East, and British forces in place were expected to hold off any attack until its Royal Navy could come to the rescue. The British assumption was their forces in Singapore could withstand any siege for 70 days. The British believed they could get their fleet any- where in the world within that time frame. Unfortunately, they didn't account for the fact that England itself might be under attack, requiring the fleet to protect the homeland. The Royal Navy was taking heavy losses in the Atlantic due to the war with Germany; so ships of the British Mediterranean Fleet, as well as warships of Australia and New Zealand, were engaged in the Mediterranean against the Italians and the

The Ulysses Flight/ Paul Wankowicz

North African campaign, and so not available to send additional maritime protection to Singapore.

However, east of Kuantan, Pahang, Malaya, Britain's two best battleships, the H.M.S. *Prince of Wales* and the H.M.S. *Repulse,* were assigned to protect the island of Singapore with four other ships, H.M.S. *Express, Electra, Tenedos* and *Vampire,* and 11 Brewster *Buffalo* planes in the air, all together, comprised the re-designated Force Z of the British Royal Navy. Originally, an aircraft carrier, the H.M.S. *Indemnable* was to be part of the Force, but it ran aground in the Caribbean and was damaged.

On December 10, 1941, within hours of the Japanese attack in the South China Sea by its 85 aircraft, 37 cruisers, and one submarine, both British battleships were sunk, 327 men died on the battleship H.M.S. *Prince of Wales* and 513 men died on the battleship H.M.S. *Repulse.* The Japanese lost only 18 men. Coming soon after the attack on Pearl Harbor, these were the first capital ships to be sunk by an air attack operating on the high seas.

This left the other ships without air cover.

The United Kingdom's overwhelming defeat demonstrated that it was a new era of aviation, where ships at sea could no longer be invincible without the protection of aircraft and anti-aircraft armaments.

Prepared with their jungle-warfare training, the Japanese forces invaded Malaya, and overwhelmed the British. Nearly 100,000 British soldiers were forced to surrender to about 60,000 Japanese. It was the most humiliating defeat in the history of the British Army.

Meanwhile, with Singapore conquered on February 15, 1942, and the British and subsequently Dutch Navies (Indonesia/Dutch East Indies) annihilated, there was nothing to stop the Japanese advance.

The Japanese occupation of French Indo-China was a strategic coup for Imperial Japan, placing its army, air, and naval forces within 800 miles of Singapore, Britain's main military and naval base in the Far East.

Japan targeted Burma, a British colony, because of its mineral wealth and its strategic position as the geographical gateway to British India.

In Burma, the British put up feeble resistance and, basically, withdrew to protect India. It was in what is now Bangladesh that the British were finally able to halt the Japanese attack.

These series of military disasters spelled the end of European Colonialism in Asia.

Mark A. Gager

Dedication

This story is dedicated to those who flew and fought in the Curtiss P-40 fighter planes on the Allied side, and those who flew on the enemy's side. May their souls rest in peace.

Paul Wańkowicz

The Ulysses Flight/ **Paul Wankowicz**

Prologue: London in 1962

Sitting in my gentlemen's club, I waited for the arrival of my friends
from the Foreign Office. It was our habit to meet every Thursday
where, without fear of supervision, we could discuss the latest shifts
and rumors that did, and would, affect our work.

I ordered a whiskey and soda, and had nothing to do except sit back
and think. My thought somehow turned to Burma at the end of World
War II. . . .

Once WWII ended, the fragmentation of Burma, along with the mili-
tancy for independence, made the politics there touchy and unstable.
Under the circumstances, the British fell into the role of peacemaker.
To do this, London needed Intelligence from Agents with feet-on-the-
ground, and found it necessary to recruit people already trained in
Intelligence gathering from wherever they could be found. I was one of
them.

As I sipped my drink, I recalled three people: an American, an
Englishman, and a Dutch girl I'd never actually met, but who haunted
me for years. For no reason, they returned to my mind like ghosts to
haunt me again. There were also three American airplanes and a merchant steamer, a ship with the improbable name of S.S. *Nike Victory*.

When my friends arrived, I had to turn my thoughts elsewhere.

The day after the meeting at the club, I ran into Air Vice-Marshal John
Laws, Distinguished Flying Cross-and-Bar. Once the war was over,
Johnny, as he preferred to be called, was one of the few surviving
Battle of Britain pilots who chose to stay in the British Royal Air Force
(R.A.F.), and thus, had to fight the many bitter battles defending the
need for an air force against the peacetime political establishment
which seemed out to ruin British Aviation.

The Ulysses Flight/ Paul Wankowicz

Johnny and I had squared off over some bit of funding, which I felt should go to the Foreign Office, while Laws wanted it for his beloved R.A.F.

Despite our differences over the negotiating table, after it was all over, Johnny invited me for dinner at his home in Lyall Square.

Johnny's wife, Mia, was from Malaysia. She prepared a traditional Malaysian cuisine. The dinner started with *Bak Ku The*, a Chinese pork rib soup seasoned with garlic and herbs. The first main dish was Satay Chicken grilled with peanuts and coconut milk. This was followed by Indian mutton curry with white rice.

The wonderful meal took me back to my time in Asia. I hadn't eaten so well since I'd left there. Later the dessert was strictly Western: ice cream and angel food cake.

During the meal, talk naturally turned to Asia and Tenasserim, Burma. The conversation revived my memories, and in the process, I mentioned Cyril Sim.

Johnny looked up sharply. "So the old reprobate survived the war, did he?"

"You knew him?"

"Quite well. If I remember correctly, he was a pirate's son, and the Royal Navy had made him Manager of the secret fueling Station and the little Tenasserim Airfield attached to it."

"Could be. Wherever he came from, I found him unusual, and better educated than most of the local Burmese."

Johnny seemed interested, so I told him of my meeting with Cyril Sim and his story of the three pilots.

Both Johnny and Mia listened in silent concentration.

"I regret that while I was in Burma, I had not been able to find out more of whom they were or what had happened to them."

After I finished, Laws said, "Let me get you a whiskey, and if you are still interested, I can tell you about them. Their story is an unusually interesting one."

Chapter 1: Aboard the S.S. *Nike Victory,* December 7, 1941 in the Asian time zone

Outside the spacious rim-stained windows of the S.S. *Nike Victory*'s bridge, the sunlight bounced off the bay's ripples, bright enough to hurt U.S. Army Captain Frank Carringer's eyes. In the windless tropical air, the crippled ship swayed with the changing tides. Now the triangle of her bow pointed directly at the jetty of the fuel depot and the hangar beyond.

Frank's friend H. Halliday was the ship's engine room officer. Halliday watched until Captain Goss left the bridge and then he walked over to join Frank on the bridge.

"The monsoon season is running unusually late this year," Halliday grumbled as a greeting. He waved his hand toward the shore outside the windows. "Where you are going, it's a might bit inhospitable, lad. . . ."

"What did Captain Goss say?"

Halliday replied, "Goss said, 'It would be a relief to put your cargo, the U.S. Army's three P-40 fighter planes ashore to get them off my ship!'"

"I gather he will be glad to get rid of me. He thinks putting me on his ship to guard the American airplanes means the U.S. Army doesn't trust him." Frank said that without bitterness. From the start, Frank was aware that the ship's Captain resented him.

"Goss insists that we finish offloading the planes by dark tomorrow. Then, he suggested that I camouflage them with palm vegetation. Ha! The old bugger didn't give you much time, did he? I hope you know what you are going to need out there. Once ashore, with us gone, you'll get bloody little help from the Village Headman. Not with mechanical things anyway," Halliday said. "I'll see to it that we get your three airplanes unloaded before dark tomorrow, as well as anything else you may need. You still think you can get one of the planes to fly?"

"Shouldn't be too difficult. In New York, the Bill of Lading said the three planes were in working order when loaded. The fighters are supposed to be ready for flight after the waterproofing is removed," Frank replied.

Halliday grunted a taciturn Scots' grunt, meaning neither assent nor negation.

"What about the ship? Do you think you can get her running again?"

"Don't know. I can probably get her moving, but no guarantee I can keep her running to get to the next port. The main shaft is fractured. I'll have to improvise something." Halliday looked away.

They focused on what the unloading would necessitate in implements and men.

From the bow of the ship, they had a good view of the fuel depot and the primitive landing field. The jetty, toward which the ship was pointing, was a concrete structure, broad enough to carry two heavy trucks abreast. *Long enough*, Frank figured, *to berth a destroyer.*

There were several valve-studded, black-painted pipes of the fueling gear along the right side of the jetty culminating onshore in a small brick pump house. A dirt road of dried mud ran from the jetty's end, curving left diagonally, through a wide cut in the thick tropical hedge. The dirt road continued to the small rectangle of land cleared of jungle as a landing field by the hanger.

Looming over the hedge row were the rusty sides of a big hangar. A thin pole atop the hangar held a scraggly, sun-bleached twist of silk as a windsock. Now, it hung limp, unstirred by even a slight breeze.

Halliday pointed to the other side of the road. "Frank, see that thatched shack? I bet it's for storage of the aviation gasoline, or avgas, as well as aircraft-engine oil for the airfield. At least you'll not have to go hunting for gas!"

In contrast to the sprightliness of the Royal Navy's installation, the neglected Tenasserim Airfield displayed an air of abandonment. Even

The Ulysses Flight/ Paul Wankowicz

the once carefully seeded grass had been overtaken by wild saw-edged, sun-parched, and ankle-high jungle varieties. Volunteer trees and saplings crowded the end of the runway.

Beyond, Frank could see tier upon tier of green jungle. In the distance, towering over it was a backbone of mountain peaks, the tallest shrouded in brilliant-white clouds.

Somewhere out here, in this uncivilized wilderness, I'll have to make my temporary quarters until one of the fighters is flyable and I can take it to Singapore to get help, Frank thought.

Standing on the bridge with Halliday beside him, Frank mentally reviewed the past few months. As the diplomatic situation between the United States and the Japanese worsened, Frank had hoped to fly to the Far East as a crew member of the B-17 bombers. The U.S. Army Air Force (U.S.A.A.F.) was sending the B-17 bombers as a deterrent to Japanese ambitions. However, the U.S. War Department had other ideas, and instead separated Frank from his unit and assigned him to escort the U.S. Army's consignment of three Curtiss P-40 *Tomahawk* fighter airplanes from New York to Clark Airfield in the Philippines.

The planes were put aboard the S.S. *Nike Victory,* a merchant cargo ship that should have been scrapped due to rust and advanced age. To serve the war effort, it had been found somewhere, and conscripted to transport military equipment.

Now the fully-loaded ship's old triple-expansion engine broke down en route to Rangoon, Burma on December 7, 1941.

As the ship's engine-room officer, it was Halliday's responsibility to get it running again, but he could not make the needed repairs because the ship lacked the required tools and welding equipment to make the complex parts. He'd patched the shaft sufficiently for the ship to crawl into Victoria Bay off the west shore of Burma, where they'd seen electric lights onshore. He hoped it indicated some sort of repair facility, but it turned out to be only a secret British Royal Navy fueling depot and an airfield. Repair facilities were nil.

Chapter 2: The S.S. *Nike Victory* at Anchor, Tenasserim Airfield, Burma, December 7 - 8, 1941

At first glimmer of the dawn, Frank Carringer and Halliday left the crippled ship and went ashore, when the alligator-back mountain ridges to the east were still a stark black against the lightening skies.

Halliday advised Frank that an European man would be meeting them. Instead, at the end of the jetty, they were greeted by the Village Headman wearing a slightly dirty, white shirt and well-worn British Army khaki pants. He introduced himself as, "Cyril Sim."

Sim lived just off the quay in a modest brick home obviously built for an European. The home was the style of a French railroad station.

Halliday asked for the station manager.

The Burmese native shrugged. "The British built this house next to the depot and planned it as the residence for an European Director. Unfortunately, they didn't realize what the climate would do to a white man. The first resident didn't last three months. After the second white one died, they gave up the idea of a British station manager."

Cyril laughed. "Reluctantly, they had to appoint *me* as manager." He had a high-pitched voice and spoke excellent English.

Frank thought he sounded like a Hollywood actor faking British ancestry. "Where did you learn to speak English?"

Cyril laughed again. "King's College, Delhi, Master of Agriculture." Then, he explained the layout of the secret base and the airfield, apologizing for the lack of repair facilities. "Perhaps the Admiralty presumes it has sufficient repair facilities in Singapore."

When the *Nike Victory*'s siren unexpectedly sounded a series of blasts, Halliday and Frank made their excuses to Cyril and left, promising to come back later.

As Frank and Halliday stepped onto the lowered gangway, the

4

The Ulysses Flight/ Paul Wankowicz

Boatswain was waiting for them at the railing. He called down to them, "The Japanese struck Pearl Harbor. Sparks says, 'They attacked on three fronts. They're landing on Malay Peninsula, too.' We're at war!"

Frank's heart leapt into his throat. He knew most of the U.S. Pacific Fleet was in Pearl Harbor. As an airman, he also knew what damage a well-led air strike could accomplish. *I hope the American troops had some warning so we could defend ourselves. If not, ...* He didn't dare contemplate it.

Frank and Halliday stepped closer to the radio room to listen to ongoing transmissions, and heard some desperate messages of British troops who were trying to defend the eastern shore of Malaya against the Japanese landings. They were only 200 miles away, not two hours flying time from where the *Nike Victory* was holed up.

Later that afternoon, when Frank was standing outside the bridge, his mind focused on several things at once. According to Sparks' decoded messages, the Japanese were rampaging through the Pacific. This made the delivery of the three P-40 fighters vital.

I accompanied the planes from the States to be sure they are delivered safely, and I will find a way to do it to justify the U.S. Army's and my nation's trust.

With the Japanese prowling on the other side of the Burmese peninsula, and the Nike Victory on its last legs, the ship cannot outrun the Japanese, even if the shaft is repaired, Frank thought, as he leaned to look out the salt-stained windows. *If the Japanese have landed on the other side of this peninsula, we must not use the radio to call for help— The Japs are probably listening to every broadcast. We are all on our own. Under the circumstances, there are a million things that need to be done.*

"Eh, laddie. Are you in there?" he heard Halliday ask.

Frank became aware of Halliday speaking to him.

"For a while, I was worried the heat's getting to you. You looked miles away," Halliday said.

The Ulysses Flight/ Paul Wankowicz

"I was daydreaming, I guess. The attack on Pearl Harbor has changed everything. I was thinking it would be best to get the planes off the ship."

"Well, if we're going to get everything unloaded by tomorrow evening, it's time we got to work," Halliday said. "Have you decided what you will need from the hold?"

"Now that there's a war on, I'll need belted-ammunition and metallic links for the machine guns on the planes, plus any tools I can lay my hands on. The airplanes are supposed to be in almost flying condition, but 'almost' can mean a lot of work before they can actually fly."

"Money?"

"There's a case consigned for delivery to the paymaster at Clark Field; it's probably pay for the troops. I'd stake my life it's full of American dollars," Halliday said.

"Yeah, but will anyone accept dollars here?"

"Yankee dollars? Everyone. Best currency in the world!"

"You'll need your own tool kit." It seemed Halliday had already thought things out. He had served in World War I, and knew the knife-edge on which survival depended.

"Yes, that too. I think what you are saying is that we'd better get to work. It's okay by me!"

Halliday grinned. *I like the Yankee lad, but he certainly takes a lot of prodding. Maybe he's in shock at the news of the attack on Pearl.*

"Right, then, off we go," Halliday said.

Throughout the day, as they worked, Sparks relayed the desperate situation of the British troops trying to defend the beaches on the eastern coast of Malaya.

The three fighters would be more than vital, Frank realized. He had to assemble them and fly them to safety as quickly as possible.

The P-40s were on the fantail of the ship because they never would have fit through the cargo hatch—their wings were integral with the fuselage and so couldn't be folded.

The Ulysses Flight/ Paul Wankowicz

"The paperwork and the manifest is confusing because you Yanks call the Curtiss P-40 a *Warhawk* and we Brits call it a *Tomahawk*. I made all the documents say *Tomahawk* because that was easier," Halliday said. He pointed out, "The major challenge will come tomorrow, when we must winch one of the six-by-six military trucks and other cargo out of the hold. You will need to use it to drag the airplanes from the jetty to the airstrip hangar. . . . And I presume the truck's battery will be flat. . . . I'll have to rig a battery charger first thing. . . . The gas tanks will be empty, too, but I can appropriate some lifeboat gas to drive the truck off the jetty. Once there, we'll work out of the avgas stores at the depot on shore."

No use asking Captain Goss about the gas, Halliday thought. *Undoubtedly, the Captain would forbid it.*

"The reason getting one of the five trucks is a problem is because in the U.S.A., the trucks were loaded onto the ship first to the back and sides of the hold. Then, all the rest of the cargo was loaded in front of them, so now they are no where near the main hatchway. Other cargo has to be moved before we can get at even one of the trucks," Halliday said.

The ship's hold had stored the heat of the day and was hot. They were both soon soaked with perspiration.

By the time Frank and Halliday located, marked, and checked off all of the other cargo Frank would need, it was close to midnight. Luckily, the smaller stuff they needed was in the forward hold.

Halliday, with his Scot's practicality, was of immense help. Once onshore, when the *Nike Victory* departed, Frank would be on his own, and he knew it. *Can't go to the store and pick up what I need.*

7

Chapter 3: The Prophecy

When the men finished in the hold, Frank suggested, "Let's go up on deck to cool off." His mind was still turning over in high gear what other cargo he would need. He knew he could not sleep until he'd relaxed and slowed down his thoughts.

On deck, it wasn't much cooler. The night had brought a slow, humid breeze rolling off the shore toward the ship. The two men walked aft until they found a bench by the midship's engine hatchway and sat down. The ventilator was open, propped up by an old 2x4, where the original support had rusted.

Frank extracted a sweat-crumpled package of Camel cigarettes from his shirt pocket and passed it to Halliday. For a while, they sat and smoked in silence, watching the drifting smoke made luminous by the fuzzy light emanating from the engine room below.

They could hear the murmur of the generators and engine-room fans. Vibration reverberated from the vertical sides of the engine-room trunk, the shaftway through which the engines had been lowered to their mounts. He smelled the hot oil and steam wafting through the ventilator. It mixed rather pleasantly with the raw odor of the jungle.

Two lights onshore burned with brilliant points in the darkness, just as the night before when the lights helped the *Nike Victory* find the inlet. Frank wondered, *How long will it take Cyril Sim to realize a war has started? Lights on after sunset are dangerous.*

Over the peaks, a thunderstorm was raging, bringing an occasional puff of cooler air onto the ship.

"End of the monsoon season seems a mite bit late this year," Halliday commented in a low voice.

Frank wondered what he was getting at. "I thought, during the monsoon, it rained all the time."

"Not around this coast. Further east, yes. But here, it's off and on. Lots of thunderstorms. You'll have a few days of sun, maybe some

8

drizzle, then all of a sudden, it'll rain like hell, dumping more than 100 inches of water a year."

Halliday paused just as flashes of lightning illuminated the bellies of the clouds, making giant Chinese lanterns of them. There was a moment of silence.

During the long voyage from New York, Frank and Halliday had formed a friendship. Halliday was the only man aboard who understood machinery. To the airplane pilot, the nautical experience of the ship's captain meant nothing, but with the diminutive Scot, Frank had found the common ground of engineering and technology. Frank knew he would miss him after he went ashore and the ship departed.

"Look, Halliday, why don't you come ashore with me? From what you said, trying to repair the fractured shaft is pretty hopeless."

"What would I do ashore? I no ken pilot one of your airplanes, lad. What would I do? Spend the rest of the war talking to the natives?"

"Getting the planes in shape would go much faster for me with you around. When one is finished, I could put you where the radio usually rides, and fly you out piggyback."

Halliday had more aeronautical acumen than Frank would have guessed. "That field looks mighty short to me, lad, and I ken you'll have yourself trouble getting out of it, even without me as an extra load. And what would you do if you run into the Japanese? We'd both be down. With me along, the machine would be too heavy for you to fly."

He paused. "I've been with this rusty bucket for six years. Guess I'll stay with her as long as she floats. But thanks anyway." As an engineer, Halliday would feel leaving the ship would be desertion.

"The offer's open anytime." Frank knew intuitively it was a hopeless request from the start. Halliday had too strong a sense of responsibility to desert his ship, even though he had no means to repair it.

The old Scot had never married and never had a son. Over the long weeks of the voyage, Frank had partly filled that gap. They had grown closer than either of them would care to admit.

The Ulysses Flight/ Paul Wankowicz

"It's okay to help you with the planes here, but my responsibility is still with the ship." Halliday took a deep breath, slapped his knee, and said gruffly, "Just fly to Singapore and send back a tug big enough to tow the *Nike Victory*. We'll probably hide it somewhere in the bay north of here and wait for the tug."

"Will do. Thanks for all the help you're giving me," Frank said.

After a pause, Halliday turned so he could look at Frank. "Listen, I'm Scots, and we're all supposed to be fey. I have a feeling neither of us will survive this. I also feel you're involved in something that will be very important to all of us. It's as if you are on a quest."

"I don't understand," Frank said.

"Truly, neither do I. In helping you, I am doing something vital, something that may change history. That should be reward enough."

He fell silent. "Bloody hell," he said, tossing his cigarette over the rail. "I'm talking too much. Let's call it a night."

Frank nodded but fumbled for another cigarette.

They walked together to the stern of the ship. Halliday disappeared into the dimly-lit companionway leading to the officers' quarters.

The thunderstorm still raged over the mountains. The breeze was steadier and cooler as if the storm were closer. Frank leaned on the rusty rail, and tried to dismiss Halliday's prediction, but he found it hard to set aside what the Engineer had said.

Getting three fighters to the Philippines, even if I manage it, cannot change history that much! But Halliday was so serious about it. . . . The word 'quest' reminds me of pictures of knights and fair ladies. Not even as a kid reading the Prince Valiant comic strip did I ever imagine myself as a knight. . . .

Shrugging his shoulders, Frank headed to his cabin.

Chapter 4: Aboard the S.S. *Nike Victory* at Anchor & Ashore at the Tenasserim Airfield, December 10, 1941

During the night, the clouds crept over the bay and, now, in the early morning light hung leaden at masthead height. Ragged, detached scud hovered heavily overhead, as if they were *Zeppelins*. The jungle-overgrown foothills, that seemed so close the previous day, were swallowed up in the fog of the low-lying clouds.

Just as Halliday predicted, the morning dawned wet, hot, and humid. To Frank, it seemed to take too much effort just to breathe.

The water around the ship was a dull slate-color instead of the bright blue of the day before. The air was filled with a fine, needle-like drizzle, which misted everything with a film of warm water, slick like cooking oil; it made the decking slippery.

Working in the rain, Frank, Halliday, and the sailors opened the forward hatch. Frank was glad they'd marked everything the evening before. It took hard work and time to clear one of the trucks, but in an hour, they'd winched it out and had it on the deck. All of the marked cases were loaded into the back of the truck.

Halliday had already added some lifeboat gas. Then, the hoist lowered the truck overboard and set it on the jetty road. When he jump-started the truck from another battery and got it running, it made clouds of fog rise from its exhaust.

At the depot avgas shed, he added more gas. Then returned to the jetty. There, Halliday stored the cases and supplies in a far corner. He carefully hid the case addressed 'To the Manila Paymaster' under some of the gear.

Frank had not realized how much he'd missed flying until he began preparing the first fighter to be lifted off. Just to touch it gave him new life. The paper tape, pasted over the seams to keep out water, zebra-striped the fuselage and wings. Even with tarpaulins covering the cockpit, the P-40 plane looked eager and beautiful to Frank's eyes.

Halliday brought out the slings used to load the three airplanes in New York. As they were fitting them to the first fighter, they were distracted by the sound of an airplane. Work stopped. Their heads swivelled upward. At first, muffled by the low-hanging cloud, it was difficult to locate the source or direction of the sound. As it grew louder, it sounded like a two-cycle washing machine.

The rhythmic noise was not like any aircraft Frank had ever heard. *Must be Japanese.*

Although the airplane could not be seen in the cloud cover, the sound became louder and came in low from seaward. Then, it made a vague turn above the ship, and clattered toward the mountains.

I hope that pilot knows his position. If that pilot doesn't turn away from the mountains soon, he'll become a flaming wreck in the jungle. Every airman, dreaded contact with rock-stuffed clouds, and Frank felt sympathy for the other above, before he considered his own safety. *Since they hadn't been able to see the plane, the pilot could not have seen us. Luck is still with us.*

As the sound slowly faded away, Captain Goss appeared on the bridge wing, with a bullhorn in hand. "Hear that, Mr. Halliday? Better hurry."

Frank heard the engineer mutter something under his breath before he turned to fitting the sling again. It took another 90 minutes working in the slippery, warm rain to get the fighter overboard and to lash its tail-wheel to the flatbed of the truck. The workers were now wet to the skin.

Getting it off the jetty road proved to be a ticklish business. There were scant inches between the P-40's delicate starboard wing and the rivet-covered, rusty-slab side of the ship. At one point, while Frank carefully inched the truck forward, three crewmen had to lift the wing to clear an extra-tall valve.

When the truck pulled the plane away from the concrete jetty, the

The Ulysses Flight/ Paul Wankowicz

fighter's wheels mired in the fresh mud.

By early afternoon, they'd succeeded in dragging the plane across the airfield and parked it temporarily in front of the hangar. By the time the other two fighters had been pulled to the hangar, and all rolled inside, it was past midnight.

With the airplanes safely parked under shelter, and the great hangar door rolled almost shut, it was time to say farewell to the crew members who were all slick with mud, and tired to the bone. As they departed one by one, Frank felt an impending loneliness.

Halliday hung back to say good-bye. "Well, lad," he said, hand proffered forward, "I ken it's time to say good-bye. In the old-fashioned sense of the word, 'God be with ye.'"

In the light of the single kerosene lamp carefully perched on the olive-drab port wing of one of the fighters, he noticed moisture collect in Frank's eyes.

"Can I walk you back to the ship?" Frank offered.

"Hell, no! I can find the way myself," the engineer said gruffly. "But before I go, the lads and I thought we'd leave you something." He held out a bottle of prized Glenfiddich single-malt Scotch Whiskey. "Best we could do," he added in a half apology.

Frank knew the treasured bottle had come from Halliday's carefully-hoarded and hidden, personal store, but there wasn't much he could say. "Thanks. . . . And stay well." The words felt totally inadequate.

Halliday nodded before he turned away to walk toward the big doorway.

He looks older and more stooped. Will I ever see Halliday again? Frank wondered.

The words of the fey Scot's prophesy became forever stuck in the forefront of Frank's mind. He shook off morbid thoughts and feelings of loss. It was time to prepare for whatever night was left.

He carefully removed the lamp from the fighter's wing and set it on the floor where it cast long, confusing shadows. Silence descended in

13

the hangar, with only the undertone of strange, jungle noises outside.
*For now, I'll have to sleep in the cockpit of one of the fighters.
Tomorrow I'll ask Cyril for a carpenter or someone to fix up a sleeping
cubicle in one of the deserted offices on the side of the building. . . .It's
funny how I'm already willing to rely on the Village Headman. I even
remember his name.*

He rustled through the gear piled in the corner to find a blanket. He
folded it carefully to fit into the bucket seat of the cockpit. *It will have
to do for the rest of the night. At least, any rodents and snakes in the
hangar can't get me up here.*

In the strangeness of his new and lonely surroundings, the confines
of the cockpit felt like home. Dropping into the seat, he was soon
asleep.

Early the next morning, the night had dissipated the overcast sky,
leaving an extra-heavy dew hanging on the grass. The fluffy, brilliant
orange and pink cumulus clouds contrasted with the purple blue of the
sky. As the sun rose, it burnished the bay with gold.

Stiff and tired, Frank walked down the rutted road to the jetty,
hoping for a last glance of the ship.

It was gone. *Captain Goss must have ordered the crew to hide her
in some inlet last night.* The waters lay calm and undisturbed, as if the
S.S. *Nike Victory* had never been.

Chapter 5: Tenasserim Airfield, Burma, December 11, 1941

Within two days of the *Nike Victory*'s departure, Frank had established a working relationship with Cyril Sim, who was the Village Headman as well as the Resident Manager of the Depot. Any reservations that Frank could have had about this local Burmese man were dispelled on the first day, when Cyril, without being asked, showed up with a carpenter to make habitable one of the offices on the side of the hangar. Cyril seemed willing, even eager to help, although at first he asked for outrageous wages for his Burman workers.

Cyril was very interested in the three American airplanes now in the hangar.

On that first morning, Frank spent two hours showing him the aircraft and answering questions. To his surprise, Frank found himself enjoying showing Cyril around. Cyril had a quick mind and the questions he asked were to the point. The Burman had a sailor's understanding of forces on a ship's hull, and Frank didn't find it difficult to translate concepts of flight into terms Cyril could readily understand.

While Cyril and Frank were talking, the carpenter sealed all the cracks leading into the cubicle. Seeking warmth, the snakes would insinuate themselves into any openings they could find, often winding up in one's snug sleeping roll. Frank carefully supervised the carpenter's work; he had no desire to wake up some night to find a cobra or a krait sharing his lumpy bed.

Up at first light, the last cool moment of the day, Frank's morning routine quickly reduced itself to absolute simplicity. Behind the hangar, among the detritus, was a pile of rotting sawhorses. Frank had picked the best two to support a beaten-up, galvanized tub to collect rainwater. After skimming off accumulated leaves and insects, he washed in the devastatingly tepid water, but it left him feeling as if he hadn't washed at all.

When clean and shaven, he picked up whatever he'd been doing the night before and worked at it until the grass-cutters came.

He wanted to make one of the fighters flyable as quickly as possible, and fly it to Singapore to get help for the *Nike Victory*: spare parts, a mechanic, and two pilots to ferry the other two planes with him to the Philippines. He also intended to bring back a tugboat to help the *Nike Victory* get repairs.

Cyril had said, "Shortly after Pearl Harbor, the Japanese raided Clark Field and Manila, most of the Philippines, devastating any equipment the U.S. had there."

From the sketchy war news relayed by radio, it seemed to Frank to be more vital than ever that all of those things be accomplished as soon as possible.

When previously loaded in the U.S.A., the three fighters were parked on the fantail of the *Nike Victory*. At the time, they were reported to be close to flying condition, except for sealing tapes, Cosmoline™ anti-rust coating, and certain other packaging which protected them on their sea journey.

According to the Air Force, eight man-hours would be sufficient to get each fighter flight-ready, but Tenasserim was not Manila. The job of readying just one fighter in the tropical heat, the rotten hangar, and with only a meager supply of tools Halliday had been able to spare from the ship's engine room, was close to impossible.

To Frank, the delays with the fighter's overhaul were maddening. When he'd taken the cowling off the engine, he found all 24 spark plugs had been removed and dummies filled with desiccant had been substituted. After an hour's frantic search, he located the real plugs taped to the bottom of the cockpit seat.

Normally, exchanging the dummies should have presented no problem. However, the job required a special wrench which he didn't possess. He lost a half-day trying to make a wrench from a piece of tubing stripped from a derelict tractor. He had to work over a makeshift charcoal fire using a ball-peen hammer and the tractor's engine block as an anvil. He badly burned his hands in the process.

The Ulysses Flight/ Paul Wankowicz

Cyril's workmen brought Frank's breakfast of rice, fish, and a stewed vegetable of some sort. Lunch was invariably moist rice-cakes wrapped in dark-colored leaves. The three grass-cutters hired by Cyril squatted down, chain-smoked hand-rolled cigarettes, and watched him while he ate. The sight of a white man eating seemed to hold an endless fascination for them.

At first, Frank was embarrassed, but then, he assumed this was part of the accepted ritual. When he had eaten, they would quietly turn to cutting the airfield's grass. They worked like automatons of skin and muscle, unmindful of heat and humidity, in their infinitely slow, rhythmic work.

On most afternoons, there was a tropical storm and the grass-cutters would take shelter in the hangar until the rain was over. They seemed to enjoy watching Frank work. After the storm, they disappeared down the jungle path to the village.

In the evening, Cyril returned, followed by a young girl walking demurely behind him, carrying Frank's supper: more fish and rice. She placed it in front of him, picked up the empty breakfast pan, and ran back down the village path.

Cyril stayed. After Frank's supper, they would set up two rickety chairs outside on the cut grass. They sat, talked, and smoked cigarettes, while Cyril shared the latest news of the Japanese advances he'd heard over his battery-powered radio. As for Pearl Harbor, 18 American ships were sunk or damaged and 200 aircraft destroyed. They didn't yet know how many were killed. In that attack, the Japanese apparently lost 28 aircraft, 5 midget submarines, and about 50 men. The war was not going well for the Allied Forces.

Since Pearl Harbor, the Japanese had landed in strength in Malaya, and had begun advancing toward Singapore Island. The defending British had lost its two best ships, the *Repulse* and the *Prince of Wales*. From what Cyril said, the rest of the small contingent of the Allied Capital Ships was pulled out of the Pacific, leaving the Japanese in charge.

The Ulysses Flight/ Paul Wankowicz

It may be to my advantage, Frank thought, *that the Japanese were heading toward Singapore, not Rangoon. It may buy me time, desperately-needed time.*

There were also rumors of Japanese Forces pushing north from Signora, in the direction of Tenasserim, but Cyril discounted them, since the jungle between Signora and Tenasserim was close to impassable. However, the rumors did underline the need to hurry.

One particular afternoon seemed to Frank to be hotter and more punishing than usual. Maybe he was just tired. The brief, violent shower that had come earlier had done nothing to lift the heat. It had only added to the already-unbearable humidity.

The sunset following the storm was spectacular, all golds, oranges, and purples. Clouds drifted singly in the sky, pierced by shafts of sunlight in wild splendor. Frank and Cyril sat still in front of the hangar, watching brilliant reflections from the bay. The smoke from Cyril's cigarette drifted lazily over the wet grass.

Frank was letting the weariness and frustration drain out of him, while Cyril seemed sunk in his own thoughts. Eventually, Cyril asked, "How much time do you think you still need to repair one airplane?"

Frank considered the question. *I wonder if Cyril has any idea how desperately I want to be done and away. Free. To see the world as an airman should, not sitting here, hot, itchy, and shackled to the ground. There's still the mass of electrical connections behind the engine, a bewildering tangle of piping to be cleaned of rustproofing and checked.*

He'd taken a case of .30-caliber ammunition from the ship, along with a small case of links, but they still had to be assembled into the standard belts, and then, carefully folded into the ammo boxes and set beside the plane's guns. These guns each needed to be cleaned and loaded with belted-ammunition. Time and more time.

Frank had not yet found the pilot's handbook among the various assembly manuals packed with the airplane. He had searched for it, but to no avail. Operating from a well-paved airport and flying out without

The Ulysses Flight/ Paul Wankowicz

the knowledge of the manual's contents would normally pose no problem. But it could be suicidal to make a first takeoff from the rough, handkerchief-sized field without the knowledge of the unstick speed, the max engine rpms, the trim settings, and all the other details the pilot should know. The P-40 was the U.S. Army's hottest fighter, faster and more powerful than anything Frank had ever flown before.

Frank knew when the time came, he would take the risk, but he had to become as familiar with the airplane as possible before actually flying it. He needed time studying it, memorizing every curve, every line, every instrument and knob in the cockpit. Then, maybe the knowledge would translate into a subconscious feel of the machine, and tell him when it was safe to pull it off the turf and miss the clutching palm trees at the end of the airfield.

He was conscious of Cyril waiting for an answer. "Five or six days at a guess," he said.

Cyril pulled out a packet of Ruby Queens and lit one with a gilded lighter. "No good," he said.

"Why?"

"You must understand, Captain, Burma is a colonial country. We are still under the British yoke. Not free as you are in America. Most of us resent the British Raj. He is not Asian. He does not understand our people, and he has grown rich on our labors. On the other hand, the Japanese are Asians. We do not know what kind of rulers they might turn out to be, but in balance, they could be better than the British.

"Now with them just over the border, some of us feel that it might be time to help the Asian Japanese push the British out. Some of us Burmese have heard that you are here to help the British and they intend to burn the place down. Soon."

"How do you know?"

Cyril inhaled deeply, then blew a cloud of smoke, and watched it drift lazily downwind. "No matter. I know."

"Could we stand them off with guns from the planes?" Frank asked. "We have plenty of ammunition."

19

The Ulysses Flight/ Paul Wankowicz

"There's more of them than there are of us. They are armed with rifles stolen from the police," Cyril said.

"We wouldn't last long."

"Precisely put, Captain."

For several minutes, there was silence. The sun had set. Only the tops of the cumulus clouds were still illuminated by its orange rays. The line between light and shadow was knife-edge sharp, making Frank think of decapitation. Where it was not reflecting a cloud top, the bay was ominously dark. Frank wished that the *Nike Victory* would appear, pluck him up, and take him to Singapore. But the expanse of water was a desert devoid of movement. He was boxed in. It was impossible to speed up his takeoff.

"What do you suggest we do?" Frank asked.

"We could buy them off," Cyril said.

"Buy them off?"

"Give them some of that U.S. money you have stored in the back and say we are working for the Japanese."

It was an unexpected answer. Frank knew that sooner or later someone would investigate what was in the crate addressed "To the Manila Paymaster," but he hadn't expected Cyril to own up to the knowledge.

Cyril wasn't naive. There was a motive behind everything this Village Headman did. *Could the admission be a signal that Cyril was allying himself with me? But where was the advantage to Cyril from such an alliance? Cyril was an expert at head games.* Frank had already recognized that. *Cyril wouldn't reveal information no matter the price.* Frank recognized it, but couldn't thread his way through the puzzle.

"You mean tell them that we are working for the Japanese?" Frank asked.

Cyril smiled. "Oh, they will know we're not. As long as we are a source of good American money, they will make believe that what we tell them is true. Then, when the Japanese come and complain, they will

20

The Ulysses Flight/ Paul Wankowicz

act surprised. As you Westerners say, face will have been saved all the way around. And with a profit, too."

Frank paused to think. *If I organize a defense, I bet Cyril and the other villagers would melt into the jungle, leaving me, literally, to hold the fort alone. I can't blame them. I don't know how strong the factions are, or even who will win in the end.* . . . There was also another consideration. *Cyril might be an enigmatic Asian, but without him, I know I can't survive three days. My food, the workmen, and above all, my little local knowledge has come from Cyril.* . . . *But there's always the possibility this could be a sophisticated ploy to line the Asian's pockets.*

Frank looked at him sharply. Manicured hands. Impeccable clothes. White, canvas trousers, silk shirt, patent-leather shoes, even in the depth of the jungle. *It doesn't seem probable that a man as careful as Cyril would resort to blackmail. Not,* Frank realized, *where simple murder could be done to perfection. Without anyone missing the victim.*

Cyril's story, then, is probably substantially accurate. Paying off the opposition, whoever they are, could buy several badly-needed days of peace at the price of a few expendable dollars—dead weight I can avoid taking when the plane lifts off the inadequate strip. All in all, not a bad bargain.

As if divining the thoughts behind Frank's silence, Cyril spoke again. "Two nights ago, they burned a plantation not 20 miles from here."

Frank let the remark pass. "How much do you think will buy them off?"

"In American dollars, 600."

"No less?"

"I don't think so. In all truth, I promised them five. If we give them a little more, we will buy more time, and have a greater vote on our side, against the hot-heads in the crowd," Cyril said.

It was Frank's turn to smile. With the admission that he'd already talked with the terrorists, Cyril was definitely allying himself with Frank. "How can you be so sure?"

21

The Ulysses Flight/ Paul Wankowicz

"Captain, I have lived in this part of the country all my life, and my father half of his before me. He owned the village, and now I do. We are not simple villagers. We have influence. The villagers come to me for advice."

So far Cyril had delivered on everything that he had promised: workmen, materials, and food. Frank had already recognized him as sort of a local leader.

"Alright, you can have the money, but on one condition."

Cyril's cigarette paused half-way to his mouth. "And what is that?" he asked.

"That you agree to tell me what your interest is in all of this. But before you do, let me get some illumination on the scene." The sun had slid away from the peaks of the tropical clouds; twilight was rapidly setting in. Soon, it would be quite dark.

Frank used the excuse of getting the lamp to give him time to dig out the money.

Cyril may have realized this, but said nothing.

When Frank returned, Cyril leaned back and lit another Ruby Queen. In the yellowish glow of the lamplight, the exhaled smoke looked like a specter as it drifted slowly downwind.

"My interest is very simple," Cyril said. "At first I thought that you, being American, must have money. Money is something that is always useful. But now that I have watched you work, it's you that I'm interested in. I know the British. I know the Hindus, and I know the Burmese.

"Except for you, I've never met an American, other than tourists—meeting tourists does not teach one very much. From you, I have learned something already. For instance, I cannot imagine a true Britisher doing what you are now doing. Nor going at it with the energy you put into these airplanes.

"I'm only half Burmese," he said, leaning back in his chair. "My father came from the Straits of Malacca. Put quite simply: he was a pirate. But when Britain forced the states of Perak, Selengar, Nagri,

22

The Ulysses Flight/ Paul Wankowicz

Sembiland, and Pathan into federating, my father had the foresight to see that his piracy business was ending. If they had the strength to force those states into joining together, it would not take them much more time before they held the reins of government over the whole of the Malay Peninsula. When that happened, piracy would no longer be tolerated. It was time to get out.

"So my father looked for a place of retirement, and eventually, found this village. For ten years, he visited here annually, buying improvements, building his reputation until he became betrothed to the Chief's daughter, my mother. In 1908, he broke up his pirate holdings, paid off his men, bought the village, married my mother and retired. Since that time, my family has run the village, and much of the countryside."

"I'm curious," Frank motioned with his hand to interrupt, "how does one buy a village?"

Cyril laughed. "I'm being imprecise. Had there been a landlord, buying the village would have been easy. But landlords talk. This village had no landlord, just a chief, which made it interesting to my father.

"He could quietly hire an agent to bribe enough clerks and administrators so that the village disappeared from the government books. Until the British Royal Navy and the R.A.F. came here with their depots, we just didn't exist.

"Two years after I was born, my father was killed. I don't know how. My mother brought me up, . . . until she was killed by a rogue tiger . . . in 1939. Since then, I have had to take over the leadership.

"It is not easy. From pirates, we have become citizens of responsibility, all in one generation. I do not know whether I should support the British, or the Japanese Asians. I trust neither. I know the British. I have heard what the Japanese have been doing to the population of China. I must think and study. It is like in a Burmese play, being between two devils."

"Have you made the decision?"

The Ulysses Flight/ Paul Wankowicz

"Not really. I am thinking of arming some of the villagers for protection, and then, of waiting to see what happens. We can go hide in the jungle where no one will be able to find us, neither the British nor the Japanese. In the end, when both are tired, maybe we Burmese can do what you did in America in 1776."

"Throw out the British."

"Exactly. Throw out the British; but not help the Japanese, who have no sense of sportsmanship."

In his mind, Frank could imagine a New England Farmer saying something very similar in the days of King George III. Cyril could be called a sort of freedom fighter; there had been a lot mentioned about them in the recent news from Europe. Cyril seemed such an unlikely figure.

Frank counted out the money.

After Cyril left, money in hand, Frank relaxed. It was too much to think about after a hard day. Frank picked up his chair and went into the hangar.

As he got ready for sleep, Frank thought about the day. The earlier thunderstorm had not dissipated all of the energy stored in the great clouds, and they continued building up while he and Cyril had talked. By the time Frank turned in for the night, the weather outside was ominous.

Later that night, Frank was awakened by a violent eddy of wind which made the timbers of the hangar rattle and groan. A deluge of rain followed. Its noise on the tin roof drowned out all other sounds.

Sometime after that, Frank heard the main doors creak, as if someone were forcing them open, but he was sleepy enough to attribute the noise to a gust of wind.

The sound of lighter rain indicated that the storm's peak had passed, and lulled him back to sleep.

But within minutes, he was abruptly awake. Outside it was not yet dawn, though the sky was beginning to lighten. As he collected his thoughts, he realized that what woke him was the sound of an empty can rolling over the floor. Someone, or something, was in the hangar.

Cyril mentioned bandits were in the area the night before who had burned a nearby plantation. Have these bandits decided to come burn me out? Or maybe, now that the money in my cubicle has become common knowledge, has some villager decided to claim it for himself? Who or whatever it is, I have to go out there to see.

Moving as quietly as he could, he pulled on his pants. Frank groped for his Colt .45 which was on a box next to the bunk, at first not finding it, then he felt the smooth metal under his hand. He leaned back and listened. *I have eight rounds, one in the chamber and seven in the clip.* As quietly as he could, he thumbed the hammer back but also slipped the safety on. Despite the heat, he shivered. The weight of the weapon in his hand didn't give him much reassurance.

There! He heard something moving in the back corner where he'd thrown an empty oil can and some tarps. It was still too dark to see. There was no more noise. The rain had stopped.

Quietly, he reached for his flashlight, tucked it into his waistband, and made his way to where the last fighter was parked.

The parked fighters in the hangar were already shadows. They took on threatening mythological shapes, like beasts ready to spring.

His foot hit something. It rolled away clattering. Frank cursed under his breath. The clatter must have alerted whoever was hiding back there.

The silence was now an almost solid thing. The jungle noises had been stilled by the violent passage of the torrential rain.

Through the dirty panes of the windows, he saw the sky was a dark electric blue. The dawn was not far away. The increasing light could lose Frank whatever advantage the knowledge of the layout gave him. He quickened his pace feeling his way around the wing's tip of the last fighter.

Leveling his .45, he thumbed on the flashlight, saying, "Freeze!"

It was a girl standing with her back to the wall, hands splayed out against the rusty corrugated metal. The light caught her squarely in the face. It seemed to pin her against the tin like an etherized butterfly in a museum.

Frank's eyes took in the details: blond hair tied back behind her neck; dark eyebrows over slightly sloe eyes, now opened wide in fear; high cheekbones; slender; skirt torn and stained, and wet from the rain; very female.

The Colt .45 became useless in his hand. Without moving the flashlight, he reached up and laid it on the wing tip. It made a loud 'clunk' against the dural of the fighter's skinning.

The image of the near-perfect body of a half-naked dancer in a Capetown Club he and Halliday had visited sprang into his mind. He tried to push the dancer's image out, but it wouldn't leave.

The girl broke the silence first. "Can I move now?" she asked.

"Yes. Who are you?" Frank asked.

He lowered the flashlight as she pushed herself away from the tin wall, untangling her feet from the tarpaulins.

"Lisa. Lisa Van Riin." She looked desperately about her, as if seeking escape. "We own a plantation about 20 miles from here. I've been running day and night."

"The one burned by the Nationalists?"

"Probably the one." Her voice trailed off.

The dawn had now come, and Frank could see her whole, tired figure.

"Why don't you follow me to where I bunk," he suggested. "We can talk there."

"Very well." She trailed behind him as he led her through the hangar.

He cleared a chair in the still-dark cubby, and she collapsed into it. He busied himself lighting the kerosene lamp. The soft light accentuated the reddish-blond color of her hair and the bone structure of her face. Even in her obviously strained state, she was more beautiful than he'd noticed at first. She'd been crying. The tears had left streaks on her cheeks.

He was suddenly very conscious of his naked chest and pulled on his U.S. Army shirt with his pilot's wings still pinned to it. Her eyes followed that bit of silver as he buttoned his shirt.

"By the way, my name is Frank Carringer. I'm an American."

She exhaled softly but said nothing.

Frank was at a loss as to what to do. He fought the desire to look her up and down. "Water?" he asked.

"Please."

"Have you had anything to eat?"

"No."

"Would you like some?" He rummaged in the corner, and found the multi-pot affair in which supper had come. The evening had been too hot to make him hungry, and about half of the fish curry and rice was left. He washed the fork in his drinking glass, drying it on a hand towel. "It's all cold, I'm afraid. Left over from supper. All I have." He handed it to her.

"It does not matter. Thank you."

As she ate, he looked around and ruefully became aware of the disordered bed, the dirty hand towel, his careless, bachelor state of living.

He watched her wolf down the food, scraping the pan clean.

When she had finished, he asked, "What happened?"

"They came two nights ago. My father was away, just my mother and myself in the house. When my mother went out to see what they wanted, they shot her." The girl clenched her eyes as if to exclude the picture. "Our Malayan cook went out to help her. They shot him, too. It was moonlight. I could see from my room that they were both dead. I grabbed my compass and got out the way I used to sneak out when I was younger, out of the window and down a tree. I don't know if they saw me or not. They set the house on fire. I could see the glow through the trees." She shuddered.

"I ran all night, terrified they might be after me. When daylight

27

came, I slept in a tree. I had heard a rumor that someone had airplanes down here. I'm hoping to get a lift to Rangoon. I didn't know that they were all single-seaters." Her voice sank in disappointment and she fell silent.

Frank looked at her again. She was all in. Questions could wait. "Look," he said, "why don't you lie down on the bunk and catch up on your sleep. I'll pull the curtain across the door so that you'll have some privacy. I'll go to work in the hangar, and leave you alone. But if something happens, I'll be nearby. You'll be safe." He saw the look of gratitude in her eyes.

"When you wake up," he continued, "I'll still be here, working on the airplanes. I'll have food brought for you; then, we can talk again. In the meantime, the cubicle is all yours. Good night." He pulled the curtain as he left. She'd be asleep in minutes.

By the time Frank had set up the day's work in the hangar, the whole encounter had taken on a dream-like quality. But the image of her face and her slim body as she had stood against the corrugated tin of the wall, was sharp. And the .45, still lying on the wing, witnessed that it had actually taken place. He left it there, glancing at it occasionally as he worked, to reassure himself.

Frank had spent the whole of the day working on the engine: cleaning, greasing, and checking the control linkages.

He put down his wrench and wiped his hands. It was getting late, it was hot and he'd worked hard all day. There wasn't much left to do in the engine section, so he could ease up and quit. The motor was almost ready for a test run, if he could find the starting procedure. If he found himself unable to start the engine, all of his work would be in vain. The pilot's manual had not turned up, and all of his experience was with smaller radials. This engine was an in-line, with presumably different characteristics, a different starting procedure, of which he had no idea.

The girl kept intruding into his thoughts. He doubted that she'd be happy sheltering in a native village after what she'd just experienced. He had sent one of the grass-cutters back to the village with a note

The Ulysses Flight/ Paul Wankowicz

written on a scrap of paper, telling Cyril that a girl had appeared, and asked him to bring extra food. He also asked for the carpenter to come again, to fix up another cubicle for her. Cyril would probably come that evening to see who she was. Maybe he could help decide what to do about her.

Throughout the day, Frank had been tempted to look in on her, but resisted the idea. He assumed she was asleep. Her proximity was worrisome. She had been immediately and completely attractive.

Judging from the heat and the sun's slanting rays through the dirty window, it was late afternoon when Lisa awoke. Her mind was still fogged with vague feelings and dim memories of twisting through several nightmares; but she felt better for the sodden sleep in the hot, airless cubicle. At least, she was safe for a while.

A few minutes later, she was able to stagger up. The curtain was still drawn, as he had left it. She heard hammering in the hangar.

After the American had left, she'd stripped and thrown her underwear into the wash-bucket in the corner. She'd meant to wring it out and drape it over the back of the chair to dry while she slept, but sleep overcame her before she'd done it. Now the underwear, dirty and crumpled, floated in the half-clean water. It didn't matter. She'd do without. Wringing it out, she draped it over the back of the rickety chair, hoping it would eventually dry.

When the memory of her mother flashed back through Lisa's mind, she grabbed the wall for support. In her memory, she replayed the noise of the rifle shot, her mother stumbled and bent over in anguish clutching her stomach.

She stopped herself. Lisa summoned her will and forcibly rejected the memory. There would be time for that later. *This is no time for self-pity. Somehow, I have to make it on my own, until I can get word to my father. I know he's at sea. There must be some way to locate him.*

His meager, but very masculine, belongings were laid out on a crate opposite the bunk. A small, chromed mirror hung on a nail driven into a beam. The mirror distorted badly, but it told her enough for her to realize that she would have hardly recognized herself. She hoped that he hadn't peered in on her while she slept.

She picked up Frank's comb and sat down in front of the mirror to re-do her matted hair. She tied it back with a string. She'd liked to have had a brightly-colored ribbon, but there was nothing like that in the room. Having done as well as she could, she took a deep breath, straightened her skirt, and tied her shirt in front, then, she pushed the curtain aside.

Chapter 6: Frank Remembers

Frank had worked in the Oklahoma oil fields from the age of 14, and had graduated to the all-male company of pilots. When the weather was bad and time hung heavy on their hands, the seasoned pilots gathered around the pot-bellied stove in the back of the hangar and talked flying. None of them could afford a woman, or if they could, they kept it very quiet.

He'd had a couple of escapades. Both had ended in frustration. The one in the Old Madrid more than two years ago, Frank wryly thought to himself, was the last one. He'd been flying the old P-36s, part of the Panama Defense Force, and had just received his U.S. First Lieutenant's bars. Kenny had insisted they go out to celebrate.

Now, Kenny was no longer alive. He'd been decapitated when a sloppily-flown B-18 bomber slid down in a turn, crashing into Kenny's P-36. The B-18's crew had survived.

The restaurant part of the Old Madrid was not the finest in Panama City, but at the time, the floor above housed reputably the best illicit house in all of Central America. Kenny was a connoisseur; he'd made no bones about Frank's naiveté, and promised that he, Kenny, would fix all that.

The girl Frank chose was dark-haired, obviously of Spanish ancestry, with high-pointed breasts. She wore a simple school-girl dress that somehow made her all the more provocative.

According to the arrangement at the bordello, the man and girl would first drink together.

She joined him at a wrought iron, glass-topped table, set in intimate surroundings, in muted light cast from a New Orleans wrought-iron candelabra. Frank and the girl sat across from each other. He felt deeply embarrassed by his lack of knowledge of what to do next.

Kenny and his peroxide-blond girl had long disappeared.

The Ulysses Flight/ **Paul Wankowicz**

To Frank, the silence seemed to stretch to infinity.

Finally the woman looked straight at him. "What makes you think that you're the only one who wants it?" she asked. "Has it occurred to you that I might want it, too?"

Her words were just the thing to dispel his tension. He felt an overwhelming sense of gratitude toward her.

She took his hand. "Come on, let's go,"

But then, she spoiled everything by adding, "Lover boy!"

In that shabby bedroom, with its cheap, period-brass bed, it had not worked out very well. The whole effect had been just the opposite of what Frank had envisioned.

Chapter 7: Frank and Lisa

When Lisa stepped inside the hangar, it broke Frank's reverie.

It took her a minute to get her bearings. Then she saw him bare-chested, standing on a wooden scaffolding working on a big-black-bear of an engine. She stood watching the interplay of muscles across Frank's tanned back.

Looking around, she realized what she had only subliminally known was right. This was no invasion of American Troops. For some reason, he was here alone.

When she heard her, he turned around. "Hi!" he said, jumping off the scaffolding. He picked up a rag and wiped his hands. "Did you sleep well?"

"Yes, thanks."

"What did you say your name was?"

"Lisa. Lisa Van Riin." Her stomach growled and she realized she was famished.

"I'm Frank." He smiled. "There should be some food coming along soon."

"That will be nice." Looking directly at him, she saw his eyes drop to the curve of her breast, and felt very conscious of the thin material of her shirt, hardly concealing anything.

"I sent a note to the village to say I have a guest," he said. "I expect they will send an extra meal sometime around sunset."

She was hot, tired, thirsty, and very uncertain of herself. At another time, she might have reacted differently. But as she noticed his gaze return to her breasts, her nipples stiffened against her shirt. Her own body was betraying her. She couldn't even trust it any longer. Anger kindled in her, an anger she'd rarely felt before. She needed help, she needed shelter, she needed something to keep her mind off the last few days, but not what he had in mind.

She put her hands on her hips and turned toward him. "If that's all that you're thinking of," she exploded, "why don't you rape me right now? Then, maybe we can start over decently!"

Unprepared for her outburst, Frank froze. A vivid scene of him taking her on the disordered bunk in the cubicle flashed through his mind, and dissolved like a wavelet on a sandy beach. *This was no way to start.*

Although the circumstances were different, for a second time in his life, his maleness had been defused by a slip of a girl, a girl hardly taller than his shoulder. But with this one, he didn't mind. The whole thing struck him as funny and he burst out laughing.

She looked at him, her expression of anger slowly changing into bewilderment. The impact of her words had not penetrated until after she had said them. Her anger was giving way to fear when he unexpectedly burst out laughing. She took a step back when he came toward her, still laughing, looking much bigger and stronger than she.

Gently putting one hand on her shoulder, he pecked a brotherly kiss on her cheek.

"How would you like to help me assemble this iron bird?" he asked, pointing to the airplane. "Just until supper comes."

When she looked up at him, her eyes misted with tears. "I think," she said, "that's exactly what I came here for."

When Cyril visited Frank and Lisa in the evening, Frank noticed that she was visibly uncomfortable.

She struggled to be gracious and answer Cyril's questions, but her answers were terse. The whole time, her fists were clenched and her arms crossed to conceal her breasts.

He wondered, *Does she think Cyril had anything to do with her mother's murder. Was he allied with the Burmese who slaughtered her mother?*

At the first chance, pleading fatigue, Lisa excused herself from the conversation.

Frank felt gratitude that Lisa had not lost her patience and tact. Cyril had been instrumental in keeping him alive and he didn't know how this Burmese man would have tolerated a scene. Frank was thankful for the provisions, food, and workers. He did not want to offend Cyril.

After she left, Cyril stayed quiet for a long time, smoking his Ruby Queen cigarettes. Finally he said, "I am sorry about this. It does our country no good. Burma doesn't need people like that. They're brigands, not patriots."

Frank realized that Cyril was talking about the mob. "The Burmese who killed Lisa's mother?"

"Yes. I'm sure Miss Van Riin is still very upset."

Frank searched for diplomatic words. He respected Cyril more and more for his honesty.

Cyril shook his head. "Wars are no good. Things happen which shouldn't—on both sides."

"What can we do to help her?" Frank asked. "Are there any boats or planes coming down the coast that she could take? Maybe she has family somewhere. She mentioned wanting a lift to Rangoon."

"I don't think so." Cyril pulled on his cigarette. "There used to be a weekly boat, but it hasn't come for a fortnight. I would not count on any, nor on the R.A.F. I haven't seen one of their flying boats for a month. They call them *Catalinas*."

"That makes things complicated." It flashed across Frank's mind that he might be her only protection right now, and this airfield her only shelter.

"Where's her father? Is he alive? Do you know?" Cyril asked.

"I don't know. Said her father was away. That could mean anything. I don't think she'd want to go back to the ashes of their home, or even be here after what she's been through." Frank said.

"At the moment, I see no other answer. With things as they are, this depot may be completely forgotten. Could you take her out in your airplane, Captain?"

"It's only a single seater. Getting off the ground with the weight of the gasoline I need to carry to reach Singapore or to Rangoon will be dangerous just for me alone. The weight of another person could make it suicidal." He didn't mention he'd offered Halliday the option to piggyback to Rangoon for parts.

Cyril lit another cigarette. "I understand. Of course, you know these technical matters much better than I. But I foresee no boat, no airplane."

There was more silence. Then he spoke again, this time quietly, as if to himself. "They were good people, the Van Riins. Some of my villagers worked for them and they were well-liked. I will send a couple of men up there to see that her mother and any other bodies are decently buried."

He turned to Frank. "Do you have something like a shirt and a pair of trousers? My wife could cut them down for Miss Van Riin. She will need clothes."

"I wasn't thinking. I should have thought of that myself," Frank said, annoyed with himself. "Good idea. I'll get them now so that you can take them back with you to have your wife make the alterations."

Sleep came hard that night. The thought of leaving the girl behind as he flew off to Singapore kept interlacing with the realization that she was in the next cubicle. Finally, the decision came, as he had known all along it must. He would try to take her out piggyback. That meant a change of plans.

Originally, he'd planned to takeoff with sufficient fuel to reach Singapore, or possibly the R.A.F. airfield at Alor Star in British Malaya. Now the route would have to change.

Once he had the plane airworthy, he would takeoff and make a quick turn around the field to become familiar with the machine. Then he'd land, tear out the radio and whatever else was useless weight. He'd only put enough gas in the tanks to take him up north, along the coast to Moulmein, a larger town he'd found on the charts in *Nike Victory*'s bridge. However, those charts were nautical, showing no detail beyond the shoreline.

The Ulysses Flight/ Paul Wankowicz

Moulmein might have some sort of an airfield. If I can't spot one, I can land on the beach. I could leave Lisa there, once I make sure she will be taken care of. Then I'd head for Rangoon to seek help for the Nike Victory, and afterward retrace the route back to Moulmein. Better than stranding her in a village where I'll never see her again, or ever find out if she survived.

He could not just dump her and calmly proceed with his business without feeling guilty.

Perhaps she could find some sort of a steamer in Moulmein to get out, and link up with another to get her to the States, where she'd be safe. Money is no object; I can draw against the paymaster's kitty. I could give her several thousand dollars. That should help.

Frank didn't know her citizenship. *Dutch? English? Burmese? She said that she'd left the plantation with only a compass. The house was set afire right after that. Any family documents such as birth certificates and passports must have gone up in smoke.*

He'd only known her for a day, yet he felt as if she'd been around all his life. She certainly was occupying the majority of his thoughts. He had no idea what the U.S. immigration laws would require.

Maybe I should ask her to marry me. It would only be pro forma, but the immigration people would have to let her in as my wife. She could make another choice later, when the war is over, and I get back.

This plan would delay his flight to the Philippines, but he wouldn't leave her without making sure she was safe. With her mother dead and her plantation burned, he assumed nothing held her in Burma anymore.

Of course, she'd want to find out about her father. Was he alive or dead?

The promised carpenters came the next morning and were collared by Lisa, who spoke excellent Burmese. She had them clean and force open the windows along the back and sides of the building.

With added light and ventilation, the hangar had a more cheerful air.

By working side-by-side, they could have one of the fighters com-

The Ulysses Flight/ Paul Wankowicz

pletely ready and checked out by noon the next day. There was more to Lisa than he had at first thought. She understood the mechanics of airplanes with the barest of instruction. He still needed to test-run the engines. Frank wasn't going to risk a takeoff on a dud motor. The best time to run the check was early morning because any Japanese observation planes would have to fly at least 200 miles. Unless they took off in the dark, they could not arrive over this Tenasserim Airfield before 07:00 hours.

With luck, tomorrow Frank and Lisa could have the fighter out of the hangar at first light, engine tested and back in the hangar before any Japanese planes were overhead.

He and Lisa finished much earlier than he had planned. By 10:00 hours, everything had been checked and Frank was hard put to find something for her to do for the rest of the day.

There was still, however, the armament. The four 30-caliber machine guns on each plane would have to be cleaned of Cosmoline and made operational before flying anywhere. Lisa took on that job.

About noon, a girl from the village brought a brown-paper parcel tied into quarters with manila string. Lisa was kneeling on the wing with her hands deep in the inspection panels over the guns when Frank came up and laid the package on the wing next to her.

"What is it?" she asked.

"Something for you. Cyril's wife took a pair of my pants and a shirt and cut them down, so you'd have something to wear."

Frank thought she would cry, but she pulled herself together.

She held up her arms to show they were covered to the elbows, with sticky, brown Cosmoline. She had a smudge across her forehead where she'd tried to brush away an errant strand of reddish-blond hair.

"Do you mind if I don't try them on right away?" she asked.

Frank smiled. "I'd really rather you didn't. Or I'll soon be running out of uniforms."

He pushed the package out of the way as she resumed cleaning the guns.

The Ulysses Flight/ Paul Wankowicz

A little while later, Frank saw silent tears stream down her face
although she was still working. "Can I help?" he asked.

"No. Thanks. It's just that little things have become so important."
She didn't elaborate. After a few silent seconds, she looked up at him
and added: "Thanks. Thanks a lot, Frank. That was a very nice thing to
do." Without saying anything more, she went back to work.

Frank realized, *She's becoming very precious to me.*

They worked in silence for another hour.

She raised her head unexpectedly. "Listen," she said.

Frank was in the cockpit, familiarizing himself with its layout and
controls. At first, he heard nothing. Then, he recognized the sound of an
airplane muted by the tin roof of the hangar. They both leapt to the
ground and raced to the great door, earlier left opened slightly for better
ventilation.

The sunlight blinded them. Then they saw it boring low over the
bay, headed straight for the airfield. The pilot must have been following
the coast until he saw the strip and decided to investigate.

Frank and Lisa peered through the crack as the plane banked steeply
over the field, crimson circles on its wings catching the rays of the
noon-day sun. The three grass-cutters working at the far edge of the
field waved cheerily to the airplane. The pilot and observer returned
their waves. Apparently satisfied, the Japanese plane headed out to sea
again. Frank let out a breath he didn't even realize he'd been holding.
"What a shock!" he muttered.

That plane was a powerful low-wing, all-metal aircraft. Although
the gear was non-retractable, the wheels were covered by oversized
spats. The rest of the machine was thoroughly modern, not the glue-
and-canvas creations he'd been told to expect from the Japanese. The
Intelligence briefings that he had received before his departure had been
wildly inaccurate.

Lisa turned to him. "You don't look happy," she said. "He's gone."

Frank shook his head. "That was a very modern piece of flying gear
for the Japanese."

39

The Ulysses Flight/ Paul Wankowicz

"You didn't expect it?"

"From what I was led to believe before I left the U.S.A., they were supposed to be far behind anyone else in aeronautical engineering."

She looked up at him. "My father is in Intelligence with the Dutch Navy, somewhere with Admiral Doorman now. From what my father said, the Japanese have been catching up very fast." she added.

"He's Dutch?"

"Yes. He was a destroyer captain in World War I. My mother was English." She didn't say anything more.

He had learned something about her.

Chapter 8: The New Arrival, Tenasserim Airfield Hangar, December 15, 1941

Frank and Lisa fueled the fighter that afternoon. Each 5-gallon can of gasoline weighed about 35 pounds, and had to be carried from the shed to the airplane, hoisted up the side of the fighter, and the gas poured into the main tank through an angled funnel. For this model plane, the filler cap was on the side of the fuselage, instead of on the top, which would have made it easier.

It was hot, difficult work, especially in the stagnant air of the hangar, where the fumes made it almost impossible to breathe. By the time there was enough gas in the tank, Lisa was exhausted.

Twilight was beginning to fall. Frank climbed into the cockpit to familiarize himself with the instruments. Not having found the handbook, he had no idea of the starting procedure. The long, black cylinder heads and the twin, engine-mounted 50s and their blast tubes extended, seemingly, to infinity.

They buttoned up the bottom cowling, ready for the morning, but left the top open. Frank wanted the engine exposed to spot any developing fire.

That night, Frank tossed and turned having nightmares fearing the engine would never start, stranding both him and Lisa forever in Tenasserim.

The morning dawned clear and a bit cooler. A storm had already formed over the bay as the sun rose. Cyril had brought five extra workmen to help wheel the fighter out of the hangar. For the first time since the *Nike Victory* had left, they opened wide the great door. In the early morning sunlight, the fighter stood poised against the blackness of the hangar like a butterfly just out of its cocoon. Frank couldn't help but wonder if the fates would allow it to fly.

He and Lisa walked around it together, checking for leaks, making sure the palm-trunk chocks were solidly against the wheels, and the prop would not blow pebbles and small objects into the uncooled engine once it was running.

Frank climbed onto the wing and dropped into the cockpit. The controls and black-faced gauges were now in front of him. The long bulk of the engine stretched out beyond the windscreen to end in the broad-sword blade of the propeller.

Danger, in the form of Japanese planes, would come from the sky. He kept scanning the horizon looking for Japanese. Past the plane's windscreen, turbulent clouds were beginning to grow and blossom more rapidly.

Frank looked at Lisa, standing on the right wing root beside the cockpit, balancing herself by gripping the edge of the windscreen framing with her right hand. She'd put on her "new" clothes and looked trim and happier than he'd seen her before.

He motioned to Cyril to have the workmen turn the prop backwards to clear the engine. As the third blade passed in front of the cockpit, he signaled them to stop.

He said a quiet prayer that the battery would still be charged enough to turn the engine. He looked at Lisa and asked, "Ready?"

"Ready." She motioned the workmen away from the prop. In expectant silence, they moved off the runway to the grass.

Lisa turned to him. "You're clear."

In his mind, Frank ran down the checklist: *Red-and-blue-colored knobs, mounted on the left side of the cockpit, mixture and pitch, full forward on the quadrant. Throttle back, then cracked a quarter of an inch. Wobble the hand pump. Check fuel-pressure gauge; it should show between the green marks. Okay. Two shots of prime. Lock primer. Look around to see that everything is clear.*

As he gave her one more look, and he involuntarily smiled at her.

The Ulysses Flight/ Paul Wankowicz

She blushed and lowered her eyes.

Magneto switch to left. Energize switch to on. The starter flywheel began to spin. *The battery is still okay. Wait until the whine of the flywheel evens out to a plateau. Starter-engage switch to 'on.' Keep the gas pressure on with the hand pump. Stick full back to my stomach.*

Up ahead of him the prop blade, black against the sky, shivered and moved to the right. The engine clattered its protest, and coughed. Blue smoke swirled out of the exhausts and gently eddied back toward the tail. The next propeller blade came into view, shivered and stopped.

Lisa said, "Too rich, too hot."

He sat contemplating the panel.

"Over primed?" she suggested.

"I don't know."

"Try it in idle cut-off. Then you can feed fuel when the prime catches," she suggested.

"Sounds plausible, but we'll have to clear the engine again." He motioned to Cyril to have the men crank the engine backwards to clear the cylinders again. He checked the magneto switch, then looked at Lisa.

"Are you lucky?"

"I don't know. Why?" she asked.

"Because I'm going to try it the way you suggested, but there aren't that many starts in the battery."

She held up her hand with her fingers crossed. The men finished turning the engine over. "Here we go. Clear?"

At Lisa's signal, Cyril's men moved back. "Clear!"

Fuel pressure up. Two shots of prime. Energize. Contact. Engage!

The prop shuddered, started turning. There was a cough from the engine, then another. More blue smoke aft. *Now! Mixture to full rich.* When the next blade came into view, Frank saw the long, black engine rock in its mounts and felt a series of healthy thumps. Then, as if someone pulled a cork from the bottle, the engine sprang to life. It soon settled down into a steady song of power.

The Ulysses Flight/ Paul Wankowicz

Lisa was still standing on the wing beside the cockpit with one hand on the canopy. The windy blast from the propeller outlined her body under her shirt.

She was smiling.

I've never seen her smile before. It suits her.

Out of the corner of his eye, he saw the engine temperature creeping up the dial. He inched the throttle forward. The roar now became a solid thing.

Behind him, the blast was laying down the grass, like a wake from a speedboat. The Burmese, who had been squatting by the wing had dropped back in awe and murmured among themselves. Cyril looked worried.

When Frank moved the pitch lever, he heard the propeller start beating the air in coarse pitch as the engine slowed down.

He felt Lisa pound on his shoulder. She pointed straight ahead.

The clouds in front had grown to a threatening dark-gray fringe leading toward them, over the black bulk of the engine. At first he didn't see anything. Then, emerging from the scud, was the silhouette of a biplane diving straight toward them. *"Japanese!"*

Frank's heart stopped. In a pilot's reaction to danger, his hand moved automatically, cutting the switch and pulling the mixture into auto cut-off.

With a rattle of gears, the engine roar stopped, even while the engine rocked briefly in the mounts. To their battered ears, the silence became complete.

Lisa was frozen watching the biplane approach. It was now in close range, guns pointed straight at them.

Lisa deserves better than this! "Run!" he shouted.

Instead, she stood fascinated, watching the enemy biplane.

Frank braced himself, waiting for its machine-gun slugs to plow into him.

The biplane was losing height and banked to the right. As the bottom of its wings came into view, Frank saw R.A.F. rondelles at each

44

wing tip. He let out his breath and stood up in the cockpit to see better. Beyond the edge of the field, the R.A.F. pilot came down in a long, easy glide. The biplane was now over the palms bordering the edge of the field, its engine barely whispering. The sound of the flying wires cutting the air was clearly audible.

With the slightest puff of the engine, the R.A.F. pilot brought the silver aircraft level with the grass, floated a few yards, and then, with infinite economy of motion, settled it down.

Whoever is flying that airplane knows it like a lover knows his mistress, Frank thought.

With little bursts of its engine, the biplane jounced nearer as it picked its way over the grass. It crossed in front of the P-40 and swung right, pulling into line with the American fighter.

From his vantage point, Frank had a good view of the pilot of the two-seater, helmeted and goggled like a WWI aviator. The rear cockpit was empty, except for two mean-looking guns swung into a holding bracket.

The stranger went through his shutting-down check, letting the engine idle for a few seconds before cutting the switch. Slowly, wearily, he stripped off his helmet and jammed it between the windshield and the cowling. Uncoiling his lanky frame from the open cockpit, he slid down the wing. He paused to shuck off his yellow Mae-West and fling it into the rear cockpit. With a careless wave of his hand, he began walking toward the P-40.

Frank slid off the wing to meet him.

The man had the relaxed gait of an athlete. Black hair, bony face, his skin was burnt to a leathery brown. Probably about Frank's age. He wore black shoes, khaki kneesocks, and Africa-Corps shorts. Over his shirt pocket were down-turned cloth wings with a single, diagonally-striped white-and-purple ribbon underneath.

As the R.A.F. pilot came up to Frank, he extended his hand. "Flight Leftenant John Laws, R.A.F." he said. "Johnny to most bods. What-the-bloody-hell are you Yanks doing in this God-forsaken R.A.F. Depot?"

Chapter 9: R.A.F. Mingaladon Airfield, Rangoon, Burma

The very first day after Johnny Laws had disappeared, Wing Commander Hayes had taken a Brewster *Buffalo* to retrace John's flight to discover if he were down in the jungle somewhere. He did this despite knowing that with the lush growth of the Burmese jungle, there was very little chance of spotting a crash site. However, he'd only been able to fly as far as Tavoy, Tenasserim, before the cylinder-head temperature of his Wright engine started climbing into the red. He'd had to turn back to Mingaladon Airfield before the engine seized altogether and before he, himself, became a casualty.

Hayes had to presume Johnny Laws was dead. On his desk, Hayes had half a letter of condolence to Sir David, Lord Laws, John's father. He'd only gotten as far as "Dear Sir David," and had left it unfinished for lack of proper words.

Chapter 10: Alor Star Airfield, Malaya, December 15, 1941

At the same time Frank and Lisa wheeled the P-40 out of the hangar for an engine test, Captain Jiro Kashimura of the Imperial Japanese Air Force was 300 miles to the south of them.

The Captain leaned against the side of his A6M-2 *Zero* fighter, and smoked an excellent English cigarette. When he was not being observed, he perversely enjoyed breaking the "No Smoking Within 50 Meters" regulation. He decided long ago that these all-metal fighters would not explode when someone lit a cigarette.

Everyone in the squadron knew that he smoked, but being the commanding officer had its privileges.

He should have been airborne 15 minutes ago, but his wingman, Lieutenant Horikashi, discovered that his own A6M-2 had developed low-fuel pressure.

That airplane was now in front of the hangar, with mechanics scurrying around it, under the lash of Horikashi's exhortations. The mechanics would probably do a better and faster job if Horikashi left them alone.

Kashimura did not intervene. He had no desire to tangle with his wingman again. Horikashi had been thrust on him by Tokyo. He would have preferred to have one of his own sergeants as a wingman, but there could be no disputing Tokyo's wishes so he had no choice but to wait for the mechanics to fix Horikashi's plane.

On the other hand, this was the sort of tropical morning which delighted Kashimura. The jungle-covered ridge of mountains to the east hid the sun behind the crest until it fully emerged, already brilliant and golden. Its warming rays hit and dispersed the spider-like tendrils of fog clinging to the tops of the field's grasses. Captain Kashimura noticed thousands of crystal-clear droplets adhering to the bending blades of

The Ulysses Flight/ Paul Wankowicz

grass that sparkled like precious stones. *The light has given me a moment of beauty, but the sun will dry the droplets to nothingness leaving only a field of dead grass—until the sparkling dew should come again.*

The scene reminded Kashimura of the scrolls and pictures he enjoyed at the Tokyo Art Exhibit. Believing a man in uniform should not be seen enjoying art, Kashimura donned civilian clothes when on leave, to lose himself in the galleries.

He walked around his fighter and looked toward the hangars. Horikashi's *Zero* was still being worked on. He lit another cigarette before throwing away the butt end of the first. *I'm smoking too much.*

Eleven years of flying had made Kashimura feel the air with his whole body. The air was heavy, full of moisture, like a sack of wet rice on his shoulder. *There will be thunderstorms by mid-morning. The coming storms will make the flight more difficult. The steel-colored skirts of rain from the thunderheads would hide the shoreline and inlets where we are supposed to reconnoiter. A strong storm could pitch us about and try to fling us into the mountains. It would have been better to have started earlier, on time.*

He was still upset with Lieutenant Horikashi because when he'd mentioned low-fuel pressure with what Captain Kashimura felt was a strained naiveté, in the next breath he suggested they ignore it.

Kashimura could not figure out if the Lieutenant was green or playing head games.

As a pilot, Horikashi should have known that low-fuel pressure is not something ordained by the gods. Disregarding it could mean engine failure at a crucial moment, or turning the airplane into a sudden fireball. There was a mechanical reason for it. Kashimura wasn't sure he cared much for Lieutenant Horikashi, but the airplane represented thousands of hours of Japanese labor and had to be taken care of.

He lit a third cigarette and looked toward the hangar. *How much longer?*

It wasn't that Lieutenant Horikashi was overeager. Captain

48

The Ulysses Flight/ Paul Wankowicz

Kashimura knew all about eagerness. He'd started in the infantry as a cadet officer, under the patronage of his uncle. Six years later, a Lieutenant on maneuvers, he saw an awkward Japanese-made biplane, a *Tatikawa*, swoop down over the regimental headquarters to drop a message. It reminded Jiro of a blundering cow-fly. From that moment, he wanted to become a pilot for the Imperial Japanese Army. Luckily, his uncle's influence was strong.

Within the year, he was at the Hamamatsu Flying School. After graduation, he was posted a combat squadron in Manchuria.

Kashimura had been filled with dreams of conquest and eager to start his score. In 1931, the Japanese were still flying the old P-1 planes against the *Rata* fighters supplied to the Chinese by the Russians.

By virtue of his being a Lieutenant, he was given a flight on his arrival. Kashimura didn't know that the P-1 could not turn with the *Rata* fighters.

Just before his first sortie, with the engines already warmed and ticking over, idling, one of the corporal-pilots turned to him and said: "Do not worry, honorable Lieutenant. Corporal Tatsumo will see to it that you come to no harm."

Kashimura considered the Corporal's comments as insubordinate, and made a mental note to reprimand the man later. However, the flight did not go as Kashimura had imagined.

Within the first three minutes, he was in trouble with a *Rata* fighter on his tail. Its machine guns drummed on the fabric of his wings, searching for the P-1's cockpit. In blind panic, Kashimura looked behind him just in time to see a P-1 deliberately crash into the *Rata*. Spellbound, he watched the two airplanes, locked together by the violence of the crash, slowly gyrate to the green earth 2,000 meters below. They fell with the spiral motion of a maple seed, a wahoo.

Corporal Tatsumo had kept his word—at the loss of his life.

Now, in 1941, Captain Jiro Kashimura felt that, by this time, eagerness was no longer dangerous. The Ki-43 that the squadron was flying, and also the Mitsubishi A6M-2 *Zero*, as it was popularly called, had shown immense superiority over the Brewster *Buffaloes* and the Curtiss P-40s of the British and Americans. The Japanese had proven it repeatedly: over Pearl Harbor, over the Philippines and now over Malaya.

Jiro heard the engine of the other *Zero* cough, and then, begin the rhythm of a smooth-running power plant. *We will start soon.*

The Japanese Navy had asked for a survey of the west coast of Burma up to Moulmein. There were reports of a stranded merchant ship, possibly American, hiding in an inlet somewhere.

The Japanese Navy radio intercept had picked up its pleas for help. A couple of B3N observation planes had surveyed the coast, but had seen nothing. On the return flight, one of them crashed into the mountains. The other was pulled off the hunt to cover some naval emergency further south.

Now, it was up to Captain Jiro Kashimura and Lieutenant Horikashi.

The Susei engine in the other fighter had now settled into a quiet idle. The cowl was on, and Kashimura could see a mechanic refitting the last inspection panels in place. He turned toward the hangar and yelled for the line man to come with the fire extinguisher so he could start his own engine. It was time they were in the air.

Chapter 11: At the Tenasserim Airfield Hangar

Johnny unglued himself from the leading edge of the P-40's wing and walked over to where Lisa stood. Then, he turned back toward Frank. "You weren't listening," he said. "My orders from the resident were to fly back anything worthwhile and to burn the rest. The Japanese are supposed to be advancing north from Victoria Point."

"What right have you got? These are United States' airplanes!"

"May I remind you that you are a representative of a foreign power assembling munitions of war on the territory of one of the King's possessions, and without his knowledge or permission."

"I thought you Limeys were allies!"

Johnny looked at Lisa with a broad and mischievous smile . "We are, and if you will come off your perch up there, and stop being so bloody-minded, I'll tell you what we can do.

"I suggest that I stick around for a while and help you get another *Tomahawk* airworthy. Then, at least, we have two to deliver. The *Tomahawk* is more valuable than the *Hart* I flew in, much as I hate to part with the old biplane."

"*Tomahawk?*"

"These. What you Yanks call a P-40."

"That still leaves one. Could you radio for a pilot to come down and ferry it up?"

"'Fraid not, old man. The resident would have my guts for garters were I to try that. The WingCo would agree, but not the old woman of a resident. He sees Japanese under every bed. If I told them up in Rangoon what I was up to here, they'd tell me to burn the whole lot and fly back in the *Hart.*"

The conversation went dead while Frank absorbed this new information.

When they heard Cyril and the villagers leave, Lisa looked out through the crack in the big door of the hangar to see what was up. The sky was ominous. "A storm is coming," she announced.

Johnny looked over her shoulder and said to no one in particular: "It's going to be a grandfather of a storm. I saw it building up as I flew down here."

With that, John Laws, Lisa, and Frank bustled into action. They wheeled the P-40 back into the hangar and rolled shut the great door.

Then, they pushed Johnny's biplane as far into the bushes bordering the airfield as it would go. As a final act, Johnny used his mean-looking machete to cut jungle brush and bamboo, which Lisa and Frank hauled to cover the wings and fuselage of the Hawker *Hart.* The brush would break up its lines to any observer; the plane would be harder to spot from the air.

Chapter 12: Johnny's Flash-Back
to his Service in Britain

The three separated for the afternoon to wait for the storm to pass. Johnny settled his lanky frame on a heap of burlap bags and tarps.

As usual, in moments of inactivity, his mind flooded with memories of the war. Johnny had been flung into the Battle of Britain at a time when an exhausted R.A.F. Fighter Command was the sole defender of the island nation. Just after the invasion of the German military might in France, Germany turned itself against England and Scotland. The British Army was slowly rebuilding itself, but was still almost power-less after leaving most of its equipment and munitions on the beaches of France in the Dunkirk evacuation.

At that time, on paper, a fighter squadron numbered 16 aircraft. How-ever, on a memorable day in early September, 1941, Johnny's squadron was down to only five Mark I *Spitfires*. It was a day that started with disaster and was now forever etched in Johnny's memory.

Another pilot, Johnny's buddy, Stan, was on an early engine test, flying with full tanks. When landing, the plane had a brake failure and creamed his plane through a N.A.F.F.I. truck. Stan did not survive, and his *Spitfire* was a charred wreck. The impact of losing a friend on their own home airfield was shattering to the morale of the other pilots.

Only the day before, a sneak raid by a single German Dornier *Do-17Z* had dropped a 200-kilo bomb on the airfield's air shelter. Ten of the ground crew were buried, including two Women's Auxiliary Air Force (W.A.A.F.) members, who staffed the flight offices. The squad-ron was already short of everything, including people. In addition, Stan's *Spitfire* being blown up left them with only ten serviceable machines.

For the first sortie of the morning, the controller had vectored them onto a large gaggle of Heinkel He-111s, but missed warning them about the Messerschmitts hovering above. Normally, the Heinkels would have presented little difficulty, but the squadron was badly bounced by the Messerschmitt Me-109s.

Phill Deever was just sliding past in front of Johnny's *Spitfire* when Deever was hit by a burst of tracer. Helpless, Johnny watched as Deever's kite rolled lazily onto its side, a banner of flame bathing the cockpit. Deever didn't get out.

Almost at the same moment, a stream of tracer passed over Johnny's cockpit. He desperately broke to the right, and was out of the fight for a while, so he didn't see Jim Dowling and Sgt. Ray Lake bailout of their crippled machines.

A squadron pilot, Jack, flamed a Heinkel-111, but that was poor compensation for the three kites lost in almost as many minutes.

The squadron fared no better in the afternoon. They went after a formation of Dornier *Do-17Z*s. In the ensuing tangle, two more pilots died. The Dorniers were apparently a decoy to waltz planes toward a group of Ju-88s. The Junkers then hit the airfield. Two *Spitfires* undergoing maintenance were blown up in the raid, which resulted in more ground casualties.

Flying a replacement machine wrested from maintenance, Sergeant Lake was the first to spot the Ju-88s that bombed the field, but he was out of ammo. His curses over the radio warned Johnny to discontinue his approach and pull up.

By the time Johnny spotted the attacking airplanes, he had less than 2,000 feet under him and about a second's worth of ammo in his guns. It would have to be a perfect approach. Johnny studied the other airplane for a few seconds.

He spied a Ju-88 scooting away at treetop level. Its dark-green camouflage made it almost invisible. However, The German's cruciform shadow, undulating over hill and dale, gave him away.

Apparently, the German had not seen Johnny's plane stalking above. The crew was probably thinking of the successful attack and of their return home.

The Ulysses Flight/ Paul Wankowicz

Johnny decided on a high-side attack. He slowly pushed the throttle forward and laid the fighter on its side to start the dive. He held the German plane in his sights until he saw its startled gunner awaken to the danger. The gunner tried to swivel his gun in Johnny's direction.

Johnny moved the golden dot of his sight one-half of the range circle ahead of the pilot, and with a quick glance at the bank-and-turn dial, opened fire. The slugs from his *Spitfire*'s eight guns just brushed the front of the German pilot's cockpit, and then, with a final burst of tracers, the fighter's left battery ran out of ammunition.

The unbalance from the recoil momentarily swung the *Spitfire* to the left, walking the fire down the left wing of the bomber.

Then the right battery died, too. Johnny was out of ammunition.

After the angry hammering of Johnny's guns had died, for a breath, the Junkers continued on course as if undisturbed. Then, as if tired, the Ju-88 put its right wing down and cartwheeled into a hill.

At that moment, Johnny's *Spitfire* swept past it. Johnny didn't see the Ju-88's end because his own wing root covered the scene below. Even so, Johnny knew that there would be no survivors. The thought gave him a moment of sardonic pleasure, which he later regretted.

The chase after the German at low level had disoriented him. He didn't recognize any landmarks. He pulled back on the stick into a climbing turn to gain a few thousand feet, hoping to recognize something that could lead him homeward.

As he climbed through 1,500 feet, he saw a twin-engine Avro *Anson* in a desperate panic turn. A trainer. Another glance showed him the reason.

A couple of Me-109s had found the *Anson* trainer, and were taking turns attacking the awkward airplane, like sparrows at a hawk. Only, the *Anson* was no *Hawk*. With its plodding slow speed of only 180 mph, it was more of a sitting duck. It should have been nowhere near skies inhabited by Messerschmitts, Heinkels and Dorniers.

Without warning, the strands holding Johnny's temper parted. *It is all so unfair! Here I am, having fought for my life most of the day, and*

The Ulysses Flight/ Paul Wankowicz

some clueless Anson pilot is looking to me for his salvation against a pair of German fighters. Well, the hell with him! He got himself into this mess. Let him get out of it! Uncle Johnny will just wander off in the direction of home field as if I've never seen him. It will suit the bugger right!

Immediately, he regretted his outburst.

With an angry movement, Johnny laid the stick in the direction of the *Anson* trainer. He could no more abandon a fellow R.A.F. pilot in trouble, even a student, than a Boy Scout could pass up an old lady at a busy street crossing.

As he turned, he had a slight bit of altitude advantage and viewed the scene from above.

The German fighter was just completing his firing pass, long ropey fingers of tracers missing the *Anson* as its pilot continued a desperate turn, wings almost vertical to the horizon.

Both pilots were idiots, Johnny decided: the *Anson* pilot and a tyro of a German. Anyone should have been able to hit the lumbering trainer. By the same token, one had to admire the *Anson* pilot. The man was flying masterfully. As the Messerschmitt finished its gunnery pass and flashed past the *Anson*, its pilot rolled out and headed full throttle for the deck. The *Anson*'s pilot tried to force the Germans to play a cat-and-mouse game to run out of fuel.

The German fighter swung into a climbing turn. This time, he wouldn't miss.

The Anson pilot saw the German lower his undercarriage and flaps to slow down the fighter to the twin-engined trainer's speed. But, at the same time, without realizing it, he'd made it easier for Johnny to catch up. Intent on an easy kill, the German pilot was unaware of the *Spitfire* on his tail. *It should be duck soup, a piece of cake*, Johnny thought.

He held his fire until the German's wingtips were well within the range ring, then depressed the trigger. Nothing happened.

He'd spent all his ammo on the Ju-88. Fury took him. He slammed the throttle into emergency overboost. *I'll ram the bastard!*

The Ulysses Flight/ Paul Wankowicz

The reality of what he was proposing to do didn't hit Johnny until the situation was irrevocable. It took only a split second for the *Spitfire* on overboost to catch the slowed-up Messerschmitt.

Johnny saw the tail, the empennage of the plane ahead fill his windscreen, and instinctively pulled back on the stick. He kicked right rudder as he did. There was a splintering crash as the *Spitfire*'s propeller ate its way into the German's control surfaces. Pieces cracked against the armored glass of the windscreen, and grated down the fuselage. When the *Spitfire* swung to the right, its wing caught the Me-109's radio mast, tearing it out by the roots, before the two airplanes were free of each other. Johnny glanced at the Me-109 flipping over onto its back, gear and flaps still down, as it plummeted to the field below. He didn't see it hit. The crippled state of his own kite now required his whole attention.

The *Spitfire*'s engine was still running, but something under the cowl was beating itself to death. The prop was out of balance, shaking the whole airframe as it turned. The prop gave no traction. The *Spitfire*'s speed slipped away, as was its meager ration of altitude.

The *Anson* had recovered from its dive, and came briefly alongside. Out of the corner of his eye, Johnny saw the British pilot wave, and spared a millisecond to wave back. The *Anson* banked and flew away. There was nothing its pilot could do to help.

Johnny's rage was spent with the violence of the collision, and he was glad that the R.A.F. pilot survived.

John could see a field ahead within gliding distance. He cut the switches. He'd rather risk a dead-stick landing than have the engine seize up, or shake itself out of its bearers at some crucial moment. The prop stopped the moment he cut the switches, leaving one blade vertical in front of his field of view. It annoyed him. Pushing the starter switch didn't have any effect. He had to leave it that way.

Until the last moment, Johnny thought he could bring the plane in more or less intact. But as he skimmed the trees bordering the field, he saw that some eager Home Guards had driven anti-glider stakes ran-

57

domly throughout the airfield. Johnny's crippled fighter slammed through the first stake, shearing off its right wing and throwing the fuselage to the right.

After the initial shock, there was confusion: Grass, dirt, crashes, and aluminum pieces flew through the air when the fighter crushed some of the stakes and impaled itself on others. When the plane came to a stop little remained. It was a total write-off. The right wing lay where it had broken off. The tail unit had twisted 90-degrees to the cockpit section. The motor had come loose and was half-buried. A lone blade of the propeller remained, sticking upright out of the grass. Only luck, and the Sutton harness had saved Johnny from injury.

Wearily, he got out of the wreckage, and sat down on what was left of the right wing, to wait for help. Nearby, the Messerschmitt's painted-silver radio mast was miraculously welded to the leading edge of the wing, the antenna wire and the insulators now all wrapped around the wing and aileron.

Eventually a farmer drove him back to the station. However, security regulations forbade the civilian to drive any further than the gate, so Johnny had to walk the last 200 yards, parachute pack slung forlornly over his shoulder. He tossed the parachute onto the shelf in the Ready Room.

A Flight Sergeant entered. "The C.O. saw you trudge in. He would like to see you in his office," the Sergeant said.

The reception area ante-chamber to the C.O.'s office was empty. As he walked in, Johnny, hesitating slightly, tapped lightly on the door.

"Come in!" the C.O. said gruffly.

Johnny pushed the door open and walked in. The sun was just setting, slanting in through the window, bathing the room in a garish orange-red light, silhouetting the Wing Commander, who sat behind his desk continuing his telephone conversation.

As Johnny entered the office, he motioned Johnny to sit down. Johnny listened to the one-sided conversation. "Yes, sir. No, he's right here" "No, quite all right. . . ." "Yes sir, I'll tell him." "No, we're down

The Ulysses Flight/ Paul Wankowicz

to six . . ." "Can't expect too much. Not all of them are like that. . . ."
"Very gratifying. Good bye, then."

The C.O. put the telephone on its cradle, reached into the bottom
drawer for a bottle of whiskey and two glasses. He poured one for
himself and one for Johnny, and settled back. "Understand you've had
quite an afternoon of it," he said.

"Some idiot in an *Anson*, sir, out for a Sunday spin at 2,000 feet. I
almost let him get shot up, but couldn't let the German have the joy.
I'm afraid I pranged my kite. A total write-off."

The C.O. smiled. "That was your idiot on the phone just now. Air
Vice-Marshal Forbes. He read our squadron letters on your kite. Said he
was most grateful to you, and congratulated me on our squadron's
esprit de corps. As a matter of fact, he said something about putting
you in for a Distinguished Flying Cross."

"What was he doing up there in an *Anson* trainer? Looking to
commit suicide?"

"I asked him that, although not quite in those terms. It seems,
without forewarning, he was summoned to London for a conference
with Winston. His personal *Hurricane* was off on ops. They are as short
as we are. The only thing they had for him to fly was that old *Anson*.
He had to bump a couple of ferry pilots off it."

The C.O. paused. "That was a good piece of work, Johnny. It got us
another German even if it did cost us a kite."

"I also got the Ju-88 that bombed our field," Johnny added.

"Yes, Forbes told me about it. He saw the whole thing before the
Me-109 went after him. Forbes said that the fighter was going after you
until he spotted the *Anson*. Probably thought the *Faithful Annie* was
easier meat. How do you feel? Are you okay?"

"Yes, Fit. Luck and the Sutton harness kept me from bashing
about."

"Think you can fly tomorrow? We're down to six *Spitfires* and I'd
like the old staggers flying them. The replacements are losing the
planes too fast."

59

The Ulysses Flight/ Paul Wankowicz

"Right. Will do. Just a bit tired, I guess."

"Hell, we are all that. All over England. By peace-time standards, none of us should be anywhere near an aircraft." The C.O. pointed to a calendar hanging on the wall, depicting the pristine English countryside. "But we don't want the Germans and their hob-nailed boots tromping over that!"

"Is it that bad?"

"Worse. If Goering has any brains, he'll keep up the attacks against the fighter stations for another week. After that, we'll have nothing left. Not of any consequence. I just got a directive from the Air Ministry saying. 'If we have a *Tiger Moth* or two, hang bomb racks on them.' *Tiger Moth*s!" the C.O. exploded. "Top speed 100 miles an hour. Made of wood and bloody canvas. And I'm supposed to put my pilots in them! Even the Air Ministry is beginning to feel the pinch," he added with a touch of sarcasm. "That is for your ears only," the C.O. said. "I don't want to spread gloom among the bods."

Johnny recoiled at the C.O.'s words. Arming de Havilland *Tiger Moth* trainers seemed like a last stand.

"Now go over to the medical office and get the M.O. to declare you fit for flying. Tell him, 'Those are my orders.' And, you, sir, can stand me a drink later on this evening, to repay the booze I've just wasted on you." He dismissed him.

Johnny left to be checked over by the Medical Officer.

The next morning's predicted attacks never came, however. Unknown to the R.A.F., after being told that the British were still reacting to the raids in full strength, Goering decided that the battle against the British airfields was not producing sufficient results. At the very moment of decision, the Luftwaffe had lost the campaign. Goering switched strategy to attacks against London, allowing the R.A.F. to catch its breath.

Johnny would never forget the shock the C.O.'s words had given him. The possibility of defeat had never crossed his mind.

Chapter 13: Tenasserim Airfield Hangar, December 15, 1941

If Johnny could save Frank's P-40 now, he would do it no matter what the cost. It could be just the mite to swing the balance in the war. He knew that Rangoon would be hard pressed when the Japanese finally decided to come. *I must not allow the American fighters to be taken by the Japanese.*

There is no time to get a third pilot. One of the fighters will have to be sacrificed. It would hurt, but saving it's a problem with no solution. I don't want the Japanese to study it. . . . The crazy Yank, Frank, won't be of any help. He'd probably try to brain me before letting us destroy any of the P-40 fighters.

Johnny's thoughts were interrupted by Lisa who was looking out the slit in the hangar door. She said, "If anyone wants to get anything from outside, they better do it now. Another storm is almost upon us!"

As she spoke, a gust of wind slammed the great door against its stops, rattling the roof. The palm trees grated loudly against the hangar. The whole structure groaned as if in complaint. The first slashing lances of rain and wind hit the field, raising a small cloud of broken grass, and dust. That cloud hung above the field for a few seconds until driven back to the ground by the sheer force of the onslaught.

The three gathered by the vertical slit between the door and the jamb to watch the spectacle. With the noise of the storm, normal speech was impossible.

"Be pretty dicey in that storm," Johnny yelled.

"Bloody right!" Lisa yelled back . "A cockeyed boob like that would drop anybody's bundle!"

Frank looked at her. He hadn't understood a word she'd said, but noticed that her teeth were barred in an animal smile and her eyes

The Ulysses Flight/ Paul Wankowicz

alighted as she viewed the storm. *Was she drawing some kind of primitive strength from it?*

Johnny had understood. Frank heard him yell back: "*Dinkum!* You from Aussie?"

She nodded. But their speech was interrupted by a different note in the wind. Their eyes turned upward to where clouds hung low over the airfield.

They didn't have to wait long. The noise swelled to a thunder as two fighters, wing-to-wing, flashed into view. The two airplanes looked immensely powerful, but half-hidden in the boiling rain they were barely stable against the turbulence. Crimson circles on their wings and fuselages appeared as bright as arterial blood.

"Japanese," Johnny said.

"Where could they have come from?" Frank asked.

Johnny shrugged. "Nakhom Rachisma Airfield in Siam? Alor Star? Who knows? It means we haven't much time," he shouted to Frank.

"What are we going to do about the third P-40?" Frank asked. "If they saw your damned biplane, we're out of business!"

"Not my fault, old man," Johnny said. "Now, we better make up our minds. I'll help you work on the second *Tomahawk* and fly it up along with you, but the third..." He didn't finish his sentence.

"And Lisa?" Frank asked.

"I hadn't considered that. Maybe I'd better take her up in the *Hart*. Abandon the two other aircraft." He didn't have the courage to say *burn*.

Frank looked about him. In desperation, he knew damn well what Johnny meant by *abandon*.

Lisa turned. With what could be described as a puckish smile, she said, "I don't understand what the difficulty is. I'll fly the third fighter."

Barely breathing, the men shared a long stunned silence.

Lisa broke it by adding. "But if we are going to get all three into the air, we'd better start to work. As Johnny said, 'There isn't much time.'"

"Wait a minute! Did you say that YOU would fly one of the

fighters?" Frank said, still stunned.

Lisa looked directly at him. There was still a hint of a bemused smile on her lips. "I did."

He looked confused. "You fly?"

"I have about 250 hours: *Harvard*-I, CAC Wackett *Wirraways*, Avro *Ansons* and Dragon *Rapides* mostly."

"What the hell are they?"

"Aircraft," Johnny interposed. "The *Harvard*-I is what you call the AT-6, I believe. The *Wirraway* is the Aussie version."

Frank was beginning to put the pieces together. *It had been no accident that Lisa had headed for the airfield. No wonder she's been so good working on the fighters, the way she'd analyzed why the engine hadn't started on the first try. I should have seen it when she followed every move of Johnny's landing, just as I did. No pilot can pass up watching another land, mentally dissecting the other's technique. And what non-airman, would have realized that the airplanes standing in the dark hangar were single-seaters? Or used the term? I've been an idiot.*

Johnny said to Lisa. "The *Tomahawk* is not a *Harvard*-I trainer, you know."

"Would you prefer to leave me here?" she asked, with venom in her voice.

Johnny shook his head. "No, but that kite is dangerous. You haven't enough hours!"

"Wait a moment," Frank interposed. "If she says she can do it, she can. I know how competent she is! Give her a chance."

Lisa looked at him with gratitude. "Thanks, Frank," she said.

Johnny was uncomfortable. "Frank, can I see you for a moment? Alone?"

Frank knew that Johnny would try to talk him out of letting Lisa fly the P-40. Intuition told him that Lisa knew that, too. He would have to distract her. "Lisa," Frank said, "go get that bottle of scotch out of my cubicle, and set up three glasses. We have to celebrate getting that engine going. If we hadn't, . . . " He made an expressive shrug with his shoulders.

She looked straight at him. "Okay, will do," she answered, in a subdued voice.

I'm getting much too fond of that girl.

With the rain still beating on the roof, the only place for the men to talk was the back of the hangar.

"You can't let that girl go," Johnny started, as soon as they were out of earshot. "She'll pile it up at the end of the field!"

"You were going to burn it anyway," Frank said.

"I know, but I wasn't going to make a *suttee* out of it. She'll kill herself."

"What makes you so sure?"

"Bloody hell, be sensible, man. She hasn't the experience. It takes more than the hours she has to put someone into a *Tomahawk* and get them off this bloody-short field. They planned it for Gloster *Gladiator* biplanes, for heaven's sakes! And it's even tight for them!"

Frank peered over the backbone of the fighter separating them from the rest of the hangar.

Lisa sat on a trestle, bent over as if in thought. The bottle glowed amber beside her.

I will not abandon her, Frank resolved.

Chapter 14: Lisa Remembers

All along, Lisa had hoped things would work out, so she could fly one of Frank's fighters out of Tenasserim, but now she felt beaten. It was another valley, another abyss in her life. She looked at the fighter beside her. It's such a beautiful machine! Tears gathered behind her eyes. It had been too much of a dream.

While the men debated her flying competence, Lisa's mind drifted back to her school years.

At age 18, her parents had scraped together enough money to send her to a Swiss boarding school for girls. Their plantation was just beginning to pay, and they thought she should go to a 'Finishing School.' Culturally, the transition was a hard experience for Lisa. It exposed her naivete, and the cruelty of some of her classmates. She wrote home during her second year, asking her parents to bring her home. Her parents acquiesced, but also insisted she continue her higher education. After a holiday, they sent her to a university in Australia.

The university there was like a breath of spring air. Lisa was bright and did not have to *swot*, to work, as hard as her fellow students. There seemed to be no limit to her horizons.

At a spring dance, she met Bill. He danced like a dream. She liked him from the first. He was older than she, and obviously no student.

"What do you do for a living?" she asked, as they pirouetted.

"Escort wonderful things like you," he'd answered.

"No, seriously. You're not a student. What do you do?"

"I fly."

Lisa laughed. "I don't believe you!"

"I bloody-well do! I fly the *Anson* air ambulance for the medical service during the week. On weekends, I teach the lads in the University Air Training Program how to get themselves up and down without pranging their kites and killing themselves. It's the down that gets

65

them."

"I never knew anyone who flies. Normal people don't do that," she said.

"What do you mean by normal? I'm as normal as you are," he said, looking down at her breasts.

"Really?"

"Well, not quite the curves. . . . I have an idea. How are your eyes?"

"Normal."

"No. I mean, do you wear glasses?"

Lisa thought for a moment that he was being impertinent, but answered him anyway. "No, why? Should I?"

"Good. Then I bet I could teach you to fly. Come out to the airfield on Saturday. I'll give you a ride in a *Harvard*, if I can whip it away from the R.A.A.F."

She nodded her head. "Would you?" She really didn't think he would.

For the rest of the week, she vacillated: *To go or not to go?* At the last minute, she decided to go.

She had no idea as to what to wear. She finally chose a simple white shirt and a light-green skirt with a red belt.

Lisa was out at the little grassy airfield by 10:00 hours, feeling very much out of place in the unfamiliar surroundings. The airfield was empty except for two men, who were working on the engine of a biplane parked at the far end of the field. They gave her a cursory inspection and returned to their labors.

She leaned on the fence beginning to feel foolish, but it was pleasant weather. The sun was warm on her shoulders, and she could feel the light wind ruffling her hair. By 10:30 hours, nothing had happened. She was about to walk back to the bus, disappointed. It was then that a bright yellow-monoplane, sporting R.A.A.F. rondelles, came in to view, low over the fence and touched down in the middle of the field. It ran to the border, and then, with a burst of its engine raising clouds of red dust, taxied to where she was standing. It was Bill.

He shut off the engine and jumped off the wing. In his helmet and with his eyes squinting against the glare, he looked more like a hero out of a Hollywood film than someone she knew.

"I was afraid you wouldn't come," he said, in a manner of greeting.

He looked disapprovingly at her skirt. "You're going to have to wear a parachute," he told her.

She didn't catch what he meant until it came to fastening the between-the-legs straps. She managed them herself.

Once that had been mastered, he gave her a light, chamois-leather helmet, and they both clambered onto the wing where he showed her how to drop into the front seat under the long, glassed-in canopy. He pointed out the little lever that adjusted the height of her seat so that she could see over the coaming, above the panel of dials in front of her.

As he helped her with the over-the-shoulder straps of the Sutton harness, she had the fleeting thought this may be an excuse for him to be fresh; but then, she realized this was just a part of a ritual that was natural to him. As his hands adjusted the straps between her breasts, he didn't seem to have any realization that she was a girl. She never had been handled in such a disinterested manner before. It made her wonder. This seemed to be a different world.

She soon forgot, though, when he continued the explanation of the various controls that seemed to her to have been haphazardly distributed around the cockpit.

"The black knob of the throttle is just where you can reach it comfortably with your left hand," Bill said. "The stick coming up between your knees and oversize rudder pedals control the direction in which the nose is pointed."

He had her look back along the fuselage to see the rudder swing from one side to the other as she alternately pushed the pedals. Lastly, he made sure that the chamois-skin helmet's fit was snug, and he made sure her intercom was plugged in.

It was all so foreign from the square of the glare-shield over the

67

instrument panel, to the heavy, black, Bakelite grip of the stick! Yet, somehow, she felt at home.

Bill adjusted his helmet and harness, then climbed into the second seat, behind her.

Lisa heard the growl of the starter up front. The prop shuddered, moved and then disappeared in a blur. The noise of the engine came faintly through her ear pads. The wind came around the windshield, playfully tugging around her head and shoulders.

With a little more engine, and a stronger odor of gas fumes, they jounced over the dry-grass field.

The two mechanics paused to watch the yellow trainer taxi away.

When Bill lined up the plane into the wind, Lisa could see the rudder pedals move as he maneuvered into position. The throttle went forward and the engine exploded into a roar of power that seemed to penetrate her whole body. In the excitement of motion, she was hardly aware of the field rushing past. Suddenly the jouncing stopped, the airplane slid a bit to the right, as if trying the air, straightened out, and they were airborne pointing directly into the sky. She turned around and smiled at Bill. *This is living!*

Within an hour, she was doing mild, coordinated turns, fully conscious of how delicately the aerodynamic forces balanced themselves in the *Harvard*-I.

By the time she had landed, she knew exactly what she was going to do. She would leave her studies of English Literature and convince the Dean to let her take Aeronautical Engineering. Although it might take a lot of persuasion, she would convince her parents to send money for flying lessons.

Luck was with her. Two years before, six Australian companies had put up the capital of one-million pounds to found an indigenous aircraft factory. The Commonwealth Aircraft Corporation was about to wheel out its first airplane, the Wackett *Wirraway*. Australia was becoming chauvinistically air-minded.

The Dean of the Engineering School was an early investor in the

The Ulysses Flight/ Paul Wankowicz

Commonwealth. After talking with Lisa, he found no barriers to her plans. Her first hurdle fell much easily than she had anticipated.

All that year and into the next, she flew. Sometimes she flew *Tiger Moth*s; sometimes, when Bill could borrow it, on the *Harvard*-I, and once or twice on the new CAC Wackett *Wirraway*. She soon had her pilot's license. In her free time, she signed up for trips as second pilot and EMT on the air ambulance using either *Anson* or a Dragon *Rapide*. By her second year at the engineering school, even Bill admitted she was good.

Then came 1939, Hitler, tension in Burma and Malaya, and Bill was sent off to England. She learned he'd won the Distinguished Flying Cross, and then, he'd been killed in a Wellington bomber over Hamburg. It was a blow.

She would always be grateful for their time together, and his influence on her life, and their shared love of aviation.

As the year progressed, Lisa's mother wrote that her father had been recalled to active duty in the Dutch Navy, leaving her mother to run the plantation.

Lisa regretfully packed her bags, took a boat for Rangoon, Burma, and made her way back to the plantation to help her mother. In two years of flying, Lisa logged in more than 150 hours of pilotage.

The argument in the back of the hangar was not going the way Johnny wanted. *The crazy Yank is determined to let the girl fly the fighter!* . . .

Despite himself, Johnny was beginning to see his point. From what Captain Carringer said, the girl seemed bloody-competent with airplanes. If she didn't crash at the end of the field, and that was a big if, it meant they would salvage three fighters at the cost of one superannuated biplane, his *Hart*, which they could leave on the little field.

"I used to do this in England," Johnny told Frank. "Teaching replacements before they were sent out on ops. And I've flown the *Tomahawk* in some trials against the *Spitfire*."

"Incredulous! You've flown the P-40?" Frank asked.

The Ulysses Flight/ Paul Wankowicz

"About ten hours. They pulled me off the *Spits* and sent me to the Royal Aircraft Establishment to fly the *Tomahawk,* against a *Spitfire* and a captured Me-109. Frankly, the *Tomahawk* didn't match up. If you took it over 12,000 feet, with its un-supercharged engine, it just didn't have what you Yanks call, 'Enough guts'!"

Frank mentally breathed a sigh of relief, forgetting all about the argument over Lisa. "You've just solved my major problem. The airplanes came without any of the pilot's notes and I haven't flown a P-40, although I've flown the P-36. But that's a different beast. Will you remember enough to brief us?"

"Piece of cake! It would have been pretty dicey taking off this handkerchief of a field without the notes and never having flown this type of kite before."

Frank shrugged, "What else could I do?"

"You have a point," Johnny agreed.

Feeling more important to be in the role of instructor, Johnny finally yielded on the promise that he would teach Lisa and Frank the ins and outs of the P-40.

"Okay, then," Frank summarized. "She flies with us, and you teach both of us about the P-40. Shake on it!"

Shaking hands to bind a bargain was to Johnny a barbaric custom. To him, a bargain was a bargain once it was spoken. He shook hands, anyway. *Maybe the Yank is all right, despite his primitive, direct customs.*

When Frank and Johnny emerged from behind the P-40, Lisa was still sitting in the same pensive position. Her face was drawn and colorless. It wrung Frank's heart to see her so. The three glasses and the bottle remained on the wing where she'd placed them. She seemed morose and no longer interested in the morning's accomplishments.

Johnny signaled to Frank to keep quiet, and turned to Lisa. "Let's pour us all a drink," Johnny said.

Frank wondered what would happen next, but said nothing, honoring Johnny's request for silence.

The Ulysses Flight/ Paul Wankowicz

"First," Johnny started, "a toast to the King, required of all English-men." He tossed his drink down and stuck out the glass for Lisa to refill. He waited until Frank and Lisa were ready with their glasses before he continued, "Now, obligatory toast over, a real toast to the intrepid pilots, Johnny, Frank, and Lisa, who will fly three P-40 *Toma-hawk*s to Rangoon." After all glasses were raised, he called, "Bottoms up!"

"Stone the crows," she gasped. She choked as the drink hit her throat. "Strong!"

In the interval between Johnny's words and Lisa's glass getting to her lips, Frank saw her face light up as if someone had changed films on a movie projector.

Johnny added, "We're a team now, so let's get to work!"

The next five days were, for all of them, full of unremitting labor, interrupted only for sleep and Johnny's training sessions with Lisa.

The lessons started with the basics requiring her to learn the position of every dial, toggle, and switch in the P-40's cockpit—while blindfolded. Next, under Johnny's gimlet eye, he put her through "sequences" during which, while still blindfolded, she had to resolve one fictitious emergency after another. He was harsh in his criticism, even of the most minor errors in sequence or timing. Any motion she missed, toward a wrong switch or knob, brought an immediate storm of censure.

Frank could see Lisa's lips slitted in anger and a flush of temper spread over her face. He considered pulling Johnny aside to ask him to back off, but as long as Lisa didn't complain, Frank kept out of it.

Most of the time, they made a good working team.

After they had refueled and armed the first P-40, they poised it so it could be rolled out rapidly. It was their 'desperation defense' in case the Japanese came in strength. Since it was unquestionably Frank's plane, it was agreed he was to fly it in any such last-ditch stand.

In the short and infrequent times for discussion, they exchanged ideas, but now Frank and Lisa mostly listened to Johnny, who, of the three, was the only one who had fired his guns at an enemy in battle.

Johnny suggested they use the R.A.F.-style short-field takeoff procedure. It depended on holding the brakes on and opening the throttle as far as the brakes would hold, then raising the tail before releasing the brakes.

To Frank, who was accustomed to the long, paved runways in the U.S., the short-field takeoff was a novel idea.

"When you open the throttle fully, the tail will bounce twice," Johnny said, "and you can become airborne after the second bounce. However, because the P-40 is a short-coupled airplane, the torque can be a problem, making it difficult to hold the airplane straight. Lisa, you will have the best chance, being lighter than we are."

"Why don't we just cut down the palms and saplings at the end of the takeoff strip?" Lisa suggested.

"We've already had Jap planes snooping around. Seeing the airfield being manicured could bring on a full scale investigation by the Japanese," Frank said.

Johnny called it. "We leave the greenery as it is, and go with the short-field takeoff. It can be done." Then he announced, "When we do go, I have to fly north to Rangoon. Lisa, I know you wanted to get to Singapore, but I'm technically A.W.O.L. until I reappear at Rangoon's Mingaladon Airfield where my unit is posted."

Frank interjected, "Where I really have to go is Manila."

Johnny ignored the comment. "Half-way to Rangoon, above Mergui, there is an intermediate 'emergency' airfield where stocks of av fuel are kept. We should make a refueling stop there. That way we can keep the planes lighter for the takeoff from this airstrip."

"The fuel we put into my plane before was only enough for the test flight," Frank commented. "Okay, now, we can go to Mingaladon Airfield first, but then I'm heading for Singapore. I also need to get a current update on the situation in Manila."

"You can probably get an update at Mingaladon Airfield. There are

The Ulysses Flight/ Paul Wankowicz

a bunch of you Yanks there, already, who fly *Tomahawk*s. Unless, that is, they have been sent up north by Area Commander Robert Brooke-Popham. He's been threatening to do that to get them out of his hair," Johnny said.

"How many are there in the squadron?" Frank asked.

"I don't think they are a formal squadron. They're some sort of a volunteer group under an ex-colonel with a funny name, like a girl's name."

"Not Claire Lee Chennault?"

"That's the one. Funny name for a man to have."

"Lord, Johnny! I can't go to Rangoon. He'd skin me alive, have me back to private, and take these airplanes the moment he sets his eyes on me."

"You know him then?"

"No, but he knows me!"

"You sound as if you'd raped his daughter. Oops! Sorry, Lisa!"

"Not quite that bad, or maybe worse. Sometime back when he was still a light colonel, we had a fly-off in the old P-36s. I was just out of school, but according to the judges, my films showed I'd shot him down twice. Chennault's never forgiven me for that! Not the Colonel!"

"I sure hope they have been moved away from Area Commander Brooke-Popham, and sent to Magwe which is about 250 miles north of Rangoon. Chennault's group was too rowdy for Popham." Johnny said.

"If I warn him, W/C Geoffrey Hayes, my Commanding Officer, will make certain you are not spotted so that you and the good Colonel Claire will not meet. We'll just hide your kites in one of our hangars."

Later, while Johnny and Lisa were going over the routines one last time, Frank worked on a surprise project. He fashioned a crude set of pilot's wings out of a piece of brass found in the hangar, but all he'd had to use to make the wings was Halliday's ball-peen hammer and a cold chisel. From safety wire, he fashioned a pin and soldered it to the back of the wing. *The finished product looked primitive, but it will serve its purpose,* Frank thought.

73

The Ulysses Flight/ Paul Wankowicz

As the days passed, Lisa became more quiet. She realized how dangerous the undertaking would be.

To Frank, she appeared more and more drawn. He tried to find
something to say to ease her fears, but he knew the danger was real. He
prayed her competence would carry her through.

By the evening of December 20th, sitting around the kerosene lamp,
Frank, Johnny, and Lisa were killing Halliday's bottle and having their
last conference in Tenasserim. All three fighters were as ready as they
could make them: sufficiently fueled, and armed with the .30-caliber
ammunition Frank had brought from the *Nike Victory*. The cowl-
mounted 50s, which were the P-40s' main armament, would ride empty
until Rangoon where, Johnny promised, stocks of U.S.-type ammunition would be available.

In preparation, Frank took out most of the larger bills from the
paymasters' case and hid them in the baggage compartments of his P-
40. They could go for emergency rations. He tore a page from a
Stromberg manual and wrote a receipt for the rest of the money, and
signed it over to Cyril.

Lisa took it from him and scrawled something under his semi-legal
Transfer of Funds phraseology, but he didn't have the chance to see
what she'd written.

That evening one preparation remained. Frank rose dramatically and
cleared his throat. He had worked out a long speech to present the
handcrafted wings to Lisa. Now, he found himself totally tongue-tied.
"I thought you deserved these," he declared as he dropped the crude
piece of brass into her hand.

She understood what it meant.

"These are the most beautiful wings I've ever seen!" She turned
away to hide her tears. When she turned around, Frank was pleased to
see the wings were pinned to her shirt above the breast pocket. The men
cleared their throats to avoid a show of emotion. Then they shared

The Ulysses Flight/ Paul Wankowicz

toasts all around.

Their last morning at Tenasserim Field dawned clear and a little cooler.

Johnny sniffed at the air and declared, "A different air mass moved in during the night. The weather will probably deteriorate further north, but not enough to abort our plans."

At first light, with the help of Cyril and several other village men, they moved the fighters out of the hangar, and arranged them wingtip to wingtip in front of the hangar.

By then, the airfield itself was still in the inky shadow of dawn, but the sun had risen on the other side of the mountains, painting the sky overhead with blues and oranges. Dew sparkled in the grass and soaked their boots. It painted the tires of the fighters a deep, shining black.

The sight of the three fighters, powerful and ready, thrilled Frank.

Walk-around. Check the control surfaces, the underside of the flaps, the pitot tube, the static port. Frank went through his routine. *Drain a cupful of fuel from the spring-loaded cock under the wing to rid the tanks of any condensate that might have collected there overnight. Kick the tail-wheel fore and aft. Re-check the many things that could make the difference between flight and disaster.*

Johnny and Frank insisted Lisa put on Johnny's parachute. They helped her get into it.

As Lisa dropped into her cockpit, Frank saw the brief glint of the wings.

Frank got into his plane last. He had insisted on being the last in the order of takeoff. He wanted to be in a position to have the chance to rescue the girl in case she didn't make it, although he knew that there could be no rescue. He had seen modern, fully-gassed fighters burn.

With all three pilots now in place, Johnny, who would lead, raised his hand above the framing of the canopy and rotated it. *Start Engines!*

The crucial moment. Exhausts belched blue smoke, then Frank's and Johnny's engines settled into a rhythmic roar. Lisa's plane had some trouble: her engine fired rich and the propeller shuddered to a halt. Frank saw her bend down into the cockpit to recheck the engine controls.

The second time Lisa's engine coughed, balked, and then settled into a steady tick-over. She looked up with obvious relief, and waved to Frank. All three planes were running.

Johnny looked around to make sure things were clear, and advanced his throttle. The slowly-turning prop dissolved into a blur, blasting slipstream that rattled the hangar door behind. The tail bobbed up experimentally, once, twice, then, Johnny brought the fighter to horizontal.

Frank noticed Johnny was holding full-right rudder against the slipstream to try to balance out the torque.

For a second, the fighter stood poised on its wheels; then Johnny released the brakes, and the machine shot forward as if off a catapult. As he'd predicted, the tail bounced twice and he was airborne, sliding to the right, just skimming the grass, barely in control, but flying. The fighter banked left, straightened, and disappeared in the deeper band of shadow covering the far end of the field, only to triumphantly emerge into the full sunlight over the trees.

Lisa's turn next.

Frank found his chest was tight. He watched as she rolled the canopy shut. Shutting the canopy on takeoff, he knew, made rescue more difficult. They had talked about it, and decided that the slight advantage in streamlining granted by a shut canopy was worth the extra risk. Now he wondered.

She'd opened her engine and raised the tail. So far, so good. Her rudder was not as far over as Johnny's had been. Frank wondered, too, late, *Does she have the strength of hip to hold full rudder against the slipstream?* He watched her as she released her brakes. The fighter over pivoted to the left. She tried to kick it straight, and over-controlled. The plane slewed to the right, skipping over the grass in little hops. The wheels kicked up pieces of turf and shredded grass.

Frank's heart stopped. *Lisa is holding the plane on the very edge of*

The Ulysses Flight/ Paul Wankowicz

*control and could lose that edge as soon as she becomes airborne . . .
and crash.*

Frank undid his seat belt and stood up in the cockpit, ready to run to
the scene. Just as he did, he saw her propeller slow down, and her
fighter came to a stop.

She turned it around, and taxied back to the starting position for
another try. As she pulled up beside Frank, she didn't look at him, but
bent her head down, busy in the cockpit.

Soon she was ready again. This time, she held the tail down, trading
length of run against ease of control, and it went better.

Frank watched her plane gathering speed. Her plane's tail wheel left
the ground well before she was half-way down the miserable little strip.
She appears to have the torque under control this time.

From his vantage point, Frank couldn't tell if she would have
enough speed before she ran out of field. Holding his breath, he
watched her disappear into the shadow. Time stopped. Then she reap-
peared in the light above the trees, skimming their tops, almost stalled.
The struggle to increase her speed was painful to watch, and Frank
didn't dare move until she began a weak climb.

Because he had watched Frank and Lisa do their run, now his own
reflexes had learned their rote. The tail bounced twice, and he was
flying. Not well, just on the edge of stall, feeling like a ball bearing on a
sheet of greased glass, but flying. The treeline was racing toward him,
but with each revolution of the engine, the fighter was gaining life. The
coconut palms seemed a lot taller than they were, but, miraculously,
their crowns slid under him as he gently eased the control column a
fraction toward him.

Ahead, black against the morning glare of the sky, Lisa's P-40 was
climbing for altitude, while much higher, gear still down to allow them
to catch up with him, Johnny's plane orbited. Still climbing, they
formed into a rough 'V' with the coast unwinding below them, and
headed north toward Rangoon.

Chapter 15: Geoffrey Hayes & Roland Biard: From 1938 through 1941

Bangkok, Thailand (Siam) in late November 1941 was in ferment. The Japanese were everywhere. They needed Thailand for the coming offensive planned to unify all of Asia under Japan's benevolent roof. They needed Thai acquiescence to their march to the Malayan borders. Most of Bangkok's population understood what was afoot, but didn't seem to care. The diplomats were not as aware.

The British Embassy was totally in the dark since the disappearance of their Chief Analyst Edward Lyford. The Ambassador felt that a replacement was desperately needed. Thailand was 'uncovered' until a replacement arrived.

In the meantime, Lyford's effects were put into storage in the Embassy's basement. A call went out to the British Foreign Office to send a new analyst. Unknown to the Ambassador, however, there was already a British agent in Bangkok—Roland Biard, who went by the name of Pa Tim, and who worked as a taxi driver-courier. Driving a decrepit Fiat, twice a day he picked up and distributed various dispatches among the scattered Japanese establishments.

Most of these dispatches originated with Colonel Lee Pi Seki in Japanese Military Intelligence. Among the locals, it was well known that this fat Japanese Colonel was masquerading as a correspondent for the *Tokyo Times*, but was really the Chief of Japanese Military Intelligence in Thailand.

Seki made his headquarters in a large old house on Bamrung Road in the center of Bangkok. The house was ideal for the task and served both as his living quarters and his office. It was guarded by a contingent of 13 thinly-disguised Japanese soldiers under the command of an elderly sergeant.

The Ulysses Flight/ Paul Wankowicz

The house was originally set in the fashionable part of the city. As the city expanded, it had long ago been by-passed, no longer in an affluent area, but now becoming further and further away from the city center of Bangkok. In time, the frontage of the lot on which the house stood was taken over by a hodgepodge of ramshackle structures for shops. Lucky for Seki, these shops effectively screened the house itself from the curious.

Access to it was limited to a narrow lane which ran between a soap store and a rice merchant who faced Bamrung Muang Road. The lane then curved directly to the front of Seki's house. A sluggish canal protected the back of the residence from the collection of slapped-together huts on the other side of the muddy waterway.

As was then the custom in Thailand, the house itself stood on stilts with the space under the first floor being used for the storage of large 'Ali Baba' jars formerly used to collect run-off water from the roof during the monsoon. The jars used to be the house's potable water supply during the dry season. Now, they still proved useful whenever the unpredictable municipal water supply failed.

The damp-and-musty spaces beside the jars were shared by the Japanese soldiers, their women, and assorted naked and dirty children who had attached themselves to the house.

At sunset, the charcoal chappies were brought out by each small group to cook their suppers. The cooking fires shrouded the house in lazily-turning blue smoke. After supper, various rotting pieces of dirty canvas, or of shredding matting, were strung between the beams to separate the area into individual sleeping compartments.

Inside the main house, the upper floors followed Thai tradition. Both floors were divided into four apartments, each with verandas. The second-story verandas, overhanging the first-story ones, gave the house an over-balanced, cake-like appearance.

A central stairway led to the second floor, ending in a windowless room which had served as a chapel when the house was used as a mission school for orphaned girls. The Japanese, not knowing what to do with that particular room, used it for storage of odds and ends.

Four upstairs' apartments, larger than the ones below, led off from the chapel.

Colonel Seki took the second floor as his own. He made his sleeping quarters in the front of the house while the two apartments in the rear became his office and a meeting room. He usually worked by the large table in the meeting room, beside the safe in which the various documents were kept.

Into this sanctuary, Pa Tim was admitted twice a day: once at 10:00 hours, and again at 17:00 hours.

Colonel Seki would personally hand him the mail to be delivered to the Japanese Naval Intelligence Head Quarters across town, or to the Japanese Embassy on Sathorn Road.

In the beginning, a Japanese soldier in civilian clothes would accompany Pa Tim as he delivered the papers. After a few weeks, Colonel Seki apparently considered the Thai taxi driver trustworthy, and allowed Pa Tim to deliver the messages unaccompanied.

The Japanese didn't suspect that Pa Tim's real name was Roland Biard, Officer/Intel., and R.A.F.

As Pa Tim, he successfully infiltrated Seki's task force as a courier by Wing Commander Geoffrey Hayes orders. How Geoffrey Hayes had managed the *tour de force* was a secret he never revealed.

Geoffrey Hayes himself was an anomaly, even for the R.A.F. Of good Yorkshire stock, he had joined the Royal Light Cavalry at 16. By the age of 18, he was in France in charge of a troop. That year, 1914, was a bad year for cavalry. Against Hiram Maxim's new machine-gun, horsemen could accomplish little other than to become casualties. After a few abortive skirmishes, the Royal Lights found themselves in the trenches, indistinguishable from infantry. Mud didn't suit Geoffrey Hayes' temperament, and he volunteered for the R.F.C., the Royal Flying Corps. Promotion in the R.F.C. was a matter of survival. By the end of the war, Hayes, at 21, found himself a Major with a Distin-

The Ulysses Flight/ Paul Wankowicz

guished Flying Cross on his tunic. Because his rank was temporary, when the peace came he reverted to the rank of Lieutenant. Even so, he stayed in. No other career was open to him.

Between 1918 and 1930, he'd flown a wide variety of aircraft, which included SE-5As, *Grebes, Siskins, Valencias, Brisfits*. He also flew the *Supermarine* S-6 in the King's High-Speed Flight race, established especially for the Schneider Trophy Contest, but, in the end, didn't fly in the competition because he drew the short straw.

In 1930, Hayes had just touched the Hawker *Hart* when the Air Ministry saw fit to post him as crew to the R-101, the government-built *Zeppelin*, which was to establish British supremacy in the lighter-than-air field.

After one look at the R-101 monstrosity, Hayes refused the post saying, "The R-101 is dangerous."

The British Air Ministry took unkindly to any man who had no faith in their toy. Hayes fell from grace. It didn't help matters any that the R-101 crashed barely four hours after it had left its mooring mast at the especially-built base in Cardington, Bedfordshire, England, killing almost everyone aboard.

Hayes was in bad odor, along with his friend, 'Stuffy' Dowding. It was Sir Dowding who'd suggested that Hayes join the newly-formed Intelligence Branch, the "R.A.F./I." It became a good place to hide.

In the fall of 1937, Hayes worked in London in the Air Ministry, when Bob Rackham, a war-time acquaintance, phoned. "Say Geof, old chap, could you come around for lunch?" Rackham asked. "I have something to discuss."

Rackham had flown in the same squadron with Hayes in 1917, and had been 'invalided out' of the R.F.C. after the tail on his Nieuport *Bebe* failed during a low pass over the trenches.

Between the wars, as a civilian, Rackham had become a successful wine merchant. It had turned him into one of those tweedy Englishmen who finally get to look like the foreign caricatures of the British.

81

The Ulysses Flight/ Paul Wankowicz

Hayes and Rackham weren't exactly friends, but, at the time, the whole of the Intelligence Establishment ran on the 'old boy network.'

Half-way through the meal, Rackham leaned back. "You know, Geof," he said, "I'm in a spot of bother."

"Something personal?"

"Well, yes and no, but I thought you could help. Do you remember a chap called Tom Biard? He was with us in the old 97th *Camels.* Got shot down."

Hayes remembered Tom Biard well. A short, stocky man with thick black hair, he looked more like a French Buccaneer than an Englishman. Yet he descended from English ancestry, country people from Cornwall, and he was one of the best pilots in the squadron.

"Tangled with one Fokker too many. Almost didn't survive," Rackham said. "Wasn't he connected with some scandal later? Something about a princess? Do you remember?"

Hayes memory kicked in. "Right. That's the chap."

"He went off to India and got himself killed in an SE-5 fighter," Rackham said.

Hayes reflected. *Rackham is damnably inaccurate. He's managed to gloss over three very tragic and bitter years in Tom Biard's life, and that Biard had died sometime later in Thailand, not in India! . . .That wild afternoon, Tom went to the rescue of a single RE-8, which was being harried by a gaggle of Fokker D-7s and an Albatros. As soon as the RE-8 saw the Fokkers were distracted by Biard's Sopwith Camel, the RE-8 gratefully dived away toward home. Biard held out as long as he could against the overwhelming numbers. In the end, one German's expert deflection shot wounded him in the knee and hip. Tom Biard crashed between the lines, and came close to bleeding to death before the infantry got to him. It took Tom a full year to get over the wounds.*

"No, that time he survived it, but he came out of it with a permanently stiff leg," Hayes said. "He was not permitted to fly combat again, but the powers that be thought to extend his service life by sending him to Siam in the dual role of Attaché and Military Advisor."

82

The Ulysses Flight/ Paul Wankowicz

"As soon as Biard took post in Bangkok," Hayes remembered, "a deluge of telegrams arrived at the British Air Ministry, all complaining that there was nothing in Thailand which could remotely be called an airplane."

"Around 1918, with WWI winding down, someone in the British Air Ministry decided that three SE-5s could be crated up and sent out to Tom Biard, for him to "test-fly in tropical conditions". However, when they crated the engines, they forgot to include the carburetors. It took six months before some mendacious Air Ministry clerk decided to investigate why someone in Thailand would want three Rolls-Royce carburetors, and another five months before the parts were finally put on a Pacific & Orient Packet ship to the Orient.

Rackham continued his story. "The results were predictable. The wings spars of the fighter had rotted during tropical storage; on Tom Biard's first flight, the plane shed its wings, killing the pilot.

At the time, it seemed a particularly needless tragedy. "During the Inquest, however, it came to light that he had married a Thai princess of the blood. Her marriage to a foreigner had thrown her into dishonor, and his sudden death left her penniless. Unfortunately, Tom Biard's Will was still made out in favor of his English fiancée.

"The litigation was thoroughly messy, and dragged through the courts for months. It became the R.A.F. scandal of the year. In the end, a fund was quietly established for his wife and child."

Yes, Hayes thought, *'went to India, and got himself killed' was not only inaccurate, but a cruel description of a difficult period for a very honest and good man. . . . I wish Rackham would get to the point.*

"He had a posthumous son, you know," Rackham continued, "born after Tom's death. His mother named him Roland. She brought Roland to England, and enrolled him in public school using The Fund.

"Later, he somehow learned I'd flown in the same squadron as his father. He came to see me about joining R.A.F., you see."

Hayes didn't quite see. He wiped his mouth, and put down his napkin. "How can I help?"

83

The Ulysses Flight/ Paul Wankowicz

"It seems quite impossible. Maybe you could explain things to him," Rackham said.

"What's wrong with him wanting to get into the R.A.F.?"

"Wants to be a pilot. It just wouldn't do. He looks like a *wog*. Took after his mother."

Hayes decided he didn't like Rackham. "Why me?" he asked.

"Well, old man. I thought that you, being still in the Royal Air Force and all that, could tell him more easily than I. You could put on your uniform and your gongs, your medals, I mean. He'd take it more easily from a real officer."

I am being asked to be Rackham's executioner, so to speak, and I don't like the idea—but Biard's son is part of the R.A.F. family. I'll have to go through with it. "I think it can be arranged," Hayes said after a pause. "When do you think that young Biard can come in to see me?" Hayes asked.

"He's in London now. Anytime. Tomorrow?" Rackham replied.

"Not quite. I'll have to arrange for an office. I can't possibly see him in mine. Security, you know. I'll call you tomorrow, and let you know the form." He'd have to borrow the Wing Commander's office down the hall.

Fred Winterbotham had run the European Section of the new Intelligence group. Hayes had been deputized to keep an eye on Asia. His office was full of maps and reports stacked on his desk, mixed in with general Intelligence paraphernalia that he wouldn't like the visitor to see.

Hayes managed to snag the Wing Commander's office a few days later, and set up the appointment for 15:00 hours.

The office had the usual drab, military-brown linoleum. Some of the windows hadn't been opened for years. The Wing Commander, however, had tried to relieve the drabness with two photographs Hayes particularly liked. One showed six Hawker *Harts* of the County of London Squadron in tight formation over summer cumulus clouds. The other was of a *Spitfire* head on, on knife-edge, both ailerons at full deflection, and the rudder hard over. This was inscribed by "Mutt" Summers, and even in the still photograph, the Supermarine's Test Pilot's legendary skill could be discerned. Hayes knew that Mutt had unofficially "arranged" for the WingCo to have an early, and unauthorized, familiarization flight in the then-new fighter.

Punctually at 15:00 hours, the old porter shuffled in to announce that Roland Biard was out front.

Hayes' heart sank when Roland Biard strode through the doorway. The boy looked exactly like a Thai with his black hair, slitted eyes, short stature, and yellow complexion. Rackham had said that the boy was almost 18, but his Asian cast made him appear much younger.

As they shook hands, Hayes hoped his own face hadn't betrayed his disappointment. Until he saw Biard, Hayes had hoped to find some way of "taking the boy into the R.A.F. family."

The boy was quick. Hayes watched him survey the contents of the office with his first glance.

After he'd cataloged the rest of the room, his eyes returned to the pictures of the Hawkers and the *Spitfire.* He sat down awkwardly on the chair facing the desk. His jet-black eyes took in Hayes' wings with the single ribbon of the D.F.C. medal underneath.

Hayes opened the conversation. "I'm Squadron Leader Hayes. Rackham tells me you want to get into the R.A.F., and he's asked me to see if that could be arranged. Is that right?"

Hayes saw the boy's eyes go to the two-and-a-half rings on his sleeve, as if to check the accuracy of the last statement.

"Yes, sir."

"How old are you?"

"Eighteen, sir."

"And you want to go for pilot training?"

"Yes, sir."

"How tall are you?"

"About five foot two, sir."

The Ulysses Flight/ Paul Wankowicz

For an instant, Hayes said nothing, thinking. *That is below the minimum for pilots. Biard might just make air gunner, but who would fly with him on their crew? Rackham was right, he'd be called a wog wherever he went.* . . . It occurred to Hayes that the boy probably spent the whole of his life under that, or a similar epithet. *English public-school pupils are not noted for delicacy to their peers. Since the lad survived it, there's strength in him somewhere.* Then, he returned to the conversation.

"Why do you want to fly?" he asked.

"Well, sir, my father was a flyer in the last war."

"Yes. I know. I flew *Camels* with him over the Somme."

"You did, sir? Was he a good flyer?"

"One of the best. You had to be that to survive in those days." As he said that, Hayes realized that he'd dug a trap for himself; but he was beginning to like the boy.

"Excuse me, sir. Is that the Distinguished Flying Cross that you are wearing?"

"Yes."

"Aren't the stripes usually different?"

"They are nowadays, but this is the D.F.C. they gave out at first, before the R.A.F. was in existence, when we were all known as the Royal Flying Corps and were part of the Army."

"I see. Did my father have one, too?"

"He did. As a matter of fact, we met at the investiture at Bucking-ham Palace. We both got our medals on the same day and were very surprised, weeks later, to find ourselves in the same unit." *The boy is obviously idolizing his father. There could be worse motivations.* A stray thought passed through Hayes head. *Bangkok could use a sleeper. Could this boy be sent there?*

Hayes considered his next words with great care. "There's a major difficulty right now," he said. "You are below minimum height for pilot training." He saw the disappointment creep into the boy's eyes. "But," Hayes continued rapidly, "if you'd care to join the R.A.F. in a ground capacity, as an officer, there is a chance that, some time in the future, we might manage to get around that. How would you feel about it?"

After his moment of dejection, the boy was attentive again. "I'd like that, sir. If you recommend it."

"You understand it might be a job that is somewhat different from the one you visualized." Hayes felt as if he were walking through a thicket of words. "But it would be an important job, and you would be a member of the R.A.F." Hayes paused to contemplate his next sentence; he decided it was more true than false. "After you've finished the initial job, then it is quite possible we could arrange pilot training. You'd have bought yourself into it, so to speak."

"If you suggest it, sir, I'd like that very much."

"That's all right then." Hayes would have to see Winterbotham, and to put the question up; but it probably would not be difficult to get him to agree. "What are your present plans?"

"I have none, sir."

"Where are you staying?"

"Charing Cross. A hotel."

"Look. It will take a couple of days to get things sorted out and moving. In the meantime, would you like to move in with me in my flat? It would save you hotel money."

"I'd like that very much."

"It's settled then. If you'll wait in the hall, I'll give you a key, and write a note to the serving woman. I'll be home about six. In the meantime, bring your things from the hotel, and make yourself at home. Tell the woman to show you to the small room. It's more comfortable. She'll see to it being dusted and the like. All right?"

"Yes, sir."

That was how Pa Tim found himself driving a decrepit Fiat in Bangkok, unbeknownst to the ambassador, or anyone else except for Hayes and possibly Winterbotham.

Chapter 16: Bangkok, Thailand (Siam), December 8, 1941

When December, 1941 came, Roland had noticed a rising excitement among the Japanese. But today, the 8th of December, something definite had to be happening. As he entered, in the guise of Pa Tim, he noticed that the sergeant was dressed in a military uniform, no longer masquerading as a civilian.

This would be Pa Tim's last days in Bangkok. Hayes had promised him a Christmas in an English Mess, in the Mess of the two Rangoon fighter squadrons which he was now commanding. After that, Roland hoped, he would go to flying training, to fly in combat before the war ended.

Hayes' orders to Roland had been strict. He was to remain a sleeper unless he saw something that could be of great importance to the English War effort. Only then could he take part in active espionage, and only if he could see a way to escape; but Roland desperately wanted to bring something vital to Hayes to repay him for the invitation to celebrate Christmas with Hayes' Squadron in Rangoon. The day before, Roland thought that maybe his chance had come. The courier from Japan had brought Colonel Seki a little red-bordered book. Just from the way Seki handled it, the red book seemed to have been of immense importance to the Japanese. Roland decided to steal it, but before he could put anything in motion, Seki had put the book into his heavy office safe, slammed the door, and rotated the dial to make sure it was locked.

Roland's chance was gone, and he relapsed into his role as Pa Tim, the taxi driver/courier. He regretted that, after his year and-a-half stay in Thailand, he could not bring a *fait accompli* to Hayes for Christmas.

The Ulysses Flight/ Paul Wankowicz

Today was different. *Something is definitely happening among the Japanese*. It was now afternoon. Pa Tim waved cheerily to the uniformed Japanese Sergeant, and continued up the stairs for his evening document pick-up from Colonel Lee Pi Seki. The stairs led past the window-less chapel storage room, half-illuminated by one dim bulb hanging over the landing. The chapel had no real function nowadays. The Japanese now used it for the storage of odds and ends, such as kerosene, kept there in case the electricity failed, odd bits of rugs and such, and some military stores that Roland didn't recognize.

At the landing, he turned right into Seki's study. Colonel Seki hadn't finished with the dispatches. To his surprise, Pa Tim noticed that Colonel Seki had also donned his colonel's uniform, a heavy cotton tunic. It already showed sweat stains from Seki's corpulent neck.

When Pa Tim entered, Colonel Seki was intent on reading his documents and impatiently waved his hand, motioning him to wait. Pa Tim stepped behind the Japanese officer's chair and was looking around when he noticed the red-bordered book had been taken out of the safe and was on the table with other papers. With rising excitement, Pa Tim realized, *This is my chance.*

Hayes had not neglected Pa Tim's training. For a solid five weeks, Biard had been apprenticed to a certain Captain Clark, whose main interest was in how to kill bare-handed.

At first, Roland was revolted by Clark's ideas. He felt that it was not sporting to creep up behind one's enemy and to surreptitiously kill him by snapping his neck or breaking his windpipe. *Killing,* Biard had then thought, *should be done face to face with both antagonists wielding manly weapons.*

Clark had not been unprepared for this and worked on the explanation that it was unfair to one's side not to use every means at hand. It was unpatriotic, like joining an English football team when one had cheated on one's training. In the end, Roland had become a mixture of English Public School lad and a professional killer; and as Clark had

89

meant it to happen, at this moment, the killer took over.

Moving quietly, Pa Tim took a step closer to Seki's bent-over form. The silence was almost tangible, only the nervous twittering of code from the radio room below, and the brusque laugh of the sergeant at the bottom of the stairs interrupted the airlessness of the room.

As Pa Tim moved closer to Seki, he pirouetted so that he was almost back-to-back with him. Looking over his right shoulder, he drove his arm down so that the point of his elbow sank into the sweaty flesh of Seki's neck. At first, his elbow encountered no resistance, then, Pa Tim felt bone on cartilage slip, making a noise like a heavy rubber band snapping. Seki's head was now at an odd angle, and he let out a gasp. Then his body began to slip under the table, as if drunk. To prevent this and the noise of his falling from alerting someone downstairs, Pa Tim grabbed a handful of Seki's uniform, swung him around, and quietly positioned the Japanese on the floor. Seki's eyes were open in incomprehension, and his mouth was working like that of a hooked fish.

Neglecting the body, Pa Tim reached for the red book and secured it under his belt. Now, he had to move fast.

He grabbed the main dispatches, which had to be distributed everyday. That was good. Pa Tim could deliver the orders to the Japanese Navy on time and avoid arousing suspicion. He gathered the documents into the standard envelope, and tucked that, too, behind his belt.

Colonel Seki was still alive, and his eyes were following every move, beginning to understanding what was happening to him.

Pa Tim could not tell how much damage his blow had done. Would Seki regain enough movement to alert the men below?

He had to make sure that Seki died now, even though Roland knew the next moments would haunt him for the rest of his days. Kneeling down by the Japanese Officer's head, Pa Tim clamped his left hand over Seki's wet mouth. With his right hand, he pinched Seki's nostrils, at the same time pushing the head down into the rug.

Seki suddenly understood. Fear and hatred were in his eyes.

The Ulysses Flight/ Paul Wankowicz

Pa Tim couldn't look. He closed his eyes, and started a long count of 50.

Suddenly, Colonel Seki summoned the last of his strength, and sunk his teeth into the fleshy part of Pa Tim's hand. It almost made Roland let go, but he held on, clenching his teeth against the pain.

Eventually, the bite relaxed. At the end of the count, Seki had been dead for several seconds.

Without looking at the corpse, Pa Tim got up, and went into the hall to listen. There was no change in the thin noises filtering up from below. He quickly went to the chapel store room and retrieved a can of kerosene. A fire would cover his tracks.

He rucked up the rug next to Seki's body and saturated it with kerosene.

Pa Tim pulled out of his pockets a pack of Lucky Strike cigarettes and the matchbooks, which were carefully tucked under the cellophane wrapper to keep them dry in the high humidity of Bangkok. American cigarettes were full of oxidizer and would burn, no matter what. He lit two of them, and put their unlit ends against the paper match heads. Then, he closed the matchbook covers about them to keep them in place. This arrangement, Clark had taught him, made an excellent time fuse. When the cigarettes burned down to the matches, the matches would flare setting alight whatever was around.

He swept some papers off the desk onto the kerosene-soaked rug and pushed them closer to the matches set with their burning cigarettes. He crumpled more papers and put them on top. He set the half-empty kerosene can next to the bonfire.

Satisfied, Pa Tim pulled the dispatch envelope from behind his belt before he started downstairs.

The Sergeant gave him the briefest of glances as he walked past, just enough to assure himself that the courier had the usual envelope of orders in his hand. Once outside, Pa Tim strolled leisurely to his Fiat. Much to his relief, it started up at once.

He clenched his hand to control the bleeding. *My hand hurts like*

The Ulysses Flight/ Paul Wankowicz

hell, but I'll see to that later. Right now, I must deliver the dispatches to the Japanese Navy as if nothing happened.

Then I can disappear.

He'd prepared this disguise in advance, almost immediately after his arrival in Bangkok, for emergencies such as this one. Now he would use them.

As soon as he was out of Bangkok, he shaved his head and put on the robes of a Buddhist Postulant. No one in Thailand would question a Buddhist Monk. Then, he left for Rangoon.

Chapter 17: In the Air
Over Tenasserim Airfield

Johnny Laws smiled as the edge of the jungle flashed under his wings and disappeared astern. The takeoff was not quite as dicey as he'd imagined. *This is a good bird. The torque was a bit worse than I'd remembered. The P-40 is close-coupled and requires a strong boot on the rudder to keep it rolling straight.* He wondered, *How will Lisa manage it? She's competent, just as Frank had said, but will she be strong enough to man-handle the fighter? Does she have enough air experience?*

Even as the thoughts flashed through his head, Johnny's hands automatically adjusted the controls for cruise-climb, reduced the power, setting the pitch, and nudging the radiator shutters. Habit asserted itself and he skidded the machine, first right then left, while he scanned the sky behind him for any enemy. Satisfied, he gently laid the stick to the right, leading the plane into a mild climbing turn. Only then did he look back at the little, rectangular, green Tenasserim airfield hacked out of the jungle below. As he looked down he could see that Frank's plane was still parked by the hangar, engine at idle, ticking over.

Lisa apparently missed her first takeoff attempt and was taxiing back to the starting position.

Johnny held his turn automatically, reducing power to stay low. He was beginning to get the feel of the airplane. It felt sturdy and workman-like under his hand. He watched as Lisa again lined up her plane and revved up the engine.

I don't envy her. Hopefully, I've been a good instructor. First flight in an unfamiliar airplane, with much more power than she'd ever flown before, and on a much-too-short airfield. If she doesn't make it, I'll blame myself for the rest of my life. Either I should have been a better teacher, or found a way to keep her from trying.

The Ulysses Flight/ Paul Wankowicz

From his altitude, her fighter looked more like a toy plane than the real thing. She had now released the brakes and was bounding across the field.

He held his breath as the fighter below suddenly slewed to the left, but she caught it in time. Gratefully, he saw her hoist the plane off the deck, and watched it barely clear the palm trees bordering the field.

Triumphantly, she set it into a climbing turn.

Without really noticing it, Johnny saw Frank's fighter begin to move. Then, his British-trained reflexes again asserted themselves: *never fixate on anything for too long, keep checking for the enemy.* He skidded the plane right, and then, left to clear the sky behind him. Johnny had not worried about Frank's ability to make it out of that little field; he had a good feeling for male competence, but Lisa was unfamiliar ground. By the time he looked again, Frank had cleared the treeline and continued to climb. Now, all three were airborne.

Many of the women that he had met in England equated their femininity with the inability to handle anything mechanical.

If a lady's MG were to break down, she would rather stand by the side of the road to wait for some sturdy male to come look under the bonnet than try to fix the trouble herself. On the other hand, Johnny had to admit, many women took over vital jobs during the Battle of Britain and acquitted themselves marvelously well. And some in Britain were flying combat aircraft to the operational squadrons. *Neither they, nor Lisa, lacked femininity. On the contrary, their competence made them all the more attractive.*

But, at the moment, Johnny's first concern was flying. He checked the sky again for marauding Japanese, and then, shifted his attention to two olive-drab fighters pulling into a loose 'V' behind him.

Back in the hangar, it had been decided that he would lead. In case they met up with Japanese aircraft, they'd decided Frank and Johnny would take them on while Lisa was to scoot away at low altitude, and make her way to the airstrip to wait for them. He'd made a couple of

94

The Ulysses Flight/ Paul Wankowicz

sketch maps of the airfield above Mergui to use in case they got separated. He was the only one of the three with any knowledge of the country below them, or of the flying conditions they could expect to run into.

Johnny watched as Frank pulled into position a few yards to his left and slightly behind. Frank flew with the aplomb of a man who had joined a formation a thousand times before. Johnny waved with his throttle arm as Frank slid the final few inches to be in perfect alignment.

Johnny could see him concentrating on the jungle below, probably trying to spot the *Nike Victory.*

Lisa was still struggling with her airplane, experimenting with the controls before sliding in close.

Johnny smiled. *Probably her first flight in formation.*

He remembered the sheer terror of his first formation flight, watching the leader's wing tip as his instructor tucked into position bobbing terrifyingly close to his own cockpit.

He'd learned in de Havilland *Tiger Moth*s in Elementary Flying School.

The American Curtis P-40 had a generous truck-like cockpit, with the coaming below his shoulder, much more roomy, and with better visibility than that of the *Spitfire.*

As Lisa pulled up alongside, he could see most of her upper body above the framing of her canopy. With some of her reddish-blond hair escaping her helmet and catching the sunlight, she formed an intriguing picture.

He waved to her and she smiled back, not quite yet daring to let go of the throttle. He saw her nod toward the jungle. A thin veil of clouds like gauze had slid underneath them; through it, the jungle became dark and foreboding ground, over which raced their three planes' shadows.

His was surrounded by what pilots call "the glory," a luminescent double rainbow in a halo from wing tip to wing tip. It was a trick of optics that made the rainbow always surround your own shadow. It

95

must have been what delighted Lisa.

The thin layer of stratus clouds below finally focused Johnny's attention on something that had been maturing in the back of his mind for some time. The weather was changing. Now, almost every type of cloud would be crowding in over the jungle. The stratus layer warned him that the next morning's weather would be thick, probably impossible. He was doubly glad that they had left early; it would give them time to replenish whatever petrol they needed from the Nat Eidendung Strip, and then, move on to Mingaladon Airfield near Rangoon, where his own squadron of Brewster *Buffalo*es were based. He wondered, *What will happen after that? Will I have to return to flying Buffaloes under Hayes?*

If I understand the crazy Yank, Frank will insist on continuing to the Philippines alone. Johnny didn't think that Hayes, the squadron C.O., would lend him pilots to help him with his responsibility to deliver all three P-40s to Clark Field near Manila. Burma was hard-strapped as it was. Lisa would probably have to stay in Rangoon. She seemed like a good pilot, but unfortunately, no provisions existed for female pilots in the British colonial military.

With his idle thoughts came the realization that he would miss them. He hadn't realized it before, but they all had grown close during the days of danger and strenuous work.

Something above to his left caught his eye. Leaning forward, he squinted up at the blinding blue of the sky: two airplanes, approximately 40 degrees off the P-40's course, a couple of thousand feet above. As they neared, he could see their fuselages shining white by the reflections of the clouds below. The red circles on their wings seemed to glow with a light of their own.

Frank saw them, too. He pulled up close and pointed upward.

Johnny cursed the lack of a radio. If the Japanese have not seen them, it would be much safer to leave them alone to continue serenely on their business; but, back at Tenasserim Field, the three had decided if an enemy is seen, they would attack, if for nothing else, for the

The Ulysses Flight/ Paul Wankowicz

protection of Lisa. There was no way without a radio to reverse that decision.

Johnny rocked his plane from side to side to attract her attention, then pointed at her and downwards.

For a second she was confused, then understanding flashed through her and she nodded her head, already cutting power and starting her drop toward the floor of the jungle.

Johnny hoped the sketch map would be enough to lead her to Nat Eidendung airfield. He pointed toward Frank and advanced his throttle.

The sun was still fairly low to the east. Frank saw Johnny's olive-drab P-40 enter a climbing turn to the right, and at the same time Lisa's plane dropped away toward the jungle. He swung his controls after Johnny, understanding that they were headed for the classic position: up sun and slightly above the Japanese. As he climbed, Frank tried to remember all that he'd been taught, but found himself remarkably empty-brained. He toggled the gun-charging handles and, remembering the countless drills that he'd gone through in combat school, set the arming switches to 'on.'

As they came out of their climbing turn, Frank had a good look at the Japanese who were, unbelievably, continuing on their way, unaware of the danger behind them. The lead Japanese machine was the larger of the two, a two-seat bomber with oversize, spatted landing gear. It's escort was a fighter of more modern design. Both were painted olive-green on top, cowls black, colors to blend with the jungle below, which made them hard to spot. However, the red of their insignia stood out like blood.

As they came out of the turn, Frank realized Johnny would go for the bomber's rear gunner to give a dangerous 'sting in the tail.' That would leave the fighter for Frank.

The Japanese hadn't seen them.

Frank felt his guts tighten. In a minute, he would either be a victor, or dead. All of his training led him to this point, but would it be enough?

97

The Ulysses Flight/ Paul Wankowicz

He was gaining on the throttled-back Japanese single seater. He glanced around the cockpit to make sure he'd forgotten nothing vital. *Gun switches on. Gas selector to main. Pitch fine. The red mixture-knob on the quadrant full forward to auto-rich. Seat harness tight.*

Frank had done this repeatedly in practice, shooting with gun cameras, but this was for real. His muscles were screaming, unwilling to relax.

He was coming up fast. The slight dive out of the sun had given him a good speed advantage. The back of his head was tight against the head-rest. He lined up the old-fashioned ring-and-bead sight on the plane ahead. His eyes lowered to the needle-and-ball to make sure he was coordinated, that his shots would not slide wide. *Now!* His finger closed on the trigger atop the black grip of the control column and, as if angry, the P-40 juddered to the recoil. Speed fell away, and Frank was conscious of bringing up the nose just a hair. His whole being was concentrated on the silhouette ahead.

A touch of powder fumes entered the cockpit. He couldn't see if he was hitting.

I miss the tracers which weren't included in the Nike Victory's manifest, but my aim must have been good. Ahead a small silver piece detached itself from somewhere near the left wing root and rushed toward him.

This is easy, he thought. *Nothing to it.*

The tumbling, glittering piece of the plane in his view distracted his eyes into following it, a mistake rarely allowed to be made twice by a fighter pilot hoping for longevity.

When he looked again, the Japanese fighter was gone. He could see only blank sky. For an instant, he sat stupefied. *Nothing could move that fast!*

He swept a hasty glance around, but still nothing. *If the airplane's not ahead, it must be somewhere. . . .behind!*

The cold sweat of panic broke out over him. He twisted to the left, looking behind. *Nothing.* Then to his right. *There it is!* Black and

98

The Ulysses Flight/ Paul Wankowicz

menacing against the sky, just sliding into killer range, he could see the greenish-red fireflies dancing above its cowl.

Instinct took over. Frank booted full-right rudder, horsing the stick to back and left. The airplane snap-rolled violently. Frank had the impression of the gyrating horizon with the sun's rays flashing across the back, crackle-finished panel, giving him a glimpse of crazily-registering instruments. He centered the controls, hoping that the roll had thrown off his attacker.

The fighter, which had attacked him, was maneuverable to the extreme. Nothing Frank had ever flown could have looped out of the way that fast. *The P-36 I flew in Panama was a lumbering truck compared to what I've just seen!*

If that pilot had been a better shot, Frank realized, *I'd be dead now.*

In the instinctive snap-roll-break, Frank had lost sight of his opponent. All he could do was to keep the left aileron and top rudder, and to confuse the Japanese's aim by skidding. He could hear his plane's duralumin skin of the rear fuselage denting under the pressure of the unexpected strains, but the airplane was holding together.

The jungle is coming up fast. He centered the rudder and rolled into an aileron turn to the left to begin his pullout. *This is the moment of danger. If the other fighter has kept up with me, I'll make a perfect target as he eases out of the dive.*

He hunched his shoulders and waited for the slugs to rip into the thin metal behind him. *Where's the other fighter?* He felt a thin thread of admiration for the P-40 for hanging together.

The G-forces of his pullout were beginning to yellow out the periphery of his vision. Then he caught sight of something flashing above him. He eased slightly forward on the stick and fought against gravity to look up. It was a wing decorated with the red Rising Sun of Japan, flipping lazily over and over, and trailing pieces of its inner structure like viscera. It floated downward in a lazy, leaf-like motion.

As he comprehended where it had come from, he looked below to see the rest of the crippled Japanese fighter, a thin, corkscrewing vertical trail of light-blue gasoline vapor marking its path. It looked like a wounded mosquito.

Even as he watched, the nose of the fighter appeared to brush the top of the jungle's trees and the whole dissolved into an orange-and-gold fire, almost as bright as the sun, which reached up, consuming the trail of fuel it had released during its death dive.

The fire died quickly, leaving a tenuous veil of smoke floating over the jungle's canopy.

Look as he might, Frank could not see the scar of the fighter's going in. The jungle had swallowed it whole. Frank pulled the P-40 into a gentle climb, breathing for the first time since the battle began.

His knees refused to work.

For a few minutes, he flew straight over the cover of the jungle, taking big gulps of air, recovering. Then he remembered: *Johnny should be around somewhere and fuel will be getting low. Either I have to find Johnny, or orient myself with the sketch map.*

He coordinated a wide turn, scanning the sky, but it was empty. *No sign of Johnny, nor of Johnny's opponent.* An overwhelming feeling of fatigue was creeping over him. He cranked the canopy back a few inches, to let in air. The noise of the engine was loud. He could feel the force as it washed across his face. *The ridge below,* he remembered now, *runs roughly north and south. If I fly west, I should be able to see the Gulf of Martaban.* The coast ran parallel to the ridge, with a larger island, Martaban, west of Moulmein. *The airfield,* Johnny said, *was almost directly east of that, against the side of the ridge.* Frank shrugged his shoulders under his straps. *I'll have to try.*

Chapter 18: Alor Star Airfield, December 15, 1941

The sun had just set behind the black of the jungle's treeline to the west, before Captain Kashimura caught up with Lieutenant Horikashi to take him to task for wrecking the undercarriage of Horikashi's *Zero* when returning from the morning's flight.

Although he was aware that airplanes get damaged in a war, Lieutenant Horikashi's accident was sheer ham-handedness as far as Kashimura was concerned. Much of the day had gone in routine tasks of squadron command, but that didn't lessen the feelings that Horikashi was avoiding him.

When he finally found the Lieutenant, the Captain asked, "Where in heaven did you learn to handle an airplane like that?"

"But, Honorable Captain, this was not my fault. The airplane's landing gear is all wrongly-designed. The engineer put the wheels too far forward of the center of gravity, making it unstable on the ground."

"Are you trying to teach me how an airplane should be built? Or be smarter than the engineers who spent their entire lives thinking about such problems? Next time, pay attention to where the wind is coming from."

"The devil with this flying business. I'd much rather be with the General Staff in Tokyo," Lieutenant Horikashi said, as he turned to go.

Captain Kashimura looked after him. *There will be trouble for this one, for sure*, he thought. *It sounds as if Lieutenant Horikashi doesn't like to pilot an airplane. Unbelievable! For anyone who hates flying to be allowed to touch an airplane is sacrilege.*

He now looked upon Lieutenant Horikashi as the Pope would have looked at the apparition of the devil. Yet Horikashi was a brother officer and Kashimura had to remain polite, just to keep his blood pressure under control.

Kashimura felt that if a crash or an accident left him crippled and unable to fly, he would commit suicide. Without the clean air, the

The Ulysses Flight/ Paul Wankowicz

freedom, and without the comradeship of those who flew, life would not be worth keeping.

Shamefully, Captain Kashimura was as lost now as when, years ago, flying in China and still green, he'd discovered that one of his lieutenants felt much like Lieutenant Horikashi. Then, that lieutenant's doubts began affecting the effectiveness of his squadron. The man took out his frustrations and fears on the veteran-enlisted pilots in the group.

Captain Kashimura had not known what to do then, just as now. His immediate reaction would have been to post the officer out of his squadron, but under the rigid discipline of the Japanese Army, that was not possible. He could have talked with him, but Kashimura knew Horikashi would never admit to anything, and the result of such a discussion would be further tension.

Previously, he had still been wondering what action he should take, when one of the Sergeant pilots had taken the solution of the problem upon himself.

Captain Kashimura wasn't exactly certain how it had developed, but the Sergeant must have challenged the Lieutenant to an aerial duel. From his vantage 3,281 feet above, Kashimura first saw them as two little model airplanes, silver Type-95 biplanes, apparently playing a demented game of hide-and-seek around the Chinese hills. As the Commanding Officer, he was furious. Squadron equipment and precious gasoline should not be wasted on games. Kashimura cut his throttle to dive down and signal them to quit, when his ears heard the crackle of machine-gun fire. The idiots were shooting at each other!

Even before the nose of Kashimura's biplane began dropping below the horizon, he saw the lead biplane suddenly start streaming a thin, transparent veil of gray smoke, barely visible against the green of the valley below. As he watched, the head of the smoke trail blazed into a point of flame. At first only a pin-prick of light against the plane's silver fabric, but it grew rapidly, consuming the machine as it spread. The burning plane hung for a breath like a burning arrow, then as if tired, it slid down, disintegrating against the bottom of the valley.

The Ulysses Flight/ Paul Wankowicz

The so-called victor rose in a vertical chandelle. His wings flashed in the sun. Then, he nose-dived into his opponent's smouldering wreckage.

As a result, back at headquarters, Captain Kashimura had to file a report as to the loss of two Japanese pilots and two Japanese aircraft. In the end, he had decided to describe the incident as a mid-air collision. For him to admit that such lethal tensions existed in his squadron would have meant the end of his career. Nor did he want the family of the lieutenant, or of the sergeant, to know of the dishonorable manner of their deaths.

Subsequently, he was reprimanded for the sloppiness of the two pilots and the incident had been forgotten. . . .

Kashimura suddenly realized that Lieutenant Horikashi was still standing there, looking at him and scowling impatiently.

"You strongly hinted that you have something else you wanted to see me about?"

"With humble apologies, Captain. I have here your report on the *Zero* and a covering letter."

"My report?" Kashimura asked.

"Yes. Apologies, Captain, but things are so sensitive at the Ministry that they couldn't send it via regular channels. They sent it as a personal letter to me."

So I was right, Captain Kashimura thought. *The man is tied up with bureaucratic politics.* Aloud he said, "No matter. But why did they send it back?"

"They did not like it. I was asked to explain a few things," Lieutenant Horikashi replied.

Captain Kashimura suddenly felt as if he'd discovered a snake. He fought down his disgust. "Proceed."

"I find it very hard, as a lowly lieutenant, to have to tell you things." Lieutenant Horikashi didn't look uncomfortable at all. He looked as if he were enjoying the session.

"However," he continued, "the Ministry didn't care for your report

103

The Ulysses Flight/ Paul Wankowicz

at all. They thought that you should be negative about the *Zero* and were very unhappy with your glowing commendation. They would like you to re-write the report." He waved the copy toward Kashimura.

Captain Kashimura lit a cigarette. He sucked in the smoke to steady his nerves and give him a time to organize his thoughts. The situation was unreal, like a bad play.

"I wrote what I thought. The A6M-2 *Zero* is an excellent aircraft, with a range that makes it invaluable. Remember that our pilots flew it from Formosa to the Philippines on the first escort missions. Without it, we could not have won aerial supremacy over the islands and our troops would be bogged down forever. No other fighter has the range to have flown that mission. And if it weren't for that range, we would have never found the American ship, the *Nike Victory*. Not to speak of the *Zero*'s ability to handle weather, you know that yourself. The A6M-2 *Zero* is the most outstanding air machine in the world."

"Tokyo thinks that you should be more loyal to the designers who labor for the Army."

"What does that have to do with it?"

"As against manufacturers in the Navy's pay."

"Say that again."

"Captain. The attack against the American Base in Hawaii was entirely a Japanese Navy show. All of Tokyo is talking about it. Everyone has forgotten that the Japanese Army is beating the enemy back on all fronts. It is Japanese Navy all the way."

"So? Both are, after all, Japanese."

"Yes. They are both Japanese. But if our Navy keeps pushing, the Nakajima manufacturing plant will be reduced to the status of making parts for Mitsubishi. This would be a disaster in many quarters. In my report, I was much more negative on the Mitsubishi A6M-2 *Zero*, and praising of the Nakajima Ki-73. They liked that."

If the Ki-73 production goes out of favor, it will kill Horikashi's career. . . . I would have liked to have seen the paragraph in which Horikashi described the ground-handling qualities of the Zero. My

The Ulysses Flight/ Paul Wankowicz

lieutenant doesn't care about Japan, but only about his career. Now I understand, Kashimura thought wryly. Aloud, he said nothing.

After a pause, Lieutenant Horikashi said, "Don't you see, we have to be supportive of our own service, or it will be demoted to the lowest place."

"Whomever they are, what are they hoping to do with the report?"

"The feeling in the Ministry is very strong. They had planned to take the report and give it to The Lord Privy Seal to show to the Emperor. Written by you, Kashimura, one of the well-known heroes of the war in China, it would be very influential with his Highness. Then, with the Emperor's backing, the feelings about the Japanese Navy and the Mitsubishi company could be countered."

Captain Kashimura could vaguely see the machinations that would bring certain companies windfall profits. It had never occurred to him that this was what he had been fighting for. It disgusted him. "What you are saying is you want me to make false statements in the report to the Emperor."

"Not directly, of course."

Kashimura found himself angrier than he could ever remember. Only long spartan conditioning enabled him to keep his face passive, but he could feel his blood pressure rising. "Give me the report," he said. "I'll think about it." Rising, he ground his cigarette in the ash-tray which was overflowing with butts. Taking the report, and with a perfunctory "Good night," he went outside.

The darkness was no less sultry than the confines of the room had been. Over the eastern mountains, a storm was raging. Lightning flickered, illuminating the clouds as if they were hanging lanterns. The thunder was a distant background mutter. Hot, humid air carrying an odor of the jungle emanated from the distant storm. The slightest of breezes caressed his face, but offered no relief. Captain Kashimura felt dirty, tainted. He wished that Lieutenant Horikashi had never been sent to his squadron.

The request for a false report had unnerved him.

105

The Ulysses Flight/ Paul Wankowicz

*What it asked for was unthinkable. But hadn't I done it in the case
of the sergeant and the lieutenant? How can I fault Lieutenant Horikashi, having done it myself?*

*Lieutenant Horikashi had said that he, Captain Kashimura, was a
famous flyer, known even to the Emperor. Coming from any other
source, this would have been the apex of my ambitions.*

*But from Lieutenant Horikashi? On top of the realization that I,
myself, have done that which repulses me at the Lieutenant's request, it
destroys the simplicity of my own ambition to be the Emperor's tool.
Now, do I know where I stand?*

Away from the storm, the sky was clear and the stars were burning
brightly. Captain Kashimura found that his feet had automatically
carried him to the hangar where his fighter was stored. All he wanted to
do was to fly. To get into the clear, cool, crystal, uncorrupted air of the
night and fly. No matter to where.

He yelled for the Sergeant. "Get my plane out and ready for flight,"
he ordered.

Chapter 19: Airstrip above Mergui, December 20, 1941

Frank found Martaban Island on his first scan of the west coastline of Burma. It had not been difficult. Johnny's sketch map was accurate. Directly east of the island, the landing strip lay higher up the mountain as a lighter-hued rectangle hemmed in by jungle on all four sides, just as Johnny had said. One precarious dirt road snaked up the mountain to the landing strip.

He saw the sun flash off the wings of a fighter aligning itself for a landing. Even at this distance, Frank could tell it was Johnny. His skill was unmistakable.

Lisa was still further out. She curved in a wide, cautious arc, like an airliner, to give herself plenty of time and distance in which to get set for the landing. Half a mile from the field, her plane's landing gear came down, then its flaps.

Frank watched her plane's shadow undulating over the irregular canopy of the jungle. As her fighter neared the strip, it looked like a toy against the verdure.

From his height, Frank could not really judge, but it looked as if her airplane wasn't comfortable in its glide. *She should use more speed*, he thought.

So far, her landing looked good enough. The airplane and its shadow came closer together as she lost height nearing the strip.

He sucked in his breath as she crossed the last trees, *She's too high. She must have been worried about the length of the field, because when she cleared the last trees at the boundary, she cut her power.* Frank tensed. Her P-40, speed gone, began to drop the last 70-feet to the ground.

In his peripheral vision, Frank saw Johnny vault out of his cockpit and scramble down the wing to run to where Lisa would obviously pile up. But, as he watched, she gunned it.

A cloud of brown smoke belched out of the exhaust as she poured a load of gas to the cooling engine. *A second later it would have been too late, but she had reacted to it in time to regain some control.*

The plane touched down awkwardly and hard-bounced, then slewed to the right; however, cushioned by the sudden power, it remained in one piece.

Lisa caught the bounce and slammed the fighter down again. She hadn't corrected for the torque, so the fighter began a run for the trees. Somehow she controlled it with brakes and fear. Just as collision with the bordering trees seemed inevitable, she ground-looped it to stop in a welter of dirt and torn grass.

From where he was, Frank could not see any damage to the fighter as it sat at the end of the long ruts it had dug, its propeller windmilling helplessly. For several seconds, Lisa sat motionless in the cockpit. Then, without warning, she scrambled down the wing, ran to the grassy edge of the strip, and threw up.

Leaving her P-40 blocking Frank's path, Johnny ran up to steady her.

Frank had to make two low passes before Johnny understood and detached himself from the still-retching Lisa to taxi the fighter to where it should be parked. Then, he stood on the wing to watch Frank's plane land.

Frank landed easily, bouncing lightly once, and then positioned his plane beside the other two.

Lisa, still smelling of having been sick, met him as he came off the wing.

Johnny looked more serious than usual. "I saw you got him," he said to Frank, in a manner of greeting.

Watching Lisa's precarious landing had knocked the fight right out of Frank's mind, and it took him a few seconds to realize what Johnny was talking about. "He seemed to disintegrate and crash. I don't know

108

The Ulysses Flight/ Paul Wankowicz

if it was my doing."

"It was a good show."

"And yours?"

"Down, too. Took a hell of a long time with only four guns."

While they exchanged remarks, Lisa stood to the side, looking down at the grass. "I'm sorry, Frank," she finally said.

"What the hell for?"

"I nearly wrecked your P-40. And I lied to you. I only have 150 hours, not over 200 hours as I told you. I never should have gone on like that."

Frank saw Johnny give him a sharp glance of warning; but even without it, he knew that he had better be careful. If he said the wrong thing, it could mean the end of any flying Lisa would do. "But you didn't wreck it," Frank said.

"It wasn't the best start for a landing approach," he continued. "I think you were slow, but you made a hell of a good recovery. Better than I could have done."

"But I lied. I don't have 200 hours."

Frank laughed. "Look, Lisa, I don't know of anyone who doesn't double his log-book time when talking. I knew damn-well that you didn't have 200 hours."

Lisa looked relieved. "And you let me go?"

"You said you could do it, and Johnny could teach you." Lisa's eyes shifted from one to the other, with a lost expression on her face. She appeared to make up her mind about something and turned to Johnny. "There were times," she said, "when I could have killed you for making me do things over and over again, especially without ever saying a word of praise, only criticism. But if it hadn't been for that," she pointed, "I'd be at the end of the runway, dead. Thanks."

Johnny shook his head. "I hated it too, Lisa, but it had to be done. I had to get you to do the right thing automatically, like you did just now. Even if you were so angry or afraid that you couldn't think. You were scared on that approach, and yet you reacted just as you should have.

109

The Ulysses Flight/ Paul Wankowicz

I'm glad it worked."

Frank changed the subject. "That Japanese fighter," he said, "was the quickest thing I've ever seen. He looped before I could even think about it! I panicked trying to get out of his way."

"Did you hit him at all?"

"I think I got him in his left wing-root. But the thing flicked out of my sight, like a *Jungmeister.* In the end, it disintegrated trying to follow me down."

"Bods from Singapore have told me all of the Japanese kites are like that," Johnny said. "Bloody sport planes with 1,000-horsepower engines, but not very strong structurally," Johnny said. "You survived, which in the end, is all that matters."

Frank turned to Lisa. "Why don't you go lie in the shade to rest a bit? Frank and I will fuel the planes and call you when ready."

Lisa nodded dumbly and went to stretch out on the grass.

Johnny and Frank retired behind the tail of the first fighter. "I didn't want to say anything in front of her," Johnny started, "but I think her landing cracked one of the fuel lines. There was petrol dripping from under the cowl when I taxied it here. What do we have to fix it?"

Frank shook his head. "Off-hand, I don't think we have anything. I loaded some tools and some wire before we started, but that was all. Nothing to fix a fuel line."

"Well, let's take the cowl off and look."

Lisa came around from the other side of the plane. "What are you two conspiring about?" she asked, sounding worried.

"We weren't conspiring, but I think your kite has a petrol leak. We are trying to figure out how to fix it," Johnny explained. "Any ideas?"

"Soap. Soap is the only thing that is usually around that does not dissolve in gasoline. Or so my father told me. Where is the leak?"

"We were about to remove the cowl to find out."

He turned to Frank. "Have you a screwdriver?"

When they had collected all of their tools, they had very little: several pliers, various-sized screwdrivers, some wire, and the home-

The Ulysses Flight/ Paul Wankowicz

made spark-plug wrench Frank had hammered out and found impossible to leave behind. It was a souvenir of the first struggles.

With the cowl off, they found the leak without any difficulty. One of the flexible fuel connections had been made a little too tight and the shock of Lisa's landing had strained a leak in it. They stood looking at it. Ordinarily, it would have been no repair at all, but here, without tools and materials, it represented another almost insurmountable task.

"With the leak, continuing is out of the question. It would be risking a fire. Can you go to Rangoon for tools and parts?" Johnny asked, looking at Frank.

Frank countered by suggesting Johnny go.

"Hell, No!" Johnny said. "If I land there alone, they'll hold me until I can give a written report. . . . It's not the C.O., but the bloody Colonial Staff. They'll probably insist on a full-dress meeting before anyone can move." He obviously didn't want to go. "Could you go, Frank, if I drew another map?"

Frank stalled, he found that he was reluctant to leave the security of the group. "I could find it okay, but I don't think I could do much good with all the Limeys up there. . . . How about Lisa?" They both looked at her.

"Look," she said. "I have a white shirt in my kit. The one I had on when I ran away. Why don't we tear that into strips, rub some soap into it and over-wrap the tube. Wouldn't that hold? And keep us all together?"

Frank started to say that such a repair would be much too dangerous, but checked himself. There was no guarantee that the mechanics up in Mingaladon Airfield would have a proper piece of tubing anyway. "We could over-wrap the strips with wire," he suggested.

"We have nothing to lose," Frank said, "especially if we run the engine, and make sure the repair holds, before we fly."

Johnny and Lisa nodded.

They set to work. Lisa soaped the strips while Johnny and Frank wrapped them around the fuel line. In the confined space around the

111

engine, it was hot and awkward work. Threatening thunderstorms, which could melt all of their work if they came, hung off to the west. They over-wrapped the soaped strips with other strips soaked in engine oil to waterproof, and then, again with the wire. Soon, twilight was around the corner. There was no question of starting for Mingaladon Airfield or Rangoon that evening.

Lisa got into the cockpit and gingerly started the engine while Johnny and Frank inspected the fitting. To their relief, it held. It was dark by the time they replaced the cowling.

What had started out to be a day's flight had stretched to two. None of them had brought any food, but they found a small brook cascading down the hill at the far end of the field to give them water to drink. Unpacking blankets, they made nestings for the night in an old lean-to, built with a raised floor which would help keep out vermin and snakes. It was better than sleeping in the cramped confines of a fighter's cockpit. Once they had established sleeping quarters, they prepared the planes for morning departure.

By 21:00 hours, they had hand-poured 35-gallons into each fighter. They were tired, itchy from insects and sweat, and nearly sick from the fumes.

Johnny was unhappy. "The weather has changed," he said. "We may have no visibility for takeoff. What do you think, Lisa?"

Because Lisa had grown up on the west side of the Malay Peninsula, Johnny figured she'd be familiar with the weather.

"Rain and very low clouds," she said. "Probably fog at this elevation. At least that's what it would be farther south. See!" she pointed upward.

The men looked to see where she was pointing. Most of the stars were obscured by thick, low clouds coming down from the top of the ridge.

"Well, there's nothing we can do about it now," Johnny said. "Let's settle down for the night."

He paused. "I think we'd better stand watch. I'll take the first leg,

112

The Ulysses Flight/ Paul Wankowicz

from now until midnight. You and Lisa fight it out for the morning hours."

Frank looked at Johnny. Whatever light was left seemed to accentuate the other's tiredness. Johnny's shoulders drooped and his usually springy walk slowed. "Johnny," Frank said, "you've been carrying a hell of a lot of self-imposed responsibility in the past few days."

As instructor, Johnny felt responsible for Lisa. Seeing her almost kill herself on her first landing had shaken him.

Frank still felt weak-kneed when he remembered how he had set himself up as a target for the Japanese fighter. He'd been saved by the other's lousy gunnery, and an undeserved lucky shot which had weakened the Japanese fighter's main spar.

The adrenaline rushed back with the memory of how close he'd come to losing. "I won't be able to sleep for hours. Look, Johnny, I'll take the top of the shift. You roll in and get some shut-eye. It's no sacrifice. I'm not sleepy. You look exhausted. I'll wake you when I feel the need to put my head down."

In his mind, Frank figured he'd take the whole night. The other two deserved the rest.

"I can take part of the watch, too," Lisa interjected.

"Good. Let Johnny settle himself, and we'll get organized; although I think you should roll in, too. Or at least, until I get sleepy. When I do, I'll ask you to spell me. Okay?"

Lisa nodded. "*Dinkum bonzer*," she said.

It meant nothing to Frank, but it did seem to be assent.

She had regained her cheerful attitude after the scare of the afternoon.

Johnny paused from arranging his blanket. "Lisa," he said, "let me tell you something."

"Yes, Johnny?"

"Before I turn in, I have to make a confession. When Frank suggested you fly the third fighter, I was dead against it. I didn't think you'd ever make it. I was wrong. Now, having watched you, I'd stack

113

you up against any service pilot in the R.A.F."

Lisa was silent for a long time. Finally, she said, "If it hadn't been for your teaching, Johnny, I wouldn't have made it. I'd be dead now. Thanks."

"Maybe," Johnny said. Changing the subject, "You know what you are now?"

"No, what?"

"A female fighter pilot. There are bloody few of those in the world. Good night!"

"Thanks, Johnny."

Johnny raised his head. "Hear anything, Frank, wake us. Right?"

"Okay." Frank said. He watched them idly through the darkness as they arranged the blankets for sleep in the lean-to.

Once they had settled themselves, Frank pulled a sawn-off palm-tree trunk back to the lean-to entrance. He settled on it to watch the deserted airstrip. The sky above was almost milky, clouded over with the mist coming down from the ridge top. *It will be a long night*, he thought.

The weather shift that Johnny had noticed earlier, before his takeoff from Tenasserim Field, was beginning to bring change, evident in the mist rolling down upon the little airstrip above Mergui.

The slight shift in the location of the high pressure area driving the monsoon onto the west coast meant that, instead of the rapid lift up the slopes of Burma's mountains, the air would be lifted more gently. It would then release all the moisture gathered in its sweep over the hot Indian Ocean and the Andaman Sea more slowly, without the violence that Frank had seen from the airstrip at Tenasserim Field. The thunderstorms would eventually form, but later, and be hidden in the layer of stratus clouds clinging to the mountains. The storms would generate areas of plane-wrecking turbulence that could be deadly to pilots who could not see them as they were threading their way through the clouds on instruments.

The Ulysses Flight/ Paul Wankowicz

As he rolled into his blanket, Johnny was worried. *If we don't start early enough in the morning, we will be in clouds all the way to Rangoon.* The fighters had no landing instrumentation to enable them to land safely on instruments. *We have to start early enough to avoid the dangerous storms which will mature later in the day.*

Johnny had no idea how much of Lisa' flying experience included instrument time, if any, so he still had doubts about the extent of her training, although she'd done superbly well. It was unfair to her now to be catapulted into another life-or-death situation. Johnny rolled over uncomfortably, cursing his inability to shut down his brain and go to sleep. As he rolled, his elbow, hardly protected from the floor by the thin blanket, thudded painfully.

Chapter 20: Frank Stands Watch

Outside, as a backdrop to Frank's field of vision, the mist rolled in, suffused with the murky light from the moon. It had already hidden the three fighters. A solitary tree, with branches shaped like a spray of water from a fountain, was silhouetted against the mist's luminescence, like the top of a Chinese-lacquered box. Overhead the mist was still thin, revealing between its tendrils the bright points of the nearer stars.

Frank heard Johnny roll restlessly behind him, bones thudding against the wood floor of the lean-to, and he smiled. He'd slept like that on a single blanket in the Oklahoma oil camps, and knew how uncomfortable it could be. He thought about the improbabilities of fate that brought him, one Frank Carringer, ex-cook, ex-roustabout, to this tropical land with an Englishman and a British-Dutch girl for companions.

Frank was an Oklahoma boy. As long as his father had been alive, his mother, father, and Frank lived on a small farm abutting a World War I airfield, which was still used for summer training by the U.S. Air Service.

One of Frank's earliest recollections was of standing at the edge of the farm, seeing and hearing olive-drab biplanes as they whispered overhead, and came in to land in the grass beyond the barbed-wire fence.

When Frank was 14, his father died, and hard times came to the family. The farm was mortgaged to the hilt. After the bank foreclosed, the family became homeless.

Frank's early dreams of flying one of those olive-drab biplanes gave way to the need to make a living and help support his mother, who worked as a waitress. Big for his age, Frank went into the oil fields to work any job that would pay.

The Ulysses Flight/ Paul Wankowicz

In the oil camp, first he was the cook's helper. By age 19, he'd worked his way up to be a laborer on an oil rig.

Eventually, his uncle found him there.

His uncle became rich after oil was discovered on his farm. He parlayed his luck into a small, wholly-owned oil company. This was the era when another oil man, W.C. Hall, was gaining fame from the flights made by his pilot, Wiley Post. Post flew a Lockheed *Vega*, named *Winnie Mae* after Hall's daughter. In the *Winnie Mae*, Post set many flight records, including a solo flight around the world.

Learning of Wiley Post inspired Frank's uncle to get a pilot, and the least expensive way to do that was to give Frank money for flying lessons. His uncle figured that $50.00 would be sufficient to hire someone to teach Frank how to fly.

Frank took the 50-dollar bill to Highwater Field. It seemed no less miraculous to him to be clutching $50.00, destined to pay for flying lessons, than riding a pumpkin-turned-coach must have seemed to Cinderella.

Highwater Field was one of the products of Aviation's "Years of Burgeoning Promise" after WWI. It was built at the urging of Professor Newman who guaranteed "to put Highwater on the map" by building a series of revolutionary aircraft. He called his company The Apex Aircraft Company.

The airfield consisted of a 15-acre plot with a large, brick hangar set next to a concrete apron. Newman's first airplane, the Apex *Dreadnought* saved its pilot's life by refusing to leave the ground.

The second twin-boom monstrosity, designed around a brace of Davis *Air Cannon*, managed to struggle off the ground, and even flew 500 feet into the air, before it became obvious to the horrified spectators that the pilot was in trouble. The plane slid slowly off on a wing, and knifed into a grove of trees bordering the airfield. It spelled the end of Apex.

After the demise of the Apex, Highwater Field remained undis-

turbed. It was located too far from town to represent valuable real
estate. What was left of the Apex plant was on the side of the airfield
opposite the hangar.

A Swede, Johansson, acquired part of the old factory to make
window and door sashes there. He did quite well financially. The small
amount of tax revenue from New-Bilt Sash and Door Company was
used to keep the airfield open.

In 1929, the airfield had a brief moment of glory as a fueling stop
for Transcontinental & Western's *Tri-Motor Ford* planes. The coming
of the longer-ranged DC-2 in 1933 ended that, and the field settled into
its former obscurity. However, it was not deserted. Men devoted to
flight kept a collection of their airplanes in the big hangar. If the flying
business was bad that month, they'd bunk there as well to wait until
some flying work came their way.

Frank smiled as he remembered the odd assortment of aircraft
stored in that hangar, and the even more eccentric men who cared for
them.

In the very back of the building stood a Curtiss *Jenny* of WWI
vintage. Long unused, its canvas was in tatters, Mice had gnawed on its
exposed wing ribs and nested between the cylinder banks of its mon-
strous, mismatched Liberty engine.

In front of it, a bright orange *Travel Air* was powered by a leaky
OX-5 engine. Next to it stood a Buhl *Pup* powered by a three-cylinder
Anzani motor with yellowed-and-cracked, transparent, cellulon panels
inset into the wings, so the pilot could see the ground when landing.
The owner of the *Pup* was about 70, with the pallor and uncertain gait
of someone who had reached his maximum age and would grow no
older. He claimed to have F.A.I., the International Pilot's Federation's
license Number 13, and to have taken part in all of the famous meets,
including Reims, France in 1908; the Doncaster Racecourse to see
which British made aircraft could fly a circular mile course over
Doncaster, Yorkshire, England in 1909 sponsored by the *Daily Mail*;
and Nice, France in 1910. He spoke knowingly of the Greats: men like

118

The Ulysses Flight/ Paul Wankowicz

Ensault Peltier, Gabriel and Charles Voisin, Louis Blériot, Henry Farman, and Charles Royce.

Then, parked beside the Buhl *Pup* and already coated with dust, stood the field's mystery airplane, a brand-new Beech Aircraft Model D18. Speculation was that it belonged to a dope runner hiding from the Feds. It never moved while Frank was there.

In contrast, the man who owned the new Arrow *Sport* sold insurance. He'd never been out of town further than Clearwater field in all his life.

Behind the hangar, rusting among the weeds, was the bent skeleton of a Curtiss *Robin*, engine full of dirt, a perfect mold of the pilot's skull imprinted in the remains of the instrument panel. The pilot was buried nearby. No one had come forward to claim either the wreck or the pilot's remains, so they both became part of Highwater Field.

Among the pilot inhabitants was Pete, the owner of the light blue and gold Fleet biplane in which Frank learned to fly. Pete was a leathery-skinned man of uncertain age who had flown with General William "Billy" Mitchell in WWI, and remained in aviation after his discharge from the U.S. Army.

When Frank approached him about 50-dollar flying lessons, Pete replied, "Sure, I'll teach you to fly. . . . First, though, go to the back of the hangar and figure out what made that dent in the instrument panel of the Curtiss *Robin*. If you're still interested, come back and give me that 50-dollar bill."

Frank discovered Pete was a tough instructor, requiring perfection. Even after Frank was ready for his solo, Pete insisted on two more hours of flying. "Hell, that Fleet is all I got. Fifty bucks ain't going to repay me if you bend it."

Frank didn't 'bend' the plane.

Once the Fleet's wheels left the turf, Frank knew that the 12-year-old boy standing by the farm fence had been right. From that moment, he was a pilot.

119

The Ulysses Flight/ Paul Wankowicz

For a while, Frank piloted his uncle's plane to chauffeur him around the state, but the inevitable happened. Fifty bucks had not paid for the extensive training he really needed. At one point, his uncle telephoned him long distance from Philadelphia, and asked Frank to fly the Stinson from Oklahoma to come pick him up.

Frank took off from Okie City just before sunrise, not exactly sure of the best air route to Washington. He refueled at Zanesville, Ohio. He didn't hit weather until he was on the other side of Akron. The ridge dividing it from Altoona-Harrisburg was clouded over. From an altitude of 100 feet, Frank could just see a band of golden light over the crest of the hill: clear weather. He thought that there was enough room to sneak through, and decided to try it. As he neared the ridge, he felt himself sucked into the clouds as an unexpected updraft hit his plane.

He'd had no practice flying instruments, or even the rudimentary panel installed in the Stinson. The only safe thing he could do was to push the control yoke forward.

Any experienced mountain pilot would have known that a down-draft inevitably follows a ridge-caused updraft; however, all of Frank's flying time had been in the plains of Oklahoma.

As he came out of the bottom of the cloud, and the trees blossomed in his windshield, Frank hardly had time to pull back on the control yoke and blow the tail down with a burst of power. It wasn't enough. The Stinson's wheels brushed the top of the trees, causing the plane to cartwheel down the slope of the mountain, shedding parts as it went. Those trees were like spikes. Frank was lucky to have survived. The Stinson did not.

During the time he had flown for his uncle, however, Frank had saved enough money to pay for two years at Oklahoma State, enough college time to meet the entrance requirements of the U.S. Army Air Corps.

When he next touched controls of a plane, he was in the uniform of an Air Cadet. The farm boy was on his way.

The Ulysses Flight/ Paul Wankowicz

As Frank stood watch while sitting on a log, his reverie was disturbed when, somewhere off to his right, he heard the hum of an airplane engine, faint and distant. Automatically, he looked up. There was a rift in the fog. Above it, against a star-studded sky, like jewels on velvet, were the red and the green navigation lights of a solitary airplane. It was high, at least 2,000 feet above the ridge.

Frank followed the lights until the small rift in the clouds closed. *Who could be running in wartime skies with navigation lights lit?*

The sound lingered for a time longer as the pilot took a wide turn over the airfield, and then, the sound slowly faded away.

Chapter 21: That Same Night Over Mergui

Getting away from his desk and into the air was what Kashimura needed. As he walked to the plane, he noticed the moon had set. Soon aloft in the soft light of the stars, he could see below him the mist-like spume, creeping down the east side of the mountains. Up here, everything was at peace. His navigation lights were on, like long ago in school, during night-flying practice when he had first discovered the mystery, the opiate of flight. He felt calmer; his soul was at peace, although his mind still roiled.

As the plane slipped through the clean, still air of the night, he could think. The scene below his wings reminded him of the scroll entitled, *Sea Foam,* that had always hung in his family's farm cottage. It was the only painting his poverty-stricken parents owned, and was dearly treasured by his mother. It must have been handed down through the generations.

Kashimura idly wondered why he remembered it so strongly now.

He had flown the fighter out to sea and up the coast with no destination in mind. At first, he played with his fighter, flying low amongst the off-shore islets. The night was bright with moon and stars. The moonlight allowed him to use the silver, lunar light, and the softer light of the stars, which illuminated the black channels between the islands.

Occasionally, on one of the islets, a square of soft orange light from a kerosene lamp in a hut showed that someone still lived below. He flew smoothly, artistically, like a lover—not the rough, two-handed horsing of the machine in air combat, but the union of the man with the airplane as a work of art, each supplementing each other in perfect harmony. When the moon was about to set off his right wing, silvering the Bay of Bengal with its magic, Kashimura had set the nose of his fighter upwards toward the infinity of stars. He slid the canopy back, letting the warm, tropical air play around in the cockpit, caressing his

The Ulysses Flight/ Paul Wankowicz

face, ruffling his clothes.

In moments like these, Kashimura thought, *man comes as close to God as he ever would.*

He could now look at himself, to see himself for the first time. *My integrity, honesty, and honor are the keys of who I am—to myself, my identity and my impeccable reputation.* . . . But the realization that he had done the very same thing, falsified a report—a thing which had so revolted him in Lieutenant Horikashi—had cored him like an apple. He'd been a warrior, who surrounded himself with an impenetrable steel wall to keep out any other human contact.

From his very first memory, he never allowed anyone, not even his mother, to bind the hurts from his frequent conflicts at school. He would take care of them himself, no matter how painful, how deep: It was the warrior's way.

The same iron will that kept out others had kept him out, too. He had never looked at himself as a man, as a being with wants, needs, or desires. He thought himself an implement wielded by the Emperor, perfected in not having an independent will. Now it was not so. What he wanted, needed most, was another human being—another person to share his bewilderment and to help him out of the labyrinth in which he now felt trapped.

Once there had been a Chinese girl. He thought she cared, beyond the money that he paid her for bedding together. He'd entertained thoughts of marrying her, but only thoughts. There was no way an officer of the Japanese Imperial Army could marry a Chinese. After he'd been posted away, he learned that she'd killed herself, along with her unborn child. So he'd soon convinced himself that he didn't care, that she'd been a fool. In reality, although he wouldn't admit it, he'd lost a child, possibly a son, and lost her. The memory brought a feeling of sadness to his soul.

He was beginning to see many things he had hidden from himself in times past. *Is there no one I can share things with?*

Sergeant Hokai, the best of his enlisted pilots? He had noticed

123

The Ulysses Flight/ Paul Wankowicz

recently that Hokai broke the battle formation discipline to make sure that Lieutenant Horikashi didn't fail as Captain Kashimura's wingman. *Hokai was breaking formation to be in a position to protect me, the 'Old Father.'*

The enlisted pilots didn't trust Lieutenant Horikashi in a fight, and Captain Kashimura knew they were right.

He stopped himself. It was unthinkable that an officer should discuss anything about another officer with his enlisted men, or even with other officers. He doubted if any of them would care in the slightest. They preferred to go for drink and women, believed in a different kind of *Bushido*, a different kind of warrior's code. . . .

I am just as alone on the ground as I am in the cockpit of my fighter.

His thoughts turned to his third victory, a Ju-52 kill over China. The 3-engine Junkers was a clumsy freighter. This one he'd trapped trying to sneak out of beleaguered Langfong, probably with a bevy of escaping Chinese Generals and their gold on board.

Kashimura fired on the tri-motor. It was a tough old bird. It took him three passes to set its port engine afire, dooming the plane.

The pilot was a round-faced German. Kashimura had seen him as he'd pulled away from his third pass. He'd been looking at the blazing engine, resignation on the pilot's face. For the first time in his life, Kashimura felt sympathy for another, weaker human.

He knew that it would take minutes for the Junkers to spiral down before it smashed into the green hills below. Captain Kashimura understood. He had pulled away for another pass, and aiming his fire carefully, he shattered the pilot's cockpit—to save him the agonizing certainty. In this way, he had communicated with the other airman. It was a new feeling. It was disturbing. Somewhere, there must be someone with whom a human connection would happen. Again. Sometime.

Afterward, he'd set the incident aside as treasonable. He was the Emperor's.

The Ulysses Flight/ Paul Wankowicz

Instinct told him that he was close to the home field. He put the fighter
into a wide turn to port, gauging it by the indication of the softly-
glowing, phosphorescent needles of the instruments before him. He
shifted his eyes to the velvety blackness below.

A sliver of light, and another, and a third, all in a line. Then, five
more at right angles to the first three. Kerosene lamps, three at the
border of the track, and five parallel to his landing run.

Sergeant Katsuki must have stayed up for the past hours just to be
ready with 'Old Father's' landing lights. With all of the work the
Sergeant had, it wasn't fair to have kept him awake for this long.
Captain Kashimura made a mental note to thank him in the morning.

He steepened his turn to come out in line with the lights below. His
left hand pulled back the throttle, adjusted the pitch to 'full fine' and the
mixture to 'rich.'

He knew now what he would do with the report. He would just hold
it. Lieutenant Horikashi could do nothing without it. Maybe later a
better idea would come to him.

The fighter was now lined up. Captain Kashimura leaned forward
and lowered his flaps. His left hand went automatically to the trim to
keep the machine balanced. His eyes focused on the eight lights below.
How many times had he done this? Yet each time, it gave him fresh
excitement.

Standing by the second longitudinal light, Sergeant Katsuki smiled to
himself in the dim glow of the kerosene lamps as he watched the
fighter's wheels gently brush the grass before settling down.

There were few pilots, Katsuki thought, *who could bring in their
fighter so gently.* For a while, he had been worried; The Old Man had
shown signs of being nervous, over-strained. It was about that new
Lieutenant. However, the landing had proven, whatever else may be
happening, the squadron C.O. had not lost his touch.

Chapter 22: Mergui Airfield,
Night December 20-21, 1941

Just as the thin sound of the lone airplane faded out in the drizzle-shrouded distance, Frank heard movement behind him. He turned to see Lisa had come out of the lean-to. In the dark, all he could see was her silhouette.

Quietly, she dragged a palm log closer and sat down.

"Can't sleep?" Frank asked.

"I thought I heard an airplane. Was I dreaming?"

"No. One flew overhead scarcely visible through the mist."

"English?" Lisa asked.

"Doubt it. Whoever it was, he was burning his navigation lights, as if peace had been declared."

The subject seemed exhausted, and, for a while, they sat in silence, contemplating the drizzly night.

"I was thinking of you sitting here," Lisa said. "And I couldn't get back to sleep."

"You shouldn't have worried. It's been quiet and beautiful." After a long silence, Frank became very conscious of her beside him. "Lisa," he said finally.

"Yes?"

"Where did you learn to fly?"

"It was in college," she said.

"In Australia?"

"Yes." Lisa described her first flight over the Outback in the bright-yellow trainer. "I was never the same again," she said. "You have no idea how I resented going back to Burma where I'd have to give up flying. . . . Am I crazy?"

Frank smiled. "I should ask you the same thing. You could have been describing my first flight. The plane was a Fleet," Frank said.

"A Fleet?"

The Ulysses Flight/ Paul Wankowicz

"A blue-and-gold biplane, owned by a man named Pete." He countered her story with his, telling her about Highwater Field. He left out much of the poverty of his earlier years, ending with a rueful laugh over the fate of his uncle's plane, the Stinson. "I suppose my uncle could afford it, although he never spoke to me again. I think I disappointed him by not being another Wiley Post."

Lisa had barely heard of Wiley Post; she changed the conversation. She'd done some mountain flying, but always with an experienced pilot in the left seat. She quizzed Frank on the techniques of it. She easily understood his explanations of the currents, and the consequent updrafts and downdrafts around mountains.

Neither noticed that the drizzle had increased, now filling the air with thousands of tiny needles. The "ceiling" was so low Frank felt he could touch it.

As they talked, Frank realized he was in love with Lisa. It didn't surprise him. Even though he didn't believe in love at first sight—when he saw her by his flashlight's beam wide-eyed, and pinned to the rear corrugated hangar wall—he'd been instantly attracted to her.

He'd also assumed then that whatever he felt he could dismiss when the time came to resume his freedom. Now he realized he'd been dead wrong: she was here, and always would be. It was a scary thought.

Lisa interrupted his thoughts.

"Frank?"

"Yes?"

"What would you say if I told you I would stay here?" Lisa looked away as she said that.

A shock of fear flashed through him. "Here?"

"I know a couple who have a plantation within a few miles. I could ask them to put me up."

Frank recalled seeing a plantation house, on the approach to the landing field, but, preoccupied with Lisa's landing, hadn't paid attention to it.

"You mean just leave the plane and go?"

The Ulysses Flight/ Paul Wankowicz

"You could get someone from Rangoon to come up and get it. I'm sure Johnny would help you with that."

Frank felt desperate. He didn't want to lose her. "Was it the landing?"

She didn't answer right away. "Yes and no," she said. "It's just that you have done so much for me already. You need to be worrying about other things . . ."

Frank started to interrupt, but she cut him off. "I never should have suggested that I fly the third plane out."

"I don't see why not. You've done miraculously well. And isn't it my privilege to choose what I will worry about?"

"Bloody hell!" she exploded. "It's all so up a gum tree!"

"What's 'up a gum tree'?"

"Means 'complicated.'"

"What's so complicated?" Frank asked.

She overlooked the question. "You're a fighter pilot. From what I heard, in Britain, a war pilot's life expectancy is at best three months. As for me, worrying about me isn't what you should be doing. You will need all of your concentration just to stay alive. You've already risked your life once just to protect me."

"I still don't see what's so complicated. Or 'up a gum tree,' as you say."

Angrily, she turned toward him. "Being in love. I never thought it would be like this!"

He wanted to take her into his arms, but feared any sudden move would dissolve the magic. Gently, his hand found hers and they sat hand-in-hand, each overcome by a swirl of thoughts, feelings, and the beginnings of happiness.

Finally, she asked, "What are we going to do?"

He heard the 'we' and was thrilled by it. "First, 'we' have to get to Rangoon."

"And you'll leave me there while you go off . . . to the Philippines?" She'd almost said 'to war' but that sounded too melodramatic. "I don't

128

The Ulysses Flight/ Paul Wankowicz

think I could stand that. It would be better to say good-bye now."

He could hear in her voice she was close to crying. His heart went out to her in compassion; but no panaceas, no answers, made sense with the war in progress.

"I don't think I could stand being so far from you, but I'd like to see you get safely into the United States."

She didn't say anything about that. "We'll be together for a while. At least until Singapore," she said.

Frank mulled over the situation. *We have a long distance to go. North to Rangoon, and south down the Malay Peninsula to Singapore. Lord only knows where we can land to refuel. We need to go across to some field on the west coast of Borneo, across the jungle-covered island to land and refuel again. From there, we'll have to continue up the uncivilized, almost unexplored, Sulu Archipelago, cross the main islands of the Philippine Group, and finally, to land at Clark Airfield near Manila. All in tropical heat, with no navigation aids. Before the war, it would have been called 'An epic flight for single-seaters,' an historic flight followed by every newspaper in the world.* Frank was stunned by the magnitude of it. *Now, I propose to do this with the Japanese gunning for everything American in the skies. If we do this, we'll need all our wits about us.*

Johnny had let Frank know, except for the Volunteer Group under Colonel Clair Lee Chennault, no other Americans were in Rangoon. Now it was a distinct possibility none would be in Singapore either.

"We have a difficult journey ahead. We can't distract each other, but I'd like to have you along. If I can't get you to the U.S., or if you won't go there, I'll worry about you stuck on some plantation with the Japanese around. If you're game, I'd like you to go with me."

He paused as it sunk into him that, with those words, he told Lisa he would accept responsibility for her. He had committed himself. "At least, we'll be together until we run into Uncle Sam's Army. At that point, I'll have to go soldiering solo, but it won't happen for a while yet. We'll have to push ourselves unmercifully even to get half-way,

129

but like all adventures, it's going to be a rough business until it's all over. Do you think you can do it?"

"You aren't leaving me in Rangoon? You won't make me stay there?"

"I doubt if the Limeys will spare me another pilot, so I need you to fly the second plane. And two more U.S. fighter planes in the Philippines will be worth their weight in gold." He took a deep breath and said softly. "I don't want to leave you, Lisa. Ever." Then, trying to lighten the moment, he added, "This may all turn out to be an adventure we can tell to captivate our grandchildren and hold them spellbound; but like all adventures, it's going to be challenging."

They stood pressed against each other, like two small children terrified by an approaching thunderstorm. He could feel her body against his, even her tears on her cheeks.

She broke away first. "Lord," she said breathlessly, "this is exactly what we shouldn't do!"

"But, I like it!" He wanted to feel the warm pressure of her against him for the rest of his life.

"I know," she said. "Can we agree not until we get to the Philippines? We'll need to keep our minds sharp."

"You're right, but promise me, you'll stop being sensible as soon as we get to Manila."

"You haven't even told me you love me," she said.

"I thought that was obvious."

"A girl likes to hear it! . . . Even needs to hear it. . . ." Her voice sounded as if she were laughing and yearning at the same time.

"Lisa, I love you," he said, pulling her close. It was a contract, a moment of time standing still.

"I love you, too. Much too much." Then she leaned away from him. "Now, to be sensible aviators again. What do you think the weather will do tomorrow?" she asked.

He heard the strain in her voice, the strain of returning to 'business as usual' after they'd just made the most significant pledge of their lives. Frank wanted to tell her a million things more about their love, but the words wouldn't come.

"Fog?" he responded lamely.

"If we don't take off, I'll starve to death," she replied. "It's okay for you two, you kept your breakfasts after landing." She tried to keep her voice matter-of-fact, but her effort showed.

He loved her.

"Johnny will give you better 'gen.'" He used the British expression on purpose. "My expertise is in the U.S.A. over plains and the eastern mountains!"

She laughed. A clear, natural sound.

He'd never heard her laugh. It was dark. He wished he could see her face. Laughing suited her.

He was very conscious of her nearness, and now proud of his new-found responsibility. They sat down again on the damp logs and fell into comfortable silence, neither aware of the passage of time until Johnny emerged from the lean-to behind them.

"Heavens, people," he said, "you should have woken me up hours ago. We're flying in the morning and the weather looks rotten. I'll take over! Get some sleep, you'll need it!"

"We weren't sleepy and thought you could use the shut-eye."

"Too right! But now the shoe is on the other foot. Away with you! Everything been quiet?"

"Like a churchyard."

"Good night, then."

"Good night!"

Frank and Lisa each had a blanket apiece, enough for the tropical temperatures. Lisa used her parachute as a head rest.

Frank, who had assembled all of his spare clothes into a bundle, was using that as a makeshift pillow, and now realized how sleepy he was. After his long absence from flying, the battle with the Japanese earlier in the day had drained him more than he had imagined. Despite their proclamations of love, Frank and Lisa quickly fell asleep.

Chapter 23: Mergui Airfield

Early the next morning, it seemed like only a few minutes since he fell asleep, when Frank felt Johnny shaking his shoulder.

"Wake up! Wake up! We have company!" Johnny's whisper had an urgency that jerked Frank awake.

"Company?" Frank asked softly.

"Burmese. I can hear them talking, but can't make out what they're saying."

"Wake Lisa. She speaks the language!"

Frank glanced outside. The drizzle hadn't let up, but there was an aura of starlight filtering through the mist. A weak pre-sunrise breeze had sprung up, carrying the sounds of those men outside audibly into the lean-to.

Gently, he shook Lisa's shoulder.

She sat up, instantly awake. "What is it?"

"Burmese. In the middle of the field. Can you make out what they are saying?"

All three listened, holding their breaths to maintain silence.

"They're talking about our airplanes. They must be another group of 'Nationalists.'" Her voice was bitter with her recent memories. "They think we are British." She fell silent, listening. "They're arguing among themselves. . . . They want to destroy the airplanes, but don't quite know how, because they are scared of the machines," Lisa relayed.

She looked up at Frank. "What do we do?" Her whisper was absolutely steady.

"I don't know," Frank replied. He admired her self-control. *She must be made of steel. . . .* "Johnny, do you have your pistol? How many rounds do you have?"

"Six. And you?"

"Seven. It's a hell of a long walk to Rangoon if we don't do some-

132

thing," Frank said.

"Thirteen rounds in the dead of night against Lord-knows-how-many fanatical Nationalists. Hardly the odds anyone would have chosen," Johnny commented.

"We've got to do something," Lisa said.

"How many do you figure there are?" Johnny whispered to Lisa.

"At least five or six. And, if the last band I ran into is any indication, they will be armed," Lisa answered.

"We could melt into the jungle," Frank said.

"Abandon the planes? We'd never make it to Moulmein alive, much less to Rangoon. Might as well save the bother and shoot ourselves now," Johnny said.

Looking off into the distance, Frank asked, "Lisa, how far is it to your friends' plantation?"

"Two or three miles. However, if there are Nationalists roaming the countryside, my friends may have already had their throats slit, or if lucky, escaped to Rangoon."

Although her voice was level, Frank realized the very statement must have revived memories. It hit him how much he loved her.

"How about the machine guns in the fighters? Could we do something with them?"

"If we had the time. But to do any good, we'd have to prop the tails up so that the guns' trajectories would be parallel to the ground. Not much good. . . . The rounds will go over their heads. " Frank said.

"Wait a second," Johnny said, and reached for his Webley Revolver, and broke it open to make sure that all six chambers of the cylinder were loaded. "If you were mucking about in the dark, with a guilty conscience to boot, and someone fired a brace of armament in your direction, would you wait to see where the bloody rounds were going?"

"You're right!" Frank hesitated. "I'll go."

As quietly as he could, Frank worked the slide of his Colt .45 to chamber a round, and then snapped on the safety.

133

The Ulysses Flight/ Paul Wankowicz

Feeling in the dark for Lisa's hand, Frank put the weapon into it.
"Ever fire a pistol?"

"No. Only rifles."

"Johnny, could you show her? The safety's on. You know the Colt automatic? It's equivalent to the Webley."

"Where's the safety?" Johnny asked.

"Left side, just under the slide. It pushes down to fire. The Colt also has a grip safety," Frank replied.

"Like a Parabellum?"

Frank didn't know what a Parabellum was, but there was no time left. "Right! I'm going!" Bent double, Frank headed in the direction of the parked fighters.

Lisa whispered, "Frank, be careful!"

Conscious of the luminescent mist, Frank felt vulnerable, as if there were a target on his back. He zig-zagged through the wet, ankle-deep grass, but the expected shots didn't come.

The Burmese must still be talking. They may have taken him for a flushed animal. *It's vital that they do not touch the machines. Without the planes, we're dead!*

As Frank came close to the fighters, he felt another's presence. He froze, hardly daring to breathe. He heard a man say something in Burmese.

Frank crouched, silent, and waited. . . . He heard the sound of a rifle's bolt slide back and the clink as a round fed into the chamber. Then silence. An unbearably long period during which Frank's breathing was as loud as an express train.

After his eyes got used to the darkness, in the distance, Frank saw a turbaned head outlined against the lighter sky. For a fleeting instant, he saw two figures, one with a rifle, the other bare-handed, facing each other in the grass. The view gave him the orientation he'd needed.

Frank sprang up and his shoulder hit flesh. At the same moment, the Burman's rifle went off with a blinding flash and a hot blast. Then he felt the S.M.L.E's hardware scrape his back and again the Burmese slammed the barrel of his weapon into Frank's back. Both men fell.

Frank felt a numbing shock of pain, followed by the acrid smell of cordite mixed with the Asian man's pungent body odor. *Tumeric?* Frank had no time to wonder. Both men grappled blindly at each other. He twisted to land atop his assailant.

When he brought up his knee, he felt it hit soft flesh. The other gasped. With no time to grab his knife, Frank jammed his elbow against the other's windpipe, but the man twisted free and struggled to get up.

As the assailant raised his head, Frank wrenched the rifle out of the other man's grasp. Holding it by its muzzle, he chopped the butt at the man's skull, once, twice, until he felt something break like an eggshell, and the man fell limp under him.

There was no time to lose. As Frank rose painfully, he heard the other Burmese Nationalist men in agitated discussion. One called something in Frank's direction.

Stumbling over the first two steps, Frank took off at a run toward the first P-40, scarcely visible against the mist. He ducked under the wing and swung up beside the cockpit. As he climbed, his fingers desperately sought the exterior, emergency-canopy release. He found it, ripped it down to slide back the canopy, and vaulted into the seat in one continuous movement.

He hit the gun-arming switches and flipped the main switch. He heard the 'clunk' of the main relay in the fuselage behind him. Closing his eyes, he visualized the position of the gun-selector switch. He felt for it and set it.

Frank had been subconsciously holding the control column as if for flight, his finger depressing the trigger. As the selector switch clicked into position, the wing guns exploded. Frank jumped. The flare from the guns outlined several Burmese huddled together in the middle of the field. From the corner of his eye, Frank saw the starlike flashes of the guns flame from the lean-to, as Johnny and Lisa fired.

Frank waited through a slow count of ten and pressed the trigger again. This time the light of the guns showed emptiness.

135

The Ulysses Flight/ Paul Wankowicz

Before leaving the cockpit, Frank performed the entire post-flight check, remembering to set the guns to "safe" and reset the selector switches. Then painfully, he climbed onto the wing root and pushed the canopy shut. His back was beginning to seize up where it had been hit with the rifle.

Now the field around him was quiet, as if awed by the holocaust of noise and fire it had just witnessed.

Frank walked back slowly, detouring around the place where he had just fought the Burmese. Near the hut, he gently called: "Lisa, Johnny! It's me, don't shoot!"

"Frank! Are you all right?"

That's Lisa's voice.

Before he could answer, she ran to him and embraced him tightly. Handing him his Colt .45, Lisa asked breathlessly, "What happened?"

He automatically ejected the round from the chamber and made sure the safety was on. "I got jumped."

"We heard a shot. Was it at you?"

"Yeah, but he missed. I didn't," Frank said.

"What do you mean?" Lisa asked.

"I think I killed him. It felt like I did."

Her hand kept a grip on him as if to draw strength.

Frank put his hand on her waist, feeling a great wave of tenderness engulf him.

Johnny approached. "I heard you talking out here, so I guess it went all right. That was a bloody-good show. What happened?"

Frank told the story as they walked back to the hut.

"Did you kill him?" Johnny asked.

"I don't know. We'll have to go out in the morning to see."

"When we heard the first shot, Lisa nearly went round the bend," Johnny said. "She wanted to run out there. I had to physically restrain her!"

Lisa laughed. "He's right. My ambulance team reflex, you know. I was sure you'd been shot and needed help. Johnny convinced me to wait a bit. Said you could take care of yourself. You scared them off, and they're gone." She added, "Then maybe we can get some sleep now."

All three of them were too keyed up to be able to settle down. They sat talking, while Lisa, aided by Frank's dimming flashlight, cleaned the cuts and scrapes on his back caused by the assailant's rifle.

Chapter 24: From Mergui, Over the Gulf of Martaban, to Mingaladon Airfield, December 22, 1941

The dawn came and the fog had turned milky-white.

"Are we flying today, Johnny?" Lisa asked. "I'm getting awfully hungry."

Johnny squinted up at the weather. "I don't know. If I were the meteorological officer, I'd say no; but it's time for all of us to bloody-well move out of here. Are the rest of you game?"

Both Frank and Lisa nodded assent.

Johnny turned to Lisa. "Have you done any instrument work? Needle-and-ball stuff?"

She nodded. "About three hours under the hood. Honest ones this time. And an occasional storm in the *Anson* ambulance plane. Why?"

"Because today, it will have to be an instrument takeoff. That means we will be taking a chance. From here to the west, the mountain slopes down. It's a pretty smooth slope; there are no ridges to snag you. If we takeoff and turn left, slow count to 15, and then lose 300-hundred-feet per minute, we should come out of the overcast somewhere south, close to Moulmein. I'd guess the cloud base is no lower than 800 feet. After Moulmein, we should be in the clear.

"The 800-foot figure is strictly guess work," Johnny continued. "I could be wrong, and it could be fogged in all the way down to the sea, making it difficult."

Frank knew what Johnny meant: it would make it difficult. *They'd either fly into the sea or stumble around, lost in the fog, until one or all of them hit a solid object. The threat of rock-stuffed clouds. . . .* He looked a question at Lisa.

"I'm hungry," she simply said.

The Ulysses Flight/ Paul Wankowicz

The girl was brave. He loved her. "Okay, field altitude here is 2,450," Johnny continued. "Set your altimeter to that. Zero your D.I., your gyro compass, when lined up. Once clear, turn to 280 degrees and start the descent. I figure this to be an updraft fog caused by the mountains so it should be clear over the sea.

"When you come out of the overcast, you should be able to see the coast. Head for Moulmein. It has a railroad south of it. The trains are ferried from Rangoon farther north. In the center of Moulmein, there is a red-brick clock tower set on a knoll. Take up an orbit around that and wait for us. You can't miss it. Got that?"

Frank nodded, *Johnny's invaluable. Without him,* Frank thought, *I'd be dead by now.* He wondered, *How will Lisa and I manage once we leave Johnny in Rangoon?*

"Whoever gets to Moulmein first, orbit 300 feet under the overcast and wait for the others." Johnny repeated, "Go closer to the bottom of the clouds if there isn't 300 feet. Okay?"

"Order of takeoff, same as last time?" Frank asked.

Johnny and Lisa nodded.

"One more detail," Johnny said. "The bod who shot at you last night—We need to see if he's still there. Want me to do it?"

Frank would have preferred Johnny do it, but felt that it was his business. He shook his head. "No thanks, Johnny. I'll see to it." Frank headed toward the parked airplanes.

"I'm coming with you," Lisa said. Johnny decided to follow them.

All three of them stood around the already-bloating corpse. The dead assailant was lying face down with a dent in the left side of his head where the force of the rifle's butt had crushed his skull.

"Turn him over," Lisa said. "I want to see his face."

Fighting revulsion, Frank reached down, grabbed a handful of dew-wet shirt, and pulled the corpse over. Ants were at its eyes, filling them, ringing them with a moving mass.

Straightening up, he looked at Lisa. She stood there, looking at the

The Ulysses Flight/ Paul Wankowicz

corpse, impassively. This was a part of her he didn't understand.

Finally, with a visible effort, she shook off whatever thoughts were holding her and, without saying a word, turned away. Her head bent down, she walked toward the lean-to.

Johnny looked at her retreating figure, and turned to Frank. "Go back to her. I'll take care of things down here." He bent over and picked up the rifle. "Police issue. The buggers must have knocked over a police station. Well, they'll never use this one again."

With practiced motion, he removed the bolt and flung it, wide-armed, into the bushes. "Damn it, Frank. Go to her. She needs you!"

"Thanks, Johnny. I didn't mean to stick you with the dirty work."

Frank jogged to her. When he was beside her, he said nothing. He put his arm around her shoulders.

Tears streamed down her cheeks. They walked over to some coconut logs and sat down, side by side.

She was still crying. He held her. Finally, her tears subsided. "I didn't mean to fall apart like this," she said. "It's just that looking at him, I realized this: the war has totally destroyed the world I knew. He looked just like any of our workers, with whom I had played when I was a child." She paused. "Why must we suffer it?"

"I don't know." He took a deep breath. "But if it wasn't for the war, we wouldn't have met. That's all the answer I need. You understand?"

She looked at him, her face still wet with tears, looking as if she'd just woken up from a deep nightmare. "That must be my answer, too," she said. "Thanks." She wiped her tears, and straightened her shirt.

"I think we better get ourselves organized and start thinking of flying to Rangoon. Where's Johnny?"

"Just coming now."

As if on cue, Johnny appeared. "I got rid of the rest of the rifle and ammunition in the bushes," he said.

"Now, it's time to get airborne. Are you ready?"

Within minutes, they'd loaded the miscellaneous pieces of personal gear and went through the ritual walk-around inspection. Once or twice,

140

The Ulysses Flight/ Paul Wankowicz

Frank glanced at Lisa. She worked through the checklist with calm professionalism.

When she was done and in the cockpit, Frank and Johnny clambered onto the wings to either side of her to make sure her Gyro Compass was set, and the Artificial Horizon was uncaged and level. She was ready to go. Conversation was difficult over the crackling exhaust of her idling engine.

"From here on in," Johnny yelled, "you're on your own. Good luck!"

Frank didn't trust himself to say anything. He just squeezed her shoulder in farewell and slid down the wing. He felt tears forming behind his eyes.

Johnny was soon ready for takeoff. The fog was still thick, but the light had grown stronger and one could see the trees, in a darker shade of gray, on each side of the field.

Johnny moved out, checked his magnetos for drop, and with a farewell wave of his hand, rolled his plane down the field.

Frank watched the fighter kick up clouds of spray from the wet grass as its engine roared to full power, and then, gray as it rolled away from them.

Two minutes later, Lisa opened the throttle, and slowly accelerated straight down the field.

Frank held his breath and watched her lift easily over the far trees and put her left wing down for her turn. He gave her a slow count of ten to avoid the danger of collision in the fog. Then, cranking his canopy shut, he moved down the field, engine roaring. *I hope Johnny's feel for the weather is good.*

After his turn, the jungle below him was indistinct in the fog. It began to slope away from view. At 1,200 feet, the clouds ended, as if he'd dropped out of the bottom of a mattress. With a monochrome view of the coast in the distance, Frank found himself following the mountain slope. Moulmein would soon be in view. He banked toward it, still losing height to the prescribed 900 feet.

The Ulysses Flight/ Paul Wankowicz

For a while, he couldn't see the others, but then, way across the town, he saw the silhouettes of the two planes banking lazily, and he sighed in relief.

The red-brick clock tower jutted out of the knoll between their planes and his own. He increased his turn to cut across the diameter of the orbit and join them. When he passed over the knoll, he saw a bright light appear at the base of the tower and slowly soar up toward him. For a second, he watched, fascinated. Another appeared. His mind becoming aware, yelled *Tracer! Some idiot is trying to shoot me down!* The reaction was instinctive: Full stick and rudder as he broke to the left, out of the area. He felt like a crow, near-missed by a .22 rifle.

Johnny and Lisa had been watching.

As Frank pulled into position beside them, they were laughing.

Lisa waved through her laughter.

They set me up, I'm sure, Frank thought. Frank shook his fist, and laughed to himself. *Yes, indeed, such flack is not all that accurate.*

In a flash, he realized he loved them, and that here in these fighters beside him, he had everything he ever wanted, or would.

The same spark, the same elan, also touched the others. They were kindred spirits.

The overcast still hung low in the direction of Rangoon. Patches of sunlight showed on the water. The sun's rays slanted toward them like blessings from heaven.

Johnny's home base was just a touch away. Without need for communication, all three planes playfully nosed down just above the choppy waters of the Martaban Bay. They skimmed over the surface, and delighted in the yellow and brown colors of the various currents from the confluence of rivers: the Salween, the Sittang, the Pegu, and the mother of them all, the Irrawaddy. They flew from sunshine to shadow and back again with their propeller tips just over the wavelets, glorying in the speed and freedom. They left behind little wakes in the water that disappeared as the air smoothed out after their noisy passage.

When they came to the green crescent of the far shore, they lifted

The Ulysses Flight/ Paul Wankowicz

slightly. They hurtled over the muddy mouth of the Pegu and the emerald green of its surrounding fields at 150 feet over the grain. The green of the rice below rapidly melted into the disease-like gray of the city as they flew over Rangoon's outskirts.

Frank recognized the usual shantytown on the edge of Rangoon proper. Then a glimpse of the crowded streets, relieved here and there by the green squares of urban parks, and startling in its size, the great golden dome of the central pagoda whipped past his left wingtip.

Before they had time for another look, Frank saw Johnny's fighter rise into a speed-killing climb at the apex of which Johnny dropped his gear, and then, swung the fighter toward a long runway flanked by tubby Brewster *Buffalo* fighters in R.A.F. colors. Mingaladon.

Still in loose formation, the planes slid down the long slope of the approach, wheels and flaps down, as if reaching for the security of the earth below. One after the other they touched the runway; and, with blips of the engines, taxied toward the yawning mouth of a hangar. There, a group of R.A.F. men in tropical khaki waited to see who the visitors were. They've arrived!

Chapter 25: Mingaladon Airfield, Rangoon, December 21, 1941

Two squadrons of British Royal Air Force *Buffalo* fighters, both led by Wing Commander Geoffrey Hayes, comprised the only air defense that Rangoon possessed. Most of its pilots were young, untried, and uncertain of why they were in Burma when, in their minds, the real war was in Europe. These pilots would become part of the price paid.

A group of American volunteers, the Flying Tigers, flying in the markings of the Chinese Air Force, were led by Colonel Claire Lee Chennault, and had been moved down to Magwe in West Central Burma on the Irrawaddy River. Colonel Chennault was reputed to be an excellent tactician. However, no one could tell how well his adventurer pilots would fight.

The Area Commander Robert Brooke-Popham didn't want the American Volunteers in Rangoon, lest their presence there antagonize the Japanese.

There was no certainty that the Allies would be victorious. With respect to Burma, it appeared the opposite. So far, whenever the Japanese attacked, the Allies could muster no real defense of their country. The only possibility was to buy time with their sacrifice to allow the Allies to work out some sort of defense for India, the real prize according to the British hierarchy.

Three days earlier, dressed in the ragged remains of a Buddhist Monk's saffron-colored habit, Roland Biard staggered into the Mingaladon Airfield gate, delirious, but still with sufficient control of himself to ask for Wing Commander Geoffrey Hayes.

Impressed that he spoke the King's English impeccably, the First Sergeant had the brains not to dismiss the bedraggled monk. The First

The Ulysses Flight/ Paul Wankowicz

Sergeant rang the Wing Commander's office and was told to send the monk up right away.

As Roland Biard approached Wing Commander Hayes, he apologized for his appearance. "It has taken me nine days to get from Bangkok to Rangoon, some by bus, by bullock cart, but mostly on foot. My hand is infected and I'm ill. I am sorry to present myself to you in such a state."

Hayes realized Roland had gotten there by strength of will alone.

Roland retained consciousness just long enough to hand Hayes the red-bordered Japanese military's book, hidden in the folds of his muddy robes.

Hayes gave the book a cursory glance before tucking it in a desk drawer to look at later. Under the circumstances, Hayes was more alarmed by young Biard's condition and made rapid arrangements to have Roland Biard transported to the hospital in Rangoon, hoping the hospital's English doctor could restore him to health. Hayes felt deeply responsible for Biard, as if he were Hayes' own son.

Now, Hayes sat by Roland's hospital bed in the stifling-hot room. In the humidity, medical staff were sugar-glazed with their own perspiration.

The hospital in Rangoon had been built on the river to catch the faintest of breezes, but all the location had accomplished was to guarantee the patients would be tormented by the humidity of the low-lying swamp.

All, that is, except Roland Biard, who was burning up with dry fever, and lay limp in the hospital bed as if already in his coffin.

Even while attending Roland, the sorry state of Burma's defenses and the sacrifices that would be required as soon as the Japanese attack would come, was uppermost in Wing Commander Hayes' mind. It formed the background for his anger. However, at the moment, most of Hayes' temper was directed toward the English doctor, a small, wizened man who turned out to be powerless as a healer.

145

The Ulysses Flight/ Paul Wankowicz

In Hayes' eyes, the nurse was an accomplice. She sat on the other side of the hospital bed, mindlessly swabbing Roland's forehead with alcohol. The room reeked with the odor.

Roland was dying from blood poisoning right in front of them, with no one able to cure him.

There was no way to reverse the course of infection. For the last days in that hot, stuffy room, Roland had struggled to hold onto his life.

The two years' inadequate nutrition, while working in the role of Pa Tim, had left the man's body little reserve of strength with which to fight the infection resulting from Seki's bite. And now, just days before Christmas, it was obvious that Roland would not survive until twilight.

The reek of medicine, the heat, the impersonal faces of the doctor and the nurse, all cried death.

Hayes hated it all to the depths of his soul. He saw Roland's lips move, and he bent to listen better.

"Wing Commander," Roland asked, "I did all right, didn't I?"

"You did all right, Roland. The R.A.F. and the spirit of your father can be proud of you. You did very well, indeed!"

"Really, Sir?"

"No doubt about it. No doubt whatsoever!" Hayes said.

During the moment of silence, Hayes heard a large insect battering itself against the screen in the window.

Then, Roland whispered again. "Sir?"

"Yes, Roland?"

"I'm not going to live. I'm going to die. Isn't that right?"

Hayes' heart stopped.

Roland trusted Hayes completely in all things, and he was giving his life for what Hayes believed in. To tell him anything less than the truth now would be to break that trust, to do a disservice which could never be set right.

"Yes, Roland," Hayes said, as gently as he could. "Unfortunately, we don't think you will survive this one."

Hayes felt the nurse's eyes burning into him with dislike. The nurse would have given a false answer. She probably already had.

The Wing Commander had long ago forgotten how to weep although he felt close to tears now. However, he'd not forgotten how to feel anger, and it rose in him like a sour tide. He looked up and glared back at the nurse.

Roland had fallen silent, listening. Suddenly, he opened his eyes. "Aircraft!" he said, loudly. "Look out the window and tell me what they are . . ."

Now that Roland mentioned it, Hayes listened. He could hear the rapidly-swelling hum of aero-engines at close to full throttle, flying low. The sound grew until it seemed to fill the whole room. The walls rattled.

Hayes glanced worriedly at Roland. Although his eyes were closed, a ghost of a smile was formed by his lips, as if a symphony were filling the room.

Looking out of the window just in time, Hayes saw three olive-drab P-40s with the blue-and-white-and-red stars of the U.S.A.A.F. on their sides, hurtling low over the paddy bordering the river.

Now it was the English doctor's turn to glare at Hayes. *I hate airplanes—Their infernal noise disturbs my patients.* The doctor didn't feel kindly toward Hayes either. In the last four weeks, three of Hayes' men had died in crashed planes, reducing these splendid young bodies to traumatized meat. *It's reprehensible. Completely criminal! Such mutilation is a sin worse than blasphemy.* The doctor seethed.

The sound of the airplanes died out in the distance and Hayes bent over Roland. There was no doubt of it now. Roland's life force was running out as fast as hydrogen out of a torn balloon. There were only minutes left.

"What were they, sir?" Roland asked.

"*Tomahawks*, the American P-40s. Not the Volunteers, either. They had the American insignia on their fuselages."

"Jolly good! The Yanks have arrived. Should be of some help to you."

The Ulysses Flight/ Paul Wankowicz

Picking his way through the threads of his previous thoughts, he
asked again: "You said that I did all right, sir?"

"Yes, you did very well, Roland."

"Then it's all right. Thank you very much, sir."

He opened his eyes wide and looked around the room as if trying to
memorize the scene forever, then stiffened his body. He relaxed slowly,
his head lolling back on the pillow. It was over.

The nurse stopped her mechanical swabbing and the English doctor,
still glowering at Hayes, dropped Roland's wrist, which he had been
holding to feel the pulse.

Without a word, Hayes got up and walked to the doorway and into
the hall. *It would be very easy*, Hayes thought, *to learn to cry again.* He
walked a few steps and stopped.

The hall was long, lined with doors to rooms like the one he had just
left. At the far end, a louvered door let in bright sunlight from the
outside; the shadows of the slats patterned the tiled floor. He stopped in
the long hospital hall and leaned his forehead against the wall for relief,
to clear his mind, but the wall was hot, and no relief came. *First Johnny, and now Roland. Am I a Jonah to my men? No! Both Roland and
Johnny Laws were casualties of the bloody war.* Standing in the shadows, Hayes realized that he was getting morbid.

With an effort of will, he forced his mind away from their deaths,
anchoring his focus on the three American fighters he'd briefly
glimpsed through the window. *Where have these come from? The
nearest U.S. base is in the Philippines.*

Hayes knew Colonel Chennault was not expecting a shipment of
airplanes, yet these planes were marked with U.S. insignia. Chennault's
Flying Tigers' aircraft carried the blue-and-white chrysanthemum of the
Chinese Air Force, not the U.S. star.

The new planes were a mystery, just like the slim red book Roland
had given him. Roland knew the book was important, but he didn't
know what it was. The book was written in Japanese, which Hayes
could not translate. *I'll have to see that it gets to the proper people who*

148

The Ulysses Flight/ Paul Wankowicz

can decipher its contents and make use of it.

The fighters would be his business. The three U.S. fighters had been heading for Mingaladon Airfield. He'd have to go there fast to see what they . . . *After all, I am Air Officer commanding Burma.*

His Humber was parked in the drive. Wincing at its inner heat, Hayes slid his bulk under the hard-rubber steering wheel and stomped on the starter. The steering wheel was burning hot in his hands. *I'd better get back to Mingaladon and take control.*

He'd deal with the incoming planes first, and then, return to the hospital to oversee Roland's burial arrangements.

Chapter 26: Mingaladon Airfield, Rangoon

In the morning, Frank saw a different Johnny Laws after the landing. They landed in a burst of sunlight. Johnny led their three taxiing airplanes, by following the hand signals of the ground crew, to the front of the maintenance hangar. They angled their planes into a precise wing-to-wing line. It was a far cry from the primitive conditions of Tenasserim Field.

Johnny completed his post-flight check and vaulted to the ground, where he was surrounded by a grinning crowd. Everyone was obviously delighted to see him back and alive.

Frank watched Lisa get out onto the wing, strip off her helmet and shake out her reddish-blond hair.

She jumped lightly off the wing and joined Johnny. Lisa had a broad, relaxed grin on her face, and an assurance in her walk—the walk of a fighter pilot. The group around Johnny opened to admire her. Her acceptance was immediate.

Johnny gave orders with ease, as if born to it.

By the time Frank joined the other two pilots, Johnny had everything arranged. The P-40s would be wheeled into the R.A.F.'s hangar so that local members of the America Voluntary Group (A.V.G.) would not be tempted to requisition them.

The three were invited to breakfast in the mess hall, a large, airy room with wide windows overlooking the airfield. Outside, a covered walkway shaded the hall from the direct sun. Inside, white-washed walls added to the cool feeling. Rolled bamboo screens hung above each window. The mess tables were arranged into a "U" layout with the head table elevated on a dais.

From the mess hall, Frank had a glimpse of a bar in the next room. The bar was accessible through a nearby doorway, with a massive pair of dark-teak doors, swung back against the wall. Groupings of easy

The Ulysses Flight/ Paul Wankowicz

chairs and sofas, upholstered in a dark leather, landscaped the room. Ceiling fans circulated the air.

The walls of both rooms were decorated with pictures, paintings, and photographs of planes. Some depicted people in odd-looking flying togs or WWI maternity jackets posed in front of the rotary engines and wooden propellers.

Frank recognized some of the airplanes: a Sopwith *Camel* here, a Nieuport *Bebe* there, an SE-5, an RE-8. But others, the more modern ones, he'd never seen before. That surprised him because he'd always considered himself as well-versed in aviation history.

When they were seated in the mess hall, two Burmese boys in spotless, white jackets above their ragged pants and bare feet, took orders and scurried to bring coffee for Frank, and tea for Lisa and Johnny. Frank picked up his mug of coffee in both hands and savored it. When Wing Commander Hayes joined them, Johnny made the introductions.

From the previous discussion with Johnny, Frank knew that Wing Commander Hayes was already a legend. Hayes was not tall. He had a square, athletic figure which belied his 47 years. He was betrayed, however, by a slight paunch—what Johnny called "the Air-Vice-Marshal bulge." Hayes' hair was short and quite gray, and his mustache was patterned after Sir Hugh Dowding, who was the Chief of the Fighter Command during the Battle of Britain. It still retained the bright-red color which matched Hayes' ruddy complexion. Eyes shone a hue somewhere between lead and polished-steel blue. Crinkles showed at the corners of his eyes from hours spent in the cockpit squinting against the sun and its glare. Frank guessed Hayes' eyes could be very cold when the owner wished. However, the moment Hayes spied Johnny, they twinkled.

"Johnny," Hayes said, in a manner of greeting, "for a while, I thought you had bought the farm."

"No chance of that, sir. I'm a city boy and wouldn't know what to do with it!"

151

The Ulysses Flight/ Paul Wankowicz

"Glad to hear it. Now that you are back, you can straighten out the
mess Flight Lieutenant Bose has made of the daily reports. He writes
like Omar the Tentmaker!"

Johnny smiled. Frank thought, *This must be a sort of ritual between
the two, masking deeper feelings.*

"Roger. Could I requisition a couple of quills and some parchment
to match the thinking at H.Q.?"

Hayes laughed. "You've put your finger on it, lad! Parchment!"
Then he turned serious. "What have you been doing all this time, Johnny? And how did you meet up with your friends?"

Johnny quickly sketched how the P-40s and Frank and Lisa had
gotten to Tenasserim, and of their flight to Rangoon.

Hayes listened in silence.

When Johnny stopped, Hayes asked: "The Flight Sergeant told me
that all three kites showed evidence their guns were fired. What happened?"

Johnny had completely forgotten about the encounter with the
Japanese planes, and quickly described the fights, and the earlier
encounter with the Burmese Nationalist patriots. In telling the story,
Johnny called Lisa by her last name, Van Riin, to make sure she would
not be differentiated from the other pilots. In an American airbase, a
woman being allowed to fly a 'hot' fighter would have raised howls of
protest from the cocky, male fighter pilots who felt a female pilot was a
threat to their virility, even though women pilots flew planes from
repair to return to service.

Johnny remembered that, during the Battle of Britain and afterwards, hundreds of dedicated women flew dangerous missions—
everything from fighters to four-engine bombers—and successfully
kept the delivery lines open to the R.A.F.

The R.A.F. had become quite used to seeing a long-haired girl
alight from a just-delivered *Spitfire,* or a four-engine *Stirling* bomber. It
hurt no one's ego. In the U.S.A., women pilots even flew the military
planes men felt were too risky to fly.

152

The Ulysses Flight/ Paul Wankowicz

Frank listened idly as Johnny described the flight. However, the rich breakfast, on top of his lack of sleep, took effect.

Hayes noticed. "Finish the story later, lads," he said, and turned to one of the Burmese boys: "Take the guests to their quarters."

The boy led them down a long, cool corridor which paralleled the front veranda of the building. Opening a heavy teakwood door, "Captain here," he said.

"Bathroom in between the Captain's and missy's room." Through the doorway, all Frank could see was the quilted bed coverlet under a tent of white mosquito netting, and an electric fan oscillating slowly in the corner.

Frank waved good-bye to Lisa as she followed the guide down the hall. Throwing his clothes on a convenient chair, he fell into the bed and was asleep within seconds.

He awoke from his nap hot and sweaty. Someone had been in the room while he slept because his clothing had been washed and ironed and carefully laid out on the chair.

A bath and the newly-clean clothes made him feel better. When he knocked on Lisa's door, he heard no answer, so he gently pushed it open. The bed was in disarray, but she wasn't there. Unhappy at missing her, he headed for the mess hall and ordered a cup of tea. The whole base seemed to be taking an afternoon nap. What he needed now was someone to talk to.

He wandered over to the maintenance hangar. The atmosphere within was totally different from the sagging, mildewed place in Tenasserim. Pursuant to Hayes' orders, the three P-40s, their cowls off, were already being worked on. Beyond them stood two of the reserve *Buffaloes* having their engines overhauled. Equipment was scattered about. A quietly-efficient ground staff went about their duties as if it were at Mitchel Field in New York.

Technical talk was what Frank sought to dispel his gloomy mood. He enjoyed at least an hour talking with the leading Flight Sergeant. He

153

was so engrossed that he didn't notice Lisa enter.

She tapped him on the shoulder. "As soon as you're through, Hayes would like to see us."

Now that she was here, Frank felt his mood lifting, now even cheerful. He realized part of his irritation was from the fact that he hadn't known where she was, or what she was doing.

When he tried to introduce her to the mechanics, he found the news of her arrival had spread rapidly, and everyone already knew of her as the pilot of the third Yank fighter.

The sun was beginning to set and the tropical humidity rose. While talking, Frank had forgotten the temperature, but now, as they crossed the apron, he again became aware of the steamy tropical heat radiating from the tarmac. Perspiration spread across his shirt.

He looked admiringly at Lisa. "How can you look so cool?"

Lisa smiled, "I grew up here, remember? Think cool."

"I missed you. Where did you disappear to?"

"Hayes had to go into Rangoon and he offered to take me along. I had been hoping to find some people that I knew. Friends."

"Did you?"

Lisa shrugged her shoulders. "A few. They had all heard what had happened at our plantation. I had a feeling I was an embarrassment, a possible burden. Most were worried about how to save their gold, and their skins." She paused. "No, not friends, not really. I felt more at ease with my mother's Burmese hairdresser. Of course, he is too poor to run."

"Are you sure?"

She looked at him with fire in her eyes. "Of course I'm bloody sure! I've never had such a rotten time in my life!" She took a deep breath and stopped. . . . "Oh Frank, I'm sorry. You had nothing to do with it. Just that it was beastly with everybody being so hypocritically polite, but not wanting to help. It almost made me sick. I suppose it's this stupid war!" She was close to tears.

Frank looked at her. He wanted to put his arms about her to reassure

154

The Ulysses Flight/ Paul Wankowicz

her that he was here for support, but it was not possible in the middle of the airfield with half the R.A.F. watching.

He swore under his breath. Being in love was damned complicated, just as she'd said.

Lisa guided him past the building where they were quartered to a larger one, identified as the headquarters by the flagpole in front, on which the light-blue R.A.F. flag hung limply in the stale air. They climbed the white-washed steps to the entrance. Verandas flanked both sides. Lisa led him down a corridor, already darkening with the coming twilight, to the door marked: Commanding Officer. She knocked gently.

Hayes' office was large. One corner was occupied by a 'military issue' desk, found anywhere in the world. Frank wondered if some Japanese C.O. sat behind its twin, a Japanese 'military issue' desk somewhere to the east of them. The other corner of the room, in contrast, was occupied by very non-issue wicker chairs, beside them two decanters and a silver bucket of ice sat on a round glass-topped table. Hayes and Johnny sat each with drinks in hand. Above them, on the wall, Frank saw a large framed photograph of three R.A.F. biplanes in tight formation, photographed against inhospitable, snow-covered crags which reared high above the machines.

Hayes noticed him eyeing it. "Hawker *Harts,*" he said. "India Squadron, taken at 25,000 feet, and we still weren't clear of the bloody peaks. Damned cold besides!" He waved toward the table. "Sit down and have a drink. Scotch or gin? Soda water is on the sideboard."

Frank poured two drinks, handed one to Lisa, and sat down. He turned to Hayes.

"You wanted me, sir?" he asked.

"Right. Johnny tells me your intention, Captain, is to ferry the three *Tomahawks* to the Philippines. Lord knows, they need them."

"Call me Frank, sir." It was hard to visualize, but the man talking to him would be the equivalent of a Lieutenant Colonel in the U.S.A.A.F. He struck Frank more as a relaxed host entertaining a guest. Hayes

155

lacked the inflated self-importance Frank had come to expect of British Field-Grade Officers.

"The fighters, sir, were originally scheduled to Clark Field, near Manila. They should be delivered there."

"Do you have a route planned?"

"Not precisely, sir. I relied on local knowledge. The P-40 has a long range, and I planned to stretch it as far as I could. I had thought to fly to Singapore, and then, across to Borneo, but that was before Johnny suggested we go to Rangoon first."

"Things may be quite difficult. The news is that the British troops on the Malay Peninsula have fallen back to the Perak Line."

"The Perak Line?"

Hayes walked to a map on the wall. He put his hand about half-way down Malaya. "Right about here. The Japanese have all of the country north of the line. That includes Penang, the airfields at Alor Star and Kota Bharu. Flying south, the nearest place where you will be able to refuel is Kuala Lumpur, about 1,000 miles from here. Do you have the range?"

Frank shook his head. "No. I doubt it."

On the map, the crescent of Sumatra hung just below the bulge of the Malay Peninsula, like a waxing moon. Were there an airfield on the northern tip, it would be a shorter lap than straight down to Singapore.

Lisa had seen that. "How about Sumatra?" she asked.

"No joy. There is a ferry field at Tjalang, but I don't know anything about it. It may not have proper petrol available. We get very little information from the Dutch," Hayes replied.

Johnny went over to the desk and picked up a piece of string, which he carefully measured against a ruler. He cut it and marked the ends with knots. "About the *Tomahawk*'s range, 850 miles," he said, holding the string against the map. He measured the distance to Sumatra with it. The island's tip came just about at the end of the string. "The route is all over water. That disqualifies it as far as I'm concerned."

Frank went to the map and measured it himself. "Johnny's right.

The Ulysses Flight/ Paul Wankowicz

Tjalang is out." The Japanese had out-ranged them. There was no place to go. The realization struck them hard.

"After all the work and danger, we are stuck in Rangoon. It doesn't seem fair," Frank said. He picked up the string and stretched it in a segment of a circle centered on Mingaladon Airfield. Tenasserim Airfield fell well on the inside, approximately 400 miles. From there to Kuala Lumpur, another 700. But a stop at Tenasserim Airfield represented a fully-loaded takeoff from that miserable little airstrip.

He heard Lisa groan. "Oh, no!"

For a long time, all three of them faced the map, silent with their own thoughts. Johnny broke the morbid silence. "There should be a 15-mile on-shore breeze at this time of the year," he said to no one in particular. "And I asked Cyril to cut the seaward palms after we left. That should make a difference."

Frank looked at Lisa. She was the color of khaki. He turned to Hayes. "If we can't make it out of that field, we're marooned here?"

"Something of that sort."

"As the bloody Royal Navy says: 'One can't live forever.' I'll have a go," Johnny said.

It startled Frank. "Wait a dog-gone minute. You're part of this Limey Squadron. How come you're so damn quick to volunteer?"

Hayes spoke up, a ghost of a smile on his face. "If you people can make it out of that field at Tenasserim and on to Kuala Lumpur, you represent the last secure transport out of here. I have detached Johnny to act as your R.A.F. escort. After all, you are traveling through the King's Colonies. But it all depends on your ability to reach Kuala Lumpur."

Frank felt a weight lift off his shoulders. *Impossible or not, Johnny is coming with us!*

Looking directly at Frank, color fighting to return to Lisa's features, she said, "I'm not about to break up a good team." The way she said it, it was a challenge.

Hayes looked from one to the other. "I'll tell the Padre to pray for a wind." He paused. "Johnny, call the mess. Ask them to send us sandwiches and tea." Hayes turned back to Frank. "You may feel that I'm rushing things. I am, but the news is bad. Intelligence informed me the Japanese are ready to move against Burma anytime now. They will probably start with an air action. The sooner you plan to get your kites away, the better.

"I have asked for your aircraft to be overhauled and armed. I also ordered the armament section to install our Mark IV reflex sight, and make your radios serviceable taking from our stock of U.S. spares for the Brewsters. Radios will give you some protection in case you are jumped and allow you to communicate one with another. Everything should be complete by the day after tomorrow. Make that your departure time, unless there is some business here that can't be rushed?"

Hayes looked from Frank to Lisa. "No? . . . Good! Ah, here come the sandwiches!"

A barefoot Burmese boy, the same one who'd guided Frank and Lisa to their quarters, brought a tray covered with a red-checkered cloth. Hayes made room for it on the table, then served another round of drinks.

After the boy had gently closed the door behind him, Hayes continued, "You may all wonder what this monkey's dance is all about. Johnny does. I told him that he's to accompany you down to Singapore, without explaining anything further. But before I do, let me ask again. It's over a 1,000-mile flight from Rangoon to Singapore, with the Japanese in control of the air almost all the way. Frank, you know how maneuverable the Japanese planes are. Are you willing to risk it?"

"Hell, yes."

"Johnny?"

"I'd rather have a go at it in one of Frank's iron birds than in the bloody *Buffalo*."

"Too right. Miss Van Riin?"

Lisa nodded her head without saying anything.

Frank knew that she was still struggling with the thought of taking

The Ulysses Flight/ Paul Wankowicz

off from Tenasserim Field in a fully-loaded airplane.

"Are you sure? The others have been through combat training. It will be much more risky for you."

"I've come this far," she said. "I'm not about to quit now." Her voice was brittle; she didn't like being singled out as a woman.

Frank was startled. *It hadn't occurred to me I might lose Lisa through combat. That she may be hit, or traumatized in a dog fight.*

She saw his look. "I'll take my chances! Just because I'm female," she said, "does not mean I expect to be treated differently." There was a hint of anger in her voice. She'd voluntarily entered a man's world and would not be challenged out of it.

One part of Frank wanted her with him. The other asked him to keep her out of danger's way. *Wouldn't it be better to find some other way for Lisa to leave Rangoon? But I know she'd object to that.*

Hayes levered himself out of his chair and went over to his desk. He fumbled in a drawer, withdrew a slim red book, and plopped it on the table.

The lettering on the cover was Japanese. Frank recognized it as some sort of military manual.

"Two men died so that this might get to us," Hayes said. "But it does the Allies no good sitting here in Rangoon where the Japanese might find out we have it and recapture it. I'd like you three to fly it down to Singapore so British Intelligence can take a good look at it."

"What is it?" Lisa asked.

"I can't read Japanese," Hayes replied, "and I don't dare ask anyone to interpret. There's too much 5th Column around. However, I feel it's important. So did the man who gave his life to get it to me."

Johnny looked up. "Roland? The one who goes by the alias Pa Tim?"

For an instant, Hayes looked much older than his years. "Yes," he said wearily.

Lisa hesitated. She wanted to ask who was this Roland, but thought better of it.

159

The Ulysses Flight/ Paul Wankowicz

"What is more important," Hayes continued, "is that the Japanese don't yet know we have it. Roland Biard was successful in burning down the house from which he took it. I hoped to get it out by a *Catalina* flying boat, but I learned they are not able to fly to Rangoon anymore." He shook his head. "If, indeed, there are any flying boats left."

He walked across the room and opened a Chinese-lacquered cabinet from which he retrieved three canisters of film. "I photographed the pages of the red book and made three sets of Leica film, purposely left undeveloped, which I've put in a small canister for each of you."

As they followed him, Frank thought, *The bastard knew all along that we'd take a chance and agree to go*. His admiration of Hayes as a reader of character grew.

Hayes continued, "I will give each of you one roll to take to British Intelligence in Singapore. If there is any chance of being captured, take it out of the canister, and unroll the film to expose it to light. This will wipe out what's on it. We must keep secret whatever it is we have. "If you do get to Singapore, find a British officer who knows Wing Commander Winterbotham personally. I say again, *Only to someone who knows Winterbotham personally*. I don't expect you to be able to find Winterbotham yourself because his base of operations isn't in Singapore. I will burn the original red book as soon as you leave." Still standing, he leaned forward, knuckles on his desk, and looked around the group. "Any further questions?"

The pilots made eye contact with one another, but said nothing. Then Frank said, "My mission, I'm supposed to deliver these planes to Manila."

"This takes priority. You can do that after." Wing Commander Hayes' voice had an unmistakable sound of command. Frank decided that if he wanted to get anywhere, it would be better not to challenge him.

Hayes straightened up and finished his drink. "Next on the list: now that you will have radios, you'll need a call name to use for you three. I'd like you to sound like a completely new unit. Like reinforcements.

The Ulysses Flight/ Paul Wankowicz

The Japanese Intelligence in Rangoon knows what we are about here before we think of it, but if we come up with a new unit they haven't reported, it will confuse the devil out of them! We need all the advantage around here we can get."

Frank felt everyone looking at him, but his mind was a blank.

Lisa broke the silence. "We're not exactly after the golden fleece, but we're wandering back and forth like the classical Greeks. How about *The Ulysses Flight?*"

Johnny nodded his head. "Unlike the Greeks, we do have a goal, but I cede the point. Frank?"

"Better than anything I'd think of."

"'The Ulysses Flight' it is then." Hayes sat back. "Johnny, you be the Red Leader. Miss Van Riin, you be the Blue Leader. That will make them think there are more of us than we really are. Make yourselves sound like an entire squadron. Okay?"

"Roger." Johnny spoke for the group.

"One more thing," Hayes said. "There isn't much peacetime left for this squadron, so I'd like to declare tomorrow night Squadron Night. Full dress if possible. And a special invitation to you, Miss Van Riin. It will give the younger pilots something to remember."

"Sort of a Farewell Party," Johnny said.

Hayes nodded. "That too."

Thinking of the Burmese situation, Frank wondered whether there was a deeper meaning to the word: Farewell. "What's Squadron Night?" he asked.

Johnny held up his glass against the light and turned toward Frank. "When the R.A.F. was first established," he said, "its Chief, Hugh Montague 'Boom' Trenchard, realized that being the junior service, it would lose out in the competition for the able, traditionally-minded young men which the Air Force desperately needed to recruit. The only counter was to build traditions in a hurry, to mimic the 'Regimental Nights' or wardroom parties on board Royal Navy ships. Establishing 'Squadron Nights' was one of the ways he accomplished it."

161

The Ulysses Flight/ Paul Wankowicz

"I'm afraid I'll look a little naked," Frank said. "All the uniform I have is what I'm wearing."

Hayes smiled. "Just having a Yank ally here will be enough. What's more, with Miss Van Riin along, I don't think anyone will be looking at you. "By the way, Frank, can you stay behind for a minute? I have a question."

Hayes' request did not require an answer.

As Lisa and Johnny filed out, Hayes turned to Frank. "The Chiefy tells me you have a stash of money in your kite."

Frank started an explanation, but Hayes cut him short. "I have no doubt it's honest," he said. "But have you thought of giving Miss Van Riin some? I understand she hasn't a farthing to her name. I offered to give her five pounds out of the recreation fund, but she only took one pound, and that in native currency. Maybe you can do better. I think she'd appreciate it."

Frank felt foolish. This was the second time that someone had suggested something for Lisa which he should have thought of himself. He nodded his head.

Hayes flicked his wrist to indicate Frank could depart.

Frank hesitated, thinking that this was a good chance to get briefed on the general war situation, and more about the situation in the Philippines.

Hayes noticed. "Pour yourself another drink," he said. "What is it?"

"I wonder if you could bring me up-to-date, sir. I was aboard ship when the news of Pearl Harbor came. Since then, I've been pretty much isolated in the jungle, away from regular radio contact. I don't even know how badly we were hurt in the Pearl Harbor attack. From what I've been able to pick up, things do not appear to be going too well."

Hayes looked at him sharply. "Your government has been pretty closed-mouth about it. From what I have heard, you lost most of your American fleet on day one. All your battle-wagons in the Pacific, and some of the cruisers. Only the aircraft carriers didn't get damaged. They were out on an exercise when the attack came." Hayes paused to

The Ulysses Flight/ Paul Wankowicz

let that sink in. "We, the British, haven't fared any better. Some damn fool in Whitehall sent Admiral Tom Phillips here with the *Prince of Wales* and the *Repulse*. Only Whitehall forgot to send an aircraft carrier to give them protection. I was told they made a proud show in Singapore Harbor. Then Admiral Phillips went on his first patrol without air cover, and it took the Japanese only 120 minutes to sink those two ships off Kuantan, Malaya. It was a bloody shambles. The Japanese had it all their own way."

"Know anything about the Philippines?" Frank asked.

"Not much. Clark Field was bombed December 8th. The Japanese landed on Luzon on the 10th. The Yank Army there is putting up a good show, but with no U.S. Navy in Pearl Harbor, there can be no reinforcements. It looks like only a matter of time before the Philippine Islands will be taken over; but don't go spreading the gloom about, demoralizing the troops."

Hayes was not a pessimist, so the tone of the interview had Frank worried. It was obvious the Allies were losing badly. It would continue downward before things could be turned around. He wondered how much of Asia would still be left in Allied hands before their luck finally changed.

During the interview, Frank also learned that the 18th British Division was originally scheduled to go to Rangoon, Burma as reinforcements. Instead, the Division had been turned around to head for Singapore, Malaya.

Hayes said, "Like other troops, they'd be sent piecemeal into the jungle. There were few troops, beyond the remnants of the fighter force and the American Irregulars, with which Burma could be defended.

Hayes was not bitter; that was, after all, part of what he had risked when he joined the military. But he held no trust in either Air Vice-Marshal Robert Brooke-Popham, Commander in Chief Far East, or in General Anthony E. Percival, the man in charge of the defense of Malaya.

Hayes considered General Percival a man of inaction. "Can't make

163

The Ulysses Flight/ Paul Wankowicz

up his bloody mind much of the time," Hayes said. "And Singapore is more of a trap than a fortress. Don't plan to stay there long," he warned. Hayes smiled a grim straight-across smile. "I guess that's about all I can tell you."

The briefing left Frank with one clear idea. *There are damned few places to which we could run, and the list is shrinking fast.*

For the first time, the possibility of their not getting to the Philippines crossed his mind.

Running would be a lousy way to die, Frank thought. *Lisa and Johnny deserve better than that.*

Frank looked at Hayes. "Thank you, sir. I'll see to the money thing in the morning. And good night."

Johnny and Lisa had already disappeared, so Frank walked to his quarters alone. Night had fallen. Thick, warm clouds obscured the stars. Waves of heat still radiated from the concrete underfoot. Frank walked with his head bent down, heavy with thoughts of his own inadequacy, intermingled with the dangers he'd invited Lisa to share.

He wished he'd never mentioned flying to the Philippines to her. At the time, he'd thought of it as an epic flight. It had seemed fun to commit her to that, but exposing her to the dangers of Japanese bullets in a dog fight was another matter altogether. Frank knew that if he asked Hayes to see Lisa to safety, the 'old man' would find some way of doing it; but he was also aware that no power on earth would convince her to follow that course.

As he entered his quarters and undressed, he was very conscious that only two doors separated her from him. He got ready for sleep. He'd never understand her, or her sometimes iron control of herself, combined with her mercurial mood changes. But he knew he loved her, even more so because she insisted on standing level with him and Johnny. Of the last, he was very sure.

Chapter 27: The Shopping Trip into Rangoon

Frank was awakened by a gentle knock on the door. He opened his eyes to see a smiling Lisa.

The sun was already streaming in through his window, promising a hot, steamy day. "Wing Commander Hayes has lent me the Station's Ford for the day, and I need to go into Rangoon. Would you like to come along?" she asked.

"I'd love to. Give me 30 minutes, and I'll meet you in front. I have to get dressed and need to see the maintenance people for a minute. Pick me up there."

Frank remembered Hayes' suggestion of the previous evening. Going to the maintenance people would give him a chance to get some cash out of the baggage compartment of his P-40, U.S. money to give to her.

After a cup of tea with Chiefy, Frank emerged from the hangar to find Lisa waiting for him in the Ford. As they turned onto the road, he noticed that she drove with the same relaxed precision with which she flew.

Burma was a British Colony so they drove on the left side of the road, which Frank found disconcerting. The wind coming through the open window of the Ford was hot and gave no relief. The causeway-style road, built up on an embankment, lanced straight through a rice paddy. Across the muddy rice fields, a railroad track lay parallel to it. A small train engine spewed clouds of black smoke intermingled with white steam. It pulled a long string of freight cars.

"I'd hate to be the engineer of that train," Frank said. "It must be roasting hot inside there."

The Ulysses Flight/ Paul Wankowicz

"Rice," Lisa said. "The rice export season in Burma starts in December and runs through the middle of May. The Japanese need all the grain they can get. Time for Rangoon is growing short. The Japanese aren't going to let much more of it be loaded onto the ships to be exported."

"How do you know?"

"I was in town yesterday," Lisa said. "All the local people, the natives and the merchants, know about the Japanese and the rice."

The railroad tracks curved to the east. With nothing new of interest to distract him, Frank returned to studying her profile. He'd never get enough of it.

They were now coming into the first tin-shanty shacks on the borders of Rangoon, where she had to slow down to avoid the pedestrians' carts and animals that began to crowd the road.

Frank remembered the money, and twisted around in his seat. He pulled out five 50-dollar bills which he proffered.

"What's this?"

"Your pay for ferrying the P-40. Ten days at $25 dollars a day. I'm sorry that I didn't get it to you earlier."

She expertly cut around a stalled, rusty taxi, and straightened out. "Look, you don't have to pay me for that. I'm not doing it for the money!"

The crowds in the streets thickened, and she needed to devote her full attention to driving. When they were in the clear again, she gave him a quick sideways glance. Then, with a shrug, she took the bills and stuffed them into her shirt pocket and buttoned the flap. "You've been talking with Hayes," she said. "Thanks!" At the next corner, she took a sharp left into a side street, almost too narrow for the Ford. She threaded the car through more narrow alleys. Apparently satisfied, she drove the left wheels up onto the mud sidewalk and parked. The car was immediately surrounded by a group of Chinese boys, curious while at the same time hesitant and shy of the foreigners.

"Here," Lisa called out to the eldest and tossed him a coin which he

The Ulysses Flight / Paul Wankowicz

deftly plucked out of the air. "Watch car. More money when we back."
The boy nodded agreement. "Watch good," he said.

When they were a few feet away from the car, she stopped to orient herself. Then she remembered and turned in the direction the car was pointing. They had to force a path through all the people.

The crowd along the street was like nothing Frank had ever seen. Every color of the rainbow, with everyone going every-which-way, using the sidewalk or the street, while carrying bundles, baskets, and pots slung on shoulder poles. People pushed wheelbarrows, rode bicycles, pulled carts, or even led miniature horses. There were Chinese, Malays, Burmese, Hindi, all races and creeds, jostling each other as they hurried on errands and commerce.

Frank found that he could identify some of the people by their clothing. Burmese men wore turbans, spotless white shirts, and colored skirts. Chinese wore equally bright materials and embroidered silks for those who could afford it. The Hindus wore a cheaper unbleached muslin garb, which showed the dirt more readily. The Arabs sported yellowing, flowing robes, all with a variety of styles of beard and turban, each chattered in his own dialect. Frank noticed a few men who looked capable of slitting his and Lisa's throats at the slightest provocation.

The combination of odors was also totally foreign. Above the body odors, Frank could identify turmeric, curry, and saffron, overlaid by sharper and more pungent spices with which he had no familiarity. Mixed with the odors were hints of Indian perfume, burning joss incense sticks, of food cooking, all permeated with the rankness of open sewers.

Frank's sense of confusion and overcrowding was compounded by the narrowness of the roadway. The over-hanging two-story buildings, with roofs almost touching overhead, shut out the sunlight. Here and there were facades of rusty, flaking, corrugated metal.

Brightly-colored signs in Burmese and Chinese vied with each other to attract customers.

167

The Ulysses Flight/ Paul Wankowicz

Drainage runnels carved into the clay of the walkway ran from the front of the buildings. These, in turn, drained into the common gutters which separated the rough packed-mud walkway from the cobbles of the roadway itself.

Vendors' kiosks offered everything from jewels to stale, fly-covered meat. Flies were everywhere.

"They hang the heads of the animals over the carcass meat," Lisa said, "so the customers can tell if the animal has been freshly killed. The eyes lose tension if the head has been dead for too long."

Small, naked, or nearly-naked children ran among the legs of the pedestrians or played in the middle of the street. Frank and Lisa were followed by crowds of chattering boys, who would melt into the background whenever Frank turned his head to look at them. He was amazed to see that none of this appeared to bother Lisa. *She must be used to it.*

When they turned left at the next corner, the buildings were more substantial, two-storied, and faced with stucco. Brightly-colored flags, some with Chinese script on them, hung from the second stories. The flags screened much of the light, but their multi-colored bunting gave the street a party-like appearance.

Lisa pointed up to them and said: "Advertisements. Each denotes a different store, a different family."

There was less crowding here. Most of the pedestrians were Chinese. The urchins, who followed them up to now, had disappeared.

Sitting on a cane chair on the sidewalk, as if in his own living room, was an elderly Chinese man. Frank thought he was attired in a Hollywood Charlie Chan movie's version of what a Mandarin would wear. His robes were green silk with a dragon embroidered in gold thread. He wore a skull cap of the same material. His long mustache and hair were a wispy gray. A rickety bridge table in front of him supported a carved, wooden box. An abacus was carefully positioned on the table beside the box.

The only "alive" thing about him were his eyes. Accentuated by

The Ulysses Flight/ Paul Wankowicz

heavy horn-rimmed glasses, his eyes gazed steadily at Frank and Lisa as they approached. He took them in slowly, as one would sip a hot cup of tea.

Lisa came up to him, made a sort of half-curtsy and half-bow, and said something in Burmese. The old man folded his hands in front of him and bowed back.

It was like a choreographed ceremony. They started a dialogue between them; Lisa first, speaking in clipped sentences.

He replied either with single syllables or just a nod of his head. Frank had no idea what it was about.

After a few exchanges, the tone of his voice changed. Apparently they'd struck a bargain.

Lisa reached into her shirt pocket and produced most of the money Frank had given her. She placed it on the table in front of the Chinese man.

He, in turn, opened the wooden chest and withdrew a large magnifying glass to scrutinize two or three random bills through it. His inspection completed, he reached deeper into the box and withdrew a handful of Burmese Notes which he counted and put on the table for Lisa.

She picked them up, and without checking, put them in her pocket, and turned to Frank. "Would you like to change some of your money?" she asked.

Frank extracted two 50s from his wallet and gave them to the money-changer.

The Mandarin moneychanger did a quick sum on his abacus and withdrew another bundle of notes from the box.

Frank picked them up and, following Lisa's example, backed away a few steps before turning around.

When they were what seemed a polite distance away, he turned to Lisa: "Who was that?"

"The family's elder and Rangoon's chief moneychanger."

"Shouldn't we count our money?" Frank had the Occidental's

169

distrust of anything Oriental.

"If he agrees to a figure, he delivers to the penny," Lisa said. "Count if you want to, but you'll find it exact—and at the right rate, too. I don't know how he does it, but he knows the daily rate on all of the currencies that are liable to crop up in Rangoon—usually faster than the banks.

"My father always went to him when in the city. That's how he knew me, knew us. And here we are!"

She swung into a large airy store. It was a simple room with whitewashed walls, mostly bare of furnishings, except for shelves displaying bolts of fabric.

A slender Burmese man, who'd been sitting by a deal table in one corner, got up to greet them. "Miss Van Riin," he said. "How nice to see you again. What can I do for you?" His face showed real pleasure as he said it.

"I need a dress."

The store owner called toward the rear of the room and a woman emerged. She greeted Lisa with the same pleasure that her husband had shown.

"For when do you require the dress?" he asked. Lisa explained about the Squadron Night. "I need it this afternoon," she said.

The owner turned to his wife, and there was a spate of rapid-fire Burmese.

"Can do," he finally said. "Make it simple, and you can have it in four hours."

"Do you have your style book?"

The three of them bent over a thick volume of clippings, a compilation of dog-eared dress pictures cut from newspapers, magazines, and mail-order catalogs. They spent some time over it.

Frank tried to keep himself occupied by looking at the bolts of fabric on the crude, but smooth unpainted shelves. Occasionally, he glanced back at them to see if they made progress.

They were deep in discussion of sewing technicalities, all of it over

170

The Ulysses Flight/ Paul Wankowicz

Frank's head.

When the decisions were made, Lisa and the woman disappeared in the back room for her to be measured.

When they emerged a few minutes later, Lisa said, "All finished. Now we have four hours to burn. What would you like to do?"

The cup of tea Frank had for breakfast wasn't nearly enough to keep him going. He was now very hungry. "How about an early lunch?" he suggested.

She looked at him. "Good idea. I know a Chinese Restaurant nearby. Would you like that?"

"Very much."

The restaurant had one small, semi-private alcove set outdoors beside a compact garden, full of greenery and decoration. Lanterns were hung above, while bunches of young lace-like bamboo plants crowded against oriental flowers growing thick around a white-stone fountain. Its water splashed half-heartedly into a circular pool stocked with golden carp. A gilded cage, suspended from an arch on the side of the compound, housed a brightly-plumed bird.

The whole was a suitable setting for some exotic romance: one could easily imagine a bevy of scantily-clad dancing girls, or a procession of Sinbad's sailors, emerging from behind the opposite archway.

As if in expectation of them, a small, round table near the archway was set for two with gaily-colored linen, water glasses, smaller glasses for rice wine, and two sets of ivory chopsticks which rested on a carving of a pale-celadon-colored jade, leaping fish.

Holding up the chopsticks, he said, "I don't know how to operate with these. I don't even know how to hold them."

"It's simple. Like this."

Frank tried to imitate her grip, but all he accomplished was to have one chopstick roll out of his hand and clatter to the tile floor.

"Like this, you idiot," she smiled, showing him again. The waiter brought him another pair.

But the sticks were still elusive. "You'll have to show me again."

171

The Ulysses Flight/ Paul Wankowicz

She came around the table and picked up his hand.

He was sharply aware of her nearness, the softness of her touch, the warmth of her body over his shoulder, and the scent of her hair as she leaned her head close to his.

"You're not concentrating," she said and laughed.

"There are certain distractions."

"Well, how hungry are you?"

"Very, in many ways."

She laughed again. "In that case, you'll learn to use chopsticks fast enough."

She moved back to her side of the table. "What else shall we talk about? We have four hours."

As with all pilots, the conversation soon swung to flying. Both of them swapped their favorite humorous stories of what happened to them or to friends who flew. Frank listened with interest to her stories of ambulance flying in Australia, a concept then unknown in the United States.

Frank said, "I don't think that a woman pilot could have gained such acceptance in commercial flying in the United States."

"I admit it would have been difficult in Australia had it not been for Bill, my Instructor." She laughed, "Remember your bewilderment back in the Tenasserim Field hangar, when I first announced I am a pilot? I don't know why, at first, I couldn't bring myself to tell you right away. It was enough to be close to the machine, to be working on it."

Frank nodded. "I needed your help."

She simply thanked him for taking her on. "How close I'd come to hating Johnny and his instructional sessions! After that landing in Mergui, I realized I owed my life to his instruction, tough as it was."

Then, Lisa said pensively, almost to herself, "Even if you love it, flying is not just a game. The airplane doesn't care, does it? It would as soon kill you, as deliver you safely."

They both fell silent, remembering their struggles in Tenasserim.

After eating, they became more serious.

The Ulysses Flight/ Paul Wankowicz

"You know we are only playing hooky from the war," she said. "I wish that we could keep on doing it forever." She lowered her eyes and studied the marble surface of the table top. "But we can't," she added simply.

"You can, you know, Lisa. All you have to do is to get onto any boat in the harbor. The money for your fare is there, anytime."

"If I went, would you come?"

"I can't. You know that!"

"Yes, I know," she said heavily. Her finger traced designs around a droplet of water. She looked up. "I know all the reasons, too. You're honest, stubborn, and brave, all at once. All the virtues that are going out of style!" She paused. "And I can't leave either, not if I'm going to be in love with you. I have to be just as stubborn and as brave!" As she said that, she reached out across the table and put her hand on top of his.

"I can't bear the thought of losing you, or of endangering you. If something happened to you through some flying mischance. . . " Frank said, then started again. "For me, would you take that boat?"

"Do you think it's any different? Do you think I could be sitting on some boat, wondering if you're still alive? Or wounded somewhere?" She didn't continue.

They both sat silent with her hand still on top of his.

"When we get to the Philippines," he began, but didn't continue.

"Or before," she said.

"No. It's going to be done properly. Padre and all. It's the least that you deserve," he insisted.

"Some day," she said, "there will be peace. Peace and civilization again. Will you still want me then?"

"More than ever!"

"Then, it's all right." She said that, as if to herself. "Until that time, I'll try to be patient. I'll be air crew." She laughed, but it was a bit forced. "And now, we still have time to fill and a dress to pick up. Let's take the long way around and sightsee from a tri-shaw pedicab. Game?"

The Ulysses Flight/ Paul Wankowicz

After they arrived at the tailors, she put on the dress to make sure it fit. She emerged from the back room and pirouetted in front of Frank. "Is it all right?"

Frank had not realized how long ago it was since he'd last seen a woman wearing a Western-style dress. To have Lisa be the first was more than he could stand.

"If you do that once more, all you'll get from me is heavy breathing," he said, trying to hide the flow of emotion that flooded over him.

She flashed a big smile, showing her white teeth, and pirouetted again, letting the hem of her skirt fly like a Spanish dancer's.

Frank appreciated the seductive glimpse of her shapely legs.

She laughed. "From the way you look," she said, "you won't last until the Philippines." She paused, as if listening to a mental echo of her words. "No," she said. "I won't make that a challenge. I love you too much."

Then, she deliberately broke the spell. "I have to change. We have to get back. Hayes will be furious if his Ford isn't returned before evening."

On the way back, they returned to the Chinese money changer. Customary bows were exchanged. From hidden under his robes, the proprietor brought out a wrapped package, and handed it to her.

She thanked him in Burmese. She tucked it under her arm along with the dress which was wrapped up in brown paper.

As they were leaving, Frank asked, "What is that?"

At first she didn't answer, but when he repeated the question outside, she stopped and looked at him with an expression of annoyance. "If you must know, it's a gun."

"What the hell for?"

"What do you think for? So I can protect myself in case I get shot down. The Japanese are not known for their chivalry to white women, or white prisoners." Before he had a chance to say anything, she added, "You carry one. Why shouldn't I?"

The Ulysses Flight/ Paul Wankowicz

Frank was taken aback. Somehow, his mind refused to see the situation in terms other than his upbringing. He was the protector and she was the woman. But her logic was irrefutable. In an aerial fight, there was damn little he could do to protect her. He'd probably have his hands full trying to avoid being shot down. Reluctantly, he admitted to himself that, were she a man, he would have no objections to her carrying a side arm. He felt angry at his critical, unthinking reaction.

"Is it any good?" he asked. "Do you know how to use it?"

"I did pretty well with yours the other night," she said.

"So you did. I shouldn't have jumped down your throat like that."

"You know," she said, turning around to face him and matching her tone to his, "This is war and this role is as hard on me as it is on you. We've had years of benevolent civilization; now, it is time for real survival. We must try." With that, she obviously considered the discussion closed.

He had to agree, she was right.

To Frank's amazement, they found the Ford with no trouble and after thanking and tipping the youth who'd watched it, Lisa drove back to Mingaladon well in time for afternoon tea, and to dress for the Squadron Night.

The Squadron Night party was not the riotous gathering Frank had visualized. By the time he and Lisa arrived, all of the other pilots and ground-staff officers were gathered around the bar, mandatory glasses in hand, cigarette and pipe smoke hazing the air. Over all of it came the burble of many conversations, with Wing Commander Hayes surveying the scene, making sure that everyone was having a good time.

In her new dress, Lisa looked stunning. She soon joined a cluster of the younger pilots, who were like a bunch of shy, pink-faced school-boys. Frank watched her engage one of them in conversation, and then, slowly pull the rest of the group into it. He smiled: judging from their hand motions, she obviously was pumping them on deflection shooting. She would never give up her ambition to be a full-fledged fighter pilot,

The Ulysses Flight/ Paul Wankowicz

equal to Frank and Johnny.

Hayes had been watching, too. "Quite a girl," he said to Frank. "We're bloody lucky you got her out of the jungle. She gives the juniors something to hang onto, something to remember. Every one of them is in love with her. They have so damn little else," he added.

Mentally, Frank agreed with him. They all looked much too young to be thrown into the war like this.

There was one bad moment. The room was full of noisy, talking officers. Snatches of conversation burbled through the air like storm-excited thunder clouds: "It's useless. The 236 is no good. Couldn't get it over twelve thou . . . "

"Bloody undercarriage broke just as I touched down. The kite settled on the runway like a tired hen. . . ."

"Never saw anything like it. The *Spitfire* plowed into a whacking great oak, and his wingman folded up right on top of him. . . . "

It was all flying talk when the Chaplain arrived.

Johnny was the first to see him peer around the doorframe. "Oh no," he muttered. "Here comes 'Old Complication.'"

Frank had seen him once before. Among all the young men, he looked like a relic, a wispy-haired prophet from the Old Testament.

In a low voice, Johnny said, "The Chaplain originally flew as a pilot with the R.F.C. After WWI, in the Great Depression, he went into the ministry. When WWII broke out, he reentered the R.A.F., this time as a chaplain. The casualties in his squadron during the Battle of Britain left an indelible mark on his mind. It wasn't the fighting and the dying that was the main thing with pilots. It was love. The Chaplain blamed their deaths on the young women for being a distraction to the pilots. He's totally 'round the bend' about that."

In the distance, Frank could see the Chaplain, with his scraggly white hair and bemused smile, dressed in a flowing white robe. Instead the Padre wore an odd assortment of uniform pieces.

"Most of the squadron tolerates the Padre, calling him '*Heavenly Bowser*' behind his back, instead of 'Padre,'" Johnny said.

176

The Ulysses Flight/ Paul Wankowicz

The Padre navigated through the crowd, making his way through the throng without effort, as if Providence were clearing the way for him to get to Hayes.

"Geoff," the Chaplain said, in a loud voice, "you should not allow that female into Squadron Night."

Lisa had turned away from the group, and was now watching.

Johnny nudged Frank with his elbow. "Watch this," he said. "Hayes is the only one up to handling the Padre. They're friends from the first war, which is why he's kept 'old *Bowser*' around."

"She's not a female, Padre."

The Padre rolled his eyes, as though looking to heaven for strength. "Not a female?"

"She's a pilot, a damned-good one. She's here in that capacity!"

"Oh." The Padre looked at Lisa.

Having heard Hayes' answer, she turned back to the junior pilots and resumed her animated conversation, still almost totally surrounded by the junior members of the mess.

Hayes, in the meantime, surreptitiously signaled a Burmese boy to give the Chaplain the large pink gin on his tray.

The Chaplain took the glass, and turned to Hayes. "Maybe you're right, Geoff. She's the one who brought in one of those American fighters, isn't she?" He looked at the group around her again. "She does seem to infuse some kind of spirit in the lads. Wish I could do that on Sundays."

Flight Lieutenant Hari Bose worked his way over to Hayes hoping to hear the exchange between Hayes and the Padre.

"Haven't seen you in church yet," the Padre said to Bose.

"Ah, but I am a Buddhist," Bose answered, a glimmer of a smile on his face.

"Right! Quite right! We must sit down one of these days and discuss religion." With that, the Padre took the Indian by the elbow and happily wandered into the crowd with him, Lisa already forgotten.

Frank noticed that Hayes carefully orchestrated the relaxation of the

177

The Ulysses Flight/ Paul Wankowicz

Squadron Night against the condition of his pilots in the morning. He obviously didn't want to risk the alertness of his pilots by having them drink too much, or to stay up too late. No telling when the first blow would fall.

The rest of the evening was a series of impressions to Frank. R.A.F. silver, wine, civilized conversations, and some not-long speeches that appeared a formality. A quick drink after the meal and people began to depart, starting with the crew who would fly at sunrise, the first patrol of the day.

When the event ended, Frank walked hand-in-hand with Lisa through the dark to their quarters.

"I'm sorry there wasn't dancing. I guess there never is on a Squadron Night," she said. "I have a childish dream of attending an Air Force Dance with my best man. But, in the dream, I assumed he'd be in Aussie blue, not in U.S. Army khakis!"

He'd learned a little more about her—*the death of Bill over Hamburg must have meant a lot more to her than she had admitted.*

Then, she became serious. "Oh, Frank! All those boys tonight! Some of them don't look older than seventeen. What will happen to them when the hour of carnage comes?"

Frank shrugged his shoulders. There was no answer.

They had come to the head of the hall from which both their rooms stemmed. He took her gently in his arms and kissed her. Impulsively, she pressed her body against his. He felt her warmth, the softness of her breasts. They kissed again, less gently this time.

Catching his breath he said: "You ought not to do that; it gives a man ideas!"

"A girl, too!" She pecked him on the cheek and twisted away. "We've got a long flight yet," she said. "So, . . . good night, Frank!"

"Good night, Lisa." He watched her go down the twilight of the hall, wishing he and she were a bit more drunk, less inhibited. It would be so easy at this point to . . .

Her door closed with a final click. Standing all alone under the dim

The Ulysses Flight/ Paul Wankowicz

light, Frank grimaced. *Other men might have done otherwise, but I am the way I am, and the time will come.*

In his room undressing, he felt the little canister of film in his pocket. Without thinking, he put the canister into the top drawer of the dresser, his mind still preoccupied with Lisa.

Chapter 28: Mingaladon Airfield, Rangoon, December 24, 1941

The Japanese made their first raid against the city and port of Rangoon early on December 24, 1941.

Frank was awakened by the scream of the entire complement of *Buffalo*es taking off. In the dawn's half-light, neither asleep nor yet awake, he was still evaluating what he had heard when a violent pounding on the door brought him upright. It was one of the Burmese boys.

"Colonel says, 'You go to shelter. Japanese airplanes come!'"

Frank was already pulling on his trousers.

The first of the bombs to fall shook the ground making the bedsprings jangle. It was followed by a deluge of bombs, making the whole of the building writhe like an animal in torment. There was no mistaking it.

Shirt unbuttoned and shoes in hand, Frank ran down the hall to hammer on Lisa's door yelling: "Air Raid! Wake up!"

They ran down the corridor and onto the airfield.

Outdoors, they could hear the steady drone of the bombers cruising over the city, accompanied by the rising whine of the fighters—the sounds punctuated by machine-gun fire. At that distance, it sounded like ripping canvas. To the south, Frank saw a flash, followed by a corkscrewing trail of smoke against the otherwise cloudless sky. He watched an unidentified airplane going down, its agony etched against the blue of the sky, until the roofs of the adjoining cottages mercifully obscured the end.

The airfield appeared deserted. Two *Buffalo* fighters, probably unserviceable, stood at random angles to the runway, like patient tethered beasts. Half-hidden in the hangar's early-morning shadow, the Station's vehicles waited: the gas truck, the armorer's wagon, and the ambulance. The crews lounged against the running boards in relaxed

The Ulysses Flight/ Paul Wankowicz

watchfulness, ready to service any returning fighter that needed it. But
the airfield, itself, appeared abandoned. The fighters were already
airborne.

The rumble of bombs was now a constant shaking. Clouds of smoke
boiled over far-off cottage rooftops. He heard the clang of a single fire
engine, as well as the insect-like drone of the distant dueling aircraft.

Frank and Lisa jogged to the Station's vehicles. The men there only
knew what they'd just seen. Settle down and wait. The armorer pointed
to the far hangar. "Better get your lady to the bombproof on the far side
of that hanger. It will be safer there."

Frank looked in the direction that the armorer pointed.

"Better to stay with the crew and wait for whatever happens next. I
don't want to be cooped up in the pile of brick and sandbags that passes
for a shelter."

They didn't have to wait long. A crewman wildly pointed toward
the end of the runway, shouting, "Look out!" Etched knife-sharp
against the sky were two low-wing fighters coming in right at them.

A hoarse voice yelled: "Japanese! Hit the ground!"

But no one moved. All watched, fascinated by the ease with which
the approaching fighters skimmed over the ground. As the two planes
crossed the fence, the cowl of the leader sparkled greenish-yellow.
Grass and dirt erupted around the nearest parked *Buffalo*.

But, even as the Japanese fighter registered his first hits, from
several thousand feet above, another lone *Buffalo* arrowed down its
engine whining in combat pitch. It flattened its dive in a great 'S' curve,
guns leaving little puffs of smoke in its wake. Bright brass cartridge
cases sparkled in the sunlight as they tumbled from the fighter's guns.

The leading Japanese plane flinched, like a shot duck, and burst
upward into a climb, engine smoking.

The Japanese pilot's wingman had been lining up for his own run,
but was unable to bring his guns onto the attacker. With no apparent
effort, the Japanese pilot brought the racing fighter into a loop, coming
out behind the flat-hating *Buffalo*. That pilot flew his machine with the

The Ulysses Flight/ Paul Wankowicz

agility of an airshow's acrobatic machine.

Frank saw the Japanese wingman give a vicious shot at the *Buffalo*. To Frank, it looked as if the burst might have hit.

Then, the Jap used his momentum to climb 1,500 feet to his leader, who was now faltering with his engine smoking heavily, the machine no longer comfortable in the air.

Frank watched in fascination as the smoking plane slowly banked and, like a fire arrow, nosed down. It exploded in flame and smoke on a cottage just off the airfield's boundary.

The *Buffalo*'s pilot brought his fighter around to the end of the runway, lowering flaps and wheels as he lined up. The plane began to wallow with the nose sloppily working up and down.

Lisa and Frank watched the *Buffalo*'s uncertain approach with bated breaths. As it crossed the fence, the plane looked as if the pilot had regained control. With a little throttle, he set it down for a smooth wheel landing.

For a while, the *Buffalo's* rollout looked normal, but with a catch. Frank realized that the R.A.F. pilot had failed to reduce power and was going much too fast. The fighter would not stop before it ran out of runway.

The ambulance driver had seen this, too. There was a shout from him, and the grind of the ambulance's starter as the crew and Lisa piled in. It raced toward the anticipated crash-landing spot of the hurtling plane.

The Chaplain saw the forthcoming crash and ran toward it in a futile race with the ambulance.

At the end of the runway, the *Buffalo* continued down the grassy, overshoot strip. Then, still traveling at speed, it hit the ditch, and the undercarriage tore away. The plane settled on its belly, the still-turning propeller threw great chunks of turf into the air. One blade tumbled upwards, black against the sky, and disappeared into the expanse beyond.

The fighter slid along the ground for a few more yards, seemingly

The Ulysses Flight/ Paul Wankowicz

undamaged. Then, the right wing hit the airfield fence and tore away. The fuselage slewed around, and with a diamond-like spark, the fuel ignited. Fire quickly engulfed the aircraft.

As the plane spun around, Frank had a glimpse of the pilot suddenly awake to the reality of the crash. Then the flames, mercifully, hid the man's end. Frank looked away, sick with the knowledge that there was nothing that could have been done. As he turned, he was aware of two things at once.

The Japanese wingman was swinging around to repeat the run on which his leader had been shot down.

Frank yelled a warning, even though he knew that it would be lost in the crackle of burning ammunition and the din of the now-attacking fighter. He watched helplessly.

The Japanese pilot saw the Chaplain running across his field of view, with the ambulance beyond. He turned his fighter away from the ambulance to come at the Chaplain. Shots kicked up spurts of dirt at the Chaplain's feet. Then, the Japanese lifted the nose slightly, and his next rounds hit the running figure squarely in the back. The force of the shot picked up the Chaplain's already-dead body and then slammed it into the ground.

By the hangar, one of the Allied airmen sitting on a truck shook his fist at the departing Japanese, yelling: "What the hell did you do that for? The bugger meant nobody any harm!" That would have to do for his epitaph; the still figure of the Chaplain was already a pile of blood-sodden clothing.

Kicking up a trail of torn sod and grass, the Japanese fighter tried to correct toward the ambulance. Frank's heart stopped.

The Japanese had taken too long to get his sights to bear on the Chaplain to be able to register again on the ambulance. He swept by in the thunder of his engine.

Frank breathed a sigh of relief when he saw Lisa move out from the ambulance with the rest of the medical crew, all hopelessly trying to get closer to the burning *Buffalo*. If the Japanese fighter hadn't gone for the

Chaplain, it would have hit the ambulance and Lisa. Anti-feminist as the Padre was, the Chaplain had been a sacrifice for her.

Another *Buffalo* was already on its landing approach. It touched down lightly before running to the end of the runway, where it swung off toward the armament crew. As it neared the truck, its pilot switched off the engine. Even before the propeller stopped turning, the men were on its wings, opening panels, pulling out spent ammunition boxes and hosing fuel into its tanks.

Frank went up the wing to check on the pilot, who was sitting immobile in the cockpit. He tapped the pilot on the shoulder. "Want something?" Frank asked.

The pilot turned to face him.

Frank found himself looking at an unrecognizable old man, with pale blue eyes staring out of white flesh, bloodless lips around a slack mouth. The whole side of the Pilot's coverall was soaked in red, almost black, sticky blood. There were brown smears of it all over the cockpit.

"The bugger had no sense of humor," the *Buffalo* Pilot said, in an almost-whisper. "I cocked my snoot at him, and he shot me!"

Apparently, saying just that took too much effort, and his face fell slack again. He made an effort. "I did him in," he said, in a sepulchral voice. "Shot his bloody wing off, I did." He relapsed into silence, and his face fell slack again.

Frank remembered seeing the pilot in conversation with Lisa the night before. He recognized him as one of the young Aussies.

He yelled for the armorer. The armorer clambered onto the wing. "Over here," Frank said. "Give me a hand."

Together they groped for the harness-release pin under a fold of flight suit. The whole thing was made slippery by congealing blood.

Someone else motioned for the ambulance to return. Its crew left the Padre's body half on and half off a stretcher in the middle of the field and sped back.

The medics picked the Aussie out of Frank's arms and carried him down the wing, where they tenderly laid him on another gurney.

The Ulysses Flight/ Paul Wankowicz

For an instant, the Aussie's eyes found Lisa, who was hovering over him. He smiled weakly. "I did the bugger in," he repeated. Then, he lapsed into unconsciousness.

While the drama was being played out, the handling crew finished refueling and rearming the Aussie's fighter. An airman climbed onto the wing, and with shredded towels, wiped most of the smears of blood off the controls and from around the cockpit.

Frank walked around the plane. When he looked up, he recognized one of the crew, Ted Archer, the chief rigger, with whom he'd spoken in the hangar earlier. Archer was on the other side of the fighter, hammering shut the entrance hole of the bullet which had wounded the Australian.

"Who is the next pilot up?" Frank asked, looking around.

"No one's ready," Archer said.

The pilot's parachute still lay on the grass where the ambulance crew had thrown it. Seeing the parachute crystallized Frank's thinking. He turned to Archer and asked again. "Is there anyone scheduled to take the plane up?"

"Our pilots are all up except for the four men off on leave, and two others ill. We're shorthanded."

Frank shrugged himself into the parachute. It fit, although badly. He'd be in trouble if he had to bailout. "Crank her up. I'll take it."

Ted Archer looked around, hesitated, then said, "Very good!" He turned to one of the airmen. "Here, Eric. See the Yank into the cockpit."

Then, he turned to ask Frank, "Ever fly one of these bloody things?"

"No. They're U.S. Navy planes. I'm with the U.S. Army," Frank explained.

"It's different in the States, eh? Like our Fleet Air Arm, yes? You're lucky. These are a suicide on the way to happen." He paused. "I'll give you a quick run-down of the cockpit."

After Frank settled down into the pilot's seat, Archer climbed onto the left wing.

The Ulysses Flight/ Paul Wankowicz

"Gun-sight switch and gun switches over here," Archer started the litany, while pointing. "These handles are the Graviner pulls. Over here are the gun-charging pulls. Two pulls for the guns; one to strip the cartridge; and one to charge. Okay?"

Frank nodded.

"The throttle gate is standard British pattern with auto rich to the back here, unlike for you Yanks. Keep it in auto for all the flying that you are going to do. Main switch: for testing mags, 1,500 rpms. Allow 300-rpm drop, no more. Got it all, Yank?"

Without waiting for an answer, Archer pulled a starter cartridge out of his pocket, and leaning into the cockpit fed it into the Coffman starter breech under the panel. There was a muffled explosion and dark-brown smoke poured out from under the cowl. The still-warm engine turned over and settled into a clattery, fast idle. Archer pulled back the throttle. "Chocks away, sir?"

Frank scanned the gages. Everything, except the cylinder head temperature was in the green. They would warm up as he taxied. "Roger, chocks away!"

He watched the ground-crewman disappear under the wing, and then emerged with the bright-orange wooden chocks in plain sight, to make sure the pilot could see that chocks and men were out from under the wheels. The plane was ready to taxi.

"She's all yours, Yank. Good Luck!" Archer slipped off the wing, stepped back, and threw a salute, half-military, half-friendly.

Frank waved back and inched the throttle forward. The clatter of the Wright engine up front was a far cry from the reassuring, dry bellow of the P-40's Allison. Frank shrugged his shoulders. It was an airplane.

The takeoff was surprising. The *Buffalo* broke ground long before Frank expected it to be ready. Built for ship-board use, its takeoff performance verged on spectacular to anyone accustomed only to Army aircraft built for runways.

At first, Frank stayed low over the countryside, heading west, concentrating on hugging the ground. He needed to be out of the

The Ulysses Flight/ Paul Wankowicz

immediate vicinity of the battle while he climbed to some useful altitude. In an unfamiliar airplane and in a climb from a low altitude, being jumped by the enemy could be a quick ticket to eternity.

The first few minutes' flying brought him over the great emerald-colored plain between Rangoon and Mau-bin, a town 15 miles west of Rangoon.

Reflecting the sun, the many delta mouths of the Irrawaddy cut sinuous dark-blue paths, reflecting the sky, to the Gulf of Martaban. A careful check of the skies showed everything clear. He saw no other airplanes, friendly or Japanese.

First time up and heading for combat is a hell of a way to become familiar with an airplane, he mused. However, there had been damned-little choice.

He turned south toward the Gulf. To familiarize himself with the intricacies of the *Buffalo*'s cockpit, he started a maximum-performance climb. By the time he had reached 12,000 feet, he thought, *I'm about as ready as I can be.* Below, spread out in the sunshine, was the city of Rangoon. From the air, it appeared as a gray splotch on the emerald of the paddy, shouldered against the blue-brown of the gulf. It reminded him of a diorama in a museum. From that altitude, it looked immensely peaceful. Even the columns of smoke rising from within the city and from ships in the roadstead seemed static. They reminded him of black tufts of wool used to represent smoke in the diorama.

Frank took several lazy circles over Rangoon. He didn't see any airplanes in the skies above it. The battle had moved somewhere else; no telling where. Running a single-plane patrol above the city seemed ridiculous. *I'd be more useful over the airfield in case any more Japanese fighters come back to strafe it.* He turned, heading north toward the Station.

He made three wide orbits over the airfield and countryside, but saw nothing. All was peaceful. He was beginning to think the battle was over and that it was time for him to descend.

Then, he saw them: a brace of three Japanese twin-engine bombers,

The Ulysses Flight/ Paul Wankowicz

flying in a tight V-formation several thousand feet below. Dark, splotched with jungle green, they were almost invisible against the vegetation—a white flake of light against the green below until sunlight glinted off a windscreen or a propeller, to give them away. They looked odd to Frank's eyes, what with the broad wings and double tails, the rudders looking as if they were the designer's afterthought.

Atop the fuselage, a single Japanese gunner sat perched in a cupola. Frank noted the details automatically. The bombers were just beginning to turn onto their Initial Point (I.P.) for what would be a bomb run on Mingaladon Airfield.

Tricky, Frank thought. *Draw away the fighters, and then, blast the hell out of the airfield.*

He remembered Hayes telling him that the Japanese master bomber rode in the lead ship in the apex of the "V" formation, and that the Japanese had too few bomb-aimers, so allowed only one to a formation. The other planes in the formation would salvo their loads only when they saw the leader's bombs drop.

He'd go for the leader. Frank thought them to be only minutes from the release point. They were in no hurry, convinced that the R.A.F. fighter defense for Mingaladon had been drawn off to some other part of the sky. He'd have time to get into position while they were busy sorting out their run. *Up sun, 1,500 feet above.*

In his mind, Frank could see the great curve of his approach. His hands and feet put him on it automatically.

He glanced behind. The sky was clear.

The Japanese never saw him until he was on top of them. The *Buffalo* came out of the sun, guns hammering. As he pulled into position, he had a glimpse of the startled gunner in the lead plane, who knew that he was staring death in the face. The man was desperately trying to wrestle the gun against the slipstream. Frank's bullets chewed into the coaming around him and he disappeared.

Easing the stick, Frank shifted his aim between the bomber's engine and the fuselage to a spot where the gasoline tanks should be.

188

The Ulysses Flight/ Paul Wankowicz

The Japanese plane jerked into a roll toward him, stabilized for an instant, and then, began slipping down, away from its mates. A thin finger of bright fire grew from where Frank had seen his rounds go in. It moved along the trailing edge of the port wing, outlining it and the aileron with the sheer, pure light of burning fuel. Frank had never seen anything like it. He had only a brief glance before his *Buffalo*'s wing obscured the image.

Gunfire from the other two bombers was now rattling through his wings like gravel against a tin roof.

Frank tightened his turn again, working it into a crazy loop, that brought him upside-down behind and above the two Japanese bombers.

The leader, which Frank had attacked on the first pass, was now nowhere to be seen.

He Immelmanned out of the loop and slid down behind, pulled up under the bombers' bellies giving them a parting burst. It went into empty bomb-bays. They had jettisoned their loads during Frank's first attack.

The last maneuver spent all of the momentum that the Brewster had built up in the dive. The tubby fighter had no more to give. The machine betrayed Frank going into a hammer-head stall. The noise of the slipstream died, and an eerie, almost dream-like silence settled around him.

With both hands, he locked the stick in neutral and jammed on full-right rudder, in a desperate attempt to avoid sliding backwards. A slide could tear the control surfaces off as if they were paper.

Gratefully, he felt the nose start a slow drop to the right. His plane was coming out of the stall and the speed began to build up. When he'd recovered, the Japanese bombers were 3,000 feet above him, specks heading for home.

Frank had damn-little ammo left. *Time to head for the barn.* Down below, against the tracery of the roads and canals, contrasted with the green of the paddies, he could see other *Buffalo*es coming in to land. They looked like minnows in a mountain stream.

189

The Ulysses Flight/ Paul Wankowicz

He spiraled down to take his place in the queue. He brought the fighter to the runway nose high, U.S. Navy style, flaring out easily and touching the ground with hardly a bounce.

Eric was by the ammo truck ready to help him out of his harness. "That was a good show you put on, sir," he said, as Frank undid the parachute release. "We were all watching from below, ready to run if any of the bombers looked like they were going to hit close. Old Man Hayes will be grateful to you."

After the tension of the battle, the hut in which the post-fight debriefing was held was full of tobacco smoke and chatter as the pilots cooled their nerves. Frank found Hayes in a corner. "How did we make out?" he asked.

"Bloody shambles. They got more of us than we of them. Against the Japanese," Hayes said, "the poor *Buffalo* has no class." He took another drag on his cigarette. "You'd better plan to leave as soon as possible. We'll have your kites ready tomorrow at dawn. Rangoon is not safe anymore, and I'd like to get those films out."

"Been thinking very much the same thing, sir. But if you think our planes would be of more use here, we can stay a bit longer." Frank was surprised to feel an irrational loyalty to Hayes and a reluctance to leave.

Hayes looked at him. "Thanks for the offer, but we have to sort this out ourselves. The films may be just as vital. Why don't you plan to leave tomorrow at first light?" It was a dismissal.

He's entirely right, Frank thought. *It's time we get out of Rangoon, before we are trapped by the Japanese tide.*

Chapter 29: Alor Star, Malaya, December 26, 1941

To make sure he would not be disturbed, Captain Kashimura had jammed a chair against the door. It was scarred by a bullet hole, put there by some rampaging Japanese infantryman during a victory celebration. The hole had been sloppily patched over with a piece of adhesive tape from the infirmary. A single bulb hung under a shattered shade glowing golden, throwing confused light and shadows around the cubicle. The same bullet had shattered the lamp shade.

Alone in his quarters, Kashimura sat by the unpainted wooden deal table, staring at the half-full bottle of excellent English whiskey. "I am drunk, *Baka* drunk, " he said to himself, "a disgrace to the Japanese Officer Corps."

Surprisingly, the last didn't seem to bother him much. He no longer gave a damn for the Japanese Officer Corps. He reached for the glass and threw the neat whiskey down his throat. "Drunk and a disgrace," he repeated, with no one to hear.

Until quite recently, the room had been occupied by a R.A.F. pilot. All that was left of his tenure was a picture of his wife and child taken in England during a picnic at some happier time. Kashimura could almost feel the presence of the Englishman's ghost.

It was midnight. The others slept.

His soul was falling apart. Shredding. He had to talk with someone, but who? He felt soul sick, overcome by *han*.

Now, the officer corps, and Lieutenant Horikashi, disgusted him. The enlisted pilots? Some had flown with him in China, but talking with them would be sacrilegious to the structure of discipline in the Japanese Army.

He wondered if the prior owner of the cubicle would understand.

This afternoon, he had an antiquated Fairey *Albacore* biplane

The Ulysses Flight/ Paul Wankowicz

escorted by a *Buffalo* fighter. Both sacrifices, but for what? The British general staff? The English pilot of the Brewster *Buffalo* had been brilliant. Had he been given something other than junk to fly, Kashimura knew things might have turned dangerous. Fighting an A6M-2 *Zero* from a *Buffalo* was an impossibility. The Japanese fighter could out-climb, out-maneuver and out-dive the Brewster. Once caught, the American plane had no place to go. The pilot must have known that, yet he valiantly tried to protect the *Albacore*. After his cockpit was riddled by cannon fire, he went down in the first minute of the battle.

Out of deference to the bravery of the *Buffalo*'s pilot, Kashimura had wanted to let the silver-painted *Albacore* biplane go—a relic out of a museum which had no chance against the *Zero*, a modern 1,000-horsepower fighter with the agility of a dragonfly. Any pictures that the *Albacore* may have taken could not have had much strategic value to the British. The Japanese Army was overwhelming them faster than they could maneuver.

The *Albacore*'s gunner had fired at the A6M-2, hitting it in the wing, forcing Kashimura to accept the challenge. He'd taken a position astern of the *Albacore*, weaving from side to side, firing a burst of cannon at the tip of every weave.

The doomed *Albacore* skimmed the jungle's trees, jinking, flying its evasive turns just over the treetops.

At Kashimura's third burst, flames whipped out from under the cowl and raced along the left side of the fuselage. The sour taste of vomit in his mouth hit him as he remembered the end. He tried to hold it back and almost choked.

The *Albacore* pilot was an old hand at the game. Instead of climbing for height where the crew and he could safely bailout, he chose an alternate course. The instant that the fire burst out, he cut his throttle and stood the ancient biplane on its left wing, aiming to ram the A6M-2 *Zero*.

For a horror-gripped moment, Captain Kashimura found himself racing to a collision with the unwieldy Britisher. He had a glimpse of

The Ulysses Flight/ Paul Wankowicz

the observer's slack face. When Kashimura saw him, the unfortunate gunner had already loosened his retaining harness making ready to jump when the sudden lurching of his plane lifted him out of the cockpit.

It all appeared as if in slow motion.

Kashimura was ruddering hard, forcing the stick forward to pass between the jungle and the burning Englishman. He felt a solid thump, causing the fighter to yaw dangerously. Kashimura forced it back into level flight just inches above the trees. For an instant, he thought that he had hit the *Albacore*. Streaks of red appeared down the right side of his canopy. Only then did he realize the unfortunate observer had not made it to the ground.

Later, wedged between the cylinders of the Sakae engine, the mechanics found a left hand, complete with a gold ring. They'd laughed over it.

Kashimura didn't understand what was happening to him. *Is it the break-up that comes to all fighter pilots? So far, I've kept my mental state from affecting my flying, but no one can do that indefinitely. Not even me. I must stop thinking of the enemy as men. They're only enemy machines to be beaten into the ground.*

Still at the deal table, as sleep overtook him, he thought of his Chinese girlfriend. She had been the only happy interlude in his adult life. He wished she were with him now.

Chapter 30: Leaving Rangoon for Singapore, December 26, 1941

The sun had not yet risen, the day was but a thin red line on the eastern horizon, although the sky had paled enough to wash out all but the brightest of stars. Tropical dew hung heavy in the air, raising odors of wet mud and new-mown hay, all intermingled with the smell of dope and fumes of fuel-rich exhaust. The air was breathlessly still as if waiting for the heat of the day. Hints of what the day would be like could be felt from the warmth radiating from the cement hardstand.

Hayes stood in the middle of the group of squadron officers talking with Johnny. It was time to go.

The mechanics had already been working for an hour. Now the three olive-drab fighters stood clustered on the tarmac. In the dim but growing light, the three fighters looked larger than life.

Warmed up by the ground crew, their engines cracked and ticked as they stood; the sound was so familiar to Frank that he would have noticed its absence, rather than being conscious of hearing it.

Frank thought of the preparations at the start of the epic flights he'd seen at the movies back home. *Here, in front of me, are the planes, the crews, and the ever-busy mechanics, making last-minute checks, as well as a small knot of well-wishers. It could be anywhere, anytime.* Hayes had given small canisters of undeveloped film to all of them, and also made sure they had memorized Wing Commander Fred Winterbotham's name.

Lisa broke away from Hari Bose to preflight check her machine. Johnny followed suit.

Frank felt sure that the mechanics had missed nothing, but the walk-around was part of the ritual designed to keep pilots alive, and not to be waived. He ducked under the wing and flipped the spring-loaded cock, draining a scant cupful of fuel from the tanks. He felt the last bit of it between his fingers to make sure that it contained no water or grit. He looked at the level of the landing gear oleos. He continued around the machine, checking the control surfaces, the underside of the flaps, the pitot tube, the gas-filler caps and the cowl.

When he had finished, a mechanic carrying a clipboard approached him. "Would you sign the 700?" he asked.

Frank smiled. The Form 700 must have been the R.A.F. equivalent of the U.S.A.A.F. Pilot's Release Form. Frank signed it, wondering *What, in the end, will happen to the piece of paper? Would anyone read it? Ask questions? Realize that the airplane was an orphan? It would probably be passed on without being noticed. It was inconceivable for the military to do anything to an airplane without a suitable piece of paper to be signed.*

The three P-40s had arrived without any documents: the ground-lings must have started by generating false logs, records of arrival, of maintenance and such. Records no one would ever read.

Frank saw Hayes smile. Apparently the C.O. knew exactly what Frank was thinking, and agreed.

The sun had begun showing its rays above the horizon. They cast a pink light about the wreckage of the *Buffalo* at the end of the runway, a souvenir of yesterday. Frank noticed the thin smoke, from the smoldering, blackened-tangle of wreckage, was still rising straight up into the air.

Almost everything about this flight was a journey into the unknown. He shrugged his shoulders. *Time to say good-bye.*

He found himself at a loss for words. He went over to Hayes and offered his hand. "I'm sorry to be leaving, sir," he said. "I'll miss the lot." He'd been with the squadron for a scant few days, yet he felt as if he'd known them all his adult years.

In the back of his mind, he realized he was speaking like an Eng-lishman. Already, their slang had taken over his thought and speech.

"The lads will miss you, too. Now that they have seen you work, they will have a higher opinion of our American Allies. Before that, Yanks were a joke. Good luck, and keep Johnny out of trouble!"

"He's more likely to keep me out of it, sir." Frank paused. "Good-bye, and good luck to you!"

He probably would never see Hayes again. Moisture gathered

behind his eyes. Silently, he blamed himself for being a sentimental fool.

Bose, the junior pilots, and the Aussie whose name Frank had never learned, all came over to shake his hand. They were different from when Frank had first met them. They were veterans now. They'd lost that pink-cheeked look.

From this time on, as long as the equipment lasts, Frank thought, *the Japanese will not have it all their own way.*

He wondered what these men could do if they were given decent fighter planes. As it was, they were being sacrificed. But there was no use thinking about it.

The ground crew had laid out his parachute on the fighter's tail, making it easy to shrug himself into it. Archer, the rigger, helped him with the cockpit straps, and made sure that the new microphone lead from his helmet was plugged into the proper receptacle.

They were planning to stay below 10,000 feet, so no need for oxygen. When Archer was clear, Frank called for start, and hit the starter switch.

By the time they had taxied to the end of the runway, the sun was well over the horizon, its rays golden. They had discussed the procedure and elected to do the takeoff in formation, with Frank leading.

It would be Lisa's first formation takeoff, and she was game for it.

There was plenty of runway. They could apply power slowly, making it easy to stay together during the takeoff roll.

He went through the process himself. *Now, stop at 45 degrees to the runway. Check the magneto drop. Cycle propeller from fine to coarse and back again. Set trim, 10 degrees of flap. Look around.* Johnny and Lisa each gave a thumbs up. *They are ready. Look up at the approach to make sure no one is landing. Release brakes, toe the right one. Align with the takeoff roll.* Toggle transmit switch: "Ulysses Leader, ready to roll!"

"Red Leader, ready." *That was Johnny.*

"Blue, ready." *Lisa.*

The Ulysses Flight/ Paul Wankowicz

Hand on throttle. Full-right rudder. Here we go!

No matter how many times Frank had taken off before, it was always a thrill.

When the lumbering weight of the airplane changed into a thing of freedom and lightness, his soul suddenly threw off the problems of earth-bound existence, and it found a freedom of its own. It became a magical time when man and machine fused into a single, free being.

Frank advanced the throttle further up the quadrant. The flat crackling of the exhausts in front of him took on a deeper note as the propeller bit into the morning air. The machine rolled faster. Slowly the tail came up, and feeling crept into the controls.

Now he could see the hedge at the end of the airport rushing toward him. The grass under his wings was streaking past in a blur. The noise of the engine was a solid thing. The plane was alive, ready for flight!

He held it down by gentle pressure forward on the stick, making sure that Johnny and Lisa had ample speed before they broke ground. As the hedge came up, he eased the pressure on the control column. The jouncing of the gear over the ground ceased as the machine felt flight.

He looked over his shoulder. Lisa was exactly in position. He could see her clearly, bent forward as she operated the switch to retract the gear. She looked up and flashed a grin at him. With the R.A.F. issue helmet and the collar of her Mae West life jacket, she looked heartbreakingly young.

Frank waved to her with his left hand, and looked forward again. In that brief time, they'd already gained 200 feet and had started a mild turn to the right. They eased out of the climb at 1,000 feet. He signaled a turn to the right and down. Keeping power on, he brought the formation around in a great, descending turn, until they were nearly grazing the tops of the cottages surrounding the airfield, to do a farewell flyby.

As he straightened out from the turn, they were heading directly for the tarmac, engines howling in the slipstream. Johnny and Lisa maintained position as if glued.

The Ulysses Flight/ Paul Wankowicz

Frank dropped his fighter to within feet of the airfield's grass, the air speed indicator steady somewhere over 300 mph. He had a glimpse of the group in front of the hangars. Hayes was waving. When the far edge of the field came up, he hauled back on the stick. Clear sky filled his windscreen. At 1,000 feet, he eased the stick forward and set course for Tenasserim Field. They continued their climb, more gently now.

As they crossed over Rangoon, shredded smoke whipped past their wings. The three fighters rocked to the thermals caused by the fires still raging in the city. They cleared over the harbor and, with the sun on their left, continued over the dark-blue waters of Martaban bay, with the inlet off Moulmein just coming into view.

Frank opened up the formation to make it easier to navigate. Even at 7,000 feet, their cockpits still retained the smell of charred wood and burned rubber. Frank remembered Lisa's words, and decided she was right: The Japanese aren't going to let any of Burma's rice get away.

He scanned around him, above and below. *We are the only ones in the sky. It's going to be a long trip.* He loosened his harness, and settled comfortably in the cockpit.

Like any other aircraft, the fighter is a compromise. It must be sufficiently steady to be a good gun platform, yet not so stiff that its pilot cannot dodge the fire of an attacking fighter. By some standards the Curtiss P- 40 *Tomahawk*, which was basically a peacetime design, was too stable to have good fighting qualities. That didn't mean, however, it could be flown hands-off. The pilots had to devote constant attention to keep it on course and at altitude, as well as continuously monitor the engine. It was an amazingly-compact package for the 1,100 horsepower the engine developed. Temperatures, pressures, fuel status, and other parameters had to be watched. Last but not least, a continuous look-out for the Japanese had to be maintained, so that the Ulysses Flight would not be jumped and shot down, before realizing they were sharing the sky with the enemy.

Every item but the last was fully automatic with Frank, a habit generated over hundreds of hours of peacetime flying. It occupied only

The Ulysses Flight/ Paul Wankowicz

a small fragment of his mind, which had long ago taught his body to react to the need for routine adjustments without having to process it through his conscious mind.

In these war time conditions, until he developed the life-saving habit of continuously scanning the sky, Frank had to will himself to do it. *Scan from right to left, then look into the rearview mirror mounted above the cockpit frame.* He forced himself to do it every time the second hand on the cockpit clock passed through the 12 o'clock position. He knew that Johnny and Lisa were doing the same: Johnny searching the right quadrant, Lisa the left. In this way, they could keep sight of each other without neglecting the air around them. It didn't take him long to pick up the rhythm, so he could turn his mind to other things.

He found himself seriously thinking of marriage and wondered if it would be fair to Lisa. He did not have what his father would call 'job prospects.' It was all right for him to be sort of a military bum while he was single, but marriage would change that. He was in love with her. Getting married to Lisa would not release him from the Army. He had already heard from her about waiting while he fought. They would have to consider the future seriously.

Would it be her decision? What he really wanted was to be able to magically transport her to the United States where she could wait out the war in safety. Then he had a foolish thought: *Lisa's absence would break up the team. Some team! One U.S. Army captain of doubtful combat value, one crackerjack R.A.F. veteran on a sort of detached duty, probably highly illegal, and one civilian, a female to boot! All of them flying what amounted to stolen or "appropriated" fighters equipped with false papers! And a film of a stolen Japanese codebook. Part of the Japanese Air Force was only hours away. Some team!* But he wouldn't change it for the world.

During the past 30 minutes of their flight, the small sheep-shaped clouds they'd encountered opposite Tavoy, had thickened and co-

199

alesced. No longer sheep-like, they now formed tall, seemingly impenetrable ramparts on both sides of the Ulysses Flight. Crenelation piled on crenelation until they stretched from the 2,000-foot level to way up overhead 20,000 feet.

Against their hugeness, Johnny's and Lisa's P-40s looked like olive-colored minnows. The clouds stood in long rows, aligned north-south, like gigantic furrows. Their sides sunward were a translucent purple; the sides opposite, a brilliant, eye-hurting white. In the cleft below flowed the dark-blue of the Bay of Bengal, like mountain melt-water runoff cutting past sunlit snows of some enchanted land.

For the thousandth time, Frank felt that this is exactly where he belonged. However, as if disassociated from himself, he was aware of the beginnings of a throbbing headache. The clock on the instrument panel told him that they had been flying for 90 minutes. They'd elected to fly directly south from Rangoon, then to cut east when they would be opposite the landing field in Tenasserim. He hoped that flying such a track would avoid meeting any Japanese heading for Rangoon coming from further south.

Now it was time to turn east. The cloud ramparts stood in their way; it would be safer to drop under the clouds than to risk the turbulence within.

Reluctantly, unwilling to leave the enchantment of the sky, Frank pulled back on the throttle. The engine quieted, and the long, slim nose of the fighter dropped. As the aerodynamic forces on the plane changed, his hand automatically found the trim wheel and wound it back a couple of notches. He glanced over his shoulder. Both fighters were following him down.

At 2,000 feet, they passed the brow of the cloud, and Frank swung the formation toward the shore. After 15 minutes, they were over Ross Island, with its northern mate shaped like a green fish swimming eastward.

After another 20 minutes of flying over the bay, they saw the beach below them with the inlet that sheltered the Tenasserim Field. He had

The Ulysses Flight/ Paul Wankowicz

hoped that he could catch a glimpse of the *Nike Victory* as he orbited; but, at his altitude, the jungle flashed past his wings too fast for him to see under the treetop canopy or any camouflage.

Frank depressed the transmit switch: "Ulysses leader. My flight will top cover. Red and Blue Flights determine your own priorities." He watched as Johnny and Lisa acknowledged the transmission with a wave, and then, cut the remains of their power and arrowed downward.

Lisa passed smoothly astern of Johnny, giving him landing priority. Her flowing, competent precision made Frank feel awkward.

From his perch at 2,000 feet, he watched Johnny come in over the treeline, nose high, speed cut to minimum, with the fighter in a slight sideslip so that he could see past the nose. Under perfect control, just clear of the trees, he leveled off and dropped easily, if a bit hard, and ran to the far side.

Lisa followed him, cutting her turn a bit lower, avoiding the necessity of slipping and risking a tip-stall. Her landing was just as easy. She parked it next to where Johnny had stopped. *Two down.*

When he had come over on the first orbit, Frank noticed the change in the field. The large hangar, in which they had lived and worked on the fighters, was no longer there. In its place stood a rubble of burned timbers and already-rusting steel sheets, now bent into surrealistic shapes by the heat of the fire.

Frank held his breath as he searched for the all-important fuel shack on the other side of the road. Without it, they were marooned, or, at best, condemned to a return to Mingaladon Airfield. To his relief, the shed still stood, untouched. He also noticed Cyril had cut down the seaward palms, making the run in from that direction a little longer and safer. After a last look at the cloud-darkened horizon, he put his wing down in a slipping-turn to the left. Losing altitude fast, he straightened out just over the jungle, and followed the route of Johnny and Lisa.

All three were down now.

As Frank had seen from the air, the main hangar was a total ruin. Among the tangle of charred wood, the burned outline of the truck that they had off-loaded from the *Nike Victory* could be seen. The fine tracery of the skeleton of the *Hart*'s fuselage stood beside the truck's carcass, part of it crushed by the fallen roof. Their old home was no more.

They had taken about 120 minutes to fly from Rangoon to Tenasserim Field. Their fuel consumption worked out to about 60 gallons, or about 12 of the Shell 5-gallon fuel-tins per airplane. The fighters have to be refueled and time was short, a murderous task to do by hand.

There was no sign of Cyril, or of the villagers, who should have been able to help. They must have withdrawn into the jungle as Cyril had planned. Frank, Johnny and Lisa were on their own.

This was now Japanese country. Before they could get the cans of gas, they had to camouflage the fighters, using bamboo shoots to break up the airplanes' outlines and make them difficult to spot from the air.

Frank, Johnny, and Lisa worked at it for a hard, sweaty hour. At one point, just after they'd begun cutting the bamboo, they heard the murmur of airplanes, many of them. They paused and Lisa dropped her bamboo.

Listening, Frank thought, *If we are discovered now, all will be lost.* Seeming to read his thoughts, Lisa added, "I haven't forgotten the day the two fighters cut over the airfield."

"When was that? It seems like years ago," Johnny said, as he hefted more bamboo branches onto a plane.

For a while, the sound grew as if it were heading directly for them, but then, it passed seaward and began to diminish. "Heading for Rangoon," Lisa commented as she bent down to pick up the bundle of bamboo she'd dropped when they heard the airplanes.

"I'm bloody-glad we didn't run into that lot," Johnny said. Finished with the camouflage, they started on the refueling. Lisa went into the fuel hut to pick out cans that weren't too rusted, and handed them to Johnny who carried them from the hut to the fighters. Frank stood on a wing, hoisting the cans up and pouring the avgas into a chamois-lined funnel. As he poured, Frank kept a tally, watching the fuel swirl over the buff-colored chamois, depositing little black flecks of rust on the filter cloth.

At the rate they were going, they could count on about three to four hours for the fueling, if they could keep up the pace, and the heat didn't slow them down, and if the promised on-shore breeze came. Only then could they be ready to takeoff for Singapore.

Frank picked up another can from Johnny and slowly tipped it into the funnel. More rust accumulated on the chamois. There was not a breath of wind, and the fumes above the lip of the funnel seemed to seek him out.

He still had the headache and the fumes were making him feel queasy. Doggedly he picked up another can from Johnny and began pouring. He was having trouble focusing. His vision was blurring, and it seemed to be getting worse. It hit him suddenly. He leapt off the wing and ran into the bushes to be sick.

Johnny heard him and, glad of the respite, put down his can. Leaning against the fuselage, he waited for Frank to finish retching. When Frank emerged from the bushes, cold sweat was pouring off him.

Johnny took one look at him and shook his head. He reached to put his hand on Frank's forehead. "You're burning up."

"I feel like hell. I have a headache like I've never had before." Frank leaned against the wing, ready to collapse.

Johnny called Lisa. She came running.

"Frank is very sick," he said. "He has a high fever."

She put her hand up to Frank's cheek. "Damn," she said. "I should have thought of that. Malaria. We landed here without any medicine, any quinine. Stupid! I wonder if Cyril has left any." However, one look at the hangar's remains dispelled that hope.

"How long is the incubation period?" Johnny asked.

"About eleven days to two weeks." She looked despairingly at Johnny. "What do we do now? He's in no shape to fly."

Johnny turned to Frank. "How do you feel? Fit to continue?"

Frank had found the interaction between Johnny and Lisa too fast for him to follow. "To continue what?"

Lisa turned back to Johnny. "He's out of it. I think we'd better get him down somewhere in the shade."

She looked around, but, with the hangar burned down, there was no ready shelter.

"Under the wing. I'll get a blanket from my kite."

"Thanks, Johnny." She turned to Frank. "Lie down and try to sleep. Sometimes these attacks don't last very long. Johnny and I will continue with the fueling. When you wake up, I'll give you a couple of aspirin, and we'll see what's next. Don't worry."

"I'm still capable of going on with the fueling."

"Like hell you are. Now, damn it, lie down."

Frank lay down without any further resistance. The bamboo that they'd cut and set about the wing for camouflage made a sort of a green room about him. It felt cooler there out of the sun.

An hour ago, Frank had been thinking of what a good team they made. Like people bonded to one another by danger and emotion, each one was always on the mind of the others. They thought in tandem.

Now Frank was the first to collapse and to endanger it. It was a bitter thought.

He heard the sounds of Johnny and Lisa slowly pouring fuel; but soon, his headache drove the sounds away, and he fell into a troubled sleep.

When he awoke, he could see through the tracery of the bamboo that the shadows had moved and the clouds had gone. The early afternoon sky was blue again.

The next time he awoke, Lisa was kneeling by him shaking him by the shoulder. "Frank, take these pills to break the fever." She handed him aspirins and a cup of water.

He choked them down.

After a few minutes, she asked, "How do you feel now?"

"Awful." The headache had spread to every nook and cranny in his skull. Frank focused on his watch. It read 3 o'clock. *Lord! They really*

The Ulysses Flight/ Paul Wankowicz

must have worked! He felt unclean and ashamed. His clothes were permeated with sleep-sweat and he stank.

A few minutes later, she put her hand on his forehead. It was hot and sweaty. Being diplomatic, Lisa said cheerfully, "You look a bit better. The aspirin's taking hold. Some of your fever is gone. Do you think you can come out for a quick conference?"

"I'll try."

Tired and hot, Johnny was standing by the wing, waiting for them as they crawled out. "We've fueled the three kites. Do you feel up to flying one of them?" he asked Frank. "If not, we'll try to take you out piggyback."

Frank knew there was no way that a fully-fueled P-40 could make it out of that field with the weight of an extra passenger. Not even with the seaward palms cut down and Johnny as the pilot. The alternative being offered was impossible. Understanding the unspoken, Frank replied, "I guess I can make it."

"Good. We'll spot the aircraft for takeoff and Lisa will help you get settled in it. She thinks that you'll be all right for the next few hours while the aspirin lasts. There's a slight breeze off the bay; but it won't last long, so we'd better get cracking. Okay?"

Frank nodded his head. *They have it all neatly arranged*, he thought. He knew, however, that he'd never make it past the tree stumps. He was too sick. Still, that was better than killing Johnny as well as himself, or being abandoned here.

He'd sometimes wondered what had led up to the deaths of some of his friends. Now he knew. It seemed of interest, somehow; but at least he thought, *Johnny and Lisa would have a shot at getting away.*

To Frank, the rest of the afternoon was lost in a blur of scenes, some sharp, some irretrievable. He remembered watching, disinterestedly, as the two started all three fighters.

Then Lisa helped him into the cockpit and, leaning over, adjusted the controls. "I've set the elevator trim at Red two, rudder full-right. Mixture rich, pitch fine, both mags on. Flaps 10 degrees. All set?"

205

The Ulysses Flight/ Paul Wankowicz

Frank nodded.

"Right, then. You're first, then me, then Johnny. He will fly top
cover. I'll try to shepherd you along through the radio. We'll head 190
degrees after takeoff. In an hour, we'll swing to 140 degrees. This will
avoid the Japanese line. Johnny will navigate, giving course changes
over the radio. I guess that's all."

As she talked, Frank instinctively wound the trim all the way back
and then reset it to 'Red two,' just where she'd had it. It wasn't a lack
of trust in her, he just needed the contact with the machine. He put his
hand on the canopy handle and hesitated. It didn't seem to matter if it
were left open or shut.

Lisa was still standing on the wing beside him, just like on that day
they got the first P-40 going. Suddenly, she leaned over and kissed him.

"See you in Singapore," she said. For an instant longer, she stood
there as if to say something more, but it wouldn't come. He watched
her scramble off and jog over to her fighter.

Frank settled himself into his seat and took another look at the far
boundary. He'd done this takeoff once before, ages ago.

Three minutes ago, he thought nothing of the idea that he would not
survive the takeoff. It would be a quick-and-easy full-power run into
the tree stumps, followed by a ball of fire, and that would be it, without
difficult good-byes. But now, he wanted to live. Very much. Well, he
would do it. The aspirin should help.

He slowly wound the canopy shut and tried to focus on his instruments. It was painful and they were scarcely legible. He stabbed the
knob of his directional gyro, uncaging it.

She must have forgotten it.

The kiss had shaken him. Her lips had been cold, but soft. It must
have been the fever. He could still feel their imprint.

Without looking at Lisa, he advanced his throttle. His brain was still
woolly. He'd never been so tired, so reluctant before, but as soon as the
slipstream buffeted his rudder the procedure came to him automatically.
The P-40 felt leaden in his hands. Half-way down the field, almost

The Ulysses Flight/ Paul Wankowicz

flying, he must have pulled the stick back too sharply. The airplane mushed upwards, controls flabby, and then, began imperceptibly sinking back toward the grass.

Disregarding all the warnings against over-boosting the engine, in a fever-bred action, Frank slammed the throttle forward through the safety gate and as far as it would go, hands and feet bracing for the torque. The fighter felt as if it were sliding on warm butter, but had stopped sinking. The bellow of the engine turned into a scream of mechanical anguish. Feel crept into the controls. Slowly, ever so slowly, the plane allowed itself to be nursed upward, inch by inch. Everything happened in slow-motion. Frank didn't dare look at the stumps ahead.

In the end, he cleared them by four feet and a couple of miles of airspeed. He took a painful breath. He still had the rest of the distance to do. At 300 feet, he remembered the undercarriage and the flaps. He tried to turn to 190 degrees true, but couldn't focus on the direction indicator. It seemed too much trouble to remember to apply the deviation, but somehow he managed to turn to an approximation of the course.

He saw Lisa's plane's great shadow pull up to his right wing and her radio crackled in his ears. She repeated the post-takeoff check, to make sure he hadn't forgotten anything, then had him turn 10 degrees to the right.

Frank felt a great surge of emotion toward her. He was very grateful that Lisa was along. Johnny was close behind and above, flying cover.

As the aspirin wore off, sometimes the horizon was an undulating rubberband, snaking across Frank's field of vision without order or reason.

Then, Lisa's voice boomed through his earphones: "Frank! Frank! You're in a spiral: raise your right wing!"

He forced himself to comply, willing the horizon to become normal for a while. At times in his delirium, she would be in the cockpit beside him, flying co-pilot. He wondered, *How is it we could both fit in the*

The Ulysses Flight/ Paul Wankowicz

cramped confines of a single-seat fighter's cockpit? How come the stick has abruptly changed into the control yoke?

The flight stretched interminably, until Singapore felt like a mythical world: a world to which they would have to fly in punishment for an unspecified insult to the gods. Time seemed to stretch to infinity on both ends, punctuated only by Lisa's voice telling him to change tanks or to level the airplane.

Without warning, Johnny's voice came over the air: "Bogey, 8 o'clock, low!"

Lisa acknowledged: "Roger. See it."

Frank looked down, as if through the eye-piece of a microscope, to see, clearly outlined against the dark of the sea, a single-float seaplane. The crimson-sun insignias were visible on both wing tips. It was flying about 2,000 feet below.

"Don't do anything. Act as if you don't see him," Johnny's voice said.

The Japanese floatplane kept on, crossing under them and bearing off to the right until it became a speck on the horizon and disappeared.

Frank would never know if the sight of three fighters of unknown type convinced the pilot that, in this case, discretion was the better part of valor. Or whether, improbable as it might be, the pilot, busy scanning the sea below, had missed them.

Shortly after seeing the floatplane, they turned east. Finally, the east coast of the Andaman Sea swam into view. A dark-green plain was bordered on one side by the white ribbon of beaches; on the other, by tier upon tier of jungle-covered mountains rising almost vertically.

Johnny called for their fuel state. All three seemed to have more than they figured on having at this stage of the flight.

"Kuala Lumpur is almost directly below," Johnny said. "I vote we keep flying directly to R.A.F. Squadron's Airfield at Sewang Naval Air Station on the north side of Singapore Island, without landing here. Anyone disagree? It's about 60 minutes away."

Frank wondered if he could make it, . . . but he remembered from

The Ulysses Flight/ Paul Wankowicz

Hayes' briefing that Kuala Lumpur was very close to the fighting. Medical facilities would be almost nil.

"Don't you mean 'Sembawang Airfield,' Johnny?" Lisa asked.

"We Brits are in the habit of calling it, 'Sewang.' I stand corrected," Johnny said.

"Frank, can you make it to Kallang?" asked Lisa, "Sembawang is still quite a ways from the city—from the doctors."

"We go on," Frank mumbled, feeling his voice was more of a croak. "Get as far as we can."

"To Kallang then," said Johnny.

Sometime afterwards, a pair of R.A.F. *Buffalo*es came up beside them to look them over. They must have been satisfied by the P-40s' appearance because they didn't stay long. They peeled off to look for fresher, and more exciting game. Slowly the hills moved under them, and the arrow-shaped tip of the Malay Peninsula began creeping toward their spinners.

"Kallang dead ahead," Johnny announced. "Start your let down."

Frank leaned forward trying to spot the airfield, but couldn't pick it out in the blur. Hours of flying and fever were eating into his abilities. His strength was ebbing. All he could see was the gray splotch of a city: Singapore. His eyes were not focusing, and there was still a landing to go.

Lisa must have been reading his thoughts. "Do you see the airport, Frank?" she asked.

"No."

"East of the city, just past that inlet with the sandbar across it. It's beyond the inlet. All grass, a large circle, just like a bull's eye. No runways, just hangars and a seaplane slip. See it?"

Frank strained forward, but couldn't spot it. "Don't see it yet."

Lisa was infinite patience. "It's okay. Just head to the left of the inlet. I'll stay on your wing and talk you down. We'll do a wide wheel from the north and a straight-in approach. Got that?"

Frank acknowledged with a click of his transmit switch. It had

209

occurred to him that, while he was sitting there like a sack of meal, and feeling sorry for himself, she'd done four hours of tight formation flying, shepherding him, doing his thinking for him. It must have been grueling, and yet she sounded cheerful and buoyant.

Frank wondered how much fuel she had; she'd probably used more jockeying for position while flying formation on him. He hoped each of them had enough.

There seems to be a clear, grass-covered space ahead. The airfield? He was having trouble concentrating again. The ground seemed more like the rolling surface of a green sea.

"Back on power, trim back a couple of notches. Full flap, gear down!" That was Lisa.

Relief is coming! Soon it will be all over, one way or the other, and I can relax. For a couple of seconds, he couldn't find the flap-gear control. Then, he remembered: it was aft of the trim. As the wheels locked in place, he flipped the transmit switch and sang out: "Two green!" as if he were in a multi-engine. Then he remembered that the P-40 had no undercarriage indicator lights. He was confused.

"Roger. I have them!" She was talking like a co-pilot.

The ground below was moving faster, coming closer. His eyes still didn't focus. He felt a pang of fear. *I'm not going to make it!*

"Back on power!" There was urgency in Lisa's voice now.

Something solid flashed under his wings.

Lisa shouted, "Power off! Back with your stick! Hold off, hold off!"

He saw her, a huge shadow, detach itself from his right wing. Over the sibilance of his idling propeller, he heard her engine go to full power. At the same time, his wheels slammed into the turf.

Lurking around the periphery of his vision, darkness began creeping inwards. He tried to keep the fighter rolling straight, but it was beyond him. He couldn't see. His physical coin had run out. Things were going wrong. He could feel the fighter bouncing and swinging over uneven ground. More by instinct than by volition, he reached forward and cut the switches just as total darkness settled over him.

Chapter 31: The Beach Hotel, Singapore, January 9, 1942

The surroundings were unfamiliar to Frank. An open window framed by white gauze curtains let in the late-morning sun, its rays streaming almost straight down. Beyond the window, against the blue of the sky, Frank could see the tops of palm trees. Long ribbed leaves stood absolutely still in the tropical air. From somewhere beyond them, he heard the sound of surf rolling onto a beach. An art deco chair, and a table made of bent bamboo and cane, stood beside the window. A couple of magazines and a newspaper lay carelessly on the table top.

Frank's angle of sight forbade his making out any of the titles. He felt immensely tired. What seemed to be, must have been scenes from recent nightmares, intermingled with reality. There had been hundreds of small, bat-like creatures with drops of blood on their stretched-skin wings nibbling at him as he flew his fighter with controls frozen in cement. Somehow this was all mixed up with strange faces peering, and memories of a despairingly-serious Lisa bending over him.

Cutting cleanly through his delirium was the image of the Japanese floatplane disappearing toward the horizon near Kuala Lumpur as if the Japanese pilot had not seen the three P-40s. Then, above Kuala Lumpur he envisioned the R.A.F. *Buffalo*es coming up beside them, their British rondelles surrounded by a yellow circle. Overall there was the sensation of a fever's heat. He was beginning to remember. Already, some of the visions were taking on a tenuous quality, as if they were being dissolved by the air itself. Others, such as the Japanese floatplane and the *Buffalo*es, retained more clarity and sharpness. The clear ones, he decided, were memories; the others, part of some long convoluted dream.

His last landing was etched in his memory. Frank could still feel the long glide down to the grass, and see the shadow of Lisa's plane as she

The Ulysses Flight/ Paul Wankowicz

pulled away from his wing tip, having guided him as far as she could. He remembered the jolt as his wheels slammed hard into the turf, and the long, desperate roll, his vision fading. He remembered seeing his hand reach forward to cut the switches as unconsciousness enveloped him, and the cockpit began to rock.

Did I ruin the landing? After all that effort and strain to get it this far, did I wreck the P-40? Lying in that unfamiliar room, despair flooded him. *Had the darkness been a crash? Had I finally done it? Mucked it up?. . . I must be in a hospital room, recovering from injuries of a crash.*

In his despair, he realized the surroundings couldn't be a hospital room—not with filmy curtains, and newspapers and magazines on the table. Still, what other rational explanation could there be?

When he tried to move, he was too weak, and felt as if he were tied down. He could, and did, begin a thorough mental check of his body to find the injuries. No broken bones.

He heard a door open, and Lisa entered his field of vision. His heart jumped. *At least, she's real!* She looked careworn. He'd never seen her like that before, not even that night in the hangar after she'd escaped from the burning plantation.

He tried to say, "Hello," but it came out like a raspy croak.

When she heard it, Lisa almost dropped the tray she was carrying. "Frank! Oh, Frank, you're awake!" She burst into tears, the crying rapidly replaced by laughter.

She came over, took his hand, and laid her face next to his. "Frank, you're awake," she kept repeating.

Nothing made sense to him, but it was wonderful to feel Lisa's cheek against his. To take in the scent of her. To know she was not a figment of his fevered dreams.

"How do you feel?"

"Rotten." It came out better this time, but it was all his vocal cords could manage.

"What's today's date?" he asked.

The Ulysses Flight/ Paul Wankowicz

"January 9th," she said.

They heard a knock on the door.

Despite his abominable bedside manner, the doctor came in before they could say anything more. A brisk young man with nervous, but expert hands. He looked at Frank. "So you're awake. That's good," was his greeting. After that, he was all business. The examination was perfunctory: tongue, pulse, temperature, eye whites. "You had a combination of malaria and black-water fever. Should have killed you. Nearly did. What you need now is sleep. No exertion for at least a week. What you do after that is your concern. I don't give a bloody tinker's damn."

Before going to him, Lisa made inquiries about the doctor's abilities, and learned he was an expert in tropical medicine.

The doctor obviously wasn't wasting any of his bed-side manner on Frank. He picked up his doctor's bag, and then he relented. "I'd advise you," he said, "to hang on to that woman of yours. She threatened to shoot me with her nickel-plated revolver if I didn't come to attend you. If she hadn't led me here at gunpoint, you'd be dead. I don't know how she found me, but I happen to be an expert on tropical diseases." He said that without any conceit. "The war and a draft to Singapore had interrupted the start of my brilliant career in London."

"How did I get here?" Frank asked.

Lisa told him, "You ground-looped, but without damage."

The news that Frank hadn't crashed the P-40 on that last landing did much to counter-balance Frank's sense of failure.

His instinctive cutting of the magnetos just before he blacked out saved his life; had he not done so, the fighter would have continued beyond the airfield boundary and crashed, like the *Buffalo* in Rangoon.

Frank had a thousand questions to ask, but sleep quickly set in. Before Lisa came back from seeing the doctor out, he was asleep—a good, healthy sleep—without any nightmarish bats.

As the week wore on, his recovery progressed slowly. Lisa brought him up-to-date on the news. "You've been delirious for almost two weeks,

213

during which time the Allies suffered major losses. Manila officially fell to the Japanese on January 2nd. American forces who survived are making a stand on the Luzon Peninsula, around the village of Bataan. There seems to be no hope of relief, and it's obvious they can't hold out much longer."

"Closer to home, the British lost Hong Kong on Christmas Day, December 25th, 1941. Kuala Lumpur is about to be abandoned. Only Johor Province and the shallow waters of Johor Strait yet stand between the Japanese and Singapore."

Lisa also told him, "The Singapore government is beginning to talk of 'defending the Bastion that is Singapore to the last bullet'—a bad omen." She thought, *Worse for those of us who understand governmentalese.*

To Frank the heaviest blow was the news that Manila and Clark Field in the Philippines had fallen January 2nd. It pulled the rug from under his plans. He had failed.

Lisa continued, "There are rumors that a Unified Command will be formed on Java, which will include Americans. The fighters could be useful there. Java is well within range of the P-40."

She was also eager to go to Java, because there was a chance her father, who was serving in the Royal Dutch Navy, could be somewhere on that island.

Chapter 32: Johnny

While waiting for Frank to recover, Johnny had attached himself as a liaison officer to the Australians, working with the R.A.F. squadron, or rather what was left of it. Command had no idea what to do with him, and Hayes' orders detaching him from regular service still stood.

When he heard Frank was awake, Johnny came for a visit on January 10th. He brought the assurance that the three fighters were safe. "Yes, the Japanese bombed the hell out of the Squadron's Sewang Airfield once, but haven't come back. I suspect they are saving it for their own use after they occupy the city." To Johnny, the eventual occupation of Singapore by the Japanese was a sure thing.

"Are you sure?" Frank asked.

"Our forces no longer use it, so there is no reason for them to come back. [See Singapore Island map at Appendix III-D.]

"The P-40 *Tomahawk*s are hidden under a half-collapsed hangar roof at Kallang Airfield. From the air, it doesn't look worth hitting again. Your kites are quite safe." Johnny took a deep breath. "Although you'll need another pilot."

"How come?" Frank felt his heart sink. "Can't you come to Java with us?"

"No. I'm getting married. She's a wizard girl. You'll like her when you meet her. Because she's half Chinese, the damn authorities don't want to evacuate her, so I'm staying behind to keep the Japs from her."

Frank had already heard rumors of what the Japanese soldiers were capable of doing to women prisoners, especially to half-Asian women.

Although the Singapore government had tried to stop the news of the massacre that followed the occupation of Hong Kong, details leaked out, painting a grim picture of rape and torture. Frank could understand Johnny's apprehension and bitter attitude.

"This means the Ulysses Flight is breaking up. We've been together

The Ulysses Flight/ Paul Wankowicz

for less than a month; and yet, with you gone, things will never be the same," Frank said, before he had a chance to think. The Ulysses Flight had functioned better than anything else with which Frank had ever been connected. It felt like breaking up a family. He'd been looking forward to introducing Johnny to an American mess. In Frank's mind, that would be almost tantamount to a victory parade.

Johnny was still talking. "I met her on an elevator," he said. "Her name is Mia. She's a refugee who single-handedly escaped from the Japanese." He sat down on the cane chair. . . .

It was obvious to both Frank and Lisa that nothing would stop him from telling them about Mia. Neither minded.

Johnny Shares Mia's Story,
George Town, Malaya, 1922

Lisa and Frank gave Johnny all their attention, as Johnny shared Mia's life story and how she came to be in Singapore at the same time he was.

Johnny said:

Mia was born and grew up in George Town, the main port on the island of Penang, off the west coast of Malaya. Her father was originally a member of one of the most influential Chinese families on the island. He raised Mia and gave her a good education. Mia lived with him in a cottage on the edge of the Chinese section of the city.

Their home was a small, compact house on one level. A public sidewalk crossed their frontage of the fence. The yard was enclosed by a neat picket fence, painted a dazzling white. From the wicket in the fence, a cement walk led to a massive front door, painted green. In the front yard, flowering shrubs were surrounded by dark-green, tropical grass.

Inside, there were four large rooms: Mia and her father each had a bedroom. There was a sitting room that housed her father's collection

216

of books and small ivory figurines. The fourth room was used for storage.

It was a simple house, not nearly as palatial as some of the houses of their more-affluent neighbors, but Mia loved it, and loved the peaceful life within it. The roof was red French tile. Guttering collected the rain water and sluiced it into a cistern beside the house.

A tin shed attached to the back of the house served as the kitchen. The outhouse for the toilet was separated from the house, and was in an Asian style. A small walled-off section by the cistern served as the bathhouse.

At the start of WWI, Mia's father's family intended for him to take part in the profitable business of supplying troops during the build up, but he defied his family's wishes by enlisting in the British Colonial Forces. He served both in India and, for six months, on the Western Front. His dedication and bravery during the War won him a lieutenancy, a rare happening among the caste-conscious British military.

When his military service and the war ended, his honors almost brought him back into the extended-family fold, but he refused to apologize to his father and the other elders for not following their wishes, and so remained disinherited. The increased family fortunes took the rest of the clan to Singapore, leaving him alone on Penang. He didn't seem to mind.

He was employed by the British Civil Service when he accepted a minor job in the office of Harbor Master of George Town. One of his early assignments was to supervise the transfer of some Russian refugees from a leaky tub of a boat that had taken shelter in the harbor. They had been on the seas for over a year, fleeing from the Bolsheviks, asking for asylum in harbor after harbor. No one had wanted them.

One of the refugees, who later became Mia's mother, was a tall and blond-haired woman, who carried herself like a ballerina. Among all the other miserable people on the boat, she stood out like the constellation of Orion stands out among the lesser stars. No one seemed to know anything about her.

217

The Ulysses Flight/ Paul Wankowicz

When she fell ill, he took her home. Soon he fell in love with her, and they were married.

Marriage to a foreign person, especially one his family considered to be 'a waif' or 'one of those Russian refugee boat people' was the final straw. He was permanently disinherited.

It didn't matter to him. He didn't miss his family of origin because his life with his new bride was ideal.

However, their idyll didn't last long. His wife died in childbirth with their first child, Mia.

Mia's father, brokenhearted, had never remarried.

With the exception of one uncle, who broke family rules to come on an occasional visit from Singapore, Mia knew none of her father's close family. Her paternal uncle was fond of Mia, occasionally brought her small toys from the big city, but otherwise kept his distance, as if to protect himself from the rest of the family's ire, were his visits ever to be discovered. The family had written off Mia's family as if they didn't exist.

When Mia was nine, disaster struck again. A runaway truck trapped her father against a warehouse wall, crushing his pelvis, paralyzing his legs. The accident left her father wheelchair bound.

Neither were Christians.

The English Minister of a near-by mission chapel, himself the veteran of the Gallipoli Campaign, became a generous friend and a frequent visitor.

On many nights, Mia fell asleep to the sounds of a murmured religious or historical discussion coming through the bedroom wall.

The Minister saw to it that Mia received a good, Western-oriented education. Her best subject was history.

When she had completed her elementary and secondary education at the age of 16, the Minister arranged for her to become the teacher at the neighborhood Christian school.

That meant Mia had two jobs, caring for her disabled father and teaching school. Although he was able to take care of some needs

The Ulysses Flight/ Paul Wankowicz

himself, she took care of the cleaning, laundry, marketing, and cooking. After each school day, she would go home to spend evenings with her father. It was a quiet, loving life. She had learned from her father to find pleasure in the smallest of things.

As she grew up, Mia gained all the beauty of an Euro-Asian. She had the grace of her mother and her perfectly symmetrical face, with high, Russian cheekbones. Her shapely, willowy body was tall for a Chinese. Her hair, a crowning glory, was chestnut-colored with reddish highlights. She wore it tied back at the neck but flowing down to her waist. Her quiet, graceful demeanor enhanced her natural beauty.

While George Town youths admired her, they kept their distance. Within the strict Chinese family system, any idea of marriage to her would have brought immediate chastisement: A half-caste, with no support network from extended family and no personal fortune, Mia was not considered to be marriageable.

The lack of genuine suitors didn't bother her. She believed when the time came, she would, in the natural course of events, find someone that she would love. In the meantime, her patience, which had stood her in good stead, shaped her life for her.

The protection of the chapel and the Christian school where she taught kept other young men from plotting means of bedding her.

In the meantime, she taught and was homemaker and nurse to her father. Those two pre-occupations filled her life as much as she wanted it filled.

With the coming of the Japanese campaign against Malaya, the quiet pace would not last for them.

Japanese Army General Yamashita Tomoyuki, the 'Tiger of Malaya,' realized that Penang, left to itself, would become a thorn in the side of the Japanese. He began his operations and conquest of Penang on December 19, 1941 by air attacks to reduce the fighting strength of Penang.

On the island of Penang, it wasn't the British troops who bore the brunt of the Japanese attack, it was the civilian population, mostly

219

indigenous people.

"So as not to arouse defeatism," the British General David Murray-Lyons, in charge of Penang Island, had done very little to prepare George Town for the possibility of air attacks. Shelters had not been built. The government of Malaya had not supplied the island with any kind of anti-aircraft defense.

When the Japanese airplanes first came over, Mia was at the docks, bargaining for catch-of-the-day fish. No one recognized the planes as Japanese. The population stood in the middle of the streets admiring the mass flyover, a sight never before seen in George Town.

The first rounds, fired by a Japanese fighter plane, buzz-sawing down Victoria Avenue, dispelled the mood. Bystanders, who, moments before, were gaily waving at the airplanes, now stood immobile and in shock, staring down at the bloodied bodies of their friends lying at their feet. Panic seized the town.

When she realized what was happening, Mia knew she must get home to her father. As she ran through the wall of noise, panic infested her. She had the overwhelming desire to cover her ears and cringe in the shadow of some dark corner, but the necessity of tending to her father overrode all.

She needn't have hurried. One of the first bombs that had fallen hit the concrete slab underlying the oriental toilet. Fragments blasted from the bomb had scythed through the thin walls of the cottage, turning it into a shambles. In the middle of his study, surrounded by toppled books and broken ivories, beside his overturned chair, lay her father. He was dead.

For several minutes, Mia stood stark still, hands hanging limply by her side, bewildered. Automatically, she lifted his body and half-carried and half-dragged him to his sleeping mat. Having done that, she cleaned up.

It wasn't until she brought the room to a semblance of its former order that the realization of what had happened struck her. Her life was changed forever. She was now on her own.

The Ulysses Flight/ Paul Wankowicz

Fortunately, the bomb fragments had spared the cistern, so there
was water. She carefully stripped her father of his blood-encrusted
clothing, washed him with care, and dressed him in the finest robe from
his closet. With effort, she returned his body to a sleeping mat. It was
too late at night to do more. She would have to see to his burial in the
morning.

After the Japanese bombing and strafing attack, civilian corpses
numbered in the hundreds. The British troops collected the bodies and
stacked them in piles, doused the bodies with gasoline, and torched
them. By evening, the whole town was permeated with the sickly smell
of burnt, already-decomposing, human flesh mixed with gasoline
fumes, an odor that once experienced, is never forgotten.

Later, surplus small-caliber ammunition was laid in the center of the
town's main street and touched off, giving it all the air of an oriental
New Year's. Long belts of machine-gun ammunition went off like
Chinese firecrackers. During all the confusion, the ammunition touched
off in the street continued to explode, making the natives think it was
another air raid and adding to their terror.

After a series of poor decisions leading to military disasters, on the
night of December 19, 1941, General David Murray-Lyons had caved
in. Secretly assembling his troops and Europeans, he commandeered
the two ferry boats that normally linked the islands with the mainland.
When they decamped, the British took all the available boats, leaving
the locals too isolated to shift for themselves.

Exhausted, Mia slept until early afternoon on December 20th.
Closing the front door of her home carefully, she left to go over to the
mission chapel.

The Minister met her at the door of the chapel. When she was
younger, his cadaverous features and gimlet eyes, under the shadow of
bushy brows, used to scare her; but now, he looked to her like a benign
Samaritan.

Mia knew that he was past 60 and had a bad heart.

Before she could formulate any words, he knew. "We'll have to bury him soon," he suggested. "Unfortunately, my helpers have disappeared somewhere."

He pointed to the little cemetery which abutted the right wall of the chapel. "Do you think that you could manage to dig the hole? Things are such an awful mess at the moment. You will find a shovel and pick stored in a small closet built into the outside wall of the chapel."

Mia got the tools and began to dig. Soon, however, she found the heat and exertion were defeating her. She was flagging before she was a quarter of the way down.

A passing British soldier, somehow left behind by the night's evacuation, saw her struggling with a shovel that was too big for her, and he offered to give her a hand.

In 30 minutes, he had the trench dug. Mia never learned his name.

Under a cloudless sky, she and the old Minister said the prayers of burial for her father. It was all unreal, as if she were living a part in a film. After the ritual was over, the Minister asked her, as if it happened everyday, "You will stay for tea, won't you?"

Mia and the Minister went into the red-tiled parish house. He produced a thoroughly-battered, aluminum, water kettle in which he boiled water above a gas-fueled cooking ring. Miraculously, the hot-plate still worked.

Once the water boiled, he ceremoniously poured it into a just-as-battered white-porcelain tea set. They took their cups and the china teapot into a walled garden on the other side of the parish house and sat down on the lawn benches under the trees to wait for the tea to steep.

"What are you going to do now?" the Minister asked.

"I don't know, Father. The attack . . . The changes are sudden and have come so fast, there are many things to be done. . . . his books, for instance."

The Minister looked at her sharply. "What has to be done?"

"I don't know, but we can't leave his things like they are, with the roof holed by the bomb and leaking. Someone should put his books in order. He loved them so."

The Ulysses Flight/ Paul Wankowicz

Conversation eventually turned to his own experiences of war. At one time, during the first war, the Minister had been posted ashore at Gallipoli as a naval artillery spotter with the Anzacs. He was a lieutenant in the Royal Navy at the time. His trip ashore had been a grim education, a first-hand look at the waste and cruelty of war. It had made him hate all parts of it. Once the armistice had come, he had gladly turned his back on his naval career and had gone into the ministry. He had not allowed his new calling, however, to dull his military sense; and he'd early seen that the Japanese could not afford to leave Penang on their right flank as they advanced southward. They would have to mount an invasion of the island at the earliest opportunity. This bombing was only a preamble to it. He did not have a high opinion of the way the Japanese treated conquered peoples. At one time in his ministry, he had helped resettle refugees from the Rape of Nanking in 1937 and 1938. He knew that the sally into colonial lands would do nothing toward civilizing the Japanese soldiery, and he'd been in Asia long enough to know that their racial theories made for particular scorn of Euro-Asians.

"Leave the books to me, girl," he said. "The Japanese will be here sooner than either you or I think. They will not take kindly to children of mixed marriages—especially young women. Were I you, I'd take the first boat south and be well out of here. If you want it, I can give you an address in Singapore where you can be safe."

"My father's brother also lives in Singapore. I'll think about it, Father."

"I wish you would. Now, enjoy your tea," he said. "I'll be back in a minute."

When he returned, he brought two white pills pinched between his nicotine-stained fingers. "Take this before you go to bed tonight, dear," he said. "It will help you sleep."

"I don't need them."

"Do it anyway. Come back in the morning if you feel like it. It doesn't look like there will be many of my parish left to keep me

223

company. I can give you an address in Singapore then."

She didn't see him the next morning. By the time the effect of the sleeping pills had worn off, it was again early afternoon, and she felt listless and unmotivated. Rather than to go see the Minister, she set about patching the holes in the cottage roof.

Then the Japanese came. Remembering the Minister's warning, she was afraid to go out into the street before the newly-arrived troops had settled into some sort of routine.

Her neighbor asked, "Did you hear? The British up and left, taking our only two ferry boats with them. What are we going to do to get off the island with no boats to take us?"

Mia didn't know how to react.

"The Brits got out and betrayed us. They should be ashamed!"

But Mia, remembering the kindness of the soldier who had helped her with digging the grave, couldn't bring herself to feel angry. She hoped the soldier had escaped. "Surely, not all of them are bad," was the best comment she could make.

On the following day, she finally worked up her nerve to walk through the town to go see the Minister. By the time she got there, the Japanese had taken him away and posted a guard by the parish door to trap any British parishioner who might have stayed behind.

Mia felt fortunate she'd noticed the guard first. She was careful to fade behind the corner of a house without attracting his attention. Instinct told her why he was there.

The fear that she felt when she first saw the face of the Japanese guard in the un-pressed uniform and with his oversized rifle catalyzed her thoughts. *I must leave. My father used to hate the Japanese. I never understood that hatred before. Now I think I do. I have to think.* She remembered the Minister saying the Japanese were closing in around the town of Perak, half-way down the Malay Peninsula, and more south than Penang. *With their troops on the island already, and the ferry boats gone to the mainland, there's no easy way to the mainland. I'll have to steal a small boat. I'll sail it well south to be sure I'm free of*

The Ulysses Flight/ Paul Wankowicz

the Japanese. It won't be simple.

The only outing that she'd ever been on was a day's walk up the mountain to see the Ayer Itam Temple above George Town. The day trip had been a school-sponsored outing. They'd been instructed to carry sandwiches in their pockets.

To get off the island, and find the protection of the British in Singapore, I'll have to do much more preparation than that. I'll need a haversack, a backpack, like the one I used to carry schoolbooks.

Back at the cottage, she found a sturdy blanket—cutting and sewing it carefully, she created a workable backpack. For a while, making the straps that went over her shoulders had her stumped; but in the end, she used a sash to one of her father's bathrobes. It had a design of deep purple with dragons embroidered in gold thread woven into it. It looked garish attached to the blanket, but it made suitable straps. She sewed a button to the back of the pack along with a loop at the edge of the flap. When she had finished, she was proud of her accomplishment.

With the problem of how to carry things resolved, she started collecting what she would take. First came the two silver-framed pictures of her mother from the table in the library. She wrapped them up in a sarong. For good measure, she rolled up another sarong and placed it in the bottom of the pack.

In the kitchen, she retrieved two cans of Golden Syrup, a tin of carrots, several tins of tea, and of rice.

As she put those into her makeshift backpack, she realized that she hadn't eaten since the tea with the Minister. She found a crust of bread and about half-a-pound of still-good pickled fish. She brewed some tea to help wash it down.

When she'd eaten, she cleaned up methodically, wrapping the remains of the fish in oiled paper and putting it at the top of the haversack. She laid out two good knives, a large one and a small one, both with a keen edge and wrapped the big one in several layers of newspaper. She put it on top of the pack beside the fish. Aside from a few personal items, there was nothing else that she could think of as being

225

absolutely necessary.

The small knife would fit between her breasts, taped down with adhesive tape. She could use it to kill herself if threatened by the Japanese. She was still a virgin and would not be raped.

Making the pack took most of the afternoon. She had already decided that she would not start her journey until the night was well advanced. It was still an hour before sunset. Restless, with nothing more to do but to wait, she tried on the loaded pack and looked at herself in the mirror. It seemed to fit quite well.

Seeing herself in the mirror, however, reminded her of her long hair. *I must cut it off. It will be too inconvenient traveling through the bush.* For as long as she could remember, she had worn her hair long. It was part of her, part of who she was. Her very soul rebelled against cutting it. Finally, she compromised and trimmed it to shoulder-length. She could not bear to look at the chestnut cuttings when she was finished. Gathering them up quickly, she threw them out of the open window.

She went into the kitchen and made herself another mug of strong tea. Without consciously thinking about it, she had maintained the charcoal fire in the chappy and had kept the kettle boiling. It saddened her to think that, after she left, the charcoal would slowly turn to a white powder and disappear, and the battered aluminum kettle would no longer stay hot. That kettle had been on the chappy for as long as she could remember. Symbolically, when it cooled, her youth—the youth of a carefree half-Chinese half-European chestnut-haired girl— would be gone.

Mia reviewed her plans. She would make her way in the dark through the Chinese section of the town to where the street changed from cobbles to macadam, lost its sidewalks, and became the road which ran south along the shoreline.

A fishing village was at the elbow of the road, where it turned sharply west in its circumnavigation of the island. She'd often dealt with merchant boats from that village when buying fish at the quay. Their boats always looked well-kept and seaworthy. *I must steal one of*

The Ulysses Flight/ Paul Wankowicz

them to get to the mainland.

She restocked the charcoal, as if to extend the memory of the house for as long as she could. After washing the mug, she hung it on its accustomed peg. That done, she stretched out on the sleeping mat to rest.

When Mia awoke, it was dark. She lay on her back for several minutes, feeling indescribably sad. Then, with a Herculean effort of will, she got up, shouldered her homemade knapsack, blew out the lamp and quietly let herself out the front door. Later on, there would be a slim, fingernail-shaped moon; but now, the darkness was completely solid.

There was no electricity in George Town; the new masters had not yet taken over the powerhouse. The city was dark. Only here and there, the pumpkin-colored glow of a kerosene lamp or candle showed behind an un-shuttered window. Except for those flickering lights, the town was lifeless in the grim dark. The usually boisterous and crowded streets had been swept clean.

As she made her way nervously from corner to corner, her hearing became more acute by the weird silence. Mia felt as if she'd been transported to another world.

When she reached the road, it was also silent and deserted. Mia's heart was beating almost in panic. Twice she thought she heard something, and hid in the thickets by the side of the road, sometimes stumbling over branches. She snagged her legs on thorns, but both times turned out to be false alarms. Nothing moved. She had the road all to herself. By the time she reached the westward bend, a thin moon was up. She could make out the path that led off to the left by its weak light. The path ran among the trees. She hoped it led to the village.

A few feet down it, she saw the glimmer of dying fires between the huts. She realized she didn't know what she was going to do next; her thinking back in George Town had only carried her this far.

The village dogs barked and she paused to consider. She had not thought of dogs. Her legs smarted from where the thorns had dug into

227

her. Her feet hurt from the roughness of the road. She had not visualized things quite like this. Mia began having doubts. The Japanese
couldn't be as bad as she had thought. Was she running away from
imaginary terrors?

It was too late to turn back now. Dawn would catch her still on the
road and, surely, the Japanese would wonder why a solitary young girl
with a knapsack had been traveling in the dark, heedless of the curfew.
She must hide during the day, and in hiding, think out her next move.

She stepped a few yards off the path and found, mostly by touch, a
clump of vegetation which would conceal her. Looking through the
fronds she could see the dying fires. She heard someone irritably quiet
the dogs. She would have to make her decision before the next night.
She knew that she could not stay betwixt and between forever. In the
meantime, she decided the thing to do was to make herself comfortable
and await the morning. She curled up in a clear space using the knapsack as a pillow. She had not realized how tired she was or how wearing her walk had been. Within minutes, she was asleep.

The noise of a car laboring through the sandy ruts, almost by her
head, woke her. The sun was well up. For an instant she was disoriented, but then, memories came flooding back, and she knew it was
December 23rd. She was terrified, not daring to move until long after the
car had passed. Finally, she gathered her courage and raised her head.
She had an almost clear view; the growth was not as lush as she had
thought.

A dusty Ford Phaeton was parked in the middle of this village. The
driver, in the uniform of a Japanese soldier, hurried around the front to
open the door for the officer in the tonneau. As the officer got out of the
car, the driver obsequiously bowed.

Mia's first impulse was to laugh. The officer was short and dumpy
with the ceremonial sword trailing behind him like a misplaced monkey's tail. She watched with interest as the Village Headman came out
of his hut, bowed to the Japanese in Malayan fashion, hands joined in
front. The Japanese answered with a perfunctory nod, and launched

The Ulysses Flight/ Paul Wankowicz

into a peroration, waving his arms as if to take in the entire shore in
front of him.

The Headman listened, nodding at intervals.

Mia strained to hear, but they were too far away, playing out their
roles in pantomime. After a few minutes the Japanese seemed satisfied.
He brusquely signaled his driver, who came running to open the door.
As the Malayan watched, the car churned up the sand turning around
and headed back up the track, back to the road. Mia feared that as the
car turned past her, the Japanese might be able to see her in her hiding
place. She couldn't breathe; her heart was pounding loud enough for
them to hear.

The car ground past at a creeping rate, but didn't stop. It reached the
main road and she heard it accelerate toward town. She could breathe
again.

A few minutes later, a village girl came up the track and stopped
opposite to where Mia was hiding.

"The Chief says that you can come out now," the girl said to no one
in particular.

Mia's heart stopped again. The Headman must have known that she
was hiding there all through his conversation with the Japanese officer.
Had he given her away? There was nothing to be done, however, but to
pick up the haversack and to come out of the bush, suffering the cold
stare of the village girl as she stood impatiently waiting.

Without a word, the girl led Mia to where the Headman still stood.

Mia bowed to him, Malayan fashion, without speaking. She knew
the custom and waited for him to speak first. She recognized him as
one of the fishermen with whom she had, at least a hundred times,
bargained for fish back on the George Town quay. She had never
imagined that he was the Village Headman.

He had been her favorite. He had a sense of humor which didn't
permit him to sell her the fish without a bit of bargaining and banter.
She had always looked for him, and anticipated the few minutes of
friendly chit-chat and contention before she could turn back toward

229

home with her purchase; but if he recognized her now, she saw no sign of it in his impassive face.

"You have been hiding on the edge of the village since this morning." He said that as a statement rather than an accusation.

"Yes."

"Thinking, maybe, to steal a boat and escape the Japanese?"

A dozen answers, none of them true, none of them seeming to fit, passed through her head. "Yes, I was."

He smiled a half-smile. "The Japanese Major who was just here came to tell me that people like you are bad, that I should hold you, and turn you over to him when he comes back."

"And you agreed with him?"

He shrugged, Western fashion. "I agreed, but that doesn't mean that I will do it. One of his airplanes came over two days ago and killed three of my villagers. If I didn't know that such things are impossible, I would have thought that the airplane pilot had done it on purpose. That he enjoyed killing. I am not sure that I should listen to the Japanese Major."

"You will help me then?" Everything hung on that question.

He pointed to the haversack which hung limply from her hand. "Are you carrying anything in that which would pay me for a boat?" he asked. "Open your pack and let me see."

They both squatted on the sand as she turned out the meager contents of the sack. In an untidy heap on the beach, they reflected the depth of her poverty. It was all that she owned in the world.

He looked at the scattered belongings in silence. Finally he pointed at the frames. "Are these real silver?" he asked.

"You can't have them. They are pictures of my mother."

"For two cans of Golden Syrup and two frames, you can have a boat." He thought for an instant. "I don't want the pictures, just the frames. I will give you some paper to wrap the pictures in so that they don't get damaged."

It was very much like bargaining for a fish. In the end, he settled for one frame and the two cans of syrup. He seemed satisfied.

"When the British return," he said, "you must come back and tell us the story of your voyage. You can then claim the silver frame and we will give it back to you. We will have a feast, because you are like a daughter to me. I have watched you grow up ever since, as a little girl, you came for the first time to my boat to buy a fish for your father."

He smiled down at her. "And now you will go back into my hut to hide, because I do not wish for the Japanese to see you. Maybe you can sleep, because tonight will be long for you. And I have a lot to do before sunset."

It was a plain dismissal. She picked up the rest of her things from the sand and stuffing them into the pack went into the hut.

Mia dozed in the hut through part of the morning. For the rest of the day, she sat in the sweltering heat quite alone. Just before sunset, the Chief called her out onto the beach where a boat had been drawn up on the sand. It was a normal Malay boat about 14-feet long. The mast was well-forward, lateen rigged. Aft of the mast was a rounded roof, woven out of thin strips of wood to allow ventilation, but keep out the sun's murderous rays.

The whole of the village gathered around it to see her off.

The Chief and his family had supplied it with rations of rice and fish wrapped in leaves, as well as with two large earthenware jugs of drinking water. The Chief himself spent the next hour drilling her on the use of the sail and the steering paddle.

She'd never sailed before and was ashamed of her ignorance. She knew that she would never remember half of what he told her. Mia marveled at his patience as he went over each important item time and time again, making sure that she understood.

When the stars came out, he showed her the southern constellations by which she could steer. Arcing his arm, he explained to her how the stars rotated from the east to set in the west, just like the sun.

When it was late enough, he said she should go. "Steer east until you smell the shore, then turn south," he told her. "When you see the first rays of the sun on your left, find a hiding place so the Japanese don't see you. Sleep in the day, sail by night. And may the gods protect you on your journey."

With the watching villagers, he pushed the boat into the water. She began paddling away, reluctant to hoist the sail where they all could see her ineptitude. A few feet out the tide took the boat, and within minutes, the village was lost to sight in the darkness beneath the trees lining the shore. She was on her own.

When she wasn't paddling to keep the boat heading in the right direction, she struggled with the unfamiliar rig. Mia didn't make much headway on the first night. When the first rays of the sun revealed a dragon back of the mainland mountains, she could still see the island of Penang, blue in the haze behind her. She was lucky and found a jungle-covered inlet large enough to accommodate her boat before anyone onshore challenged her.

She discovered that she had no rope with which to tie up to the bushes lining the bank; she bent some palms and bamboo and tangled them in the rigging to hold the boat.

Once temporarily secured against the sluggish current, she spent the morning ripping one of her sarongs into strips which she plaited into a workable rope with which she moored the boat. She had not dared borrow a line from any part of the rig; she wasn't sure she could replace it correctly once she decided to move on. With the boat secured, she had some of the drinking water and one packet of rice and fish.

Refreshed, she lay down under the plaited-wood canopy and slept until darkness. Things worked more smoothly on the second night. Mia had become familiar with the rig and, although the stars in the south were obscured by clouds, she found that the Chief had been right, that she could steer by the smell of the land on her left. She would tack outwards until she lost the smell, then tack back until it came strongly at her.

Once, coming too close to the shore, she heard Japanese talking. Twice that night, she heard the sound of aircraft in the darkness above.

232

The Ulysses Flight/ Paul Wankowicz

Toward dawn, looking southward, she saw the flicker of artillery fire reflected from the bellies of the clouds, and she became conscious of an underlying murmur being carried by the breeze. The fighting was still well ahead of her.

Just as the early dawn crept behind the mountains, she anchored in another inlet. She was running low on rice, although her drinking water supply was holding up well.

The next night was a repetition of the last, with the exception that the artillery fire was almost abeam now. She was getting close to the line of the Japanese advance. She felt a desperate need to get as far as possible.

Each night the moon was growing in brilliance, and rising earlier, forcing her to anchor long before the night was done. Despite her caution, the moonrise found her well out to sea. The moonlight made her feel very conspicuous; she felt naked, exposed by the light.

She dropped her sail and quietly paddled, hoping to find another inlet. With the battle drawing closer, she felt anxious, unsure. The moon's light had found her much too far out.

Soon a bay appeared, more of a gut, a narrow creek, than a bay, and slightly different from the previous hiding places she'd found before. As she glided in, she noticed a small beach was on the right bank. It was silver-white in the moonlight, contrasting against the still blackness of the mangrove overhanging its edges. From what she could see, the shoreline curved sharply behind the beach, forming a cove within the gut itself. There was no time to hunt for another inlet; she had to find concealment in the cove. The sun would soon be up.

As she passed the white shadow that was the beach, she thought she heard a voice. Her heart was thumping. Something black against the sand seemed to stir. An evil spirit?

The angle of the shore screened her from anyone who could be watching from the other side of the creek. She wasn't sure what she'd heard or saw as she glided past the beach.

As fast as she could, Mia dove into the tangle of an overhanging

233

bank of vegetation. It gave her some shelter in the cove to hide under.

She slept fitfully for what seemed a few minutes, then awoke, aware that her mind would not leave it alone.

With the boat secured to overhanging greenery, she decided to explore along the shore on foot and make sure that the beach was deserted. She felt for her little knife, still securely taped between her breasts. Its feel gave her a sense of security, of control over her destiny. A talisman.

The twisted mangrove grew tall and thick to the water as well as onshore. It was hard going and was almost impossible to penetrate. She waded, supporting herself on overhanging bushes. Her mind imagined the water full of leeches and carnivorous fish.

The sun was just beginning to paint the sky a translucent blue when, drooping with exhaustion, she reached the small crescent of the beach and found them. Two men were dead, sprawled in unnatural attitudes on the edge of the sand. The other two miraculously were still alive. All wore the khaki of British soldiers. The one nearest to her, wearing the stripes of a corporal, seemed alive but just barely. A huge black patch of dried blood on his shirt showed where a rifle round had gone through. As he breathed, his wound made sucking noises, like a baby at a dry breast.

She knelt beside him.

"Help me to a tree, Miss, so I can sit up," he whispered. "I want to see the sun once more."

She looked at him in despair. He was heavy. The nearest palm was yards away, up the slope of the sand dune. She doubted she had the strength, but there was no way she could refuse. Cradling his head in her arms, she dragged him uphill. His legs made weak swimming motions to help.

She saw every movement that she made reflected a grimace of pain on his face. Halfway up, feeling winded and awkward, she stopped, hoping to save him further anguish. *It is not worth it.*

He opened his eyes and looked straight at her.

234

The Ulysses Flight/ Paul Wankowicz

"Don't give up now, girl. Let's see the thing through."

Desperately, she grabbed him by a bunch of uniform at his shoulders and started anew. She didn't know how long it took, but the sun was well up by the time she had him propped against a tree.

His wound was bleeding again, bright red with flecks of pink foam against the black of matted blood. She reached to look at it, maybe to staunch it.

"Let it be," he said. "Can I ask you one more thing?"

"Yes?"

"Go down the beach and get me a rifle. If I'm going to die in this bloody country, it will be as a soldier with a weapon in my hands."

With the rifle in his lap, one hand on the metal of the receiver as if to draw strength from the weapon, he seemed comfortable. "Thank you, Miss," he said, and closed his eyes.

For a second, she thought he had died; but then saw that his chest was still moving, still sucking air. She looked at him again, realizing the craggy strength that had carried him this far. She thought of quietly slipping away while the Corporal's eyes were closed.

As she had struggled to drag him up the beach, she noticed that the other casualty had noiselessly followed her every move with his eyes. At first, it made her feel eerie. Now, she felt the desperate need to go to the other quiet boy; but as she took a step to move away, the Corporal opened his eyes.

"Wait," he said. "Someone has to know how it was. We were told to hold the shore road outside of Taiping, Perak, for at least 24 hours while the main force made its escape down the railroad tracks. Then, we were to make our own way to the beach to be picked up by the Royal Navy. There were 120 of us altogether, the rest of the company, and some odd sods and bods we'd picked up along the way. The Lieutenant had bought it the day before, so we were now all under Sergeant Clark."

His voice was getting weaker so that Mia had to lean toward him to hear what he was saying.

The Ulysses Flight/ Paul Wankowicz

"We bloody-well held our position for 36 hours. The Japs were all around when we finally gave up. By the time we got to the beach to be evacuated, there were only four of us: 'Red' Taylor, me, and the other two bods—I never learned their names.

"When a boat came down the shore, we thought it was coming for us. It was flying a bloody great big British ensign, you see. The Japs must have captured it somewhere. We all got out of the bush and waved. The boat was full of Japs. The bastards opened up on us with machine-gun fire. They had been cruising up and down the shore looking for sods like us." He paused, his hands clenching at the re-lived experience. "But it's all down the river now. Tell the Captain that we did splendidly. Bloody-damn splendidly. That is, if he's still alive. Tell him Sergeant Clark's men. Don't forget.

"You can go now, thanks. It would have been unbearable without you." He closed his eyes.

Mia ran to a red-headed figure who was still following her with his eyes. The day was getting hot. She knelt in the sand beside him and examined his wound. It didn't seem to be as bad. The slug had gone through the soft part of his side, below where the ribs ended, a combination of dried blood, sand and torn clothing; but it had been neglected for hours, already beginning to smell. When Mia gently rolled him over, it was worse where the bullet had exited.

She wondered why she wasn't sick. She had never gone beyond putting Mercurochrome on a cut finger, and now regretted her lack of knowledge. She didn't know, for certain, what to do; but it seemed obvious that the wounds should be cleaned somehow, and a dressing made. Mia carefully explained to the silent figure what she was going to do. She gave him a drink of water.

His expressive, brown eyes were the only sign that he understood. The remains of her sarong were in the boat. She'd have to go get them. She could feel him mutely watching as she walked down to the corner of the beach.

She made pads out of the material and soaked them in seawater. It

236

The Ulysses Flight/ Paul Wankowicz

appeared to her that seawater was somewhat cleaner, or better, than the remains of the drinking water in her jug. After an hour of alternately soaking the wound and rubbing off the scab and the enclosed sand, she felt that she had cleaned the hurt as well as she could. The grayish edges of traumatized flesh scared her. She felt that if she worked any more on the wound, it would start bleeding heavily again and she wouldn't be able to stop it.

It was close to midday by the time she had bandaged his side. The sun was fierce. She had to move him off the beach and into the shade of the boat's shelter. Otherwise the heat would kill him. She went around the point again, and brought the craft to the beach, wondering how she could manhandle him over the gunwale and into the bottom. She knew that if the Japanese were to show, she stood no chance—but in her single-minded work, she felt no terror.

The little knife still nestled comfortably against her flesh, and she didn't think she'd mind using it, were the necessity to arise. The Japanese didn't show, and somehow she eased his inert body into the bottom of the boat. Then, she led the craft back under the bushes where she had first hidden it. It was cooler in the shadow there.

The wounded boy didn't speak although Mia was under the impression that he was fully aware of what was happening. After she had led the boat into the bushes and made him more comfortable, there was nothing more she could do.

She sat in the stern and watched him. He was young. He could have been the brother she had always wished for while she was growing up.

Sunset came, and then, the night. Mia realized that she should be moving on, but the wounded boy's condition hadn't changed. As long as he lay there, she wouldn't move, as if she were waiting for something.

When the moon rose, its wan light crept in under the hood. She tried to sleep, all hunched up, but sleep wouldn't come. She must be growing light-headed. She imagined this now wounded soldier as her brother, and pictures came to her like memories out of a broken kaleidoscope. In

237

her mind, she saw his father coming in through the rough doorway of the farm house with a freshly-cut evergreen tree, a Christmas Tree, over his shoulder. In the dream, his much-younger red-haired sister clapped with glee. The smell of goose cooking. The father explained the symbolism of a small carved-ivory statuette while she looked on. Had she known him all her life? Where?

When she heard the soldier stirring, she awoke and crawled forward in the boat. In the pale moonlight, she saw tears glistening down his cheeks. He was crying. She felt helpless. She took his head in her lap and cradled it against her chest. She had no idea how long she sat there like that.

Sometime in the night, his breathing became shallower and shallower. Finally it stopped, as if he'd looked within himself and found all exhausted.

Gently, she laid his head back against the bottom boards and crawled to the stern.

She spent the rest of the night crying silently to herself. For her father, for this soldier-boy brother whom she had almost saved, for herself. Washing her soul.

The body of the Corporal was still propped against the far tree, his face now black in death. She chose a spot as far away from him as the small beach allowed. When the hole in the sand was ready, she dragged the boy's body up to it, wrapped it in her other sarong and, as gently as she could, lowered it into the cavity. She knew she never could bring herself to throw sand onto his face without having covered it up first.

When she had buried them both, she fashioned two crosses out of straight sticks and put them over the mound. It was not much, she knew, but the best she could do. She felt placing the crosses was a sort of period, a final step to the first part of her life.

Daylight or not, she could not stay. She pushed the boat into the water and laboriously paddled out of the little inlet. Within a quarter mile she found another thin jungle stream and pulled into that. It would shelter her until the evening.

The Ulysses Flight/ Paul Wankowicz

Once during the afternoon, she was awakened to hear planes overhead. She leaned out to see three of them heading roughly south-east.
Two were close together and a third a bit behind, as if he were a shepherd, a protector. Somehow she knew they weren't Japanese and, as
they passed to seaward, she waved, following their flight in her imagination, wishing them luck.

By sunset, she was out in the bay under sail. From what the Corporal had said, she figured that the English could not be too far away. Mia
knew it was imperative she reach them that night. She'd had no food
and she felt she wouldn't be able to stand another 24 hours in the boat.

She sailed close to the shore, listening. About midnight, she heard
unmistakably British voices and headed toward them. As she rounded
the last point, she saw a small fishing village, partly burned, with dark
canvas tents beside it. The scene was illuminated by dying fires and,
here and there, the diamond point of a hooded hurricane lantern. Khaki
figures moved purposefully between the tents.

Although she didn't know it, it was the village of Kota Bhara. Here
the British Army was desperately mustering part of its strength after the
defeat at the Perak River. Further south, threatened by the Japanese,
and already evacuated by the R.A.F., lay the Telok Anson Airfield, the
last good landing field on the mainland.

A Sergeant took efficient charge of her as soon as the boat's keel
touched the sand and he led her to the ranking officer's tent. Inside of
the tent unbearably hot; the heavy, military-issue impervious canvas
kept the air from moving.

Two hissing hurricane lanterns hung from makeshift hooks on the
tent poles. The lamps sent clouds of heated air upwards into the peak.
Two tables had been set up. A large, ornate mahogany one with three
legs stood at one end, its missing leg replaced by a pile of khaki ammunition boxes with rope handles. A field telephone and a welter of maps
and order chits, thin oblongs of rice paper, covered its top. A hollow-
eyed Lieutenant and a Sergeant were apparently trying to make sense
out of some of the chits, occasionally pulling a map out of the pile in

239

The Ulysses Flight/ Paul Wankowicz

front of them and referring to it. A battered card table stood at the other
end of the tent, its top taken over by a pile of military kit. A Major
stood beside it, just as hollow-eyed as the Lieutenant. However, the
Major's uniform was spotless, as if it had just come back from the
cleaners. Standing, hands behind him at parade rest, he listened to
Mia's story in silence.

When she had finished, he snorted, "I don't believe you."

Mia was sleepless, hungry and, above all, out of reserves. His
statement hit her like a right to the jaw. She had done her best for the
soldiers on the beach. She had always felt an attachment to the British
Military since her father had served in it. Nor had she forgotten the
kindness of the lonely soldier who had helped her dig her father's
grave. She felt a part of the military family. His words cut a cruel
rejection.

She fought back. "You can find Sergeant Clark if you want, sir, and
check my statements. All I know is, there were two dead and two
wounded on the beach. The wounded died, despite what help I could
give them. Before he died, the Corporal told me the Japanese had come
around the point in a boat that was flying the British flag. Because he
thought the boat was British, he took his men out of hiding. He thought
the launch was the Royal Navy coming to get them. The Japanese are
using the British ensign to lure stragglers like him out of the jungle and
to kill them. He told me that."

"Very well. Did you get any of the men's identity disks?"

"Identity disks?"

"Yes. Identity disks. The tags they had around their necks. One of
those is supposed to be buried with the body and the other to be returned to headquarters for the record."

"I didn't know. I thought the tags had something to do with their
religion and should be buried with the men."

Mia had thought that the plastic medals on olive-drab cords were
amulets of some kind. *My father had an amulet around his neck when I
had buried him.* She avoided saying the word aloud, however, not

240

The Ulysses Flight/ Paul Wankowicz

wanting to sound superstitious in front of the Major.

"As to their using the Union Jack to lure men out of hiding, that's sheer fabrication. Poppycock! I know. I was a military attaché in the Tokyo Embassy. The Japanese have a very strict code of honor that forbids them to do such a thing. They call it *Bushido*. A very strict code."

Obviously, the Major had been in the field since the start of the campaign and had not heard of the Rape of Hong Kong.

"That's what the Corporal told me, sir, before he died. If he made it up, it does not explain the wounds on him and the other men."

The Major pointed a bony finger at her. "You made it all up! I think that you're a native spy for the Japanese. I don't know why, but that's what I think! You ought to be taken out and shot!"

As his words sank in, Mia found to her surprise, that it didn't make much difference anymore. She was too tired, too hungry, and too low of spirits to care what happened.

Before the Major had finished his accusatory rant, the field telephone buzzed and the Sergeant offered the phone to the Major.

Abruptly swinging around, the Major barked, "Take that call, Lieutenant!"

The Lieutenant, apparently in the last stages of exhaustion, had used the distraction caused by Mia's arrival to rest face down on the card table amid the welter of chits and maps. He was fast asleep.

The Major stood up and angrily picked up the handset and barked: "Headquarters here!" His face was still hardened in a scowl, as he listened to a tinny voice from the other end.

"I don't care what you think!" he shouted. "When you are told to hold, that's exactly what it means! We have to control the junction until the train, the one with. . . " He trailed off as his glance fell on Mia.

He put his hand over the mouthpiece. "Sergeant, get this native woman out of here before she learns our dispositions. Chop! Chop!"

The Sergeant, who had first brought Mia to the tent, and had quietly stayed through the interview, now came forward. He gently touched

241

Mia on the shoulder. "Come, Miss," he said. "Time we were out of here."

He led her to the outskirts of the village, and sat her down by a small fire smoldering in a hollow dug in the sand. A soot-blackened billy of tea was gently steaming beside it.

"Wait here, Miss," he said. "You could probably do with some kip. I'll be back in a minute."

As he disappeared in the darkness, Mia realized just how tired she was. She felt a deep sense of gratitude to the Sergeant for having led her to this place of peace, where there were no more demands on her. She was depleted. Sitting comfortably before the fire, her head drooped; however, before she was totally asleep, the Sergeant returned carrying a steaming mess tin.

"Here. Eat this," he offered. "It'll do you good."

She hadn't needed the invitation. It tasted great.

"Sorry that it's only Cookie's stew, but it is all that's going this time of night." The Sergeant paused while she ate. "It's Singapore that you're going to, I'm thinking. Right?"

She nodded again, mouth full.

"I'll tell you what. We're sending a lorry to the city tonight to get some ammo and replacements. The driver is a friend of mine. I can put you with him. Will that suit?"

She almost asked him to leave her there, where she didn't have to make another decision, but reason won over. She nodded her head.

"We've been told the city is so full of refugees, we shouldn't send any more in by train. But they didn't think to say we couldn't send refugees by lorries." He smiled broadly at his logic.

Although she was totally drained, Mia understood the Sergeant was taking a chance with the arrangement.

"Won't it be bad for you or the driver if the Major discovers me?" she asked.

He looked at her. "You've done well by our army," he said. "I figure the army owes you something for it. The Major, he don't know sweet Fannie Adams, so don't mind him."

Mia didn't know who, or what, Fannie Adams was, but the meaning was clear. She had an ally. "You did more for us than the brass with their fancy education. Now if me and my chums have to run, we'll know to look over any boat before breaking cover. That, an' tending to our wounded. I'll go find the lorry driver now," he added, embarrassed by his outburst.

That trip took two days of jouncing over bad roads. Mia and the driver drove past mile upon mile of monotonous jungle, sometimes relieved by neatly combed rows of rubber plantation trees, or some poor native village with it huts crowding the road. Nothing seemed capable of stopping the driver as long as every few hours, he could pause by the roadside to have a billy of strong tea, which he shared with Mia. Twice they came to way-side army camps. Mia hid in the back of the truck while the driver went to the cook and got rations for himself and his 'helper,' thick beef sandwiches and more sweet, strong tea.

By the time they crossed the causeway from Johor to Singapore Island, Mia felt as if every bone in her body had been jarred loose by the rutted roads.

Sensing Mia's state of physical depletion, the driver laughed and admitted, "I feel a little like that too, but a good night's sleep in the barracks, and 'a bit of recreation' will fix that," he winked. He was looking to get back to his mates as quickly as possible.

Mia wondered at his resilience.

He let her off at the end of Bukit Timah Road. She shouldered the knapsack, waved good-bye to him, and began walking to town.

The Ulysses Flight/ Paul Wankowicz

No one paid Mia any attention: Singapore was already full of refugees, so one more was no novelty. A passerby gave her directions to her uncle's place in Singapore. She had the address from a letter to her father she found in his desk.

I must find them. As she climbed the narrow stairs to her uncle's apartment, she was worried. *Suppose they've moved? Or won't take me in?* She had no other resource.

But her worry was unnecessary. The moment he saw her chestnut hair, he knew who she was. He and his wife made her welcome. Food, a warm bath, clean clothes, and then, sleep, and more sleep.

She thought she would never return to normality.

However, by the end of the week, Mia grew restless. She discovered that she couldn't stand the formlessness of having nothing to do, nothing about which to hinge her days.

She asked her uncle, "Is there anything I can help with? Some place where I can be useful?"

He listened to her question. He owned the Orient Hotel, now taken over by the Australians for their headquarters. Sundry liaison offices with the other forces in Singapore were also headquartered there. "Do you think that you could learn to run an elevator? My elevator boy was killed in a raid yesterday, and I have been wondering where I could find a replacement. Could you do it even for a few days? It is not difficult."

Mia nodded. It would fill her time.

Johnny paused the story so Frank, Lisa, and Johnny could eat something. When the sandwiches were ready, he returned to the story of how he met Mia.

244

Chapter 33: The Orient Hotel's Elevator, Singapore

Johnny was angry. By January 10th, the Malayan situation was worsening day by day. Everything was piling up on him. In Singapore, he could not find any officer who had knowledge of a Wing Commander Fred Winterbotham, much less one who knew him personally.

Frank was still delirious, suffering from the effects of malaria combined with black-water fever. It would be a long time before he was totally fit again.

Understandably, Lisa had refused to leave Frank's care. If Frank wasn't well enough to fly out, Lisa would stay with him. Of that, Johnny was sure. He felt responsible for them both, as if they were members of his own family. The government didn't see it that way.

Frank and Lisa didn't exist as far as the bureaucrats were concerned. Because they didn't have passports properly stamped at the port of entry, they therefore didn't exist.

Frank might not even be well enough to be evacuated before the Japanese came. Were that to happen, both he and Lisa, but especially Lisa, would be on Johnny's conscience.

The Japanese were now pushing toward Johor, part of Malaya and the last province before the island of Singapore itself. It's only a short walk across the causeway from Johor to Singapore; the water is only about 4 feet deep if they were to wade across.

No amount of cheerful general staff prognostications could change that. Nor could they change Johnny's opinion. The city of Singapore was doomed, no matter what they said.

Once in Johor, the Japanese would make short work of the "Bastion of the East" as Churchill had called Singapore. The Japanese would be in artillery range of the city's water supply, and thereby be in control.

Mia's elevator was a true antique, even for Singapore. It was a giant wrought-iron birdcage. A red plush seat ran around three sides of it. On one side the seat was a bit shorter, allowing Mia to stand by the big brass quadrant, on the face of which was spelled out 'Otis,' indubitably a deity of the elevator world.

The cage itself hung in a wrought-iron shaft. The outside of the passenger box was decorated with tall, gilded papyri growing out of bas-relief, ornately chased pots. The whole reeked of 'splendor of the past.' It was placed in the center of a hollow marble staircase, treads now worn concave and grayish with dirt.

At first, Mia was overwhelmed with timidity. She had never been in a room as large, and as plush, even if it was a bit seedy around the edges. She had never heard of the concept of 'good taste,' but she did wonder if 'civilization' was like this. She preferred the simplicity of the cottage she'd left in George Town. The operation of the elevator proved simple; in 30 minutes, she had mastered it, and had become a full-fledged 'elevator boy.'

Johnny's story jumped to how he actually met Mia in the elevator. After the Ulysses Flight landed at Kallang Airfield just outside of Singapore and arrangements were made for the planes, Johnny showed Frank and Lisa to the Beach Hotel. When they were situated, he arranged for Frank to be put under the care of a doctor. Satisfied that they would be okay, Johnny then attached himself to a R.A.F. *Buffalo* Squadron stationed at Sewang (Sembawang) Airfield, 18 miles north.

Commanding Officer Richardson was delighted to have another experienced pilot on his staff, and asked Johnny to run liaison with the Aussie Defense Force stationed around the airfield.

Johnny found them, as all green Aussies were, irritatingly independent. The morning's show was, for Johnny, the straw that broke the camel's back. Early that morning, a lone *Buffalo* pilot on patrol had spotted a Japanese Unit moving down a rubber-plantation road just below Tanduk Malim.

While attempting to strafe, the Aussie pilot had been jumped by a pair of Japanese Army *Nakajima*s and had barely shaken them off. His

246

The Ulysses Flight/ Paul Wankowicz

badly shot up fighter limped back to Sewang Airfield. He himself was
wounded in the melee. At the edge of the airfield, while he was making
his approach, the Aussies shot him down.

That they had shot down a British Fighter didn't perturb the Australian Lieutenant in charge. "Oh, you mean that the boys have finally hit
something? Bloody-good show!" he'd answered to Johnny's complaint.

During the argument, Johnny told the Aussie Lieutenant that he's
bloody-well going to have to find someone else to relieve your bloody
crew, even if you have to go to bloody King George VI yourself.

The Lieutenant told him, " It doesn't matter to me, I don't like the
Bryll Cream Boys," (a derogatory name for the R.A.F.) and, "You can
go to hell."

Johnny almost turned his back to him and marched out of the room.
Instead, Johnny requisitioned the squadron transport and was driven
from the airfield straight to the Australian H.Q. located in the ancient
Oriental Hotel.

As he strode into the well-worn foyer of the hotel, he was still
angry. He headed for the stairs, intending to take them two at a time,
but then, his glance fell on the Chinese girl in the wrought-iron elevator. In contrast to the shabbiness about her, she had a freshness that
made him stop and look at her. She had chestnut hair, and was altogether the prettiest girl he had ever seen.

She smiled at him as he walked toward the lift.

On the way up in the lift, Johnny saw that the bridge of her nose
was sunburned, peeling. He had not realized that the Chinese were
subject to sunburn. He was sorry when the creeping elevator arrived at
his floor.

The officer in charge of the Australian anti-aircraft was a Captain.
"There's no need to get excited, Lieutenant. I'm sure the lads meant
well. It could have been Japanese, you know."

The R.A.F.'s rank of Flight Lieutenant was equivalent to that of a
Captain, equal in rank to Johnny. He was being intentionally insulting

247

The Ulysses Flight/ Paul Wankowicz

in addressing Johnny, by using only half of his rank to address him
while still just within the bounds of military legality.

"Damn it, Captain, are your people on our side?" Johnny demanded.
A supercilious bastard.

"If you think we like Pommies, the answer is No, and we don't take
orders from them either, Lieutenant!" the Aussie snapped back.

Johnny considered what pleasure it would give him to bash the
Captain's perfect smile past his Adam's apple. He'd just about had
enough.

In the end, military discipline and good breeding won out. Johnny
forced himself to turn away before he lost control. As he did so, he
nearly collided with a smallish man smoking a pipe and wearing the
pips of major general. Johnny recognized him from newspaper pictures:
He was Major General Gordon Bennett, G.O.C. Australian Forces,
Malaya.

Bennett looked at both of them. Johnny was conscious that the
General had probably heard every word of their argument.

"What's going on here?" Bennett asked.

The Australian Captain started to explain, but Bennett cut him off
with a brusque motion of his hand and pointed at Johnny.

Johnny briefly ran over his story.

"Where was the pilot when he spotted the Japanese unit?" the General asked.

"About ten miles below Tanduk Malim." Johnny had flown the
patrol himself and knew the location described by the wounded airman.

"Show me." Bennett walked over to a large map pinned to the wall.

"About here, where the unimproved road parallels the edge of the
plantation. At least, I think that's where the pilot saw them. He was in a
pretty bad way when we pulled him from the machine, sir."

The General turned to the Captain. "As I thought, they are trying to
outflank us, get to the main road."

He turned to Johnny, his finger stabbing at the chart. "We're trying
to hold the junction HERE. I guessed they went down the road your

248

The Ulysses Flight/ Paul Wankowicz

man saw them on, and would get behind us through HERE. I don't
know where our flank guard was, but the *Buffalo* pilot did us a favor."

He turned to the Captain. "You will change that crew, and order
whoever is in charge of them to report to me before the afternoon is out.
Is that clear?"

Johnny thanked the General. A man who could make decisions
without vacillating. One of the few.

Johnny's mind turned to the girl again. As he was walking out,
however, he heard his rank called. He swivelled around to see a Wing
Commander, behind the desk in one of the jury-rigged cubicles lining
the room. A miniature blue R.A.F. flag on a chromed standard was the
only thing on the desk-top in front of the Wing Commander.

"What was the flap about, Lieutenant?"

As Johnny started into the whole dreary story again, he was waved
into silence.

"It'll keep," the W/C said.

"Sir?"

"I don't care who you are, or what this is all about. My name is
Wing Commander Porteous. Among other duties, I am the R.A.F.
Liaison Officer to the Australian Forces. Complaints come to me.
Understand? We have a real war on our hands here, not some Service
Flying Training School where you can do as you wish. And we expect
the members of our service to behave with this in mind. Where did you
come from?"

Johnny glanced down at his shirt. He was not wearing his D.F.C.
ribbon. Among the garrison troops still in Singapore, it was more of a
mark of Cain then a decoration. Richardson had pointed out that ribbons like the D.F.C. tended to remind the brass that there had been a
real war going on while they had sat on their hands, playing at being
colonials; not getting ready for what was obviously coming. Porteous
was obviously one of those. A ground officer. Johnny regretted not
wearing the ribbon.

"Yes sir. I guess that the Battle of Britain was a sort of an Elemen-

249

The Ulysses Flight/ Paul Wankowicz

tary Flying Training School, run in preparation for the real war here?" As soon as he said it, Johnny regretted the words; he saw the words had struck home.

The WingCo reddened."That is all, Lieutenant. And I'll thank you to keep a civil tongue in your head. Dismissed!" Johnny knew that within the hour, Porteous would know who and from where he had come. He'd made an enemy.

One more minute, however, and the frustrations of the day would have proven too much. He would have reached across the desk and struck. A court-martial offense. It had been that close.

Johnny forced himself to take a few deep breaths as he walked toward the elevator.

Within a few days, Mia was taken for granted as 'the new elevator operator.' Although she'd never run machinery before, the concept fascinated her. During lulls she experimented, trying to gain ascendancy over the antiquated equipment, trying to jiggle the handle just enough to make little corrective jumps that would place the sill of the elevator just where she wanted it.

Because of the number of military who daily went in and out of her elevator, she'd taken to studying ranks and badges in a book of her uncle's. It was during one of those lulls that Mia saw an R.A.F. officer, boiling-angry, come out from the Australian H.Q. in the hotel. She recognized him as both a flight lieutenant and a pilot. She had learned that only pilots wore symmetrical wings; the other air crew just wore one wing on the side of the medallion. The letters in the medallions, she knew, spelled out the trade: "AG" for air gunner, "N" for navigator, "O" for observer, and so forth. Only the pilots had the service monogram surmounted by the royal crown in the center of the badge.

Mia saw him start for the stairway.

When he saw her standing by the Otis quadrant, he hesitated and changed his direction toward her. . . .

She smiled at him as he stepped on. They rode down in silence,

250

The Ulysses Flight/ Paul Wankowicz

Johnny was unable to think of anything to say to open a conversation. As they came to the ground floor, she swung the handle to stop. Nothing happened. Catching herself, she rapidly jammed the control to 'up.' There was a clatter of relays from above and the elevator stopped with a jerk, inches below the floor level. She turned to him: "Sorry, Flight Lieutenant. The elevator seems to have died. I'll have to get the concierge to reset the machine. Not quite the landing I had hoped to make."

"Better landing than some of mine."

She looked meaningfully at the wings on his shirt. He wondered if she could see the holes where a D.F.C. had been pinned. "If I may say so, sir, I have grave doubts about that."

Her expression was elfin. He warmed toward her. After the day's tensions, the conversation struck him as funny. He burst into a peal of laughter.

For an instant, she looked startled, lost; but then, she must have decided that it was all right, and broke out in a smile of relief.

It wasn't like any smile that Johnny had seen before. Her whole being was in it.

He'd not seen anyone so radiantly beautiful. He couldn't just walk out and never see her again.

"What time do you get off work here?" he asked.

"At 6:30," she had answered, without thinking.

"Why?"

"Because I'll be here. To walk you home. I'll have to hurry to make it to Sewang Airfield and back, but by heaven, I'll be here. If I'm late, wait a bit for me."

Mia looked after him as his broad back disappeared in the sunlight outside. Had it been anyone else, one of those self-important officers who rode up and down her elevator, she would have known what they were after, what they called 'a lay.' With him, she wasn't sure. She'd cross any difficulty when it came up. In the meantime, she realized, she was happier than she'd been for a long time.

Chapter 34: Johnny Reminisces

Just after the defeat of the Germans in the Battle of Britain and their switch to night bombing of London and nearby cities, Johnny went on leave. For Johnny, this leave turned out to be a disaster. He'd gone to Settle in Ribblesdale, Northern Yorkshire, where his family had a manor home, a turn-of-the-century brick. A long, curved drive led up to it. There was a formal park behind it, now taken up with growing food for the war effort.

It had been ages since he had been away from the ever-same routine of eating, flying, sleeping, and then, starting over again. This unanticipated leisure of the leave made him start thinking about the war, something he didn't want to do.

Since he'd joined the R.A.F., just before the start of the war, the demands on him had never let up. Johnny was tired. Deadly tired. He'd been on flying duty from the very beginning.

Service Flying Training School had been followed by operational training on *Lysander*s in an Army Cooperation School, and then, a direct posting to France, where the planes, the "poor, bloody *Lysanders*" had been totally inadequate to the work asked of them.

Under the pressure of the developing Luftwaffe attacks against England, he had been taken off his duties in France and sent in a hurried conversion to *Spitfire*s. With a significant ammunition shortage in England, Johnny was allowed only one gunnery run against a ground target before being sent to operations. Then he was pitched directly into the Battle of Britain and, while himself surviving almost by a miracle, he watched his inadequately-trained fellow-pilots go down one by one.

Johnny only had six hours training in an obsolete Mark I *Spitfire* before being posted to the 11 Group. There his experience in France on the *Lysander* quickly made him senior to most other pilots.

The Ulysses Flight/ Paul Wankowicz

Flying in 11 Group, the main defense of London, Johnny had never learned the names of many of the men with whom he flew. Often, those who had arrived in the morning were dead or in the hospital by the afternoon. Watching faces of fellow airmen come and disappear, he had tried not to wonder if his luck would hold.

When the squadron was finally pulled out of line, he'd been given two-weeks' leave before being reassigned to the Pacific.

While at home on leave, he found himself desperate to establish some connection with his father, and to explore what his old man's experiences had been and what he'd thought of his military service in the British Expeditionary Force in France in 1917; but it didn't happen.

His father, David, Lord Laws, was Victorian to the core, as Victorian as the manor in which he lived, and as tightly sealed as a green walnut. Although for some reason which he never disclosed, he hated Churchill sufficiently to have resigned from the Conservative party; but he carried on his anti-Churchillian politics through the newspaper he owned, spending most of his time in London playing what would be petty politics.

When Johnny came home to the market town of Settle, his father was full of invective against 'that man Winston.' It was the only thing Lord Laws would talk about—perhaps a ploy to shield himself from his son's needs.

In the end, Johnny gave up trying to connect with the man.

His mother, on the other hand, was neutral in her political outlook and very proud of her boy. As a member of 11 Group, R.A.F., Johnny was one of 'the few' of whom Prime Minister Winston Churchill said, in August, 1940, "Never in the field of human conflict, have so many owed so much to so few."

Lady Laws, occupied by her charitable work in the countryside, had no idea of the dangers that her Johnny faced. Although she was rolling bandages for the Red Cross, the perils experienced by the aviators were beyond her.

Johnny had been truly embarrassed by his mother as she showed

253

him off to the various charitable organizations of which she was a member, and pushed him toward the spinster daughters of her women friends.

In the end, Johnny's leave was cut short by a summons to London because Johnny's medal, the Distinguished Flying Cross, had been approved. He was ordered to the palace to be presented to the King.

When the ceremony was over, Lord Laws finally paid some attention to his son by taking Johnny to the club; but it had all been too late and they had remained strangers.

Then came the blessed relief, for Johnny, of the journey back to the airfield to his military family, now clearly closer to him than his parents.

Six days after the King had pinned the medal on him, Johnny was on a *Catalina* flying boat to Rangoon. Then he was pitched into flying the *Buffalo*es, which handled like a truck after the *Spitfire*s, the heat of Burma, and always the grinding responsibility for the green pilots who, but for the war, would still be studying in school.

In contrast to his leave after the battle, the time he spent with Frank and Lisa, in that overheated hangar in Tenasserim, was the best respite he'd ever had.

Johnny enjoyed Frank's naive dash and his belief that everything would always turn out alright, and he admired Lisa for her bravery, competence and for her ability to be a comrade-in-arms, without any loss of her femininity. Johnny realized that they had become his family.

Now, Johnny was in a much more desperate fight than the Battle of Britain ever had been. At least, while he flew against the Germans, there was a chance of winning. Here, against the Japanese, there was none. He felt trapped in a senseless tragedy as he watched pilots come and go.

He'd kept going out of habit and on the traditions that he'd learned which became a part of every member of the R.A.F. The tradition that

The Ulysses Flight/ Paul Wankowicz

said that no R.A.F. pilot ever gave up, no matter what the circumstances.

Years ago, when he was about ten years old, Johnny had walked away from his picnicking parents and went off on his own, exploring. He had discovered an abandoned foundry which had been shut down shortly after the First World War. The roof had partially caved in, and grass and fungi were growing among rotting timbers. Assorted unidentifiable pieces of rusting metal were scattered around.

Off on one side of the decaying ruin stood the cupola, partly caved in. Its inside was filled with black clinkers, intermingled with a cold, white, powdery ash. Absolutely nothing had taken root among the ash left in the cupola.

In contrast, the rest of the building's remains had grass, weeds and young trees growing among the collapsed beams.

Looking inwardly, until recently, Johnny felt his soul was like that abandoned cupola: Burned out, cold, and done in by war. Meeting Mia resurrected some flicker of heat among the wreckage—a springtime among the ashes.

He found he was spending more and more time worrying about her. When he wasn't on duty, he would be at the P & O office trying to wrangle an evacuation permit for her. An impossible task. There were not enough places for the not-needed government officials, nor for the wives of Europeans. A half-caste native girl just didn't count.

During one of his visits to the steamship office, the clerk never bothered to look up. "You can't expect us, sir, to give out chits for 'female *wogs*,'" he declared.

As he walked out, Johnny thought he heard snickering remarks about his being tied to his *native mistress.*

His helplessness even to buy her a ticket made him furious. There was nowhere to dissipate his anger, furthered by the radio's hypocritical announcements about "standing shoulder to shoulder with the natives."

If he had money, maybe he could bribe a clerk. It was being done all around him, but he didn't have any here, so there wasn't much use thinking about it. Whenever he could, Johnny would meet Mia at the hotel and walk her home after her shift operating the elevator.

Once, they went to the movies. Films were still in full swing despite the ever-tightening ring of Japanese about the city. Bob Hope delighted her, even though Johnny had to explain most of the jokes.

Chapter 35: Downtown Singapore

On one occasion, Mia and Johnny had gone out to a Chinese Restaurant with her uncle. During the meal, much to Mia's embarrassment, her uncle insisted on re-telling the story of her trip from Penang.

When he had finished telling her story, Mia said demurely: "My uncle exaggerates. It was nothing difficult. I couldn't stay in George Town any longer."

"I don't think it was 'nothing,'" Johnny said. "How many others could have made a journey like yours successfully, with the Japanese holding the coast?"

She was silent for a moment. "They weren't as lucky as I was."

Then casting for a change of subject: "That ribbon under your wings is the Distinguished Flying Cross, isn't it?" she asked, but she already knew the answer.

She must have looked it up, or button-holed some other officer, Johnny realized. He had only recently started wearing the ribbon. He didn't care what others thought of it; he was proud of it himself and that was what mattered. It was a badge of brotherhood with friends who hadn't survived the Battle.

He had also hoped the men at the ticket office might take it into account.

"What was it given for?" her uncle asked.

Johnny thought of the many flippant replies he could make and discarded them all. "For saving the life of a brave, but foolish Air Vice-Marshal during the time the Germans were attacking England. But then, I crashed a perfectly good *Spitfire* saving him; so, in the end, it wasn't very great."

"And you got it from the King-Emperor in the Buck Palace?" she asked.

Johnny smiled inwardly. *Of course, out here it would be the King-*

The Ulysses Flight/ Paul Wankowicz

Emperor. I've never heard King George called that before. And I doubt if many in London ever referred to his town's royal residence as 'the Buck Palace.' "That's right," Johnny smiled.

"When he gave it to you, did the King-Emperor say anything? What did he look like?" Mia asked.

Johnny laughed. "The King said: 'How clumsy of me!' He'd stuck his thumb on the pin behind the medal. Then, put his thumb in his mouth and apologized in case he got any blood on my tunic."

"And what did you say?" Mia asked with genuine interest.

"I said: 'Oh, that's all right, Your Majesty.' . . . He was just like anyone else, not at all distant."

"Did he really say that?" Mia asked. "Is he like his pictures? Were you very close to him? He sounds so much nicer than the officers who ride my elevator everyday."

She is sometimes fascinated, like a little girl. To Johnny's relief, they spent the rest of the meal talking about the Royal Family.

She had managed, Johnny thought wryly to himself, *to turn the subject away from her own exploits.* But knowing about them made her that much more precious to him. He would not forget.

He renewed his efforts to get her evacuated, but now, the panic to leave the island was setting in. The bribe price was a hundred times higher and the chances much, much worse. All the requests had to go through the Governor's clerk. He would be expensive. No dice there. *Even if she were evacuated, even if she managed somehow to get off the island,* Johnny realized, with a tightening of his heart, *what would she do? Were she to get to Java, or Sumatra, or even Australia, then what?* She'd be just another person tossed up in the backwash of the war. Penniless. Without protection. Not knowing the customs. There's only one solution. Thinking of it, he leapt at it gladly.

After supper at a restaurant bordering the native section where she lived, as they walked arm in arm, "Mia," he said, "I've been trying to get you evacuated, to get you safely off Singapore Island before the

258

The Ulysses Flight/ Paul Wankowicz

Japanese come." He felt her body stiffen, as if she knew what he was going to say.

"Why, Johnny?"

He stopped. After he turned toward her, he put his hands on her shoulders. In the dim light of the blacked-out city, a distant fire started by a Japanese bomb, painted her features in a candle-like glow, making her unbearably beautiful. Johnny had difficulty keeping his voice level. "Because I love you!"

She looked up at him. What moonlight there was glistened in her eyes.

"Johnny, don't be foolish!"

"I've never been less foolish in my life, Mia."

"Not on the street, Johnny. Let's talk of this in the apartment."

When they got there, Mia's aunt and uncle were away. They had the apartment to themselves. He started the subject again. "You have to get out of Singapore before the Japanese come."

"But surely there is much time. On the radio, the Governor says that everyone will fight to the last bullet, to the last man. Surely they will not let the Japanese in."

"There is no more time, Mia. The Japanese are already in Johor. It's only a matter of weeks. When they come, if you haven't gotten out, what will you do?"

"I will manage somehow. It's you who should be getting out."

"Mia. You don't know the Japanese. They have cut a swath of cruelty across the country wherever they have come." Johnny had heard the stories out of Hong Kong. "I can't leave you here."

She looked at him as if judging her own thoughts, and then, said: "Come upstairs for a second."

He followed her up the narrow cement stairs. Over the landing, a single bulb hung spreading dim light into her bedroom. It was a small narrow room with crudely white-washed walls. A sleeping futon was on the floor, leaving just enough room for one person to pass. A wooden box with a candle on it served as a bedside table. Beside the candle was a silver-framed picture of a blond-haired woman in a 1920s dress, the photo, sepia with age.

After the rich, over-stuffed comfort of the living room, these surroundings screamed poverty. He wanted to take her into his arms and comfort her. She deserved better than this.

As they entered, Mia picked up something from the low table and held it out to him. It was a small paring knife. "See this? I carried it taped between my breasts through the whole journey, in case the Japanese caught me. They may be cruel, but they will never rape me, nor torture me, so there's no worry about it," she said.

No words would pass through his constricted throat. She'd believed every word that she'd said.

As if making conversation, she finally broke the silence. "Don't look so sad, Johnny. It has happened to thousands before. Wars are cruel. You will soon forget!"

"Mia, would you marry me? Then, you would be my dependent, and the R.A.F. would have to take care of you."

Even as he said it, he realized that it hadn't come out at all as if he'd meant it. It had sounded like a business proposition! But he had said it. He found he couldn't breathe.

"Johnny, you are a good man, but you are being foolish. You don't want to marry me, a half-caste Chinese girl." She looked up at him. "If you want me, you can have me anytime. Even now," and she flung her hand toward the futon. "I love you, Johnny. I love you very much, but I couldn't marry you."

He felt something inside him collapse like a shot balloon. "Mia, why?"

"As soon as you go back to England, you would find someone more to your liking than me. I'd be in the way then. I want you to be happy, not just now, but always."

"You're wrong, Mia. I have had plenty of chances before. English girls pale in comparison with you."

The Ulysses Flight/ Paul Wankowicz

He saw her smile at his unconscious joke, and hurried on. "You're very wrong. You're the only one I've ever wanted to marry, and not just to keep you safe. I love you!"

He looked around the room, it depressed him. "Let's go downstairs. Being up here gives me ideas!" He said that as a half-joke.

She laughed and took his hand. "It's supposed to, Johnny. You are a fine man, but you know little of the physical side of things. I could teach you. On your terms. Now, if you want. From what you say, we might not have much time left."

He reached for her wrist and gently spun her around. Taking her into his arms, he put his lips against hers. For a brief instant, he felt her body stiffen; then, she relaxed, molding herself against him. Neither knew how long they stood like that before coming up for air.

"Will you marry me?" he asked again.

She looked at him with an impish smile. "Either we use the bed," she said, "or we go downstairs!"

"Before we go, you have to answer me, Mia."

"You have a one-track mind!"

He looked at the futon. "It's on the wrong track at the moment!"

She followed his gaze and laughed.

"Please marry me!" Again it didn't sound quite like what he meant.

She came up to him and put her head on his chest. A gesture of surrender?

"Yes, but under one condition."

He bent down to stroke her chestnut hair. He couldn't see her face, but thought she had started crying.

"What condition?"

She had difficulty getting the words out. They came so quietly that he had to strain to hear them. "That when you get to England, and meet that woman, you will give me a divorce."

"Never."

"That's the condition, Johnny." She was crying. *Was she thinking of that distant day?*

The Ulysses Flight/ Paul Wankowicz

He pressed her to him. "All right, but it will never happen."

She looked up at him, tears still glistening on her cheeks. "Oh, Johnny," she said, but apparently, couldn't say anything more.

He took her fully into his arms and they stood there, again saying nothing. He couldn't imagine anyone else could ever be as happy as he was.

Chapter 36: Singapore Cathedral

Their wedding on January 20, 1942, was not a large wedding party. Mia's uncle had delayed it by a week, insisting that they be married in the Cathedral, legally secure in both Chinese and English law, to make sure Johnny was sincere. There were many British leaving their Chinese girls, concubines, and even wives, in the lurch as they fled the city.

The more formal the arrangements, the uncle thought, the more difficult for Johnny to abandon Mia. She, of course, didn't tell him of the one condition she had put to the marriage.

The inside of the Cathedral was cool. A gentle sea-breeze had unexpectedly arrived, reminding Johnny of an European spring. As if for the event, the debilitating tropics and the war could be forgotten or set aside, although not in totality. Near-misses had left little of the stained glass in the tall Gothic windows. A few colored shards still clung to the frames here and there, but the rest of the openings showed the cruel blue of the sky. Sunlight lanced through shrapnel holes in the roof, dappling the floors and the wedding party in strange patterns.

Frank and Lisa were there. Frank was still drawn and walking with a cane; Lisa tired and worried. Johnny had asked Andy Rogers, the Aussie C.O. from Sembawang Airfield to be his best man. Andy looked very much like a craggier edition of Johnny; he had one more half-ring on the epaulets of his tropical khakis than Johnny, making him a Squadron Leader while Johnny was still a Flight Lieutenant.

He had delegated four pink-cheeked pilot officers to be the guard of honor, and had even found swords for them.

When Frank expressed his surprise at swords being found in Singapore, he quipped, "Hell, half the ruddy staff is fighting the war with them. Probably have warehouses full of the damn things, waiting to be issued!"

The Ulysses Flight/ Paul Wankowicz

Lisa had liked Andy Rogers the moment she met him, and heard him tell how it was that he'd joined the "Royal Air Farce," as he called it. "Three years before Johnny, here. Hoping to fly some real kites, so they put me on the oldest, most decrepit planes they had: Fairey *Battles*! How I missed the prang at the Belgian bridges, I don't know!"

Lisa knew that at the war's outbreak, the R.A.F. had refused to see that the *Battle* was a dangerously obsolete plane. Until, that is, a whole squadron of them had been wiped out on one raid on the Belgian bridges early in the campaign in France; but, for many months, there was nothing else.

Rogers had been lucky to survive the period called "The Phoney War" flying the *Battle*. Most *Battle* pilots didn't. He'd eventually flown *Hurricanes* during the Battle of Britain and had won a D.F.C. at about the same time that Johnny had.

Johnny and Rogers had never met in England, but had an immediate respect for the friendship with one another from the moment Johnny had arrived at Sembawang Airfield.

"I thought he'd be some bloody-ground type. Then, this fellow walks in, looking like me, only uglier. I had to like him!"

Yes, Lisa liked Rogers quite well. From somewhere Andy Rogers had found an Aussie who could play the organ, and the procession took their places to the strains of Mendelssohn's *Wedding March*. This was followed by a twiddly version of *Where Sheep May Safely Graze,* but this seemed to exhaust the repertoire, or possibly, his patriotism got the better of him.

Soon Mia and a laughing Johnny, now Mr. and Mrs. Laws, went back down the aisle under a booming rendition of the Aussie anthem, *Waltzing Matilda*. Rogers was cheering, and Mia looked bewildered. As Johnny and Mia entered the ceremonial arch of swords, Frank saw Rogers turn around and wave to the organist. It made absolutely no difference. They ducked under the swords to the second verse of the song.

In the sacristy, the Bishop was already changing his stole; some of

The Ulysses Flight/ Paul Wankowicz

the casualties from the temporary hospital next door were waiting to be buried. As he took the black fabric from the peg, he was reproaching himself for being an old, sentimental fool. He shook his head. The bride and the young officer she was marrying both looked so radiantly happy.

He'd never seen a Chinese girl so beautiful. She'd had chestnut hair. Odd for a Chinese. Too bad she'd cut it in a pageboy; it would have been so beautiful had she let it grow long.

How long would they last? How long can anyone in these times? He'd buried several mangled bodies still wearing the R.A.F. light-gray-and-blue insignia of rank.

He picked up his prayer book with the worn gilt cross on the cover and the frayed black ribbon marking the burial service and turned toward the back door. They were waiting for him out there.

The after-wedding party at Sewang Airfield was all that Rogers had promised. It went on long after Johnny and Mia had disappeared in the direction of their rented bungalow. From the quantity of empties and the number of collapsed airmen when the party ended, there wouldn't be much flying the following day.

Four days after the wedding, Johnny sat down to write to his parents. It was a difficult letter, especially because he was counting on his father to take care of Mia after she was evacuated. His father would be furious at his only child marrying a "native girl, a half-caste Chinese." It could not be helped. He picked up the pen, wrote the date, and followed it with the usual salutation: "Dear Pater" didn't sound right. He leaned back to look at it again.

All of a sudden it struck him: The image of his parents as he'd see them if he'd just met them, without the pain of being their only child. Without automatically looking for support, for guidance. As one sees two strangers at some party. He'd have liked them. That was something to think about. Had he changed? The marriage? Independence?

He picked up the sheet and crumpled it into the wastepaper basket;

265

then, leaned forward and started again. "Dear Mum and Dad," sounded better. He continued writing. By noon, he'd finished seven pages. The longest letter he'd ever written them. He'd now have to see that the letter got onto the Java-bound *Catalina*. Too many ships leaving the harbor were being sunk. He found that he was feeling much better. His relationship with his parents had been on his conscience. His father, like an irate volcano, would rail about his new daughter-in-law, but he would eventually subside. His mother, Johnny knew, would like her right away, though probably never understand her.

Johnny knew that he had made no mistake marrying Mia. . . .

Chapter 37: Singapore

By January 25, 1942, Frank found himself sufficiently recovered to get around, and felt restless. He now spent his days fiddling on the P-40s to return some normalcy to his day.

The R.A.F. had left a crew of five men to guard the Kellang Airfield. They had little to do and willingly helped the Yank in whatever he was doing.

Frank found abandoned long-range gas tanks, originally meant for *Albacore* torpedo bombers, but now surplus as there were no more *Albacore*s. Fitting the gas tanks to the P-40s would increase the fighters' endurance by almost three hours, so he set about adapting them to the American fighters.

While he was trying to determine what he would need for the job, the telephone in the guard hut rang. It was Lisa. He could tell from her voice it was something important. "Frank, could you come back here? Johnny is here and needs to talk with you."

Frank's heart sank. "Mia?"

"No, she's all right. It's Andy Rogers. He's been shot down." Lisa would say nothing more over the phone.

"I'll be there as fast as I can." The airfield crew had requisitioned a Chevrolet.

Johnny had not been the only one to have seen the writing on the wall.

As people not wanting to be captured by the Japanese fled the island, they had to leave most of their possessions behind. Around the docks, abandoned cars were beginning to clutter the street, free for anyone to pick up. Some had pathetic little notes pinned to the ignition keys, notes saying: "Be kind to my Ford, it's been kind to me," or, "You're welcome to this malevolent wreck!" It made transport easy if, like the airport crew, you had access to gasoline.

267

The Ulysses Flight/ Paul Wankowicz

As the Sergeant drove him out the arched gate that marked the entrance to Sembawang Airfield, Frank was deep in thought. He was back to his old dilemma.

Johnny's marriage to Mia had brought it on again.

Frank knew he loved Lisa, but also that he had nothing to offer her, neither family, nor fortune. She deserved more than he could give, and it had been somewhat of a relief, although painful, to see how well she got along with Rogers. Andy Rogers could give her so much more. Now Andy was dead, or, at best, a POW. Gone.

Frank couldn't visualize what his relationship with Lisa would be, especially now that lately he found her irritable, harder to get along with.

He had not long to worry. The hotel was a scant two miles down the road and now had ample parking. In less than five minutes, he was knocking on their door.

"Its me, Frank."

"Come in, its unlocked." Johnny called back.

When he entered the suite, Frank found Johnny and Mia sitting opposite each other, dead silent and preoccupied. Johnny's expression was grim.

Johnny looked up as Frank entered. "I would like to borrow one of your kites," he said.

"What for?" Frank asked.

"Andy Rogers had cleanly bailedout of his *Buffalo* and was parachuting down when a Japanese riddled him. We know the Jap pilot came from Kuantan, and some of us are going to fly there to shoot up the bastard's airfield."

"Where?"

"Kuantan, about 200 miles north, up the coast. I have taken over command and already organized the raid. I'd like to borrow a P-40 to use when I lead the raid. I'll go to Kallang to get one, then come back here to form up—We have five serviceable *Buffalo*es, but because all of the pilots want to join in, I'd like to add a *Tomahawk* to the foray."

268

The Ulysses Flight/ Paul Wankowicz

"Make it two. I'm coming with you," Frank said.

"Are you well enough?"

"For that, you bet. For Andy, it would be a pleasure to shoot up the bastard's airfield."

"Make it three," Lisa said. "Count me in."

Frank swung around, "Hardly."

"Why not?"

"Because you are . . ." He almost said 'a woman,' but checked himself, "not trained as a fighter pilot," he finished lamely.

"Why don't you say it?" she said, her eyes narrowing. "'Because you're a female.' While we're at it, let me add, . . ." but she was interrupted by Johnny holding up his hand.

"Let me get out of here while you settle your differences," he said.

"Hell, no," she answered. "You're in this, too. We stick together. 'The Ulysses Flight,' remember?" She turned to Frank. "I'm part Dutch, stubborn as hell. And I choose my own man. He doesn't make choices for me. And that applies with whom, and where I fly. Understand?"

Frank was taken aback. *How the hell did she know what he had been thinking about Rogers and her?* He remembered that they'd been over the male-female ground, and he'd lost before. He knew it was no use arguing. "I'm sorry."

Beaten, Frank turned to Johnny. "Call Kallang Airfield. Tell them to get the three P-40s ready."

Again, he had been defeated by Lisa, but he felt immensely better for it.

She looked up at him. "I didn't know how to tell you that you were being stubborn, stupid, or both."

"Look," he said, partly as an excuse. "I have no money, no family, not even a hometown. I can't give you anything." He didn't mention that as a war-time pilot, his life expectancy was not all that spectacular.

"And me?" she asked. "I'm just a refugee from Burma, remember?" Her mood had changed kaleidoscopically from anger to tears. "We've all become expendable. But if that happens, I want a chance to be with you, not sitting somewhere far away, wondering if I'll ever see you again."

Frank looked at her, feeling how much he loved her, but living with her would take some getting used to. Her lightning changes of mood, the almost uncanny way she read his mind, his actions.

He saw her eyes were still full of tears, but she was smiling. "It's all right," she said. "You'll get used to it."

It shook him.

Johnny had watched the entire sequence. He now showed obvious relief. "Three kites then?" he asked no one in particular. "The Ulysses Flight is back in business! Bloody good!" He picked up the telephone and asked for Kallang Airfield.

Chapter 38: Kuantan, Pahang, Malaya, January 25, 1942

Captain Kashimura ground out the cigarette in the already full ashtray and called: "Come in!" It would be Lieutenant Horikashi. Kashimura dreaded the interview.

Horikashi seemed nonplussed. As if nothing had happened, he asked, "You wanted to see me, Captain?" as he came in, using his best social tones.

Kashimura lit another cigarette. "Sit down. Smoke if you wish."

Horikashi said nothing.

"Sergeant Hokai tells me that something, which he wouldn't discuss, happened during the last flight. Would you like to give me a report?"

"Nothing happened. I shot down a Brewster *Buffalo*. That's all."

He was lying.

"Sergeant Hokai also tells me that you killed the pilot after he had parachuted out of his fighter. Is that true?"

"Hokai is an old woman. It's none of his business!"

"I didn't ask you that. Did you shoot down a man in a parachute?"

"What of it? He was enemy." Horikashi leaned back in his chair, remembering the pleasure. The proof of his marksmanship. *Captain Kashimura just didn't appreciate how difficult it was to shoot down a stationary object from a fast, modern fighter.*

His marksmanship had been exceptional. It had been an officer. He had flown close to the figure swinging on the thin tracery of shroud lines under the white canopy of the parachute, close enough to see the rings denoting officer rank.

The man floating in the air had watched Horikashi with interest, unaware of what was about to happen.

Horikashi had thought the man was more concerned with the Japanese fighter's appearance than anything else. It wasn't until the last

271

moments, when Horikashi's fighter had turned toward him that the Britisher realized what was about to happen and had lifted his arms across his face to shield himself from seeing the gunfire coming at him. Within split seconds, the 20-millimeter cannon shells had cut into his body, throwing a red halo of blood around him, staining his khaki uniform a dark, almost black-red.

Horikashi's only regret was that one of the slugs had cut a riser and the parachute folded on itself and streamed. This prevented Horikashi from being able to enjoy the sight of his kill longer—but it had been a thrill for him, nevertheless.

Horikashi realized that Kashimura was saying nothing, but glared at him in silence as if he were a particularly odious kind of insect.

Finally, he could stand the silence no longer. "What is this," he exploded, "a court-martial?"

"No. Unfortunately." Kashimura paused to think of what he should say next. Eventually, he broke Horikashi's arrogant silence. "Japan has a centuries-older civilization than the Westerner's. Even so, it seems sometimes we could learn from them. I have yet to hear of them mistreating a prisoner, or of shooting down any of our men in a parachute. But you!" Kashimura was using all his restraint to control his temper.

"Have you been drinking enemy whiskey?" Horikashi burst out. "It sounds as if it has gone to your brain?"

Kashimura's temper broke. He bolted up, towering over the junior officer and leaned toward his face. "I have had enough of you! I have more years in the Emperor's Service than a pup like you will ever see! My squadron and all its members will always fight like warriors, not animals! You have done something I will not pardon. You have broken our honor!" Overcome, Kashimura paused briefly. "Effective this minute, you are grounded. You will never fly with us again. You are not to go anywhere near the airplanes under any circumstances. This is an order! Understand?"

"Yes, Captain." Horikashi's voice was mocking.

"For what you did to dishonor this squadron, I would like to kill

The Ulysses Flight/ Paul Wankowicz

you!" Kashimura said. "Do you understand that?"

"Yes, but I doubt many would agree with you."

"I have no doubt," Kashimura said. "I have heard of the inglorious exploits of our Japanese Army in Hong Kong. Nurses raped and put to death. The blood of children on Samurai Swords! Enemy pilots beheaded! The Nippon shamed!" He looked down shaking his head.

"I would have liked to be there. Help tame the Chinese enemy beast!" Horikashi said flippantly.

For long seconds, Kashimura glared at him. "Get out! Get out! And stay out of my sight!" He closed his eyes until he heard the door slam. *One more word from him, just one more word, and I would have killed him. And felt good about it, too.*

He forced the thought away. He felt weary and stained forever. *Could the unit I lead ever be pardoned? I doubt it.*

Soon there were other considerations to distract him. He sat down. *Were I British, I would now be organizing a raid in retaliation.* From what Sergeant Hokai had told him, there had been plenty of time for the British fighter pilots to see what had happened to their parachuting pilot that Horikashi shot down. However, it would take time for them to organize a punitive raid properly. *I doubt if the British fighters can be over Kuantan before three in the afternoon. The thing is to set up a patrol. I will fly it, I need to get into the air. My soul needs it.*

I'll take my Zero and patrol the area between Singapore and Kuantan. That way, by radio, I can warn the airfield of any British planes approaching. If the British retaliate, Kashimura thought, *they will fly the direct route because I don't think the Brewster Buffaloes have a very great range. I can order the rest of my squadron to stand by in strength, ready to be airborne so I could signal them on my radio to 'Intercept the British.'"* It was as good a plan as he could work out in the time he had. He opened the door and bellowed down the hall for the orderly.

273

Chapter 39: Sembawang Airfield, Singapore Island, January 25, 1942

From Kallang Airfield, where the P-40s had been stored, it was about 18 miles north to Sembawang Airfield. Frank, Johnny and Lisa were flying the distance at an altitude of 200 feet, barely clearing the green of the island, flashing over small native settlements huddled among the massive trees of the semi-jungle.

This flight, even if only a few minutes, after his recuperation, was a rebirth for Frank.

After landing at Sembawang Airfield, all three went to the mess hall for a meeting Johnny had called. With Andy Rogers dead, Flight Lieutenant Johnny Laws had unofficially taken over leadership of the squadron and was organizing the raid on the Japanese' Airfield at Kuantan.

All five squadron pilots were already assembled. Johnny went to the front of the room to open the unofficial briefing: "Because the *Tomahawk*s have no bomb racks and can't carry any bombs, we'll use those planes for flak suppression. But, before we get into more details, I have to state that I have no authority to organize this raid. Thus, anyone who is afraid of trouble for taking part in this raid should drop out now."

He paused. There were no takers.

"Altogether for the raid on Kuantan airfield, we have three *Tomahawk*s and five *Buffalo*es operational." Johnny continued, "The sixth *Buffalo* is down for maintenance."

"Now, let me introduce the crew. Captain Frank Carringer is a Yank fighter pilot. Miss Van Riin flew one of the P-40 *Tomahawk*s down from Mingaladon with us. She is a crack Aussie-trained pilot so there will be no special protection of our female member, and no stooging around like moths around a candle. She is better equipped to take care of herself in the air than some of you aces-to-be."

That brought a laugh, especially since Lisa's arrival and landing in a P-40 had created quite a stir.

"The three *Tomahawks* will come in early and beat up the airfield. The five *Buffaloes* will follow in at a low altitude and do the heavy stuff. Their call sign *'Penelope'* will distinguish them from the three *Tomahawks*, call sign: *'Ulysses'*."

Johnny pointed. "On the board, there's a sketch of the Kuantan airfield made by Sergeant Parker."

"Sergeant Parker served at Kuantan airfield before we evacuated it. Note that he has marked the old anti-aircraft positions; presumably, the Japanese will have used the pits we generously dug for them, and be using them now for gun emplacements. Their guns are very much similar to our 40-mm Bofors. Penelope Group, you stay away from the gun pits if you can. The Ulysses Flight, you take care of them.

"One more thing. The Japanese may have a standing patrol guarding their Kuantan airfield. To avoid it, we will go out to sea and fly out of sight of the coast to surprise them. Any questions?"

Frank raised his hand. "I suggest I take the north flak anti-aircraft emplacement as we run in. You and Miss Van Riin take the southern one." He would team Lisa with Johnny to give her some protection. *Johnny's the more experienced of the airmen here*, Frank thought.

Johnny nodded agreement.

"Anything further?" Johnny asked.

"Just wanted to give you the latest Intel," one of the men offered. "Tenasserim Province fell to the Japanese just after January 15th, and Moulmein was captured January 20th. They are catching up to us."

The *Buffalo* pilots asked a few more questions. These were soon cleared up and the Penelope Flight jogged out to their planes.

Because the P-40s were faster, they were to give the Brewster *Buffaloes* a lead so that the Penelope Flight would be arriving when the Ulysses Flight was already working over the Japanese gunners, or while the Japanese gunners were still taking cover, giving the *Buffaloes* a

The Ulysses Flight/ Paul Wankowicz

better chance of survival. Frank, Lisa and Johnny moved to the rickety porch to watch the *Buffaloes* snarl off the field.

As the sound of the departing Penelope Flight section quieted, all three Ulysses Flight pilots shrugged on parachutes and climbed into the P-40s.

Its well-familiar odors of paint, leather, gasoline, and human sweat felt to Frank better than any medicine. He completed his checks and waved readiness to Johnny and Lisa.

Johnny raised his hand and rotated it: Start engines! The Ulysses Flight is back in business.

Sixty minutes later, Frank could see the beach-fringed coast of Malaya coming up under the spinner of his fighter. Here the shore was cut into a mammoth triple scallop. The white dot of a town hugging it had to be Kuantan. Down below, sliding against the choppy waters in a tightly-bunched formation, Frank could see the *Buffaloes*. Their over-used engines left long, smoky trails behind them.

Navigation had been perfect. They had been intentionally losing altitude for the past 30 minutes, working themselves westward toward the town.

Now they were down to 2,000 feet. *We are at the point of no return,* Frank thought. *Close enough for Japanese spotters to see us boring in, and give an alarm.*

At the Japanese airfield, engines were coughing into life, while pilots desperately struggled into their flight gear. The Japanese flak crews were running to their guns, breaking out ready ammunition and jamming it into the breech.

All the way from Sembawang Airfield, we have been keeping radio silence. Now, Frank figured, *there's no further need to.*

Johnny's voice crackled in Frank's earphones. "Tally ho! Ulysses going in!" A cloud of smoke came from Johnny's fighter's exhaust as he fire-walled the throttle.

Lisa waved, too, and pushed her engine to full power and drifted

The Ulysses Flight/ Paul Wankowicz

away, opening the formation for the run in.

Frank grinned. Just like a cavalry charge in a Western movie at the Saturday matinee. This was what he had been born for!

He reached down, turned on the armament switches, and tightened his straps. The town flashed under him. Now he could see the airfield expanding and flattening as he tore toward it.

Intensely, Frank's eyes scanned the area. He had a bare 30 seconds to find and identify his target.

There it was!—just where Parker had said it would be. Black, spidery spreaders under its slim barrel . . . The Japanese crew desperately scrambled to get it ready to fire.

Frank touched right rudder. An olive-green fighter was moving on the ground, ready for takeoff. The red of its insignia was plainly visible.

A split-second decision. Delay would mean that gun crew could have its weapon firing. If the Japanese fighter makes it off the ground, it could cut the *Buffalo*es to ribbons, and prevent proper top support by the Ulysses Flight.

Get that plane. Flak will have to wait.

Frank eased the rudder and gently dropped the nose until the gold dot of the sight touched the canopy of the fighter. When his finger brushed the trigger, the P-40 bucked to its guns.

Delicate, smoky lines of tracer lanced toward the Japanese plane. They fell short, kicking up small volcanos of dirt under the left wing of the moving plane.

Frank swore. He was running out of range. He lifted the dot a hair and touched the trigger again. This time he had a short glimpse of his tracers going into the cockpit and the left gear of the fighter. Then, the nose of the P-40 blanked out the scene.

The Japanese flak crew had won the race. He saw tracer leave their gun, deceptively slow at first, then, faster and faster until it whipped past his cockpit at express-train speed. He was now at the boundary of the airfield. His wingtip raced just above the grass in a gut-wrenching turn as he tried to come back, to line up on the gun.

277

The Ulysses Flight/ Paul Wankowicz

Craning his head back to look out of the top of his canopy, he could see the crew serving the weapon. Tracer was coming out in a steady stream. It was not accurate. *The crew was still out of balance, thrown by the suddenness of the attack. In another moment, the reprieve would be over. The crew would settle in to make themselves comfortable, and become one with the gun. Then, they couldn't miss!*

He imagined himself as the gunners saw him, a top view of a fighter, but rapidly narrowing to a razor-thin silhouette of death, growing terrifyingly larger every second.

His entire being was concentrated on that translucent golden dot in the center of his sight. With infinite patience, he brought it up until it covered the mounting of the slender barrel. Again he touched the trigger.

The fighter shook from its guns as if in anger, and the cockpit took on the tang of cordite. The tracers reached delicately toward their gun, and where they touched, they whipped the crew aside as if dolls, flaying them into so many scraps of bloody clothing.

Then, he was over and ruddering hard to the right. Climbing for height with his head well back against the head rest, he was trying to see if he could spot the others.

Everything was happening in slow motion. It felt like it had been hours ago he had fired at the Japanese fighter, but there it was, still moving, its propeller bent, and its landing gear now collapsed.

In the distance, Johnny and Lisa were banking hard left as they rose from firing at the other gun. No tracers followed.

Beyond the dying Japanese fighter, several other olive-drab planes were moving for takeoff. The Japanese must have been On Alert, ready to go before the P-40s appeared. *We must keep them from taking off.*

Frank flung the control column to the other side of the cockpit. He might not be able to get them all, but maybe, just maybe, he could delay them, and cut the odds for the unwieldy *Buffaloes*.

As he came around, he could see the portly silhouettes of the first two *Buffaloes* coming in low over the town of Kuantan. They'd help

The Ulysses Flight/ Paul Wankowicz

strafe the Japanese fighters. He pulled his turn tighter to get his sight to bear. The edge of his vision was yellowing from the force of the turn driving his blood away from his brain. He leaned forward to reduce the pull.

When he saw a third flak mount, one nobody expected, laid out by the corner of the big hangar, he rapidly straightened out of the turn. He saw its two slender barrels swinging toward the first of the racing *Buffalo*es. It would be murder. The range was point-blank.

Fighters forgotten, he again threw his controls over, banking hard right, desperate to get his own guns on the lone weapon below before the *Buffalo*es crossed its field of fire.

For an instant, he thought he had made it; but, just as his finger tensed on the trigger, he saw the first plane of the Penelope Flight flash between him and the gun. In a millisecond, a ball of orange fire, the 40-mm rapid-fire shells slammed into the *Buffalo* fighter's flank, blowing off the canopy. The chubby plane hung there for an instant, as if unaware of its wound. Then, it began a roll to the left, knifing its wing into the sod of the airfield while the rest of it went cartwheeling across the field in a banner of red-gold fire.

Frank tore his eyes away from the scene and saw his own tracer bodily throw the crew away from the gun's conical mounting. He'd left himself very little room. Desperately he horsed back on the stick, rolling into a vertical chandelle to the right. He saw the corner of the hangar flash scant feet away from his wing, and then, the force of his maneuvers proved too much for his body, and the darkness of a blackout finally closed around him.

Even so, he could still hear. As his plane's engine labored with the loss of speed, he instinctively pushed the stick forward, and with that movement, his vision came back. He was at 2,000 feet, almost level. Below him, the Kuantan airfield stood as if a still-life of disaster, with the black skeletons of Japanese fighters, shriveling insects, burning in the pool of the shot-down *Buffalo*'s fire. A column of smoke rose vertically from a jagged hole in the roof of the hangar where one of the

The Ulysses Flight/ Paul Wankowicz

following *Buffalo* fighters had dropped its 500-pound bomb.

Japanese soldiers, who minutes before were scurrying to their posts, now stood—little stick figures—immobilized with the realization of the sudden disaster that had struck their airfield. In the foreground, lying like a hit bird was the Japanese fighter that Frank had first fired on. Its wounded pilot struggled to get out of the cockpit.

Frank had spent more time than he should have looking at the scene. Johnny's voice broke through his fascination: "Frank! Break left!"

It took a few seconds for Frank to assimilate the message, seconds during which his brain had to thread through the images of what was happening below, and to return to the reality of his cockpit. Priceless time which made it all too late.

Frank saw tracer lance past his right wing, and in the mirror, a thin, black silhouette aimed straight for him, wing edges sparkling with the star-like flash of guns firing. Within seconds, the Japanese pilot, wherever he came from, would correct his deflection, and the stream of slugs would be shredding into the P-40.

The Japanese pilot would expect Frank to break left, just as Johnny had advised. Frank's hand dropped to the cast aluminum landing-gear lever and pushed it down hard. He heard the moan of the electrics pushing his wheels against the windstream. The plane decelerated as if the surrounding air had turned to molasses. The other found himself overshooting.

Frank saw the Japanese fighter slide out of the right-hand side of the mirror. Seconds later it appeared on his right, still traveling faster than Frank's slowed-down P-40, with barely yards between them. Frank's eye was attracted to the vivid green dragon painted under the cockpit framing. He remembered that particular dragon. He'd had a glimpse of it that day in Tenasserim, the same day Johnny had arrived when they had almost been sighted by the two Japanese fighters battling the thunderstorm over that miserable little field.

Now the Japanese had almost matched Frank's speed, and the two were traveling together, as if in parade formation, yet powerless against

280

each other. Frank knew that lowering the gear had been only a temporary expedient. His seconds of inattention were now calling for pay-
ment. Frank felt the acid taste of fear in his throat.

The Japanese could out turn, out climb, and, generally, more than
match the American machine in any maneuver. Frank was trapped.

Were he at 10,000 feet, Frank would have been able to escape by
diving. The sturdy P-40 could out-dive the more fragile Japanese
machine. But, with the green folds of the jungle a scant 2,000 feet
below, such an escape was not to be his.

As soon as the Japanese fighter's speed fell sufficiently, the Japanese would swing into a gunnery pass. Frank could almost feel the
other's cannon shells thudding into his P-40, like the ones that had just
disintegrated the unlucky *Buffalo* minutes before. Already his mind had
accepted the reality of the next few minutes, and was turning toward
other things. *My plane would fall into the jungle, and the trees would
hide the wreckage, possibly forever. This is the way it feels to die. Lisa
will miss me.* He felt a wave of love and sorrow for her.

Frank could see the Japanese fighter quite clearly now, flying wing-
to-wing, the pilot looking at him. It was an older man with a lined, but
sympathetic face. A man too old, by American standards, to be a fighter
pilot. He must be good to be still flying. He reminded Frank of an
oriental Gepetto. Perhaps one of their Aces?

As their eyes met, it seemed to Frank that a bridge of communication formed between them. Was the other desperately trying to tell him
something? He felt better than if it had been spoken: unity, fear, compassion, apology between brothers, all rolled into one.

They could not stay side-by-side forever. Slowly, when the greater
air resistance of the other's radial engine started taking hold, the Japanese began dropping back for the *coup de grace.*

Frank let his hand drop to the throttle. Maybe, if he fire-walled it at
the moment the other was ready to fire, he could buy a few more
precious seconds. Prolong it, to give a miracle time to happen.

As the Japanese fighter slowly slid back, he could not take his eyes off the other pilot. Now, Frank could see the detail of the radial's cylinders under the lip of the cowl.

Apparently, the Japanese pilot had arrived at some sort of decision. Frank would never know what it had been, but he saw the uncertainty leave the pilot's face and saw him wave a fighter-pilot's salute with the left hand.

Without thinking, Frank waved back, as if a bond had been established between them. Those few seconds had inexorably combined their two lives. Oddly, he knew their brief contact had lifted some sort of burden off each other's shoulders. Now, the Japanese fighter was dropping astern faster and faster. Their moment of communication had not changed the reality of war.

Although everything seemed in slow-motion, Frank's time was slipping by fast. He tensed his hand on the throttle. The duel, which he was bound to lose, had begun. He twisted in his seat to watch, to guess the second when he must pour on power, to start playing out the hopeless game.

He could now barely see the Japanese pilot's face over the cowling. The other was banking in toward the gunnery run. Frank was concentrating with all his energy to try to out-guess him.

At first, the significance of the bright-orange flash didn't penetrate his brain, until without warning, the Japanese fighter disintegrated. One moment it was there; the next, there was the emptiness of the blue sky, only broken by a brown smudge of smoke, where several pieces of that plane smoldered as they fell. Frank found it hard to comprehend. *A pardon for me, not an execution.*

An olive-drab P-40 cut through the smoke, slipped clear, and took up position on his wing.

It was a triumphant, smiling Lisa, her thumb in the air, in the exultation of victory. Weakly, Frank waved back. She had heard Johnny's call to break, and had arrowed in with a perfect deflection shot. The 50-caliber guns had torn the less-sturdy Japanese fighter, and ignited the fuel.

The Ulysses Flight/ Paul Wankowicz

Frank felt a rainbow of emotions and was left without any strength at all.

Johnny's signal to re-form crackled over the earphones.

Frank would have said that it had been years since he'd heard the same voice with the desperate, too-late call to "Break." When in reality, it was only a few minutes ago, but he'd gone through a lifetime. He clicked his transmit switch in response. Together with Lisa, they banked toward the spot where Johnny's kite loafed against the sky.

As he banked, Frank saw the remaining four *Buffaloes*. They looked like crazily-painted bumblebees as they skimmed over the jungle in seeming haste to regain their own hive.

Stronger now, Frank waved again to Lisa, and smiling, pointed down at them. It was good to be alive!

January 26, 1942

Frank thought, *This debriefing will never end. It's a cross-examination, a search for details.*

"How many aircraft did you see?". . . "What color were they?" . . . "Are you sure?" . . .

The red tape of senseless reports! But it gave Frank the chance to review mentally the whole of the raid on the Japanese airfield at Kuantan and to tabulate results, which were impressive.

The exploding *Buffalo* had taken four of the taxiing fighters with it. Frank was credited with another on the ground and Lisa with an aerial victory. Six fighters for the cost of one. Johnny thought he had also seen a twin-engine bomber through the half-open doors of the burning hangar.

Frank wondered how low Johnny must have been to be able to see into the dark maw of the hangar.

The Intelligence Officer (I/O) conducting the debriefing was very

The Ulysses Flight/ Paul Wankowicz

unhappy with Frank's presence in the raiding force. There were no
forms for reporting combat by Yank fliers. As for Lisa, the I/O blankly
refused to credit her victory or existence.

But the other pilots would have none of that! They were elated that
Lisa had successfully shot down a Japanese fighter. She had become
sort of a rallying point, and they clamored for her to be credited for it.

On Johnny's suggestion, it was decided that the credit go to "L. Van
Riin of the Royal Dutch Air Force." It had an official sound. With
everything going to hell, as it obviously was, Johnny's opinion was that
no one would read the pedantic paperwork anyway.

In the end, when it was over, the Intelligence Officer departed with
his sheaves of paper forms and scribbled notes.

One by one, the sputtering engines faded. The *Buffalo*es were being
given a post-battle tune-up by the mechanics. With the coming of
sunset, the air was cooling down, and all of the planes were pushed into
their revetments or under camouflaging trees.

The bar had opened. A Sergeant-fitter, his hands still smudged with
engine oil, set out the bottles. Someone brought a bowl of watery ice
from the last functioning refrigerator, and the party was on.

Here, the weeks of hopeless fighting with inadequate equipment had
stripped things to their essentials. Uniforms, ties, squadron silver,
natives in white jackets, all were gone. *It isn't the same,* Frank noticed,
*as it had been in Rangoon. Just a bare, scuffed floor with a makeshift
bar manned by a solitary sergeant in battle dress. . . . Tired looking
ground bods mixing with the officers here in a break with tradition.* But
there was no more time for tradition.

Their victory over Kuantan had been a rare victory that knotted the
whole staff into a single band, and provided a release from the long
strain of lost battles, of missing friends who had not returned from a
battle. This evening the group collected into half-voiced little knots,
comparing memories, re-hashing maneuvers with their hands, and
drinking. . . .

The party, such as it was, broke up early. The battle, the drink, and

The Ulysses Flight/ Paul Wankowicz

the strain all took their toll. By 21:00 hours, the pilots were leaving. Some men staggered toward their quarters by themselves. Others were led, or dragged off, by their more sober companions or by someone from their ground crew.

Frank, Johnny and Lisa were the last ones remaining. Johnny said, "I'm going back to the squadron office to get the paperwork straight, because tomorrow there will be hell to pay when H.Q. learns of our little raid.

"You know where you're staying?" Johnny asked.

Frank shook his head in negation.

"It is much too late to return to the hotel. Anything moving across the island in the dark is liable to be shot at. The rumors of 5th Column activities are rife," Johnny explained. "I've made arrangements for you and Lisa to stay in the bungalow, two down from the one Mia and I are using. And I sent someone to your cottage to spruce it up, and light some lamps. It used to belong to a government *wallah*, but he was smart and debunked from Singapore early."

Frank noticed how tired Johnny looked. *Johnny's inability to assure Mia's leaving the island is cutting deeply into him.*

"Come on, let's walk down together." Frank suggested, "Do the paperwork tomorrow."

Johnny shook his head. "I still have things to sort out. You and Lisa go. I'll be along."

The path to the bungalow led down the steps, and then, left across the access road and the track to the village. Once across the road, they could see the large, square windows of the cottage glowing invitingly. They walked slowly, picking their way through the tropical darkness. Frank was very conscious of Lisa beside him. Earlier in the day, she had saved his life. *I need to thank her for it.* But as they walked, he found he couldn't put the phrases together. The silence stretched between them.

Since she didn't make conversation, he assumed Lisa didn't feel like conversation either. Frank thought he noticed a reflection of his

285

own tension in her.

Somehow, the idea of spending the night in a bungalow with her made her that much more desirable. His thirst for her had not abated.

He kept reminding himself of his promise that they would wait until they could have a proper marriage, complete with minister and all the bells and candles. But that didn't diminish his thirst for her.

They mounted the front steps and after they stepped inside, the flimsy screendoor banged shut behind them. Inside, the living room was partly-veiled in gloom. The shrouded furniture appeared ghostly against the half-lit darkness. The place smelled of dust, hot kerosene lamps, and lightly of mildew. The smell of abandonment.

Whomever Johnny had sent to 'spruce up the place' had not felt much should be done for mere, overnight guests. But the two bed-rooms, one on either side of the living room, had been better dusted. Kerosene lamps threw a cheery glow onto the well-worn flooring, and cast light onto the great luminescent cubes of mosquito-netting-shrouded beds in each sleeping room.

Frank turned to her. In the soft light of the lamp, he noticed she was wearing an enigmatic smile. Her beauty took his breath away.

"Which room would you prefer?"

She didn't hesitate. "The smaller one. You can have the big one. Okay?"

"Lisa?"

"Yes, Frank?"

"You saved my life this afternoon. Thanks." It sounded trite, dry. Not at all what he really wanted to say.

"You saved mine, back there in Tenasserim, so now we're even." She sounded disappointingly cool. Dispassionate. Women were some-thing he'd never understand, especially Lisa.

"Good night," he said, wishing he knew to say more.

"Good night." She picked up her lamp which had been left by the door and turned toward the bedroom. "Sleep well." She was still smil-ing that enigmatic smile.

The Ulysses Flight/ Paul Wankowicz

As if on second thought, she came over and gave him a sisterly kiss.
He wanted desperately to take her in his arms, kiss her properly, but
with her holding the hot lamp, there was no way. *Another proof of my
ineptness*, he thought. The moment passed. "Good night," he said.
She went into the room she had chosen.

His room was larger than hers, with unglazed windows set near both
corners. Screens against insects let in the nocturnal breeze, keeping the
temperature in the room bearable. Rain-shutters hung above them like
eyebrows. The furniture was all heavy Victorian. Originally the room
must have been the master bedroom. What furniture he could see in the
wan light of the lamp was overly ornate. As Johnny had said, the
property had belonged to some pompous colonial official. The huge
oversize, four-poster bed must have been his prized possession.

Looking at it, Frank wondered how many women had been rolled in
it. It was, like the furniture, massive. Four spiral-carved mahogany
pillars supported a baldachin of heavy, Victorian fabric. All of it contrasted blackly with the luminescence of the white-muslin, mosquito
netting which hung between the four posts like a tent.

Frank was tired. He turned the lamp low so it would last through the
night. Without much ado, he stripped naked, and stretched out on the
bed under the netting. Despite his fatigue, sleep failed to come. Pictures
flashed of the day's battle, invading his mind. . . . The Brewster exploding in a globe of flame cartwheeling into the Japanese. . . . That third
gun, more sinister in his imagination, all black with its splayed out legs,
like a malevolent spider. . . . A vivid picture of the Japanese fighter
spinning around its collapsing undercarriage, as its wounded pilot
struggled to clear the cockpit. . . . The face of the Japanese pilot, intent
on getting some sort of message across to him before resuming their
deadly dance. . . . And the memory of Lisa smiling, holding thumbs up,
as a reprieve from the death he'd already accepted as inevitable.

Lisa. . . . What could he do about her? He wanted her desperately,
but did she want him? *She had seemed so distant tonight, as if she'd
found someone else. Her smile could have meant anything, as if she*

The Ulysses Flight/ Paul Wankowicz

were bearing a decision, a secret—and yet so beautiful!
Frank rolled onto his back, his eyes still wide open. *I have to get some sleep. I have no idea of what tomorrow will bring.*

They could join Johnny's bunch at Sembawang, or stay in Kallang; however, it would not be safe in Kallang for long. Where could he connect with American forces? Now that Lisa was blooded, he wondered what she would do next. That smile bothered him. . . . And then there was the issue of the film. They still had not been able to locate anyone who knew the mysterious Fred Winterbotham personally.

Johnny had been right about Singapore. Things don't look good, not with the Japanese already at the gates. Frank felt a cool breeze come through the muslin and play over his body.

I should have turned off the kerosene lamp. It's light is too bright and it adds to the heat. It made the netting around him glow, like being under water, under a phosphorescent sea.

Lisa. . . . His desire for her was overpowering. *Somehow I must find a way to talk with her.*

Eventually, he must have dozed off. He didn't hear the door open as she came in. When he opened his eyes, the first thing he saw was Lisa's sheet-draped body, ghostly through the muslin. Even draped as in a Roman toga, she looked wonderful. The torrent of emotion passing through Frank almost paralyzed him.

She saw his eyes following her and raised a conspiratorial finger to her lips.

Without a word, she parted the netting, sat down on the edge of the bed with her back to him, letting the sheet drop away from her body. She was wearing nothing underneath.

Her body is beautiful! he thought.

Gently closing the netting, she slid in beside him.

Frank had never imagined perfection. The soft light filtering through seemed to heighten the beauty, the softness, the life.

He dared not stir, lest the slightest motion break the magic. As if on its own, his hand moved gently to her breast, cupping it. He felt the nipple harden under the gentle pressure.

She had stiffened for an instant, and then, with a slow smile, relaxed. "I've never done this before," she whispered. "Be gentle."

The realization of the gift that she'd brought him flooded his being. Slowly, he leaned over and kissed her. That seemed to melt whatever restraint there had been between them.

All sense of time was lost. They made love gently. Then, with a violence that spoke of the too-long-chaste time between them. Then, tenderly again.

His hands continued to explore her perfect body, lovelier than ever now. As did hers.

Finally, totally drained, they fell back onto the sheets.

After they'd rested a time in bliss, eventually, slowly, words crept back into their world. "I thought that it would be you who broke first, before we got to the Philippines," she said. "Were you ever going to get around to making it happen?"

"I dreamt of it, but I didn't know how you would react."

"I'm not made of stone, you know."

"I found that out. Tonight."

She laughed. "Neither are you."

"You had such an enigmatic smile earlier tonight, as if you'd found someone else. I was very unhappy with that fear as I fell asleep."

"I had. You. I decided it would be tonight, or never. After all, I saved your life, so you are mine, for a while at least. I was scared stiff by the decision, but very happy—Almost as happy as I am now."

There was a moment of silence.

"Frank?"

"Yes?"

"Do you love me?"

"More than anything, I love you." It was a promise, a commitment, for the rest of his life, for eternity. "I think that without you I would have shriveled up like a weed in a flame, I love you so much!"

"It's all right then." She paused again. "You almost got killed today." She trailed off, letting the thought dangle.

"I know," he said. They were both silent for a while, each inspecting their own worlds.

"It made me realize that time could be very short, but I didn't know how you felt. I didn't know how to approach it. I was scared, too, I guess . . . of nothing," he said.

She leaned over to kiss him.

This time it was much gentler but just as tender.

Afterward, total exhaustion took them both, and within minutes, Frank was asleep smiling, with her head on his shoulder.

Lisa lay awake for a long time, a warm smile on her lips. Maybe time would not be long, but another day, even another minute, was a greater treasure than she'd ever dreamt of.

January 27, 1942

The next morning, they were late to the mess hall. Only Johnny was left in the hall, struggling with a welter of papers before him. He glanced up as they came in. "Your P-40s have been serviced and rolled out for you. I must go to H.Q. to explain yesterday. I'll have to join you later. They have already commanded my presence. My old 'friend,' Wing Commander Porteous of the R.A.F., the Liaison Officer to the Australian Forces."

He looked at them more sharply. "You ought to do it more often."

"Does it show?" Frank ginned.

"To me, it does. You're both glowing. Congratulations!" Then, Johnny's face became more serious. "Things are speeding up for Singapore. They are now talking, for the first time, of evacuating Aussie nurses. Until now, it has always been: "Why go? We can keep the enemy out of Fortress Singapore forever." The brass is beginning to realize it takes more than bluster to keep the Japs out. Were I you, I'd get those long-range tanks on your kites and do a bunk-out of here."

Frank had found some long-range gas tanks originally brought in for the Fleet Air Arm's Fairey *Albacore* airplanes, but now useless for want of airplanes to put them on.

Frank smiled. "We already appropriated them." He and Lisa had been working on adapting them to the P-40s. The tanks would almost double the fighters' range. With the Philippines gone, they might have to fly them to Australia, assumed to be the next point of Allied resistance.

"Aren't you sticking with us?"

"Only if I can get Mia transportation out. It looks like it's going to be a *sauve qui peut*, roughly translated: the devil take the hindmost. There will be no room made for Mia on any of the boats. According to them, she's a *wog*, you know." His tone was bitter. "If she can't get off the island, I'm sticking with her, and will keep trying to find some way."

He paused, as if to organize what he was going to say next. "Say, could I use some of that American money we took out of Tenasserim? As bribes it might buy someone off."

"Sure. What's left of it. Lisa used much of it to pay the hotel while I was sick, but the rest is yours. I'd guess the Manila paymaster is in no condition to object."

"If I can't repay you when the time comes, I'm sure my father will. Lord Laws. Everyone in England knows him."

"I'm sure you'll be around. So don't worry." Frank said. *It's sad that the Ulysses Flight is being broken up, but it can't be helped.*

"Worse comes to worse, we could strip your P-40 and load her behind you. Not very comfortable, but it would get you both over the 300 miles to Sumatra," Frank said.

"The piggyback scheme again. I've considered that one already. It smells of running, somehow." Johnny paused before asking, "If you go, and I wind up behind, could I have one of the *Tomahawks*? It'd be

better than having a Brewster—and even those are in short supply
nowadays!"

Frank thought: *What if I must abandon Lisa? . . . Could I do it?* He
already knew the answer to that question. He, too, would stay no matter
what the price. Aloud Frank said, "Sure. But let's do everything possible to get her evacuated. The way I understand it, you're still under
Hayes' orders, so it's on the up and up. It would not really be running."
Frank hated the way Johnny looked drawn, tired and hopeless.

"Good. If you two go without me, don't forget the film of the
codebook. You know I haven't found anyone who knows Winterbotham here, but there may be someone in Sumatra. It could be very
important. You still have it?"

"Yes." With a pang of guilty conscience, Frank remembered that
he'd thrown the little metal canister which contained the film of the red-
bordered codebook's pages into the hotel dresser's drawer, along with
his socks and a sparse supply of underwear. He hadn't thought of it in
weeks. "I'm sure if we work on it, we'll find some way of getting
passage for Mia, especially now with the money."

Lisa had been listening to the conversation, and nodded in agreement. *I've grown very fond of Mia. Now that I'm no longer a virgin, I'd
like some less-constrained conversations, some good girl-talk with Mia.
There's a lot more I'd like to know about being a woman, a wife. . . .*

Johnny looked at his watch. "Okay. I better get over to H.Q. I'm
late already. Can you ferry your kites to Kallang without me? I'll get
the adjutant to warn the Flak people so you don't get shot at."

"Would it help if we went to H.Q. with you? To shoulder some of
the bawling out?"

"Good heavens, No! All I need is Yanks at my back. Then, they'll
really drag me through it!"

If it weren't wartime, a utility airplane would have come to pick up
Johnny and had him to H.Q. within 30 minutes. That as such was not
available, not even a lumbering *Albacore*, was another sign of things to
come. Instead, Johnny had to drive a requisitioned car.

The Ulysses Flight/ Paul Wankowicz

Johnny was right. The sooner Frank and Lisa left, the better.

To her surprise, Lisa's P-40 now sported a small Japanese flag on its
side under the cockpit. As she went out to it, she was surrounded by the
ground crew, grinning over her victory.

A grizzled Corporal intercepted her and said, "This is the only
bloody cheery thing that's happened in months. The bods asked me to
tell you that and thanks!" He looked a little abashed as he said that, but
the crew crowding behind him were all grins.

Chapter 40: Johnny's Brimming with Good News

Johnny didn't return to Kallang until the afternoon. Frank and Lisa were still working on installing the long-range gas tanks when they heard the sound of Johnny's Allison engine and broke off to see him land.

The sun was pouring down from a virginally-blue sky making the scene look like a South-East Asia painting by Canalletto. Johnny came in low over the fence. He hoisted his plane into a spectacular 1,000-foot stall turn. At the peak, he throttled back dropping the undercarriage and the flaps, then he kicked the P-40 toward the airport's end. He had judged things exactly, coming out of his dive just as he crossed the fence, holding up the airplane until it touched so delicately, it was hard to tell when the fighter ceased flying and became ground-borne. Johnny's whole approach had the exuberance of a victory roll, as if he'd found new energies since Frank had seen him in the morning.

Lisa and Frank stood together in the sunlight, shoulders touching. They watched the fighter turn off half-way across the grass, and taxi toward them.

With little bursts of engine, Johnny swung it around with a final peal of power and cut the switches. Before the prop had stopped turning, he was out of the cockpit waving a bunch of papers.

"Look at what I have," Johnny said. "Guess what these papers are!" His obvious good humor was infectious.

"Can't tell, old man." Frank answered, feigning an English accent.

"Mia's sailing orders, I got them! H.Q. called me in, not to tear off a stripe because of the raid, but to give me these!"

Lisa tilted her head trying to read the papers in Johnny's hand. Before he could go further, she interrupted. "It's addressed to 'Squadron Leader John Laws.' Real? Or a mistake?"

Johnny waved his hand in dismissal. "Real. Official. Came in the

The Ulysses Flight/ Paul Wankowicz

Daily Routine Orders from the Air Ministry several days ago. No one noticed, but that's not the point. I have Evacuation Orders for Mia! I had been going about it all wrong. But now I have them!"

"Well, let's hear the story."

"Let's get into the shade first."

They retired to the ramshackle hut the security crew used when the pilots were out on a mission. Once they had settled down around the rough table, Frank said, "Congratulations, Johnny. How the hell did you manage it?"

"Remember this morning, I asked you for money? Apparently, I was going in the wrong direction. The Aussie filled me in about what had happened before I got there. Here is what I learned. When the Intelligence Assessment of yesterday's raid on Kuantan had come to Porteous' desk, the Aussie said Porteous erupted. 'Who in the-bloody-hell does Flight Lieutenant Laws think he is? Another bloody Sholto Douglas?'

"The Aussie replied, 'Squadron Leader.'

"'What?' Porteous responded.

"'Squadron Leader Laws. It was in the Daily Routine Orders. Yesterday. From London,' the Aussie reported.

"Porteous erupted; 'He'll be back to corporal by the time I'm finished with him!'

"'The Australian Flight Lieutenant said, 'I shouldn't advise it. Do you know who his father is?'

"'Who? No. Who?'

"'You've been too long in Singapore. John's father is David, Lord Laws, the pacifist newspaper owner. He'd crucify you, and the R.A.F., if you so much as touched his son. He may not be the most popular man in England, but he has his following. You remember what he did to that chap who opposed him several years ago?'

"The Aussie said, at first, Porteous was silent for a while, then muttered, 'Won't do at all. Must have something done, or it won't look too good. . .'

295

The Ulysses Flight/ Paul Wankowicz

"So by the time I arrived at his office, Porteous was all smiles," Johnny said and continued the story.

"Porteous opened with, 'Let bygones be bygones.'

"It was quite a shock," Johnny said. "I had felt like a boy summoned to the headmaster's office. Instead, he handed me a write-up of the raid.

"'Is this accurate?' he asked me. 'It's for the press.'"

Frank interrupted. "Is your father *that* influential, Johnny?"

"Not really. But he hates Winston's guts and can be quite a muckraker. Everyone in the War Office is petrified to come under his glass."

Johnny quoted the release almost to the full. It started with the usual bumpf:

Royal Air Force Headquarters, Singapore: A singularly effective raid against the Japanese Air Installations at Kuantan was led yesterday afternoon by Squadron Leader John Laws, D.F.C. The intrepid, surprise attack destroyed at least five enemy fighters on the ground, as well as a number of installations around the airfield.

"They must have read the Intelligence bod's report," Johnny interposed.

One of the Japanese fighters was destroyed in the air by Cadet Officer L. Van Riin of the Royal Dutch Air Force, in a rare show of inter-service, as well as international cooperation. Officer Van Riin was flying with the squadron as an observer.

"That makes us even in promotions, Lisa! You're now a Cadet Officer!" Johnny said. "The release ended with:

Squadron Leader John Laws, who led the raid, is the son of Sir David, Lord Laws, Northern Yorkshire and publisher.

"When I finished reading the document," Johnny said, "I told Wing Commander Porteous it seemed all right. I didn't raise the question of Lisa; it would have challenged him. I wonder who had passed on the word about my father. So as it turned out, his career, not gold, was the valuable coin among the Regulars, even when on the brink of defeat.

"Then I said,'I do need to clarify one thing, Commander. I'm still a Flight Lieutenant, not a two-and-a-half striper as it says here.'

296

The Ulysses Flight / Paul Wankowicz

"Porteous feigned surprise. 'Haven't you heard? Your promotion came through in the Daily Routine Orders. Yesterday's D.R.O.s to be exact. Let me be the first to congratulate you!'

"I thanked him before I said, 'There is, however, another discrepancy. We did lose a *Buffalo*.' . . . I feel bitter about losing the pilot from the squadron. The picture of the stricken machine, left wing low, fire streaming from the cockpit as it angled downward to explode among the Japanese, is all still fresh in my mind. It saved the rest of us from the deadly onslaught by the better and more-maneuverable Japanese planes. I am familiar with those Japanese planes from my earlier experience.'

"Porteous replied, 'Oh, that. It's for Security. No use telling the enemy of our losses.'

"I smiled to myself," Johnny said. "The tangled and probably still-smoking wreckage of the *Buffalo* was most certainly lying in the middle of the Japanese airfield. By now, they probably know everything about the machine, and about its pilot.

"Then, as if we were old friends, Porteous asked me, 'How is your father, anyway?'

"He put the question with such a studied air of unconcern that immediately it made me more alert. I realized that while money isn't the coin, I'm apparently not without power. In many ways, I hated to play Porteous' game. But I wasn't asked if I wanted to play it, nor whether I agreed with the rules, so I played my trump card since my wife's life depends on it.

"'Last heard from, sir, he was fine. Very interested in the situation here, of course. I couldn't write too much about it. Censorship, you know. . . .'

"Frank, I didn't want Porteous to know that the last letter from my father was sent to Rangoon. It was carefully written full of paternal Victorian advice. I expected an immediate and vociferous reply to the mention of my marriage to Mia. But there was only cold silence. On the other hand, I'd hoped that if my father had indeed written such a mis-

297

sile, it was lost in the tangled war-time mails. I can only imagine its tone. . . .

"I realized if Porteous was feeling open-handed, a bit of a goad wouldn't hurt. I said, 'I haven't had much time to write him, sir. . . . By the way, while we're both here, has anything happened about transport—for the evacuation of my wife?'

"'Was coming to that. Have the papers right here.' Porteous pulled open a drawer. He took out the sheaf of documents and handed them to me.

"I quickly read the top line to make sure I knew what the papers were. I was not going to be fobbed off by the pompous Wing Commander. Then, I folded them carefully and tucked them into my shirt.

"As far as Porteous was concerned, the interview was just about over. 'One more thing,' Porteous said. 'The staff here feels that the American and the girl are quite irregular, although we wish to honor Wing Commander Hayes' directions. Do you know when they plan to leave?'

"I was glad I could answer," Johnny said. "I told him 'The ground staff at Kallang is working on their planes right now, sir. Getting them ready for a flight over to Sumatra. As you know, the *Tomahawk* is not a type of aircraft common here, so spares present a problem. I shall be going with them on Wing Commander Hayes' orders as soon as the kites are ready.'

"Then, I asked him, 'When do you think my wife will be sailing?' He got my point but he didn't show it. I'd already made up my mind. Trust no one. No one was going to send me off before I saw Mia safely onto a ship and out of the harbor.'

"His reply surprised me. 'The Dutch Ship *Nieuv Hoorn* is undergoing some minor repairs, and is almost ready,' Porteous replied. He said it shouldn't take more than four or five days. I promised to push the ground staff, so the *Tomahawk*s will be ready by about that time. He dismissed me with 'Be off with you. And remember, who it was, in the end, that got you these evacuation papers!'

The Ulysses Flight/ Paul Wankowicz

"I couldn't help smiling. . . . Of course, with them, it's protecting their careers which count. Especially, if you're on the losing side!" Johnny shook his head. "I guess the hold up in her evacuation papers wasn't so much Porteous as it was my own naivete on how the professional military worked."

Johnny brightened, "Let's all celebrate tomorrow evening at my bungalow."

"Great idea," Lisa said, and Frank nodded in agreement.

Chapter 41: Making Arrangements

The evening's celebration had to be called off. With a scant four days to departure, Johnny found himself introducing a new Commanding Officer to the squadron. He was a good man, but he came straight out of the bowels of the staff and was someone who had not flown for months, if not years.

The new C.O. was also unaware of the plight of the pilots flying obsolete equipment, serviced only with makeshift maintenance, carried out despite an ever-increasing shortage of parts. The long-awaited parts had been aboard the S.S. *Australian Princess*, which was sunk by a Japanese air attack within sight of the harbor.

With Johnny tied up at Sembawang, the rigging of the long-range tanks was left to Frank and Lisa. The tanks were British, not designed to fit American planes. What had originally been a leisure-time filler had now turned into a crash project.

Johnny had talked with one of his opposite numbers in the Royal Navy who said, "The Japanese have already established a destroyer patrol running as far as the Bangka Strait, some 300 miles south. Long-range patrol boats are assisting their destroyers. Apparently, they're hoping to cut off the evacuations out of Singapore.

"The Lieutenant said all he has are some river gunboats hidden in Keppel Harbor, left over from the China Station from our Imperial days on the Yangtze. Leftovers! Hardly a match against destroyers!"

Johnny was thinking. *An air patrol would help; it could spot the Japanese ships, and allow the Nieuv Hoorn to turn away from danger. But it would mean extending the flight time to match the ship's slow progress; but Mia's life could very well depend on these larger gas tanks.*

Although they were getting willing help from the R.A.F. ground crew at Kallang, the task of designing the necessary fittings for the fuel

300

The Ulysses Flight/ Paul Wankowicz

tanks fell on Frank and Lisa, who found themselves digging deep into half-forgotten knowledge they'd gained at engineering schools. They worked well together with Lisa making the necessary drawings.

"The joint between the fuel system and the tank will have to be strong enough to withstand a rough-field takeoff, yet fall away when the release is pulled," Frank told her.

"Once we work out the details, and draw up the design," Lisa said, "the machining can be done in a downtown machine shop. I know of one which is used to do design-work for the R.A.F."

As the design progressed, Frank was again amazed by Lisa. To hear her discuss the section's thickness, Young's modulus, or to see her sketch the parts, face drawn in concentration, made it seem as if she had been born to it, that she'd always done engineering.

They completed the drawings together and handed them off to the Corporal to take downtown and supervise the manufacture.

Once the drawings were on their away, there was really nothing more they had to do. Lisa cleaned up and dressed up to go into town for an audience with the Dutch Consul.

It so happened that when the Dutch Consul had read Porteous' press release, he sent word to the Liaison Office that he wanted 'Cadet Officer Van Riin' to appear before him. The Consulate had no record of anyone by that rank or name being in Malaya, and wanted a lot more information.

Frank intended to accompany her, but at the last moment, there were difficulties with the tank-release design so he had to stay behind and work through the changes.

When she returned from the meeting, she came back breathless."I've found him!" were the first words she said as she ran to Frank in the half-ruined hangar.

"Found who?" Frank asked, still deep in concentration staring at a design.

"My father! He's with Admiral Karel Doorman as his Intelligence

301

The Ulysses Flight/ Paul Wankowicz

Officer. In Jakarta!"

"Isn't Doorman the commander of the American, British, Dutch, and Australian naval forces?"

"Well, I would have put Dutch first, before American; but yes, they are fighting in the Java Sea, trying to halt the Japanese invasion forces there."

Frank had never seen her so radiantly happy. "How did you find out?"

Lisa laughed. "The Consul read Porteous' news release and wanted to meet 'the heroic Dutchman' who shot down the Japanese fighter. The Consul was more than a little lost when I walked into his office!"

Frank couldn't bear just to look at her, so he took her in his arms. "I love you, Lisa!"

She laughed again. "It's bloody lucky you do. Considering you haven't used your bed for days! But don't interrupt!"

Lisa returned to her story. "The Consul thought he knew all of his nationals around here. He even called Johnny to ask what he knew about me. I think he thought that I was some sort of an imposter. Johnny didn't help a bit by making heavy weather of the question. It worried the Consul since he couldn't figure out Johnny or me. . . . You really should have seen his face when I walked in!

"Once he got over the shock, he recognized me. He knows my father quite well. He even offered to wire my father saying that I'm all right and a bit of a military heroine." She paused, thinking. "I really should have taken him up on it, but I knew that we'd be in Palembang within days. That's only a two-hour flight from Jakarta, or Jogjakarta as it's known locally. What fun it will be to walk in on my father with you beside me! I can hardly wait! Having both my men right there!"

The Ulysses Flight/ Paul Wankowicz

January 29, 1942

The next morning, she happily dragged Frank by the hand from under
the fighter to "forget the war for a while and 'do' Singapore."

They light-heartedly rode into town like peacetime tourists. Frank
bought himself a small Kodak box camera, and with it, he
photographed her in front of the famous statue of Sir Stamford Raffles,
the founder of Singapore. The statue was in front of the Friday Mosque.
He took another photo of her at the Meriamman Temple. They toured
the Raffles Landing Place off River Valley Road, and showed more
than a tourist's interest in the remains of a shot-down Japanese Army
fighter dragged in front of the Cathedral by the home-defense forces as
a morale-booster. When they stood in front of the wreckage, they forgot
their tourist status, as Lisa examined the machine's armament.

While she was at it, an Australian soldier standing nearby turned to
Frank. "Say *cobber*, that sheila of yours seems to know a lot about
airplanes."

Frank could not resist it. "She should," he said. "She shot it down."

Lisa gave him a dirty look, but didn't say anything.

"*Dinky die*? You're pulling my leg!"

"No, really. She didn't shoot this one down, but one just like it over
Kuantan."

It took the soldier some time to digest the statement. "Say *cobber*,
what kind of uniform is that you're wearing?"

"United States Army Air Force."

That seemed easier to digest. "Is she a Yank, too?"

"No, she's Dutch." Frank was working his brain at top speed to
remember some Aussie Slang. He turned to Lisa. "Is this man *dinkum*?"
he asked.

She smiled. "True *merino*."

The Australian shook his head in bewilderment. "A Dutch sheila
who shoots down Japs and talks Aussie. Wait until I tell my *cobbers*.

The Ulysses Flight/ Paul Wankowicz

They'll think I was full of *goog!* Shake, Yank. You too, Miss!" He wandered off, still shaking his head.

Frank and Lisa had a hard time to keep from laughing out loud.

After that, they went to Fortnum's for ice cream and tea, and then more ice cream, before returning to the hotel, hot, breathless, and twice as happy—Everything except themselves forgotten. Events were moving fast. The next day would be the last that all four of them would have together in Singapore.

The S.S. *Nieuv Hoorn* repairs were now ostensibly completed, and would be sailing this night with Mia aboard. However, the afternoon started badly, with the heaviest raid on Singapore that the Japanese had yet mounted. This time they hit the docks and the adjoining Chinese Quarter. During the raid, a 500-pound bomb made a hit near to the shop that was working on the pieces for the long-range gas tank installation, killing the Corporal who was supervising the work. Frank went into town and salvaged two of the finished assemblies, as well as a third which was still being worked on at the time the bomb hit. It would have to be completed in some other undamaged shop.

The machinist who had been working on the third set of parts was not killed in the raid. Within an hour, and with the help of some American money, Frank had him working under the supervision of the Armament Sergeant. Although the third P-40 would not be ready first thing in the morning, the crew at Kallang thought they could have things put together by noon.

On this day, the air raid attack was over by three in the afternoon, but the warehouses and a lumberyard by the river burned well into the night. It spewed up columns of superheated flame and bathed the whole city in a flickering orange-pink light. The huge stocks of rubber in the warehouses, which were stockpiled by the British for the war effort in Europe, were also set ablaze, sending up clouds of thick, black smoke from which rained down a black, greasy, slippery soot.

The volunteer firefighting services battled to contain the fires, but were defeated by the fractured water mains, shattered by earlier bomb-

The Ulysses Flight/ Paul Wankowicz

ings. By dusk, the firemen stood, beaten, watching parts of the city
burn.

With the coming of twilight, it was time to take Mia to the ship. The
four of them went in Johnny's car as far as the Cathedral and, parking
the car, set out on foot toward the quay where the S.S. *Nieuv Hoorn*
was loading. The Cathedral parking lot was as close as one could drive
toward the north pier. The bomb-created rubble and the still-burning
fires forbade driving further.

Johnny carried Mia's little string-tied suitcase. As they walked, a
stream of people, some with children, some just husbands and wives,
joined them in a silent procession toward the ship.

*These are the lucky ones, the ones who would escape the final hell
that would be Singapore,* Frank thought. He felt a twinge of guilt: he
would be an escapee, too.

By now, the gravity of Singapore Islands was obvious, even to the most
obtuse. About the same time the Ulysses Flight had flown against
Kuantan, the Japanese had entered Johor Province, the quasi-independ-
ent state that was the last way-stop before Singapore Island itself. The
channel separating Singapore from Johor was only four-feet deep. The
Japanese would make short work of that.

To an onlooker, the Pacific looked like an unmitigated disaster. In
the Philippines, abandoned without reinforcements or supplies, the U.S.
Forces were reeling after Manila was lost the previous January 2nd.

To the north, the Japanese Army was poised, ready to enter Burma.
As Wing Commander Geoffrey Hayes had foreseen, 'It would be a
lightning campaign' that would bring the Japanese Army to Myitkyina
in a week. The bombing of Rangoon resumed on February 8th and the
Japanese would take not only Rangoon, but also would force the Allied
Armies, under the command of General Joseph Warren "Vinegar Joe"
Stilwell, to retreat up the Irrawaddy all the way to India.

On February 28, 1942, the once-proud Dutch Fleet, along with the

The Ulysses Flight/ Paul Wankowicz

U.S. Cruiser *Houston*, would be lost to an ambush in the Macassar Strait, leaving the Eastern Pacific totally at the mercy of the enemy.

By that time, Geoffrey Hayes would be dead in some Burmese paddy, buried under the wreckage of his inadequate *Buffalo*. In the last frantic days of Burma's defense, his body would never be found.

The history of the next months would be one of continuous losses in Asia until the cryptographers would, through the reading of the Japanese Naval Code, allow the U.S. Navy to win a victory at Midway Island in June 1942. But that was all in the future. At the time, for the four of them, the future looked bleak.

As they walked toward the dock, with Mia and Johnny leading, glass, like crusty winter snow, crunched under their feet and sparkled with thousands of reflections from the surrounding fires. Johnny incongruously remembered seeing a Hollywood musical where the sidewalks in heaven were studded with diamonds. He remembered that the musical was also full of dancing, and scantily-clothed, very feminine angels.

On the quay itself, a Malayan wearying a P&O purser's hat had set up a deal table and a hurricane lantern. A sheaf of papers lay in front of him while he checked the passengers' permits against a grubby list clutched in his hand. Official sanction to the operation was given by the figure of a solitary British Army Corporal, complete with rifle, standing beside the table, wearing full battle kit. Johnny had no doubt that his rifle was loaded. The panic had not hit yet, but it would soon, and then it would take more than just a solitary soldier to keep the unauthorized from trying to win space aboard the last of the leaving ships. The Corporal looked as imperturbable as the Rock of Gibraltar among the milling, despairing humanity and the lurid, swaying flames behind them.

Regardless of the growing line of people, the Malayan Official went through the same painstaking routine with each passenger. He first scrutinized the list, and compared letter-by-letter, the names on the orders with the passports or papers carried by the individuals. Holding

The Ulysses Flight/ Paul Wankowicz

the papers close to the lantern, he squinted from it to the face of the permitted, as if cataloging the features for future reference. Satisfied, he would imperiously motion the person toward the ship, and then, he attended to the next person in line.

As Johnny and Mia came forward, the Malayan Official cast several glances from him to her, as if unbelieving that a native, a Chinese at that, would have the temerity to join a line of British refugees. His obvious surprise mounted when he glanced at the papers Johnny handed him, and realized that it was, in fact, only the Chinese girl who was to be evacuated. He made several painstaking comparisons of the name on the orders against the list, looking over both sides of her papers as if to spot a forgery. He double-checked her papers and picture, and finally, reluctantly, motioned her on.

Johnny, his temper boiling over at the Malayan's disdain, made as if to follow her, but was stopped by the man's peremptory motion. "It is not permitted," the Malayan Official said.

"I would like to accompany my wife to see the accommodations."

"It is not permitted."

Mia put her hand on Johnny's arm. "I guess we say good-bye here," she said gently.

Although he was still furious, Johnny realized how right she was. *This self-important clerk holds the key to Mia's, and therefore to my happiness.*

They stepped to the side where he could take her in his arms. He held her for a long, long time. Reluctantly, they broke apart.

"When I go up the gangplank, Johnny, turn around and go home," she said. "I couldn't bear to see you standing there and not be able to go to you. Please."

He nodded, dumbly. "I will, Mia. Anyway, I'll soon see you in Jakarta. Keep well."

Without another word, she walked quickly up the ramp and toward the brow.

Standing on the cement of the dock, Johnny felt old and helpless.

307

The Ulysses Flight/ Paul Wankowicz

As soon as she disappeared in the maw of the hatchway, he turned to rejoin Frank and Lisa, but the Corporal barred his way.

"Don't pay any attention to that silly bugger, sir," the Corporal said. "If you want to go on board that boat, I won't notice. An' if you don't come off, I won't notice that either, sir."

"I'd like that very much, Corporal, but I still have things to do here." He paused. "But why don't you? I wouldn't notice," Johnny said to the soldier.

The Corporal looked at him incredulously. "I'm still in the British Army, sir!" It was a simple explanation, but apparently the Corporal thought it sufficient. His eyes moved to the striped ribbon under Johnny's pilot's wings.

"I was in England in August '40, begging your pardon, sir," the Corporal said. "On a 40-mm. Bofors just outside of London. I saw you people in your *Spitfire*s and *Hurricane*s. It was a bloody-good show, sir. Not to be forgotten. Not by me." The Corporal stopped, as if embarrassed by what was probably the longest speech he'd ever made.

"I see. Thank you, Corporal." Johnny nodded. As he turned away, Johnny seemed to stand a little straighter. *Maybe it had been worthwhile, after all.*

Lisa looked at Frank, her face oddly-painted by the firelight. "I'm glad we're sticking together," she said quietly. "I don't think I could stand being separated from you, not now." He felt her hand in his.

They caught up with Johnny's solitary figure, and made the long silent walk past the burning city to where the car was parked, and passing people who were still thronging toward the quay.

308

Chapter 42: Flight from Singapore to Bangka Channel

Johnny planned to return to Kallang by noon in one of the *Buffalo*es, then he could switch to one of the P-40s. By then, Frank and Lisa would be waiting for him. As the Ulysses Flight, in the now newly modified P-40s with the longer range, they would fly the afternoon patrol over the *Nieuv Hoorn* to protect the ship, but more importantly, to protect Johnny's Mia.

"The *'Buffo*es,'" as Johnny now called them, "will be all right patrolling the ship until I get back at about noon. After that, the ship will be out of their range. The *Tomahawk*s with your long-range tanks will come in useful. It will be a long grind, so save your strength."

The plans were that Johnny and two pilots along with squadron's *Buffalo*es would fly the first patrol above the *Nieuv Hoorn* with Mia aboard. Frank had suggested that he join Johnny in the morning, but Johnny would not hear of it. "We'll need you fresh and bright-eyed," he said, "for the grind to Bangka Strait. For that leg, the three of us will be all alone," he added.

January 30, 1942

Frank awoke the next morning to see the sun already slanting past the gauze curtains and beginning to charge the room with heat.

Lisa was in the little alcove with the silver-plated tray of tea and coffee which the boy brought every morning. Tea for her, coffee for him. Lisa was humming to herself as she fussed over the tray.

Frank felt unhappy and tired. He wondered if the unhappiness was, or could be, a premonition. He remembered Halliday's words which had brought a feeling of foreboding, a feeling of being trapped in the last act of a Shakespearean drama—as if events in life had become

309

predestined. He looked out of the window at the palm trees. Time to rearrange his thoughts.

As Lisa hummed to herself, her thoughts were undoubtedly on the reunion with her father. She'd mentioned again how happy she would be to have 'both her men' beside her when they met him.

When Frank looked out of the window, he saw the three stubby fighters heading south. It had to be Johnny going out to patrol over the *Nieuv Hoorn.* Involuntarily, he glanced at his watch. Eight o'clock. "There go the *Buffalo*es," he called to Lisa. "Right on time!

"And we'll be taking off at noon!" she said. She came over to look out the window, and leaned against his shoulder, her body against his.

Very conscious of each other's presence, they watched the silhouettes of the three planes vanish in the distance.

He felt a pang of irrational, almost infinite sadness. The morning seemed out of joint.

"Johnny and Mia deserve every chance they can get," she said. "They are the best, both of them!" She added, looking at her watch. "If we are to fly at noon, we'd better get ready, and put our gear in order."

Frank looked around the room. It had served them well. He felt a pang of regret at leaving their 'honeymoon suite.'

"After the war," he said," we'll have to come back here. We'll dance and sit under the palms on the tropical beach and soak up the sun. Do what civilized people do!" But inwardly he wondered: *Would we ever come back? Will we be able to?*

They arranged their meager gear to take, and then distributed what was left among the ground crew at the hotel and a group of newly arrived R.A.F. pilots, an advance party for a *Hurricane* Squadron brought in to defend the city.

They seemed to Frank to be inordinately cheerful, unaware of what was waiting for them. One of the group told Frank a Yank by the name of Donahue was flying with the R.A.F. squadron. He would be arriving in a few days ferrying another one of the fighters in. Frank would have liked to have met him.

310

The Ulysses Flight/ Paul Wankowicz

What remaining American money Frank had went to settle the
Hotel bill. Even with the Japanese looking over their shoulder, the
accounts had to be straight!

When they got to Kallang airfield, it was almost noon. The P-40s had
been lined up on the apron, engines warm. The extra-range tanks
looked indecent to Frank's eyes. Their bulk broke up the belligerent
outline of the little fighters, making them look overly-heavy and awkward. The bottoms of the tanks were just four inches from the ground.

The Crew Chief told Frank, "The ground crew was worried about
the danger of the low-slung, gasoline-filled tanks, so we walked over
the takeoff path, inspecting it for any obstacles or craters which could
snag the tanks. Don't want any sparks that could set the airplanes
afire."

They had also hung out two white bedsheets over the fence as
markers. As long as the fighters stayed between the two, they would be
all right.

Frank and Lisa thanked them for these considerations. They discussed holding the P-40s down a little longer than normal to assure
themselves of a clean break with the ground.

While they were standing there, talking with the ground crew, the
three *Buffalo*es appeared, snarling low over the Kallang airfield.

Frank watched the lead ship detach itself and float in over the fence,
bouncing twice before finally becoming ground-borne.

As the first *Buffalo* plane taxied up, Frank checked its gun ports to
see if there had been trouble. Much to his relief, the ports were clean.
He took this to mean everything was still all right with the *Nieuv
Hoorn*.

Climbing out of the *Buffalo*, Johnny was exhausted. Starting at
dawn, he'd flown two patrols over the ship and was visibly tired.
Nevertheless, he was eager to takeoff again. Every moment the ship
Nieuv Hoorn was left unguarded with Mia aboard was agony for him.

311

The Ulysses Flight/ Paul Wankowicz

A British Navy friend of Johnny's gave the Dutch Skipper the frequency that the fighters would be using so the *Nieuv Hoorn* would be able to listen in on the Ulysses Flight as they orbited over the ship. However, while the planes could radio each other, the ship would not be able to speak with the planes.

Johnny, Frank, and Lisa stood silently, of one mind, shoulder to shoulder in the sunlight in front of the fighters, for the last few moments, temporarily reluctant to break the spell of their unity.

Goaded by Johnny's impatience, they soon broke up, each to his own machine.

Despite the glorious sunshine and the cloudless sky, and the closeness of the three of them, Frank could not shake off his earlier feeling of fatigue and foreboding. Frank should have been looking forward to the delivery of the fighters to some U.S. command, and to have some recognition of the work he'd done to accomplish that, but all he could feel now was gloom. Perhaps he was grieving that he would have to surrender what had become his three personal aircraft. That thought amused him and his mood brightened.

"Everyone have his own canister of film?" Lisa asked.

Frank tapped his shirt pocket, and Johnny nodded yes.

As soon as Frank was in the cockpit, the familiar routine took over, driving any other thoughts out of his mind. He made a quick eye-sweep of the interior, left to right, to make sure everything was in its place. He went through the checklist in his mind. *Set the trim. Pump the emergency hydraulic pump a couple of strokes to make sure there's pressure in the landing-gear system and that the gear won't suddenly collapse. Check the parking brake. Master switch on. Mixture back. Magneto to 'L.' Pump the hand fuel-pump. Sixteen pounds on the gage. Two shots of prime. Stick full back. Switch starter on. Look around to make sure the area surrounding the plane is clear. Mechanic is in front. Fire extinguisher at the ready. Listen to the rising whine of the inertia wheel. Now! Switch to engage. Keep the wobble pump going. As engine fires, mixture to Full Rich. Hand on throttle.*

The Ulysses Flight/ Paul Wankowicz

The beat of the Allison became muffled and irregular at first as the engine burned off the over-rich prime, spewing clouds of heavy, blue smoke out of the exhaust. Then, the carburetor took over and the rhythm evened out, building a solid wall of power and noise. The temperature gages began their crawl upward.

Check the parking brake again. Run up to 1,500 rpms, check mag-netos, first left, then right. Keep stick full back as it vibrates, battered by the near-solid air streaming from the propeller.

With the left hand, motion to the mechanic to pull the chocks. The fighter is ready to roll!

Frank glanced right and left to make sure both Johnny and Lisa were ready. All three olive-drab fighters had the engines running and ready. The little Japanese flag under Lisa's cockpit shone bright against the drab paint.

She and Johnny were looking toward him: the Ulysses Flight. Just like its beginnings in Tenasserim, only now they were an experienced team. Further delay was pointless, it would only overheat their engines.

Frank raised his hand, motioned ahead, releasing his parking brake as he did so. As he pulled out, he noticed the ground crew standing at rigid attention, saluting a final farewell. He returned the salute, feeling the twinge of guilt again.

Singapore would not be easy for them once the Japanese entered.

The grass looked fresh and green, speckled with small yellow flowers that he'd never noticed before. A quick glance around told him that there was no other traffic in the air, friendly or Japanese. Forward on the throttle watching the temperature.

Another glance around, Johnny and Lisa were steady on his wing as the three airplanes accelerated over the grass.

Much to his surprise, Frank was airborne before he was more than four-fifths down the field. *Wheel selector to up, push the hydraulics button on the control column.* The fuel tanks seemed only to minimally affect the flying characteristics. That was good. Above his banked wing, the long pink exterior of the Hotel flashed past. Then, he was turning toward the bay with the stone bulk of the Cathedral below. The spotless lawn of the Cathedral was now disfigured by lozenge-shaped mounds of fresh earth, new graves.

Beyond the Cathedral wound the river. A great charred expanse of the burned-out lumberyard in its bend, with the blackened skeleton of a fire engine in the middle. Blue smoke was lazily rising to meet him as he swept over.

Then, he saw the empty quay where the *Nieuv Hoorn* was moored last night. The deal table now stood abandoned in the corner of the expanse.

Out into the bay, sunlight sparkled off the wavelets, and myriads of little islands dotted the water.

Over his shoulder, Frank could see Johnny and Lisa following his slow climb. He eased the rudder to correct a few degrees to the right, onto the heading Johnny had given him just before takeoff. It was going to be a long flight.

He eased his shoulder straps and shifted himself into a more comfortable position.

Two hours later, Frank's cramped muscles were beginning to ache.

They were holding an altitude of 12,000-feet, high enough to be able to intercept any Japanese bombers if they should show at under 10,000 feet, but not so high as to be forced to use their scant supply of oxygen. Nevertheless, Frank could tell that the rarefied air was beginning to slow his reflexes.

A merciless sun beat down from the deep blue sky, the curvature of the Plexiglass canopy above him seeming to concentrate its rays on his head and itching shoulders. As with all the P-40s, hot air from the oversized radiator under the engine spilled into the cockpit ventilation system further raising the temperature.

Frank leaned forward and cranked the canopy open a turn, instantly letting in the refreshing air, but also the nerve-shattering roar of the engine's exhaust. The noise was hardly muffled by his helmet.

The Ulysses Flight/ Paul Wankowicz

They had leaned-out the mixture, cut back the propeller rpms to
stretch their range as far as they could, but that meant the engine
temperatures had to be monitored constantly and adjusted by cranking
the radiator-shutter control.

Frank's eyes were getting tired from shifting from the glare outside
to the shaded gages at the bottom of the instrument panel. His now
oxygen-starved brain was beginning to refuse to make sense of what he
saw.

Under him spread the limitless ocean. Lisa's and Johnny's fighters
were hanging in the same position that they had held for hours. Painted
planes over a painted ocean. They were flying in a great, ten-mile-wide
circle to protect the ship.

Down below, the S.S. *Nieuv Hoorn* seemed to stand still at the head
of the thin, white lines of its arrow-shaped wake. The only change in
the past hours was a hint of building clouds, dim in the heat haze, on
the southern horizon.

A glance at the map told Frank that those clouds were probably
forming over the coast of Sumatra, close to the Bangka Channel, which
was believed to be the current limit of Japanese operations.

Frank wondered if Mia's ship would ever reach it. He knew that,
even in their leaned-out setting, the fighters' fuel quantity would be
critical long before the ship was close to that channel.

*If a Japanese warship ever found the Nieuv Hoorn, what could
three fighters do against it? Even if we skimped on the reserve required
to enable us to reach and land at Palembang, it seems all so futile.*
Frank tried to shake the thought. He wondered if the Japanese had
missed the red codebook at all.

He heard the hum of a transmitter in his earphones. "Tally ho!
Below and to the right. A Kawashini flying boat." It was Johnny.

I should have seen the boat. I must be getting drowsy. Frank swung
his eyes to the indicated quarter, and there it was, 2,000-feet below. A
four-engine, high wing, painted dark olive to make it hard to spot
against the deep blue of the tropical sea or jungle. Only the Japanese

hinomarus, the red circles on its wings near its tips stood out, a round of crimson red, outlined in white.

As Frank watched, the great Japanese flying boat throttled back and started down for a closer look at Mia's ship below.

Frank was now fully alert. He pushed the transmit switch: "Ulysses Leader. Number two and three, go after it. Keep your tanks. Ulysses One will stay topside to cover."

He heard the click of Johnny's and Lisa's transmitter switches in acknowledgment as both throttled back and began dropping downward. As they went, he saw Lisa's plane slip back and cross over onto number two position on Johnny. It was smoothly done, as if she'd practiced it all her life. She'd learned fast.

He tore his eyes from the fighters below, and methodically scanned the horizon. Except for themselves and the Japanese, the sky was empty, as if evacuated. *There's no reason for the Japanese to send fighters to protect their observation aircraft.* Frank realized, *Their error.* For right now, the Ulysses Flight ruled the airspace.

Johnny's transmitter came alive again. "Detached section, arm guns. Turn on sight. Adjust reflex sight to 130 feet!"

Good man, Frank thought. *In case Lisa forgot the drill.* Down below, all three airplanes had now shrunk to model size in a panorama of battle. Frank watched his two fighters leisurely close in on the Japanese. They looked impotent and puny against the flying boat's larger bulk.

The Japanese crew must be concentrating on the ship below. There's no sign of their being aware of the death stalking behind them.

Frank remembered what Hayes had once said: "That a fighter does not fight, but murders out of stealth." He realized that he was watching the truth of those words now. Lisa was now swinging wide to give Johnny more room. She would come in scissoring from the side, disorienting the gunners, giving Johnny a clear field of fire. Frank wondered if she'd discussed maneuvers with Johnny, they were so well coordinated.

The Ulysses Flight/ Paul Wankowicz

First, there was a tentative splash of tracer from Johnny's guns, and an almost immediate reply from the flying boat. Both strings of tracers went wide. It was too late for the Japanese crew to wake up now.

Johnny's fire eased to the left, and the Japanese tail gunner fell silent.

Seen from 2,000-feet above, the battle had a fascinating, slow-motion quality. The two minuscule fighters passed under the larger aircraft like minnows playing with a dolphin.

Frank saw Johnny break off his pass to the right to give Lisa a clear field for her approach.

Before she could get into position, a small, shy flame appeared behind the cowl of the flying boat's right inboard engine.

Lisa saw it and sheered off.

For a few seconds, the fire clung there as if uncertain of its life; then, it rapidly grew bolder, expanding into a banner of fire.

The big Japanese flying boat was obviously doomed, yet it continued on its path, as if the fire was of no concern to it.

Frank tried not to imagine what must have been going on inside that hull: panic, blood, realization of sudden death.

The fire had now grown. It was flicking at the edge of the horizontal stabilizer, stripping off parts which tumbled behind in the ribbon of smoke trailing the stricken aircraft. The flame reflected a dull orange from the dark paint on the side of the boat's hull, giving it an ethereal look.

Within minutes, the fire could be seen inside the wing, melting structure. With a sudden wrench, the wing broke away and tumbled aft trailing its own golden banner of fire. The crippled flying boat rolled like a harpooned whale, and plummeted down to hit the water in a messy circle of foam.

Within an eye-blink, the sea closed over it, leaving only a lone wing still spiraling down, trailing a thin veil of smoke, a last appeal.

When they pulled into position, Frank saw Lisa and Johnny smiling. Frank signaled 'thumbs up.'

317

The Ulysses Flight/ Paul Wankowicz

They cheerfully waved back. They took up another orbit around the *Nieuv Hoorn.* Mia was still safe. But the moment of euphoria was short. Frank wondered, *Did the Japanese flying boat represent danger? Or, when it looked over the steamer then proceeded on its way, was it convinced that the rusty veteran of a ship below was not a worthwhile target? On the other hand, a fighter-escorted freighter, no matter what its condition, would excite someone's attention. And there had been enough time after Johnny and Lisa's first pass for the boat's crew to radio back a description.*

Frank now watched the northern horizon with greater care. That was the direction from which Japanese bombers would come.

He didn't have long to wait. It had taken the Japanese a scant half hour to digest the information received from the dying seaplane, and to divert whatever strike force they had in the air which was, in all probability, planned for the afternoon's raid against Singapore.

Frank could see them, a smudge on the horizon, an occasional glint from a window or propeller betraying their position.

There would be 21 of them flying at 16,500 feet.

Frank hit the transmit switch: "Tally ho! Climb, climb, climb!" He realized he'd been hanging around with Johnny too long, he was beginning to talk like an Englishman!

Frank's throttle was already at maximum power. There was no time to lose. As he climbed, the great panorama of the jungle of Sumatra emerged from beyond the horizon. The whole of Bangka Island below shone dark green against the ocean's blue.

By now, he was already on oxygen. The mask smelled of etherized rubber, a familiar smell. He leveled off at 20,000 feet, leaned forward to slide open the canopy a crack, and let in some cooler reviving air.

He could see a Japanese formation rapidly overtaking Mia's ship. Wings and fuselages glinted in the sun, 4,000 feet below.

He glanced over his shoulder. Lisa and Johnny were in position. They would depend on his timing, his judgment.

Frank flicked the switch. "Line astern! Go for number one and

318

The Ulysses Flight/ Paul Wankowicz

number two. That's where the bomb-aimers are. Turning right—Now!"

He swung the stick to the right and watched the horizon tilt and slide up on the windshield, as his P-40 started the long, falcon-like dive that would bring them level with the Japanese planes and into firing position. He could see Johnny and Lisa in the rearview mirror. The two airplanes were scissoring into position. They were moving now like professionals, a far cry from the original *ad hoc* crew that had left Tenasserim: a neophyte American, a Battle of Britain pilot and a civilian female, now his family. He switched off the belly tank, now empty and an encumbrance in battle, and pulled the makeshift release.

Lisa's transmission came almost immediately. "Ulysses Leader, your tank is clear!"

Within seconds, he heard her clear Johnny's and then, Johnny's voice telling Lisa that her fuel tank was away.

He toggled his switch: "Arm sights and guns. Set the sight to 80 feet."

Sergeant Pater had given them these settings of the reflex sight for everything operating over Singapore.

Then breaking off to the right, where the fire of the Japanese gunners was less able to reach. Re-form for another pass in a blood-draining turn.

Looking back at it, Frank realized, again, it had been a textbook approach—each fighter hurtling toward the leaders of the Japanese formation, with 50 and 30 mm guns hammering.

The lead Japanese bombardier didn't have a chance. With his wing already on fire, he slid out of formation on the Ulysses' first pass.

Number two was a little tougher. It took two passes before the Japanese plane began dropping out, but appeared unhurt. Frank watched the Japanese plane's dive steepen until the fuselage was vertical to the sea. Before that plane could lay over on its back, it came apart, leaving a long, glittering trail of aluminum following behind. Frank lost sight of him as he hauled out of range.

The remainder of the Japanese flight formation was already begin-

The Ulysses Flight/ Paul Wankowicz

ning to look more and more like a bevy of sheep. They salvoed their bombs helter-skelter, then turned for home.

Below them, the *Nieuv Hoorn* plodded on unhurt. The fight had not all been one sided: One bullet had hit Johnny's plane's cooling system. *The only thing Johnny can do now is to ditch,* Frank thought.

He watched Johnny make a long approach to the ship below, trailing a light-blue cloud of coolant vapor behind his plane. His propeller was stationary. The plane ended in a welter of white foam close to the stern of the freighter.

Frank made a low-altitude drag to make sure Johnny was not hurt. When Frank saw Johnny climb out onto the wing and wave, he was reassured. Right away a lifeboat was lowered from the *Hoorn* to pick him up, almost dry-shod. Frank heaved a sigh of relief.

Back at cruising altitude, he gave a thumbs up signal to Lisa to let her know Johnny survived okay.

Now started the dreary time. Frank was very conscious of the new gap in their formation that ditching Johnny's plane had left—almost like the "missing man flyby" had been for his friend Kenny so long ago.

Frank was glad Johnny was now safe with Mia, but it also signaled the breakup of the Ulysses Flight had started. Would it be irreversible?

They shouldn't have shot down the Japanese flying boat. *If we hadn't done that,* Frank now felt, *the freighter would still be safe and Johnny would still be in the air with us. It's all my fault.*

He looked over his shoulder. Lisa was there, bent over the controls, looking lost in her own thoughts.

Tiredness was setting in. Down below, evening was coming, darkening the surface of the sea, lengthening the shadows that were drifting off the spine of Sumatra.

Within the next 30 minutes, darkness would soon be reaching up to their altitude. They would have to find their way into Palembang Airfield at night. Frank didn't know whether that airfield would be illuminated or not. Johnny had only given him the colors of the day to be fired from his flare pistol. Hopefully, that would keep the Dutch from shooting at them, but they would still have to find the blacked-out city. Radio was useless. Palembang Airfield was operating on a radio frequency for which they didn't have crystals.

He'd been orbiting the fighter in a constant left turn. Time to break the monotony. Frank straightened the machine to start an orbit to the right.

That movement saved his life. A clutch of tracers cut past his wingtip, slicing the air where he would have been, had he continued circling to the left.

Reflexes took over. Back and over on the controls, at the same time yelling to Lisa over the radio, "Break left!"

As he fell from the apex of his turn, Frank had a quick, knife-edge-sharp glance of the Japanese fighter coming at him out of the sunset. He held desperate top rudder, letting his plane arrow into a dive.

He saw only a glimpse of Lisa's plane peeling away as the olive-drab of her fighter blended with the dark of the sea two miles below.

The Japanese fired another string of tracer, brilliant orange. It missed, but closer this time. It was just a matter of time before his opponent would get the measure of Frank's desperately-slipping fighter.

Frank kicked the rudder pedal from the hip, reversing the rudder into a left skid. The plane's speed built up as he plummeted down. *Can the plane build up enough speed to tighten the other's ailerons? And reduce the Japanese pilot's edge in maneuverability? It's a crazy, deadly chase.*

Wind was screaming past his cockpit. He's coming closer. *Time to move. Roll to the right, as if to a split-S.*

In his rearview mirror, he could see a miniature of the Japanese plane following him through the maneuver.

Tightening his stomach and hunkering down to reduce the G-forces, Frank racked his turn tighter, engine screaming in protest, wings on the point of stall.

321

The Ulysses Flight/ Paul Wankowicz

The Japanese pilot had followed Frank into the start of the split-S but recovered slowly enough to give Frank a slim edge. As Frank tightened his turn, he came out astern of the now-frantically-rolling Japanese plane.

The horizon was bisecting Frank's windshield, sliding wildly toward the floor. Frank aligned the dot of his sight just above the other's cockpit and squeezed the trigger. The brightness of the volley almost blinded him, but he saw the tracer eat into the Japanese fighter. It rolled over on its back, flames under his cowl, pilot and plane doomed.

Frank eased out of the turn, breathing heavily. He kicked the fighter into a climb, trading speed for altitude.

He thumbed his transmitter. "Lisa, where are you?"

"Seven thousand and climbing. Where are you?"

Relief swept over him. He glanced at the altimeter. "Ten and climbing."

Things were returning to normal. "Meet you over the ship. Over."

He put the fighter into a mild bank, trying to spot the *Hoorn* in the murk below. He located the ship far over to the left, making for the Bangka Channel. *Almost safe. High time, too. Our gas is pitifully low.*

When she called again, he was caught off guard.

"Frank! I've been hit! I'm on fire!"

There must have been another fighter stalking her. "Bailout! Fast!" he yelled. "Where are you?"

"Oh, Frank, I can't bailout. My legs won't work. I've been hit . . . in my back! . . . Here he comes again!"

Despair flooded over him. He horsed his fighter right and left, trying to spot where she was, at the same time waiting for her to release the transmitter switch so that he could reach her.

There was only the sea, the ship, and the islands.

Suddenly, her voice came in again, but more calmly this time. "He's gone. . . . Frank, I think this is the end."

He could hear her taking several deep breaths. In the background

The Ulysses Flight/ Paul Wankowicz

her engine beat raggedly. "Thanks for everything. It would have been great to have landed in Palembang together. It's been terrific knowing you, I couldn't have wished for more!" She paused. "I'm glad Johnny and Mia made it. That we gave them a chance. They deserve it so!" she whispered. Then her voice came strong again. "I love you, Frank, and will always!" Her transmitter's hum died.

He called "Lisa!" several times, but there was no answer. She'd switched off the set.

Automatically, he did another circle, and then, he saw her. The sea was now a deep blue with the islands blending into it like kiln-melted glaze. Only the white wake of the ship, the *Nieuv Hoorn,* showed in detail.

Against this background, he saw a flicker of light, like a carelessly thrown match. It kept straight for a few seconds while the flame grew brighter, and then, in a final arc, it swung down toward the dark blue of the sea. Just before it touched the surface of the water, Frank turned away. He couldn't bear to watch.

She was gone.

Numb. Tears streamed down his cheeks. They didn't seem to have anything to do with him. He could still see his hands on the controls. It was interesting how his hands could keep moving regardless, to correct for little variances in the air currents. Someday, he would have to think about it, figure how it was that his hands knew what to do by themselves.

Now there was something else important that he had to think about. *She'd made that takeoff from Tenasserim Field the first time. I'd nearly died watching her. And the landing at Mergui. And a cheerful Lisa waking him before the drive to Rangoon. She'd been so happy that she would soon be seeing her father. And our first night together. The last thing she'd said was that Johnny and Mia had a chance.*

But was she wrong? They didn't. How could they?

Above him, Frank could see the last flight of bombers banking lazily to line up with the ship. Black, cross-like silhouettes against the

323

evening sky.

He knew now what it was that he had to think about: what to do. With desperation, he looked at his gas gage. It read 'empty.' Instinctively, he pulled the mixture knob to 'lean.' He didn't know precisely how much fuel he had left before the last of his reserve ran out. He knew he should fine-out the pitch to keep the engine from burning up, but he didn't.

It doesn't matter. Let the engine kill itself in this last climb.

Frank pointed the nose upward. Nursing it. Getting as much height out of the near-empty tanks as he could. He prayed then. He prayed that the badly-detonating engine would not leave its bearers, that the fuel would let him reach the altitude he needed.

The coolant light was burning bright red as he brought the fighter level. Out of the corner of his eye, he could see the fuel-pressure light blinking. Viciously, he switched tanks and hit the booster pump switch. It could not quit on him now!

He could see the planes below and to his right. A malevolent organism shaped like a deadly ray, each bomber a living cell. It rippled along its whole length to the varying air currents, hinomarus marks like pockets of arterial blood under reptilian skin.

He swung down toward the head Japanese bomber. Angry red-and-orange balls came up to meet him, rising slowly out of the formation. Tracer fire. Just before flashing past, they accelerated, passing him with the speed of an express train.

Frank hardly saw the tracer. Concentrating on the glazed nose of the lead plane, where the bombardier sat hunched over his sight, Frank fired the last of his ammunition and watched it go into the Japanese' starboard engine without effect.

Until the last moment when they realized his intentions, the Japanese seemed to pay no attention to him, allowing their gunners to take care of the lonely attacker. It was only when collision couldn't be avoided that they began to turn away; too late.

Frank aimed his spinner at the bombardier crouched over his sight

The Ulysses Flight/ Paul Wankowicz

in the nose of the Japanese plane.

Just before the spinner hit, Frank ducked down behind the coaming.
The P-40 hit just aft of the plane commander's seat, an armored squab
to the right of the pilot. The fighter's propeller shredded the armor as if
it were tinsel, reducing the man within it to a bloody splash on the
cockpit's side, soon wiped clean as the wind tore the plane open,
scattering the aluminum sheets of the fuselage like silvered cardboard.

The P-40's disintegrating wing crushed the Japanese bombardier
before he had time to look up and see the olive-drab fighter which was
his doom.

Frank's overheated engine battered its way through the rest of the
bomber, scattering the structure as if it were rice paper. Slamming
midships, it collided with the neatly stacked bombs. There was a sharp
crack of a detonator.

Then the remains of the aircraft disintegrated in one brilliant flash
of exploding bombs.

An engine, torn bodily out of the wing, arced over, and dropped
through the cockpit of the second Japanese plane in the formation.

The now hurt Japanese bomber cartwheeled, burning, and cut
through the rest of its own Japanese bombers behind it.

Within seconds, the survivors were wheeling for home, shocked
into uselessness by the violence of the disaster. The air filled with
shredded wings, torn-apart fuselages, and parts of human bodies.

Down below, leaning against the bridge's railings, with the ship's
Dutch Captain, Johnny and Mia silently watched the explosion.

Behind them, the ship's radio, which had shortly before broadcast
Lisa's last agonized words, hummed gently to itself, now voiceless.

"Brave people," the ship's Captain said to no one in particular.

Gripping the rail until her knuckles were white, Mia was weeping
silently at the loss of her friends. Johnny stepped up to hold her close to
him.

Epilogue: London, 1963

Air Vice-Marshal John Laws, D.S.C., D.F.C. and bar, leaned back. "And that's the story," Johnny said. "Another drink?"

A piece of coal fell from the grate and rolled into the corner of the cooling fireplace.

"Please."

"I'm afraid the ice has all melted."

"That's all right. I'll take it warm," I said.

Johnny handed me the glass. "It was a great pity about Lisa," he said. "She was superb. A natural flyer."

"What happened afterwards?"

"The liner *Nieuw Hoorn* docked at Jakarta. There I ran into one of Group Captain Winterbotham's Majors. He took one look at the developed film and packed me with it by air to England—as straight as one went in those days—to Station X, Bletchley Park. But I suppose you know all about that, having been in Intelligence yourself.

"MI6," I nodded.

"I beat Mia by two months," he said as an aside.

Mia interrupted. "It took me nine weeks to get to England. We went by convoy from Australia, to Cape Town, South Africa, then to Gibraltar, and finally, England. Initially, I felt like a fish out of water, and wished I'd never left Malaya. The English wives were polite, but not friendly. They whispered among themselves that I'd been Johnny's "Chinese mistress."

"We arrived in Liverpool in a wet, driving snow. I didn't want to leave the ship, to leave the last link with my homeland, my youth. I was cold to the bone. And then, there he was! He looked strange under the officer's cap pulled down almost to the up-turned overcoat collar. My heart was fluttering. I could hardly breathe. I could feel my cheeks turn pink.

"I flew to him and gave him a big hug. The snow from his greatcoat melted all down the front of my clothes. It was all right. In his arms, I was home."

Johnny took up the story. "Except for Mia's arrival, it was a bloody-awful day. I was so happy she'd arrived safely I could have danced there in the wet snow.

It took a while for my father to get used to the idea of having a Malaysian daughter-in-law, but my mother eventually brought him around."

"And afterwards?" I asked.

"After I got out of Group Captain Winterbotham's clutches, I went on night intruders flying *Typhoons*. Got my own squadron in time for the invasion of Europe. I got shot down on my third mission."

I looked at him sharply. There had been something familiar about him, and it crystallized. "You were the pilot who had parachuted into the bit of country we were holding and you joined our mess that evening. I remember you!"

Johnny smiled. "I wondered how long it would take you. Of course, you have the game leg. Hard to conceal. Easy to remember. . . . So how did you meet Cyril?"

"MI6 got tired of me in England so they sent me out to the Pacific, and eventually, once the war was over, to Burma.

"After that, I went with the War Crimes' Commission to Tokyo. That's where I ran into Sergeant Hokai. He was doing orderly duties in what was left of the Japanese Army Air Force H.Q.

"When you shot up Kuantan on a raid, one of your rounds hit him in the hip, and he couldn't fly anymore.

"Hokai laboriously made out a deposition against Horikashi. He believed if it hadn't been for Horikashi, Kashimura would still be alive, and the Kuantan raid wouldn't have happened in retaliation. But we never found Horikashi. He probably got shot down somewhere, or like many others when the war turned against them, committed suicide.

"I couldn't trace Frank either. I learned who Lisa was through her dressmaker in Rangoon. And I traced Van Riin, her father, only to learn

The Ulysses Flight/ Paul Wankowicz

that he had died when the *deRuyter* went down in the Battle of Sunda
Strait. But as far as you were concerned, Johnny, there was no trace of
what had happened. You were just the R.A.F. pilot of Cyril's story," I
said. "I was haunted by my inability to find out what happened to the
three."

As I paused, I happened to glance up, and then admire two silver
frames showing a very elegant blond woman dressed in an early 1920s
wedding dress. Mia saw me looking at them.

"My mother," she said. "After the war I went back to Penang, to the
village, and they made a ceremonial feast and gave back the silver
frame that I'd traded for the boat. I had to tell them the whole story of
how I had sailed and of how I had met John. They made me a member
of the village. I'm very proud of that!"

"That seems to wind it up," I said. "Except for one more question.
The codebook film? You said it got to Bletchley Park. What was it?
What happened to it?"

Johnny smiled and paused. "I expect I can tell you now. . . .You
were in Intelligence. Anyway, I heard that Fred Winterbotham is
writing a book about it, about *Ultra.*, so it will all be out in the open. It
took him a bloody-long time to get the Government's permission to
even mention *Ultra*; but in the end, he wore them down."

I did know. *Ultra* was the wartime name for the information we got
by breaking the enemy's top codes. Originally, the Poles had broken the
German machine's code, and given their knowledge to the French and
British just before the war started.

During the war, the British codebreaker and codereading work was
being carried out in a requisitioned estate, Bletchley Park. Fred Winterbotham, then an R.A.F. Wing Commander, headed the establishment,
code named Station X.

"First, imagine what would have happened if the population of Los
Angeles, San Francisco, and the west-coast towns of the United States
became devoid of population, with everyone dead. That was what the
book Biard got from Colonel Seki was about. It was so secret that only

The Ulysses Flight/ Paul Wankowicz

a handful of Japanese knew what was in it.

"I had to go over the story of how the films got into my possession," Johnny continued, "before they would consider that the film was not a plant. Geoffrey Hayes was dead by then, so there could be no confirmation of what I told them. They were very careful. The matter dealt with the Pacific Theatre, and it would have to be turned over to the Yanks. Bletchley Park didn't want to lose face by giving them something that wasn't authentic." He took another sip of his drink.

"But what was it?" I asked.

"It's still classified and probably will be so forever. Colonel Seki must have been more important in Japanese Military Intelligence than we at first thought." Johnny paused. "You probably know, of course, during the war, the Japanese built the *Fugaku*, named after Mt. Fuji. It was a six-engine bomber, with the range to reach almost to the U.S. Rockies and return to Japan. It couldn't carry heavy bombs over that range, but it did carry weather-balloon bombs and could deliver radioactive dust which could be spread by balloon over California and Oregon. Even farther when the wind was right. They dropped some 4,000 such balloons on the U.S. west coast. The Japanese were aware of the dangers of radioactivity. Colonel Seki was to be put in charge of their A-bomb program."

"And the red book?"

"Because Japan's research into Atomic Physics had lagged behind, they swung a bargain with Germany to supply the hot dust and have it delivered via submarine. But it also showed they were quite a way into developing their own A-bomb. The red book was the special code that Seki's group was to use with Nazi Germany to get the ball rolling. The ability to read that code enabled a team section at Bletchley, including Americans, to follow developments in the program. And when the Japanese got close to making it effective, a special flight of B-29s obliterated their research laboratories, as well as the *Fugaku*. So in the end, that Scots engineer Halliday on the *Nike Victory* got it right. Without Frank and Lisa, the *Nieuv Hoorn* would have been sunk and

329

that canister of film would never have reached Allied hands," Johnny summarized.

"By the time the Japanese had it all ready, it was probably too late to affect the war, but it would have been a horrible slaughter of Americans, more than equal to the deaths at Hiroshima." Johnny said.

Mia nodded. "Frank and Lisa should not have been left in obscurity," she said. "I wish someone, some day would write about them."

THE END.

Appendix I: A WWII Aviation Glossary with Commentary by Paul Wańkowicz

-A-

* *Albacore:* See Fairey *Albacore.*
* *Albatros* **Flugverks GMB**: A series German fighter biplane, very successful in WWI with ply-covered and very streamline fuselages. These biplanes were quite fast for their time. Max. speed: 116 mph for the DV model.
* **Apex *Dreadnought*:** a fictitious plane in this story.
* **Armorer:** A crewman who was detailed to load or reload and service weapons on a fighter plane.
* **Armstrong Whitworth Company** *Siskin:* A British biplane fighter of the 1920s. First flight in 1919. Introduced into the R.A.F. in 1923. Nicely agile, it was well-liked by its pilots.
* **Arrow** *Sport* **A2-60:** Side-by-side two-person, open-cockpit biplane often used as a trainer. Built by the Arrow Aircraft and Motors Corporation of Havelock, Nebraska. First built in 1929. Engine: 60 hp *Le Blond*-60 engine. Max. speed: 105 mph. Range: 280 miles. Small, and for the times, had a high-wing loading. Arrow also built the **Arrow Sport 90.**
* **Auto Rich:** Auto Rich is a control in the cockpit. A red-knobbed handle in the throttle group. In the British system, it operates in the reverse of the American system. Therefore, pulling back the Auto Rich in the British system was like pulling full choke on a car to start it.
* **A.V.M.:** Air Vice-Marshal of the British Royal Air Force. Equivalent to a Major General in the British Army.
* **Avro** *Anson***:** British twin-engine utility aircraft and bomber, often called *Faithful Annie* by members of the R.A.F. First introduced by

Avro in 1936 as a coastal patrol plane. It was the first low-wing monoplane and the first with retractable landing gear in the R.A.F. Extensively used for training and utility, before and during WWII; it still soldiered on until the late 1950s. Max. speed: listed as 188 mph, although this was rarely reached in production aircraft.

-B-

- **B3N:** A Japanese low-wing reconnaissance aircraft used by their Navy.
- **Baldachin:** A cloth canopy fixed or carried over an important person or sacred object, also a bed canopy. (*Merriam-Webster's Collegiate Dictionary*, 10th edn., Springfield, MA: Merriam -Webster's, Inc. 1993.)
- *Baka***:** A Japanese term meaning "idiot."
- **Bay**: (As applied to biplanes) "bay" refers to the number of inter-plane struts or longitudinal pairs of struts, and thus to the number of open areas on one side of the fuselage. Therefore, if there is one pair of struts tying the upper and lower wing together on each side of the fuselage, then the machine is a one-bay biplane. Two pairs would make it a two-bay machine, and so forth.
- **Beech Aircraft Model D-18** *Twin Beech***:** A low-wing, all metal, twin-engine light transport. Built and flown in January 1937. Carried six to eight passengers. Also used as an U.S. Army Air Force C-45. Sometimes called "a little DC-3." Engines: P&W 450 hp. Max. speed: 200 mph. Cruise: 180 mph. Range: 632 miles.
- **Bell P-39** *Airacobra* **fighter:** Commonly called the *Airacobra*. Pre-WWII designed U.S. fighter, originally armed with 37-mm aerial cannon. In R.A.F. and R.A.A.F., the cannon was 20-mm caliber. Allison V-1710 was located behind the pilot, therefore making it doubly dangerous in crash-landings or crashes. Also had a reputation of entering a flat and uncontrollable spin leading to crash. Engine: 1325 hp. Max. speed: 408 mph (rarely attained).

Range: 450 miles. Armament (U.S.): (1) 35-mm Cannon, (4) .30-cal. machine guns.

- **Billy:** camp cookware; a pot with a bail handle for hanging
- above a cooking fire.
- **Blériot, Louis (1872-1936):** Pioneering French designer and pilot, first to cross the English Channel by air (1909).
- **Blooded:** scored a kill in an aerial dogfight.
- **Bowser:** Name of the company which manufactured the pumps on the R.A.F. fuel trucks; hence, in R.A.F. slang, a "fuel truck."
- **Brewster *Buffalo* (Navy F2A):** Mid-wing shipboard fighter (1941). Engine: Wright R-1820-40, 1,200 hp. Max. speed: 318 mph, rarely attained. Range: 770 miles. Armament: (6) .30-caliber machine guns midwing. Went through some improvements, but was rapidly replaced by the F4F.
- **Bristol F2B biplane fighter:** Popularly called the *Brisfit.* Max. speed: 123 mph. Engine: 275 hp. Armament: (3) 303-caliber. machine guns. It could be used as a fighter or as a bomber. Developed in 1917, it soldiered well into the late 1920s.
- **Brow:** The retractable gangplank where passengers enter the ship.
- **Buhl *Pup*:** A single-seat sports plane built in the early 1930s. Engine: Shekely 3-cylinder 90 hp. Max. speed: 90 mph. Midwing, with yellowed, transparent Cellulon pilots (lookouts) on the wings so the pilot could see the ground when landing.
- **Bumpf:** R.A.F. slang for papers from H.Q., any red tape.
- **Bunk-out:** A hasty military reassignment Sometimes it means "to flee an unpleasant duty. To make a bunk."
- **Buy the Farm:** R.A.F. slang for getting killed, or "getting the chop." Such a "Farm" was 6-foot x 3-foot x 6-foot plot in a cemetery.

-C-

- **Capital Ship:** Generally, a battleship, cruiser, or aircraft carrier; a ship of major rank.

- **Catalina flying boat:** British designation of the American de-signed PBY-5 flying boat. They were used for over-water patrol and as communication boats. Range: 2,350 miles. It was a *Catalina* that found the German Battleship *Bismarck* after the shadowing ships had lost it, leading to its being sunk.
- **Chandelle:** An abrupt climbing turn of an airplane in which the momentum of the plane is used to attain a higher rate of climb. (*Merriam-Webster's Collegiate Dictionary*, 10th edn.)
- **Chiefy:** Slang for Chief Engineer.
- **CIB:** China-India-Burma Theater of WWII.
- **CMG:** Companion of the Order of St. Michael and St. George.
- **Coffman Starter,** and **Coffman Starter Breech**: A pyrotechnic type starter. To start the engine, one fed a cartridge into the breech and fired it. The gasses generated turned over the engine via a special mechanism.
- **Control surfaces**: The control surfaces of an airplane are ailerons, elevators and rudders.
- **Control yoke**: A substitute for the "joy stick" of smaller airplanes. Usually found in larger machines, it consists of a "yoke" or wheel capable of turning (to control the ailerons) or being moved fore and aft (to control the elevators). Not usually found in fighters; the Lockheed P-38 was an exception.
- **Cosmoline™**: A brand of petroleum jelly; here, used to waterproof parts of any plane in transit by sea.
- **Curtiss *Hawk* 75**: See Curtiss P-36.
- **Curtiss *Jenny* JN-4D**: Used as trainer by the U.S. Army Signal Corps Aviation Division in WWI. With pontoon, used by the U.S. Navy. Also saw service with the Canadian and British forces.
- **Curtiss NC Boats:** Curtiss built seven flying boats for WWI. The NC-4 was the first heavier than air to cross the Atlantic via the Azores. Her companions NC-3 and NC-1 were supposed to

accompany but didn't make it. The hull of the NC-4 is in the Smithsonian Institution. They were sometimes called "Nancies."

- **Curtiss P-36**: Pre-WWII fighter built by Curtiss in the United States. Engine: Radial, 1,200 hp. The P-36 formed the basic air frame around which Don Berlin designed the P-40. It was extensively used in the U.S.A.A.F. in the late 1930s, and exported as the Curtiss *Hawk* 75.
- **Curtiss P-40 *Warhawk* a.k.a. Curtiss P-40 *Tomahawk*:** A fighter designed by Donovan Berlin for the U.S.A.A.F. A sturdy fighter, suffering partly from being designed to outdated Wright Field rules and lacking a good super-charged engine. It was the fighter with which the U.S. entered WWII. This story is about the models P-40A or P-40B. Against the Japanese Mitsubishi A6M-2 *Zero*, it was somewhat suicidal, although it could out-dive it. Colonel Clair Lee Chennault equipped his Flying Tigers with such *Tomahawks*, and developed a special tactic to suit the airplane, resulting in phenomenal kill ratios using it against the Japanese. A total of 13,733 P-40s, in various versions, were built in the U.S. during WWII. It saw service in all theaters of operation; however, sparsely used over Europe, as there, it was out-classed by the German Me-109. Used in the normal manner, dogfighting, it was also out classed by the Japanese machines. Engine: Allison V-1710, 1040 hp. Max. speed: 352 mph. Range: 1,020 miles. Armament: (2) .50-caliber machine guns on cowl, (2) .30-caliber wing machine guns.
- **Curtiss *Robin*:** Manufactured by the Curtiss Robertson Aeroplane and Motor Company of St. Louis, Missouri. It sat one in front and two side-by-side behind. Engine: Initially a 90 hp OX-5; later some used a Wright J-6 air-cooled engine.

-D-

- **Davis Air Cannon:** An experimental large-bore cannon fitted to some of the NC Boats after WWI. In order to cancel recoil, the

335

cannon fired a wad of paper-packed grease backward at the same time it fired a projectile forward—as dangerous to the aircraft structure behind it as it was to the enemy in front. In England, a similar weapon was built by the Coventry Ordinance Works and commonly referred to as the "C.O.W. Cannon," taken from the initials of the makers. To the best of the author's knowledge, the Davis, or C.O.W. Cannon, was never used operationally. Modern recoilless rifles work on a similar principle, but have not been applied to aircraft.

- **Dead-stick landing:** A landing with the engine dead resulting in the propeller not pulling.
- **Deal table:** A small unpainted wood table.
- **Debunked:** to depart.
- **Deflection (deflection shooting):** Deflection is the angular (or linear) distance that has to be allowed in front of a moving target to allow for the finite speed of the bullets. A full-deflection shot is one from 90 degrees to the target's line of flight; as the angle narrows, less and less "lead" has to be allowed. Deflection shooting was more of an art than science in WWII. Nowadays most sights compute the deflection automatically.
- **DeHavilland DH-82 *Tiger Moth*:** British primary trainer. A single-bay, two-seat biplane. Engine:130 hp air-cooled Gipsy Major. Wood and canvas construction.
- **D.F.C.:** The British Distinguished Flying Cross medal, awarded in recognition of extraordinary achievement in aerial flight, and heroism in battle.
- **D.I.:** A "D.I." is a Direction Indicator. A gyroscopic instrument on the panel that indicates the aircraft's heading. A "D.I." was steadier than the usual compass, but was given to "precession," meaning that it had to be reset every 15 to 30 minutes.
- **Doorman, Karel:** Admiral Karel Doorman, Commander of the American, British, Dutch, and Australian navel forces against the Japanese invasion fleet in the Java sea, and killed in action on

336

The Ulysses Flight/ Paul Wankowicz

February 28, 1942.

- **Dornier:** Dornier was a German aircraft manufacturer. During the Battle of Britain, the term usually referred to the Dornier *Do*-17Z, a twin-engine bomber introduced into the Luftwaffe in 1939 and used against England in the 1940s.
- **Douglas DC-2 Commercial Transport:** 3 crew and 14 passengers. Engines: (2) 875 hp. Wright cyclone engines. Range: 1,000 miles. Speed: 200 mph. Cargo capacity: 3,600 lbs. First manufactured in 1934.
- **Douglas, Sholto:** Air Marshal W. Sholto Douglas, Assistant Chief of British Air Staff (1940).
- **Dowding, Sir Hugh Caswall Tremenheere:** 1ˢᵗ Baron Dowding, GCB, GCVO, CMG (4/24/1882 - 2/15/1970). Made Air Chief Marshal in 1937, he lead the British R.A.F. Fighter Command during the Battle of Britain. He served in WWI and WWII. Awarded the Knight Grand Cross of the Order of the Bath (GCB), Knight Grand Cross of the Royal Victorian Order (GCVO), and Companion of the Order of St. Michael and St. George (CMG). Knighted in 1933. He was an early advocate for the use of radar in aviation. He is credited with introducing the 8-gun Supermarine *Spitfire* and the Hawker *Hurricane* for use by the R.A.F. before WWII.
- **Dragon *Rapide*:** A very neat series of transport planes designed by Arthur Hagg and built by the DeHavilland works in England. Graceful two-bay biplanes with extremely slender wings, they were a delight to fly and much used in varying roles in Australia as well as in other parts of the world.
- **DSO:** British Distinguished Services Order.

-E-

- **Elevator:** a moveable auxiliary airfoil usually attached to the tail plan of an airplane for controlling pitch. (*Merriam-Webster's Collegiate Dictionary*, 10ᵗʰ edn.)

- **Elevator trim**: Usually a crank or handwheel in the cockpit that adjusted the airplane's horizontal attitude. Balance of forces changes as power is varied, gas used up, etc. Adjusting the elevator trim to the new conditions relieved the pilot from having to hold pressure on the stick to maintain flight attitude.
- **Empennage**: The tail assembly of an airplane.

-F-

- **Fairey *Albacore:*** British torpedo bomber designed by Fairey Aviation (Replacement for the *Swordfish).* Engine: Bristol Taurus 1,065 hp. Max. speed: 161 mph. Range: 930 miles. Armament: (3) 8-mm machine guns; (1) 1610 lb. torpedo.
- **Fairey Aviation of England:** The manufacturer of the Fairey *Swordfish* and the Fairey *Albacore.*
- **Fairey *Swordfish*:** British-designed biplane torpedo bomber. Crew of three. Referred to as '*The Stringbag*' by the British Fleet Air Arm crews that flew them. Despite their antiquated appearance and slow speed, they proved a very successful weapon. The F.A.A. had a replacement, the Fairey *Albacore,* but '*The Stringbag*' outlived it, soldiering until the end of WWII. *Swordfish* aircrafts destroyed the Italian Navy in the night strike at Taranto.
- **Fairing:** A member or structure whose primary function it is to produce a smooth outline and to reduce drag. *(Merriam-Webster's Collegiate Dictionary,* 10ᵗʰ edn.)
- **Fantail:** An overhang on a ship shaped like a duck's bill. *(Merriam-Webster's Collegiate Dictionary,* 10ᵗʰ edn.)
- **Farman, Henry (1874-1958):** Pioneer European pilot and designer who was the first to complete a one-kilometer flight in Europe. He was holder of early distance and endurance records, and possibly the first to fly with a woman as a passenger.
- **Fey:** A Scot word meaning pre-cognition. Possessing the ability to sense the future. Extra-sensory perception.

- **Field:** In the British military system, an airstrip that is a British Royal Air Force installation, is called an "Airfield" or a "Field"; whereas, a "Station" is generally a British Royal Navy Air Station.
- **5ᵗʰ Column**: A group of secret sympathizers, or supporters of an enemy, that engage in espionage or sabotage within defense lines or national borders, to help an invading army.
- **Flap Control:** A lever in the cockpit which allowed the pilot to lower or raise the flaps preparatory to landing, or whenever needed. Usually on the right-hand side of the cockpit.
- **Fleet Air Arm:** Britain's Naval Aviation arm.
- **Fleet Aircraft Company:** In 1928, Reuben Fleet broke away from Consolidated Aviation to start his own company. Fleet Aircraft company made a successful series of aircraft for both the private market and the R.C.A.F.
- **Flight**: A unit in the air force numerically below a squadron.
- **Flying boat:** An aircraft with a ship-like hull. Sometimes also called a 'seaplane' but most often the latter term is applied to an aircraft with floats (pontoons) under the fuselage.
- **Flying wires:** Wires rigged between biplane wings to provide structured strength.
- **Fokker D-7:** German fighter of WWI vintage. It was an excellent machine and a favorite with many German pilots. Engine: either Mercedes 160 hp or BMW 185 hp. Max. speed: 120 mph (Mercedes engine) 124 mph (BMW engine). Armament: (2) 7.92 Spandau machine guns.

-G-

- **GCB:** Knight Grand Cross of the Order of the Bath.
- **GCVO:** Knight Grand Cross of the Royal Victorian Order.
- **Gen:** Short for "General Information." R.A.F. slang for any sort of information, including rumors.
- **G-Force:** G stands for gravity. When an airplane changes direc-

tion, various opposing forces acting on the air frame and the pilot are measured with respect to normal gravitational acceleration. A 170-lb. pilot experiencing a 2-G turn, has an apparent weight of 340 lbs. (170 x 2). If the force is opposite normal, then it is negative G. Positive G tends to make the blood heavier, 3 or so G (varies with the person) will drain the blood to the lower parts of a seated body, starving the brain, leading to a blackout condition which starts with loss of vision and can end in total loss of consciousness.

- **Gimlet**: an awl. "Gimlet eye" is a British expression meaning "to keep a sharp eye."
- **The glory:** A phenomenon of a luminescent double rainbow in a halo extending in an arc from wing tip to wing tip.
- **Gloster Aircraft Co. Ltd.** *Sea Gladiator* **MK-II and four other models of the Gloster** *Gladiator***:** A British biplane fighter. Engine: 830 hp Bristol Mercury. Max. speed: 258 mph. Armament: (2) Browning 0.303-inch fixed machine guns, (2) Browning repositionable machine guns.
- **Gloster Aircraft** *Grebe:* The *Grebe* was the first fighter accepted by the R.A.F. at the end of WWI. Its first flight was in 1923.
- **G.O.C.:** British military abbreviation of "General Officer Commanding"—used as part of the title of a regional commander.
- **Government** *wallah***:** Slang for a colonial government man, usually meant to be uncomplimentary.
- **Graviner:** The name of the maker of the R.A.F. aircraft-mounted fire-extinguishing system. Hence, in R.A.F. slang, the name of any internal fire system. Graviner systems were operated by pulling a handle somewhere under the instrument panel, this in turn flooded the suspected area with carbon dioxide, theoretically snuffing the fire.
- **Graviner pull:** British for fire extinguisher control. Pulling the handle flooded the engine spaces with carbon dioxide.
- **Ground bods:** ground crew.

-H-

- *Han*: In Oriental medicine, a medical-spiritual condition of soul sickness, where one feels dispirited and dejected, sometimes betrayed, but is not without hope.
- **Hardstand:** A paved area for parking an airplane.
- *Harvard*-**I:** British designation of the U.S.-built AT-6. Designed by 'Dutch' Kindleberger and Jack Northrop, the AT-6 in its many guises became the most-used advanced trainer in the Allied camp. A total of 15,000 were built. The Australians built their own version of it, called the CA-3 *Wackett Wirraway* and used many of its parts in the Australian-designed Ca-12 *Boomerang* fighter.
- **Hawker *Hart*:** A very successful British biplane two-seat fighter designed by Sydney Camm and built between WWI and WWII. It was the progenitor of the *Hurricane.* The Hart was a highly-streamlined single-bay biplane powered by a neatly-cowled Rolls-Royce inline engine. The landing fixed gear was covered by streamline spats. Although obsolete at the outbreak of WWII, it was used as a hack, especially at the colonial outposts. Greatly beloved by many pilots.
- **Hawker *Hurricane* Mark 1:** A British fighter built by Hawker Aircraft and designed by Sydney Camm who also designed the Hawker *Hart* and its derivatives. The *Hurricane* formed the backbone of the R.A.F. during the Battle of Britain, although it was inferior to the German Me-109; in consequence of its inferiority, it was supposed to go after the bombers, while the nimbler *Spitfire* 'covered' it. The *Hurricane* was a superb gun platform and heavily armed. It entered R.A.F. service in 1937. Engine: Rolls-Royce Merlin, 1030 hp. Max. speed: 322 mph. Range: 525 miles. Armament: (8) .303-cal. machine guns.
- **Heinkel He-111:** A Twin-engine bomber designed by Ernst Heinkel, used by the Luftwaffe as its mainstay in the early parts of

the Battle of Britain. Often referred to as the *Heinkel.* Basically an ugly machine, it was sturdy and reliable, but slow; as a consequence, an easier target to hit. Engine: (2) Daimler-Benz DB 601A 1,150 hp. Max. speed: 274 mph. Armament: (3) machine guns.

- **Hinomarus:** Japanese for the solid red circle painted on their aircraft as a national insignia. Often called a 'meatball' by aviators.

-I-

- **I.J.A.F.:** The Imperial Japanese Air Force.
- **Immelmann:** A maneuver developed by Max Immelmann, WWI German Ace. "Immelmann is a turn, named in 1917 for Max Immelmann, in which an airplane reverses direction by executing a half-loop upwards followed by a half of a roll. Also called an Immelmann turn." (*Merriam-Webster's Collegiate Dictionary, 10th edn.*)
- **Immelmann turn:** The turn consists of a half-loop followed by a half-roll which returns the airplane to right-side-up, thus reversing the original directional flight with a gain in altitude. The maneuver is used mainly in fighters and aerobatic displays.
- **Initial Point:** The Initial Point, or I.P., is the position from which a bomber starts its bomb-dropping run. In order to bomb accurately, WWII bombers had to have a fairly-long, straight run, during which the bomb-sight was aligned with the target. This run was started from the I.P. which is usually about a minute away from the intended target.
- **Instrument flying:** Normally, flight orientation is accomplished through reference to the horizon and the land below. However, when in the clouds, fog, or often at night neither is visible, a pilot must rely on the instruments on his panel to tell him the attitude of his aircraft. Instrument flying is a learned science, and dangerous to a novice until the technique is mastered.
- **International Pilot's Federation (F.A.I. -** *Federation*

342

The Ulysses Flight/ Paul Wankowicz

Internationale Aeronautique): First group to license pilots. F.A.I. is still the group that certifies all aeronautical records.

- **I.O.:** A British military Intelligence Officer.
- **I.P.:** See "Initial point."

-J-

- **Jinking**: To move quickly or unexpectedly with sudden turns and shifts, as in dodging. A quick evasive turn.
- **Judder**: To vibrate with intensity.
- *Jungmeister*: German training/aerobatic biplane. Famous the world over for its aerobatic capabilities. Still flown (and much treasured) into the 2000s.
- **Junkers JU-88:** German bomber built by the Junkers factory. Used extensively during the Battle of Britain, probably their most successful machine during the period. Soldiered on until the end of WWII. Engine: (2) Jumo 211B, 1,200 hp. Max. speed: 286 mph. Armament: (6) 7.9-mm machine guns. At other times other engines and armament were used.

-K-

- **Ki-10-11 "Perry" also called "TYPE 95":** An early Japanese biplane fighter. Silver in color. U.S. and R.A.F. terminology came to mean "Un Serviceable."
- **Kite**: R.A.F. slang for an airplane.

-L-

- **Landing Gear Oleos:** See "oleos."
- **Lockheed P-38** *Lightning*: U.S. Army Air Force twin-boom fighter. Engine: (2) Allison 1425 hp. Max. speed: 414 mph. Armament: (1) 20-mm cannon, (4) 12.7-mm machine guns. J-model

extensively used in the Pacific theater of operations.

- **Lockheed *Vega***: A plane made most famous by Wiley Post in his plane named *Willie Mae*, which broke many records, including a solo flight around the world. Engine: Wright J-5, 220 hp. Max. speed: 138 mph.

-M-

- **Magneto:** Equivalent to the spark ignition coil in an automobile engine. The mechanism that creates the spark used to fire the gasoline in the engine's cylinders. Usually two magnetos are used on an airplane engine, both for safety and for better combustion.
- **Magneto drop:** Before takeoff, one ran the engine separately on each magneto and if the revolutions per minute dropped below a certain limit, the air craft was deemed unfit to fly. The limit was called the magneto drop.
- **Messerschmitt Me-109:** German fighter. Designed by Willy Messerschmitt, it bore the designation either Me-109 or Bf-109, the letters changing when the factory making it became the Bavarian Aircraft Works. Generally admired as one of the best designs of early WWII, it lacked the range to stay long over England. It came close to the *Spitfire* in maneuverability. The Me-109's fuel-injection engine gave it an edge over the *Spitfire* in a diving escape. A major detraction from the design was its ultra-thin wings, which made some pilots reluctant to dive it. The design also didn't allow space for as heavy armament as was desired. The *Emil*, the E-1 model, was used during the Battle of Britain. Engine: Daimler Benz DB 601 1,050 hp. Max. speed: 342 mph. Range: 410 miles. Armament: (2) 20-mm cannon, (2) 7.9-mm machine guns.
- **Miles *Magister*:** British training aircraft. Built by Miles Aircraft Ltd. Plywood-covered, highly streamlined, designed primarily to give pilots the feel of a modern, medium-performance machine.
- **Mitchell, General William "Billy":** A visionary and controversial

pioneering aviator and military man who was the first American aviator to fly over enemy lines in Europe. He predicted the role of airplanes to be used as fighters, to drop bombs in wartime, and to be able to sink warships.

- **Mitsubishi A6M-2 *Zero*:** The Japanese fighter was designed by Kashimura Horikoshi at Mitsubishi. The official Japanese name for the plane was *Reisen*. The fighter had phenomenal maneuverability and range. It was a complete surprise to the Allies at Pearl Harbor, and for the first part of WWII. Along with the Ki-43, it dominated the Pacific. (Colonel Chennault had forewarned its existence, but his reports were buried in the U.S. War Department and not read until too late.) Engine: *Nakajima Sakae* 950 hp. Speed: 332 mph. Range: 1,930 miles. Armament: (2) 20-mm cannon, (2) 7.7-mm machine guns. The *Zero* was the popular name for the Japanese fighter A6M-2 *Reisen*, because it was built during the Year 2,000 of the Japanese calendar. Therefore, its model designation was "00"—hence the nickname "Zero."

-N-

- **N.A.A.F.I.:** Navy Army and Air Force Institute. British service organization equivalent to the American U.S.O. During the Battle of Britain, the N.A.A.F.I. organization supplied tea and snacks from special vans to the fighter squadrons.
- **Nakajima G10N1 *Fugaku*:** Japanese 6-engined bomber designed to reach the U.S. West Coast from the Japanese Islands. Engines: Nakajima radials 2,500 hp. Armament: (4) 20-mm cannon, 44,092 lb. bomb load. Max. speed: 423 mph. Very little is known about it. Under development at the war's end. Possibly one built and that was destroyed in the raids on the islands.
- **Nakajima Ki-43 *Hayabusa*:** Japanese Army fighter built by Naka-jima. Japanese name *Hayabusa* means "*Peregrine Falcon.*" De-signed by Hideo Itokawa, it was introduced into the Japanese

Army Air Force in 1940. The *Hayabusa* was highly maneuverable, almost equal to the A6M-2 *Zero*, but somewhat under armed. Engine: Nakajima Ha-25 980 hp. Max. speed: 274 mph. Range: 745 miles. Armament: (2) 12.7-mm machine guns.

- **Nieuport *Bebe "Baby"*:** A French-designed biplane for racing before WWI and used as a fighter in WWI and after.

-O-

- **Oleos:** Landing gear struts made of oil-and air-filled tubing designed to take up landing shock. Oleos replaced landing gear springs as the aircraft got heavier and faster. They have a better snubbing action than springs.
- **OM:** Order of Merit.

-P-

- **P-1:** An early Japanese Army observation/liaison aircraft.
- **P & O:** Pacific & Orient Steamship Line. The British line connecting the British Isles and the Orient. (The term "POSH" comes from the P & O boats. For maximum comfort during the journey from England to Asia, most of it in tropical temperatures, to avoid the sun, one ordered a Port cabin on the way Out, and a Starboard cabin on the way Home!) Typically 2,500 hp.
- **Parabellum:** Nickname for a Luger pistol derived from the inscription on some of them, *Pax par Bellum* meaning "peace through war."
- **Peltier, Ensault (1881-1957):** Pioneering aircraft designer. Noted for inventing the "joystick" type of control.
- **Pitch:** Up/down motion of an aircraft in relation to forward motion. Pitch also refers to the angle with which the propeller meets the air. In modern fighters, setting of the propeller pitch to match the maneuver is vitally important.

- **Pitot Tube**: A tube or open strut facing the airflow, located some-where where it can get a clean (undisturbed) flow. The pressure accumulated in the pitot tube is transmitted directly to the air-speed indicator.
- **Polish Inspectorate for Aviation:** Head Quarters of the Polish Air Force in Canada.
- **Pommies:** English immigrants. (*Merriam-Webster's Collegiate Dictionary,* 10ᵗʰ edn.)
- **Prang:** R.A.F. slang meaning "to crash" or "bend" an aircraft.

-Q-

-R-

- **R-101**: A British Government built *Zeppelin*.
- **R.A.A.F.:** Royal Australian Air Force.
- **R.A.F.:** British Royal Air Force formerly known as the Royal Flying Corps (R.F.C.).
- **R.A.F./I.:** British Royal Air Force's Intelligence arm.
- **R.A.A.F.:** Aussie slang for Royal Australian Air Force.
- **Raffles, Sir Stamford:** Founder of Singapore Island and the City of Singapore both as a settlement and an economic center.
- ***Rata*:** a Soviet inter-war fighter plane.
- **R.C.A.F:** Royal Canadian Air Force.
- **RE-8:** A British early WWI reconnaissance and bomber biplane. Armament: (1) machine gun, 1 or 2 Lewis automatic machine gun. Engine: Royal Aircraft Factory 4a, 150 hp. Max. speed: 102 mph. (1) 7.7-mm Vicker gun, (1) or (2) 7.7-mm Lewis guns.
- **Reflex sight:** A sight mounted above the instrument panel on which the aiming point was represented by a gold dot of light reflected to the pilot from a transparent glass disk. The geometry of the sight was such that no matter where the pilot's head moved the aiming point held true. The sight also had a circle concentric to the

aiming point, used to help in estimating deflection, and a pair of settable range bars which, when they touched the wingtips of the plane in front told the pilot he was in range. The reflex sight was a magnitude improvement over the old ring-and-bead sights used before WWII. It was also the first "heads-up" display.

- **R.F.C:** The British Royal Flying Corps which later became the British Royal Air Force (R.A.F.).

- **Roadstead:** A place less enclosed than a harbor where ships may ride at anchor. (*Merriam-Webster's Collegiate Dictionary*, 10th edn.)

- **Roll:** Clockwise/counterclockwise rotation of an aircraft in relation to a forward motion.

- **Rolls, Charles (Rolls-Royce):** Rolls was a self-taught mechanic who joined forces with Sir Henry Royce, a car-racer and pilot. Together they formed Rolls Royce Ltd. In 1904. Royce was unfortunately killed in an air accident in 1910, but the company continued in the motor field, building motors for the British Air Service during WWI and developing the Rolls-Royce *Merlin* that was the major engine for the R.A.F. in WWII.

- **Royal Aircraft Factory (Scout Experimental) SE-5:** British fighter of WWI vintage. Probably the best fighter of WWI. It was a cocky-looking single-bay biplane of wood frame construction that could match anything the Germans had on the Western Front. Flown by British and American forces, it was considered to be more maneuverable than the Sopwith *Camel*. Engine: Hispano-Suiza 200 hp. Max. speed:130 mph. Armament: (1) synchronized .303-in. forward-facing Vickers machine gun, and (1) swing-mounted Lewis gun on the upper wing.

- **Royal Aircraft Factory SE-5A:** This model was a modification of the SE-5, to carry (2) Cooper bombs under each wing.

- **Rpm (revolutions per minute):** An indication of engine speed. Normally kept at a given figure by the mechanism of the constant speed propeller. However, if the propeller was set to "fine pitch," the speed varied with load or engine performance. The above characteristic was used in checking out the engine's magneto function prior to flight.

-S-

- **Salient:** Area of an Infantry front.
- **Scout Experimental 5a or SE-5a**: See "Royal Aircraft Factory SE-5."
- **Seaplane:** Normally refers to an airplane with one or more floats that can alight on water. Can be used interchangeably with "flying boat" although, in normal air parlance, "seaplane" refers to a plane with floats.
- **Sembawang:** See "Sewang."
- **Sergeant-fitter:** One responsible for the airworthiness of an aircraft. Often a machinist or mechanic.
- **Sergeant-fitter armorer:** One responsible to load and maintain the armament on an aircraft.
- **Sewang:** R.A.F. nickname for the R.A.F. Squadron's Airfield at the British Royal Navy Station at Sembawang, Singapore Island.
- **Slipstream:** An area of disturbed air moving immediately around a rapidly-moving airplane.
- **S.M.L.E.:** A British issue rifle. The initials stand for Short Magazine Lee Enfield. A British-designed bolt-action rifle patterned on the American Medford action, it was extremely sturdy and went through several models. Equivalent to the U.S. Springfield '03, the S.M.L.E. was chambered to the British .303-caliber.
- **Sopwith *Camel*:** A British WWI single-seat fighter, introduced into the R.A.F. in 1917. Designed by Tom Sopwith, the plane replaced the Sopwith *Pup*. The Sopwith *Camel* was powered by a rotary engine which made it quite agile in turns, but also deadly. Called the "camel" because of the hump over the section aft of the engine. Only 5,490 were built.

- **Spats:** A type of fairing which shields most of an airplane's non-retractable wheels to reduce drag.
- **Spinner**: A streamlined cone over the propeller's hub.
- **Station**: In the British military system, a "Station" is generally a British Royal Navy Air Station. When it is a British Royal Air Force airport it would be called an "Airfield" or a "Field."
- **Stinson**: Early U.S. aircraft company run by the Stinson family. Their *Reliant* models *SR-1* through *SR-10* were the best of the series of aircraft. First flown early in 1930s. Seated 4 people. Engine: Lycoming engine 280 hp. Max. speed: 141 mph, and cruised at 130 mph.
- *Stirling*: Britain's first four-engined bomber. A good weight carrier; however, it had altitude limitations which made it easy for the German forces to shoot down. Withdrawn from service as soon as the Halifax and Lancaster four-engined bombers came along.
- **Supermarine Mark I** *Spitfire*: Legendary British fighter, designed by Reginald Mitchell for the Supermarine Company. A delight to fly, it had a classically beautiful airframe. The *Spitfire* entered R.A.F. service in 1938. Various Marks of it soldiered until well-beyond WWII. Highly maneuverable, it fought as an equal with the Me-109. Some historians consider that if the *Spitfire* had not been built, England would have lost to the Luftwaffe. Probably the most beautiful fighter of that war. Engine: Rolls-Royce Merlin, 1030 hp. Max speed: 355 mph. Range: 500 miles. Armament: Varied. During the Battle of Britain: (8) wing-mounted .303-caliber machine guns.
- *Supermarine* **Seaplane S-6:** A racing seaplane powered by a Rolls-Royce engine. Designed by Reginald G. Mitchell. The S-6 was only flown by special high-speed-flight trained pilots for racing by the R.A.F.
- *Suttee*: A Hindu custom that a widow is required to be immolated on her husband's funeral pyre as a part of her duty as wife.
- **Sutton harness:** Restraining harness named for its inventor, devel-

350

oped for British pilots in WWI and still in use. The harness is extremely simple consisting of four straps which meet at the pilot's chest and are held by one, quick-release pin.

- *Swordfish:* See Fairey *Swordfish.*

-T-

- *Tatikawa*: A Japanese biplane trainer.
- *Tomahawk*: The British designation for the Curtiss P-40 *Warhawk.*
- **Tracery:** A decorative interlacing of lines.
- **Transcontinental & Western**: The parent company for TWA. They were early transcontinental flyers using a Ford AT tri-motored airplane, commonly called, *The Tin Goose.*
- **Transmit switch:** A radio term for a switch to change from "receive" to "send."
- **Travel Air:** Early airplane builders. Built both monoplanes and biplanes, some very successful models.
- **Trenchard, Hugh Montague:** Marshal of the Royal Air Force Hugh Montague Trenchard, 1st Viscount Trenchard, GCB, OM, GCVO, DSO.
- **Tyro:** A young inexperienced soldier, British slang for "an amateur."

-U-

- **Unstick speed:** The speed necessary for an aircraft to break free of contact with the ground and liftoff.

-V-

- **Vickers-Armstrong Wellington**: A night twin-engined bomber used by the British R.A.F. Nicknamed "Wimpy" after a cartoon character. Armament: (5) machine guns in nose and tail turrets, and a ventral dustbin manufactured in at least (14) versions with modifications and engines of many manufacturers. Later models used for high altitude reconnaissance. Max. speed: approximately 255 mph. Range: approximately 1,540 miles. Armament of the Mark X: (8) 7-mm machine guns and 2,041 kg F-bombs. Handled with difficulty in take off and landing.

- **Vickers *Valentia***: A troop carrier (2 crew and 22 troops). Engine: (2) Bristol Pegasus radials 650 hp. Max. speed: 120 mph. Armament: 2,200 lb. of bombs.
- **Vertical chandelle**: An abrupt climbing turn of an airplane in which the momentum of the plane is used to attain a higher rate of climb. (*Merriam-Webster's Collegiate Dictionary*, 10th edn.)
- **Voisin, Gabriel and Charles:** Pioneering aviation pilots who designed, manufactured, and flew many of the first airplanes in France. He and his brother opened the first commercial airplane manufacturing plant.

-W-

- **W.A.A.F.:** British Woman's Auxiliary Air Force, wartime part of the R.A.F.
- **Wackett *Wirraway*:** See Harvard-I.
- **W/C**: a British R.A.F. Wing Commander.
- **Westland *Lysander*:** The Westland *Lysander* was used as a reconnaissance aircraft in WWII.
- **Wicket:** A small gate forming part of or placed near a larger gate or door. (*Merriam-Webster's Collegiate Dictionary*, 10th edn.)
- **WingCo:** British R.A.F. slang for Wing Commander.
- **Wing root:** A projection from the fuselage of an aircraft to attach the wings and allow more stability.
- **Wings:** Insignia consisting of an outspread pair of stylized bird wings which are awarded on completion of prescribed training to a qualified pilot, aircrew member, or military balloon pilot.

(*Merriam-Webster's Collegiate Dictionary,* 10th edn.)

- **Winterbotham, Frederick William:** R.A.F. Wing Commander, and Chief of the British *Ultra* intelligence project to decipher German Enigma Machine ciphers. His role is described in his memoir *The Ultra Secret* published in 1974. A British R.A.F. Officer and Group Captain during WWII.
- *Wog:* Short for *polliwog.* A British term, used disparagingly, to indicate a dark-skinned person from the Middle East or Far East. (*Merriam-Webster's Collegiate Dictionary,* 10th edn.)

-X-

-Y-

- **Yaw**: The left/ right rotation of an aircraft in relation to forward movement. To deviate erratically from course when struck. To move from side to side. To turn an aircraft by angular motion about a vertical axis.
- **Young's Modulus:** A parameter to determine the elasticity (elongation, compression) of an object using the stress to the strain ratio.

-Z-

- *Zero*: See Mitsubishi A6M-2 *Zero* the Mitsubishi A6M-2 *Reisen.*

Appendix II: The Characters

★ The narrator is a British Intelligence MI6 secret agent.

★ Air Vice-Marshal John Laws, R.A.F., D.F.C. and bar, son of Sir David, Lord Laws, M.P.

★ U.S. Army Air Force Captain Frank Carringer from Oklahoma

★ Halliday, *Nike Victory* ship's Engine Room Officer

★ Goss, Captain of the *Nike Victory*

★ Cyril Sim & Mrs. Sim, Manager of the fueling station and Tenasserim Airfield, Village Headman, and his wife

★ Sparks, the ship's radio operator on the S.S. *Nike Victory*

★ Lisa Van Riin, pilot, EMT

★ Lisa Van Riin's father served in the Royal Dutch Navy

★ Mia who became Mrs. John Laws, and her family: a Russian mother, a Chinese father; and a Chinese uncle in Singapore, owner of The Orient Hotel.

★ Initially a Wing Commander, then Air Officer Commanding Burma, Geoffrey Hayes, R.A.F. Mingaladon Airfield, Rangoon, Burma

★ British Embassy, Chief Analyst Edward Lyford, British Embassy in Bangkok, Thailand (Siam)

★ Roland Biard a.k.a. Pa Tim, son of Captain John Biard. As Pa Tim he is an undercover British spy affiliated with the R.A.F. posing as a taxi-driver/courier.

★ An ambitious Japanese Military Intelligence Officer, Colonel Lee Pi Seki is undercover as a correspondent for *The Tokyo Times.*

★ Imperial Japanese Air Force (I.J.A.F.) Pilot, Commanding Officer, Captain Jiro Kashimura

★ Imperial Japanese Air Force (I.J.A.F.) Pilots: Lieutenant Horikashi, Sergeant Hokai, Sergeant Katsuki, Corporal Tatsumo

★ Area Commander and Air Vice-Marshal Sir Robert Brooke-Popham

★ Ted Archer, the chief rigger, the mechanic

★ Aussie I.O.

★ Uncle Roy, Frank Carringer's mother's brother, and wine merchant.

The Ulysses Flight/ Paul Wankowicz

★ Bob Rackham

★ The chaplain, a.k.a. the Padre

★ Andy Rogers, the Aussie C.O. and Squadron Leader at Sembawang (a.k.a. Sewang) Airfield

★ Sergeant Parker

★ Wing Commander Frederick William Winterbotham, British R.A.F., later made Group Captain, also involved in *Ultra,* the British codebreaking project. (See Glossary)

★ First Sergeant Station Guard

★ English Doctor in Rangoon hospital

★ Nurse in Rangoon hospital

★ Pete Stern, Oklahoma flight instructor

★ Bill, Lisa's flight instructor, who flew a Wellington

★ Sir Hugh Caswall Tremenheere "Stuffy" Dowding (See Glossary)

★ Colonel Claire Lee Chennault (See Glossary)

★ Kenny, Panama Defense Force

★ Wing Commander Porteous, R.A.F. Liaison Officer to the Australian Forces.

★ Major General Gordon Bennett, G.O.C. Australian Forces, Malaya.

★ Corporal at dockside, P & O lines Official

★ Flight Lieutenant Hari Bose, a Buddhist

★ Mechanics, carpenters, and fitters

★ Sergeant Pater

★ By reference, Air Marshal W. Sholto Douglas, Assistant Chief of British Air Staff, 1940. (See Glossary)

Appendix III: Period Maps

A. The Andaman Islands and Mergui Archipelago

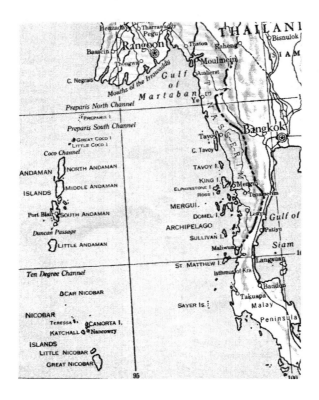

SOURCE: *Global Atlas of the World at War*, Cleveland, Ohio: The New Matthews-Northrup World Publishing Company, 1943, p. 33.

356

The Ulysses Flight/ Paul Wankowicz

B. Japanese Invasions in the China Sea, including the Philippine Islands, Burma, Thailand (Siam), New Guinea, Borneo, and Sumatra, December 7, 1941 through May, 1942

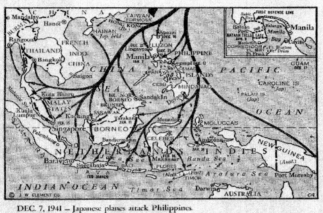

DEC. 7, 1941 — Japanese planes attack Philippines.
JAN. 2, 1942 — Manila surrenders. American and Filipino forces under Gen. MacArthur retire to Bataan Peninsula.
JAN., FEB., MARCH 1942 — Japs overrun most of Philippines and East Indies.
MARCH 21, 1942 — Gen. MacArthur arrives in Melbourne to assume full command of Allied forces.
MAY 6, 1942 — Corregidor surrenders.

SOURCE: Map of Japanese Attacks, "Dynamic Chronology of WWII" *Global Atlas of the World at War*, Cleveland, Ohio: The New Matthews-Northrup World Publishing Company, 1943, p. 53.

C. The Wandering Routes of the Ulysses Flight, December 1941 through January 30, 1942

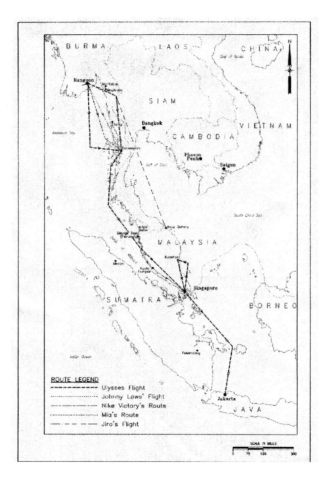

SOURCE: Created for *The Ulysses Flight* by Sally Chetwynd.

D. Airports on Singapore Island used by the R.A.F.

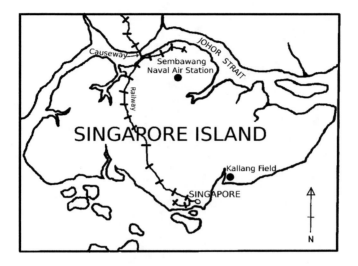

Meet the Author Paul Wańkowicz

Paul Wańkowicz has traveled widely, as well as having flown in many countries. In WWII, Paul flew with the Polish Air Force and the British R.A.F. Born in Poland, he has worked in Europe, the Middle East, the U.S.A., and Antarctica. As an engineer in anesthesia research, he is presently employed by the Massachusetts General Hospital. He and his wife now live near Boston, Massachusetts.

SOURCE: Photograph from the author's private collection showing him climbing aboard a snow track in Antarctica.

Publisher's Registered SAN: 854-1388

The Terra Sancta Press Catalog

An easy way to order: www.terrasanctapress.com

★ Paul Wańkowicz's *The Ulysses Flight, A WWII Aviation Adventure Novel of Aerial Dogfights and Love, with a Glossary* is an action-filled novel of pilots in WWII Burma and Malaya. Aerial dogfights, romance, Japanese invasions, and a secret codebook redirect their mission. Softcover book ISBN 97809653467-9-5 $24.95 USD.

★ *Kazik's Polish Navy* by Kazimierz J. Kasperek with Pat McDonough. Exciting, eye-witness account of naval battles of WWII and the Polish diaspora after the end of the war. What was the backroom deal that caused Poland to be sacrificed to Russia? Kazimierz Kasperek was the most decorated NCO in the Polish Navy in WWII. Also 84 photographs. *A Pulitzer Prize contender in 2009.* Softcover book ISBN 97809653467-2-6 $21.95 USD. Soon to be issued as an eBook entitled *Kazik's Polish Navy, The Betrayal,* ISBN 97809653467-5-7 (without photographs).

★ *He Didn't Say Good-bye* by Raymond F. Flaherty. U.S. Special Forces in Laos search for a downed U.S.A.F. pilot. What happens to the family at home when one is MIA? *A Pulitzer Prize contender in 2006.* Softcover book ISBN 97809653467-7-1 $24.95 USD.

★ *Strangers Brothers* by Raymond F. Flaherty with Pat McDonough. Immigrant boy comes to America in search of family and purpose. Joins the Army and becomes an Airborne Ranger. In the invasion of Grenada learns that he and another soldier share the same father. *A Pulitzer Prize contender in 2009.* Softcover book ISBN 97809653467-8-8 $21.95 USD.

★ ***What Made Us Who We Are Today, WWII Oral History*** by Mary Timpe Robsman. Civilians and veterans answer "What was it like for you during World War II?" More than 100 exhibits and photos. Softcover book ISBN 97809653467-4-0 $19.95 USD.

★ ***Without Keys, My 15 Weeks With the Street People*** by Pat McDonough. Two children are abducted and their mother goes in search of them. Her journal covers experience in a shelter for homeless men and gives a comprehensive assessment of homelessness and what needs to be done. *A Pulitzer Prize Semi-finalist 1998, and winner of 5 MIPA Awards.* Hardcover with Dust Jacket ISBN 97809653467-1-9; Softcover book ISBN 97809653467-0-2; Each $24.00 USD.

★ ***From Rough to Ready, an Editor's Tips for Writers***, 2nd edn., by Pat McDonough offers tips on grammar, style, and formatting based on the most frequently encountered oversights of new writers. What does a publisher expect in a well-polished manuscript? Book ISBN 97809653467-6-4 $10.00 USD; Soon to be released as an eBook ISBN 97809653467-3-3 $9.95 USD.

Some of our authors are available for book talks, events, and workshops.

The Ulysses Flight/ Paul Wankowicz

Shipping and Florida Sales Tax if applicable, not included.

Our website **www.terrasanctapress.com** uses PayPal which accepts most credit cards. We also accept orders by phone, email, and mail order. **Terra Sancta Press**, 304 Royal Palm Dr., Melbourne, FL 32935-6955. Phone orders, call 321-914-2290 (11 AM - 8 PM EST/EDT). For e-mail orders or inquiries: **books4you@cfl.rr.com**

NOTE: For bulk orders, special discounts, book talks, workshops, or international shipments, query by eMail or phone. If this contact information should change, new information will be registered with the Publisher's Standard Address Number (SAN) Directory at R. R. Bowker (Bowkerlink): www.bowker.com/index.php/supportfaq-san or www.bowkerlink.com under the Terra Sancta Press' Registered SAN 854-1388.

What others say about *The Ulysses Flight*

The Ulysses Flight by Paul Wańkowicz is a page-turner which has almost everything: a fascinating setting, believable characters, a riveting plot, history, and surprises produced by a knowledgeable author who provides authentic detail. *The Ulysses Flight* is more than a good flying story: it is an intimate picture of diverse people responding to the end of their pre-war world; and at the same time, taking courageous steps to influence the shape of the world to come. I hated to have it end.

> JOE ST. GEORGES
> THE OLD, BOLD PILOT, GLENMORE, PENNSYLVANIA

Action adventures. The Japanese invasions of Burma, Malaya, and Singapore Island. Dogfights pit Curtiss P-40 pilots against the agile Japanese *Zero*s. Daring pilots. Smart, competent, beautiful women. A spy captures a secret codebook. Impossible missions. Aviation history. Transcendent love. *The Ulysses Flight* has it all!

> ANNE MACK

This was certainly one of the best books I have ever read! The pages turned themselves once I got into the chapter that introduced Lisa to Frank! What a pair, and Mia and Johnny too! Johnny was such a technical pro, so well-organized, knew what to do ... the brains of the trio and so unassuming!

I loved how independent Lisa was, and such a forerunner of the Feminist Movement in all the good things!

I like how points of view alternated from the Japanese to the British, Australian, and U.S.

That look, the communication by the elderly Japanese fighter pilot who chose not to kill Frank, and then was killed by Lisa was especially wrenching. She being unaware of his mercy, was just looking out for Frank, and thought it was a kill or be killed situation. So much misunderstanding and lack of communication during a war and chaos. Lots of thought-provoking issues here.

I think you have an international bestseller on your hands.

MARIE E. ROMAN
POET, ARTIST, AUTHOR & EDUCATOR
TINLEY PARK, ILLINOIS

The Ulysses Flight kept me reading to the end. A beautiful Dutch refugee, a disenchanted American pilot and a distinguished British officer form an unlikely alliance to move three American planes past Japanese lines at the onset of World War II. Their mission becomes more vital when the team is must to deliver a smuggled Japanese codebook to the Allies. Paul Wańkowicz has produced a well-researched book that is partly a story of budding love; partly a story of underdog dogfight survival, and partly realistic war history. Many books offer a single viewpoint or character to describe the impact of war. But Wańkowicz shows how the war changes the lives and futures of local residents, as well as the Yanks, Brits, Aussies and even Japanese, whose lives intertwined as they fought in the Malayan Peninsula and south. "War is Hell" is proven in his pages.

LINDA JUMP
AUTHOR, JOURNALIST, PHOTOGRAPHER & AVID
READER, PALM BAY, FLORIDA

The Ulysses Flight is an historical novel that captures the atmosphere of its time—The beginning of WWII around southeast Asia: action, adventure, romance, and the reality of suffering endured by those who lived through the difficult days when Japan was expanding its empire. The lives and hardships of civilian and military personnel are described in accurate detail as background to a tragic love story. A true page-turner.

ED VON KOENIGSECK
TECHNICAL WRITING FOR PRIVATE INDUSTRY,
WEST MELBOURNE, FLORIDA